CW01111898

EXOTIC ESCAPE

EXOTIC ESCAPE

*A Tale of Sinister Encounters
and Heartfelt Romance*

PAT BOOTH-LYNCH

Copyright © 2014 by Pat Booth-Lynch

Cover Design: Pat Booth-Lynch
Editor: Jean Burmeister

Library of Congress Control Number:		2014909045
ISBN:	Hardcover	978-1-4990-1571-3
	Softcover	978-1-4990-1572-0
	eBook	978-1-4990-1570-6

All rights reserved. No part of this book may be reproduced or transmitted in any form or by any means, electronic or mechanical, including photocopying, recording, or by any information storage and retrieval system, without permission in writing from the copyright owner.

This is a work of fiction. Names, characters, places and incidents either are the product of the author's imagination or are used fictitiously, and any resemblance to any actual persons, living or dead, events, or locales is entirely coincidental.

Any people depicted in stock imagery provided by Thinkstock are models, and such images are being used for illustrative purposes only.
Certain stock imagery © Thinkstock.

This book was printed in the United States of America.

Rev. date: 06/23/2014

To order additional copies of this book, contact:
Xlibris LLC
1-888-795-4274
www.Xlibris.com
Orders@Xlibris.com
552032

Dedication

To be sure, I want to thank our daughter Kyle and our grandsons Mark and Paul for bringing us a great deal of pride and joy. As for living life's dream, I have Jack to thank for helping me fulfill that dream by sharing a cache of loving memories over the years and for his patience, his understanding and his immeasurable love.

For all those who wish to achieve such happiness my advice is to . . . Live Simply, Love Passionately and Care Deeply.

Author's Notes

Some have asked me why I write. My answer has a great deal to do with my love of travel. For travel, to me, is as much a passion as ambition or love. I've found the only way I can clear my mind's hard drive of all those faraway places is to put my thoughts on paper. It's beastly challenging, but full of gratification.

Psychics often refer to their visions as nothing but a curse. I feel similarly cursed. Yet I continue to write tales hoping that my storytelling, with all of the twists and red herrings, will give you a glimpse into a breathtaking new world filled with intriguing individuals and allow you to experience situations that thrill and stimulate your imagination.

As a tourist and writer, I find Africa, in particular, affords a glimpse into the primeval feelings that heightens one's senses. The sounds, the scents, the spectacularly varied landscape and the magnificent creatures that roam the plains seem to charm the strongest of critics.

A trip into the bush is like a sojourn into a foreign entity, one that stimulates the mind and awakens feelings of being wholeheartedly alive as never before. The wild surroundings, the majestic animals seeking their share of an evening meal, make the experience of either walking into the bush or riding in a Land Rover a chance of a lifetime to really get to know oneself and face the terror that lurks in the tall grass or the rocky outcroppings called Kopjes (pronounced copies).

The anxiety one encounters fosters an urgency that prompts all to be at the top of their game. There is no laid-back attitude when confronting any one of the Big 5, namely: The elephant, the rhino, the cape buffalo, the lion or the leopard. One must enter with the knowledge that your cunning is as clandestine as their force.

Meeting a challenge like this while still enjoying the pleasures of seeing the great beasts in their native habitat leaves a lasting impression that can only be satisfied by many more treks into the Lowvelt's golden savannahs and the rocky Highvelt of Eastern Africa, a continent still dominated by creatures of antiquity. I've traveled the world, but there is no other place on this glorious planet of ours that has touched my heart like Africa.

PBL

Greater Kruger National Park
South Africa *

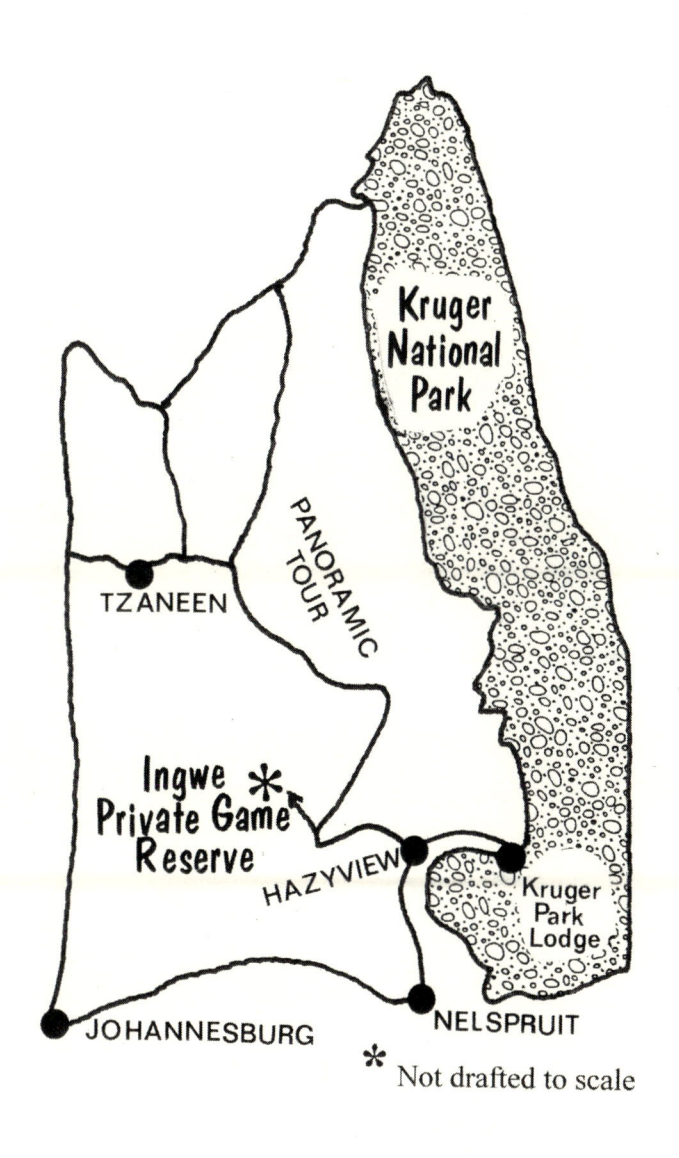

- Kruger National Park
- TZANEEN
- PANORAMIC TOUR
- Ingwe Private Game Reserve *
- HAZYVIEW
- Kruger Park Lodge
- JOHANNESBURG
- NELSPRUIT

* Not drafted to scale

Chapter 1

Thursday

"I'm so very sorry Kyle, but I can't marry you!"

Those caustic words echoed over and over in Kyle's mind as she gazed out the window of the SAA 340-600 Airbus. The cotton candy clouds that stretched across the azure sky were in such sharp contrast to the phrase uttered a few days ago when Ryan hurriedly walked out of her apartment, that she was overwhelmed with grief. In total shock, Kyle's whole life seemed to change in a millisecond leaving her smothered in disappointment.

Her teeth raked across her bottom lip and a tremor of nerves rattled through her as anxiety simmered in her stomach like toxic acid.

With eyes rimmed in red, suddenly tears rose effortlessly, riding the crest of her emotions. Even though she fought for control, droplets streamed down her cheeks. She could sense her fingers shaking as she pulled a tissue from her pocket and brushed the tears away while stifling a sob, at the same time hoping her traveling companion hadn't noticed her crying. She certainly didn't need any more lectures on choosing the right "life partner."

Kyle had done her best to lock away her fiancé's abrupt dismissal of their wedding plans, but down deep she felt devastated and more than a bit frustrated as to why Ryan had changed his mind ten days before the ceremony. He had never given her any indication that he was leaning toward such a decision. In fact, between their breathtaking romantic interludes, he'd often told her, in the most intimate ways, that they were soulmates for life, and those moments still lingered like a strong floral fragrance. She couldn't seem to shake them. *How could he do this to me?*

This mission of the heart "getaway vacation" to the most remote place Kyle could think of was decidedly an escape from the shock and disappointment she felt about Ryan's betrayal. Fortunately her best friend, Gina Austin, had come along on the adventure, notwithstanding the fact that the idea of a safari scared her to death. Gina's concept of an ideal vacation was a restful lounge by the pool on a cruise ship with a tequila martini in one hand and her gaze fixed squarely on the cabana boy. Yet she'd agreed to accompany Kyle on this sojourn as any Good Samaritan would do out of sympathy for her best friend who was in need of all the support she could offer.

And so it is that Kyle, a jet charter pilot and Gina, a spa owner, found themselves flying high above the broad Atlantic, heading for new horizons on South Africa's vast savannahs.

Aware that her left temple was throbbing, Kyle took a deep breath and looked to her right to see Gina deep in sleep, her nose in a cute pout, her mouth wide open and her eyelids fluttering as if she were experiencing some traumatic dream or perhaps a nightmare. Kyle managed a slight smile and glanced out the window at the wing of the South African Airbus, noticing how it swayed to the force of the wind, a miraculous sight indeed. How she loved the serenity one feels soaring high among the clouds. However, being a pilot herself, she was well aware of the thrill as well as the accompanying boredom that pilots face on long haul flights, and this trip fit neatly into that category.

While Kyle slept, Gina swallowed a yawn and tried to pass the time away by reading a novel, but that diversion failed to keep her interest. Her breath seemed to jam in her throat and she couldn't concentrate. She tried closing her eyes as she bit down on a sigh, but sleep wouldn't come. Finally, she secured her journal from the carry-on bag under her seat and began the entries that would someday prove she had actually experienced the excitement of seeing the great beasts outside the confines of a zoo, a dream she'd harbored for years, though she had always envisioned Ryan would be by her side at the time. That, sadly she thought as she drew in a shuddering breath, was not to be. So, pen in hand, she began to write.

Journal Entry—1 *Heading for Johannesburg via Dakar, Senegal. An hour layover for refueling. Total flight time 17 hrs, 30 minutes with arrival in South Africa approximately 5:00 P. M. Transfer to hotel. Looking forward to the next day's charter flight to The Ingwe Private Game Reserve which, according to my travel itinerary, is but a few miles from Kruger National Park and the town of Hazyview in the Province of Mpumalanga. Sounds exciting! Hope this experience will lessen my feelings of heartbreak over Ryan.*

After putting her journal into her carry-on bag, Kyle raked her fingers through her auburn curls, leaned back and observed the billowy clouds as they floated by like a sea of foam in a brilliant blue sky. *What a peaceful scene.* She closed her eyes again, hoping she, too, could enjoy some much needed sleep on this long flight, but that wasn't to be either, for the commotion caused by the breakfast cart's presence somewhere behind her was a definite distraction.

The seat belt light popped on and an attendant's voice cheerfully sliced through the air. "Please take your seats while the breakfast trolley passes through the aisles. Thank you." Kyle grinned when she heard the South African's term for the food cart. A humorous description, she thought, for the attendant referred to it as a "Trolley." She listened carefully when the attendant went on to detail the various choices on the menu, for she was certainly hungry. All of the selections sounded great to Kyle. True to form she hoped the breakfast would be as delightful as was the dinner menu. But then according to all reports, South African Airlines was well known for their delicious meals.

Kyle was just about to awaken Gina, for she knew her friend must be hungry as well, since they had little to eat after their dinner had been served, when she noticed a woman hurriedly moving along the aisle toward them. Kyle figured she'd heard the announcement and was apparently in a rush to get back to her seat.

All of a sudden the woman tripped, most likely the cause being a passenger who had stuck his or her foot out into the aisle. Her own experience told her that was usually the case. At any rate, the woman let out a loud groan and fell just shy of Kyle and Gina's seating row. Items from the woman's purse went flying, scattering across the floor of the cabin. An attendant rushed to the scene from the front of the aircraft to help the frustrated woman to her feet while, at the same time, the nearby passengers scooped up the contents of her purse and handed them back to her.

Kyle leaned back for she was positioned in a window seat and the seating rows were not exactly in alignment. With curiosity she observed the entire episode as it transpired, but could do nothing to assist the woman. As Kyle watched the mishap, she spied the young man in an aisle seat angled slightly opposite Gina who had, she'd previously noticed, appeared to be traveling alone. Now, he seemed to be acting in a furtive manner. Strangely enough she spotted him quickly scoop up something from under the seat in front of him. To Kyle it looked as if it were a bright blue card or something of the sort. Surreptitiously he slipped the item into the side pocket of his backpack. There was so much confusion at the time that Kyle presumed no one else observed the man's suspicious action for all were busy assisting in the retrieval efforts. Surprisingly though, Gina never opened her eyes, apparently oblivious to the happenings around her.

Within minutes the attendant ushered the woman back to her seat which was about three or so rows behind Kyle and Gina. At that point Kyle jokingly gave Gina a right-arm jab, chiding, "You missed the whole scene. I bet you'd sleep through a hurricane."

Gina shook her head in bewilderment and glanced at her friend. "I probably could sleep through most anythin', but what scene?" She frowned and, in a groggy voice, added, "What are you talkin' about?"

"A woman fell in the aisle and the things she had in her purse went flying, but guess what?" Kyle hunched over and whispered into Gina's ear. "When the woman fell, I think that guy across the aisle from you picked up what looked like a credit card that landed under the seat in front of him. I saw him put it into his backpack."

Gina straightened up and whipped her head about in order to get a look at the passenger. He sported a pony tail and he was wearing a dark blue jacket. When she turned back to Kyle, she loudly blurted out, "You're kiddin'?"

Kyle swiftly placed a finger over her lips. "Sh-h-h. I don't want him to hear us."

"Well, what are you goin' to do?" Gina said offering one of her animated hand gestures which often resembled the unchecked hands of a clock spinning out of control.

Kyle's teeth pulled on her bottom lip as a tidal wave of thoughts rolled through her mind. "I just can't let it go," she confided.

Gina gave a half laugh of impatience, "Well you can't accuse the guy. How can you be sure it wasn't his?"

"I can't, but I've got to tell someone. That poor woman better check her belongings carefully to be sure she isn't missing something."

"How do you know she hasn't?"

"I don't, but I know what I saw, and it just didn't look right."

"Oh jeez!" Gina went on, "You could get us in real trouble if you're wrong."

Kyle's brows narrowed in thought. "I know," she said quietly. Then without another word she unbuckled her seat belt and pushed past Gina in an effort to get to the aisle. Fortunately she didn't have to jostle past anyone else since they were on a side of the craft that accommodated a two-seat arrangement. After she maneuvered herself into the aisle, she turned back to Gina and whispered, "I'm going to tell that attendant up there in the galley."

Gina's gaze focused on Kyle. "Here we go again. You're always livin' on the edge. I swear."

"Don't remind me!" Kyle shot back. "Here goes." Kyle glanced at the man in the seat opposite Gina then took note of the seat number, 51D. She tried to see his face, but he had his head down, obscuring her view. Quickly moving forward into the first class section, she was soon at the galley where one of the attendants politely told her to please take her seat for they were attempting to serve breakfast before their arrival in Dakar.

"I know and I'm sorry," Kyle confessed, "but I feel obligated to tell you that I was in a seat opposite the woman who fell in the aisle, and I did see the man in seat number 51D pick up something from under the seat in front of him that may have fallen out of the woman's purse. He put it into his backpack." Kyle hesitated for an instant and looked down the aisle, but she couldn't see past the first-class mesh screening. When she turned back to the attendant her dark eyes flashed. "I'm sure of what I saw. It looked like a card or something that was bright blue in color."

"You said seat number 51D?"

"Yeah. All the passengers were picking up the items and handing them back, but it looked to me like the man put that card or whatever into a pocket of his backpack. I thought you should know so the woman can take a good look and see if she's got everything. It'd be a tragedy if something important is missing."

The attendant thanked Kyle and offered to check into it. It couldn't have been more than a few seconds after Kyle returned to her seat and had fastened her seat belt that she saw the same attendant heading down the aisle toward Kyle and Gina's seating row.

A puzzled look clouded Gina's face. "What's goin' on?"

"I don't know, but I did tell an attendant, and she seemed to have taken me seriously, for she's the one who just passed us going down the aisle," Kyle responded, unhooking her seat belt.

Gina watched Kyle as she twisted around and scrunched down in her seat, her body resting on her knees.

"What are 'ya doin'?"

On the tiptoe of excitement, Kyle asserted, "Sh-h-h! I want to see what's going on."

Gina sighed, "You would!" she blurted out absentmindedly as she fingered the strands of her short blond hair. "Beats me what you get involved in."

Kyle ignored her friend's comment, while noting that the attendant and the woman were talking and the woman appeared to be looking down as if she were checking something.

"Well?" Gina pressed. "What's happenin'?"

A rustle of whispers could be heard throughout the cabin as other passengers watched the proceedings. "I think the woman is checking her things," Kyle said poking Gina on her arm. "She's got her head down. That's all I can see from here." Kyle paused then let out a gasp. "Oh, my God!"

"What?"

"They've moved the breakfast cart to the section behind us, and it looks like that attendant is motioning to a man in a seat in the back of the plane. Hey, now he's coming up to where the woman's sitting."

Still remaining on her knees, Kyle grasped the seat back and pulled herself up further in order to get a better view. In the meantime, Gina continued to shake her head in disbelief. "You sure do like to push the envelope, don't you?"

"Come on. This is exciting. I just know something's happening. The man that came up from the back section is talking to the woman. She's looking down and seems to be showing him something, but I can't tell what it is." Kyle stopped suddenly. "Oh, no!"

Exasperated, Gina spouted, "What now?"

"That man's coming up the aisle with the attendant." With a decided huff, Kyle swiftly swung about in her seat, sat down and fastened her seat belt. She poked Gina again. "Pretend that you don't know what's going on, okay?"

"What do you mean pretend? I haven't a clue," Gina said, darting a swift glance at Kyle. "What did 'ya get us into?"

Kyle didn't respond. She was too busy watching the man who had accompanied the attendant up the aisle. They stopped opposite Gina. The man was obviously talking to the passenger in seat 51D as the attendant stood by. "What's he saying?" Kyle probed.

Gina twisted her head from one side to the other in an attempt to keep Kyle informed. "I can barely hear 'em . . . but wait." She cupped her hand close to her mouth and angled her head a bit to divert her comment so the attendant couldn't hear her. "I think the man asked the passenger if he had any overhead luggage."

"What'd he say?"

"Nothin'. He just shook his head. He's pickin' up his backpack and, look, he's gettin' out of the seat. Now they're all leavin'."

Kyle unhooked her seat belt, pulled herself up again and turned her head about to see the three of them moving back down the aisle toward the rear section.

"Well," Kyle said, "if there's nothing to it, why are they taking the man away? Now I'm glad I spoke up. There must be something to this."

Gina's frown turned into a smile. "I wonder if we'll ever know what happened."

"Oh, don't worry I'll ask."

"I know you will, but right now I don't give a damn about the guy. I just wish they'd serve the food. I'm starvin'. It seems like a lifetime since dinner."

Her tongue darted across her lips as Kyle echoed, "Yeah, I'm hungry, too!"

It wasn't long before the commotion subsided and the two got their wish, for the breakfast cart moved up the aisle offering a delicious breakfast of pancakes, sausage, toast, a fruit combo and juice with a flavorful cup of coffee which couldn't have been better. All the while Kyle observed that the man who had been sitting opposite Gina never returned to his seat. Her suspicious nature couldn't be dampened, though, and Kyle continued to wonder what had happened. Finally, when that same galley attendant passed them in the aisle, Kyle called out, "What happened to the young man in seat 51D?"

The attendant leaned into the row and quietly stated, "I can only say that he's being detained for questioning by the Federal Marshal on board. Beyond that, I have nothing further to report, but I do want to thank you for your astute observation." She smiled, nodded and walked on.

"Wow!" Gina piped up. "Wonder what they've got on him?"

"I guess we'll never know, but I'm glad I told her. It's got to be something serious or a marshal wouldn't be holding him for questioning, right?"

Gina cocked her head. "Maybe so, but damn I sure hope the rest of the trip'll be less hectic. Here I thought we were tryin' to get away from everythin' and relax, particularly the situation with Ryan."

"Oh please don't bring that up. I can't even bear to think about him."

"I'm sorry. I promised not to mention his name, but it was so unlike him. Whatever would make him do that? And why would he have taken a leave of absence from his job with the FAA?"

"I know he once said he wanted to go on and get his degree in aero dynamics."

"Well, that doesn't mean you couldn't get married," Gina concluded. "Besides he always said he loved that job at the FAA, and why would that change his mind about the weddin' plans on such short notice? It's all too weird if you ask me."

Fine lines etched the corners of Kyle's eyes and she braced herself against a barrage of hurtful feelings that Ryan's surprising comment had brought on. She quickly tightened her lips, unable to face the bittersweet memories as powerful images surged through her mind. Close to bursting out in tears, she turned her head and stared out the window. She hadn't noticed with all the commotion at hand and the serving of breakfast, but the billowy clouds she'd seen before now carried a dark tinge, definitely cumulous in nature and packing a decided amount of moisture with threatening up and down wind gusts. She was familiar with the affects of warm and cold air meeting in a clash of conflict, so she wasn't surprised to hear the familiar "ding" as the seat belt light popped on again.

The loudspeaker came alive with the captain's voice commenting on the weather conditions. Though calm, his voice carried a hint of authority when he warned everyone to stay in their seats and keep their seatbelts fastened. "It appears there's a storm cell brewing ahead as we approach the airport in Dakar." The captain quickly added, "And we may run into some turbulent weather."

Kyle was all too familiar with such warnings and the outcome of storms on a flight. The warning didn't worry her at all, but since the flight so far had been as smooth as a hand gliding over a patch of silk, Gina expressed her displeasure by displaying a nervous twitch in her cheek that she always exhibited when she was upset.

"Man, how I hate flyin'!" The words gushed from her mouth. "You know full well I wouldn't do this for anyone else but you."

"I know and I appreciate it, but believe me it'll be okay. Just a little bouncing around. That's all."

"Yeah sure," Gina mumbled as she rolled her eyes upward, "just a little bouncin' around all right." She paused to inhale a shuddering breath. "I'll sure be glad when we get there."

Kyle continued to monitor the weather conditions from her window seat as the sky darkened and the clouds were ever so murky. She wasn't overly concerned when the turbulence got a bit more than one experiences on any normal flight, but it soon appeared this was not going to be what is considered normal. In no time the aircraft was bobbing up and down like a kite in flight. The cloud mass thickened as did the lightning bolts that crashed all around them washing the sky, illuminating it like a Fourth of July celebration and thundering through the cabin walls. Though Kyle was used to terrifying conditions, such situations didn't usually faze her. However, now she felt her heartbeat quicken a bit, mostly because she knew what an impact this was having on Gina. And she was right. When she looked over at her friend she saw her flinch as yet another bolt of lightning slashed across the sky and the plane shook under the force of the thunder that followed. In a near state of panic Gina's face was as white as a glowing overhead street lamp against a pitch black sky.

Kyle did notice that the attendants were scurrying down the aisles to be sure all the passengers had fastened their seat belts and that the overhead bins were locked securely in place. Then, without any warning the plane suddenly plunged downward, at least a 500 foot drop Kyle surmised. One could hear a loud gasp, almost in unison, as many in the cabin were assumedly in shock. After that the only sounds that could be heard were the roar of the engines, the battering of rain against the plane's windows and the ever increasing number of lightning strikes.

Noticing that Gina was now clutching the arm rests in a death grip, Kyle tried to calm her down by saying, "All will be fine. I've been through worse storms."

"Sorry, but you're not makin' me feel any better," Gina contended in a voice filled with fear.

"I mean it. We'll be okay," Kyle added with steadfast confidence. Gina's face had turned from ashen to chalk and she was shaking so that Kyle reached out and squeezed her friend's hand ever so tightly. "You'll see. We'll make it." As the turbulence continued, an ax of lightning cleaved the sky and scarred the bellies of the clouds. The cabin passengers maintained complete silence as if they were afraid to breath. It was like everyone was seated in a vacuum.

Gina said nothing as she leaned forward, grabbed her purse from under the seat in front of her and quickly pulled out a bottle of pills. Kyle was well aware that Gina had issues regarding motion sickness, yet she felt helpless in being able to calm her. After Gina swallowed a Dramamine, she put her head back and closed her eyes. Kyle knew her friend was, in every respect, trying to cope, but it was definitely getting the best of her, for her breath was sawing hot . . . in and out of her lungs. To boot, the weather didn't seem to be improving. Without a doubt it was getting worse. Kyle continued to talk to Gina with ever more reassurances, but she knew the girl was in misery, and she braced herself against a wave of guilt. *I should have taken this trip alone.*

Kyle's kick of guilt heightened when the captain's voice cut through the air, and he uttered words she prayed she wouldn't hear. "This is your captain," he reported. The tone level of his voice was composed, but Kyle did catch an added layer of speed and urgency beyond that of the normal message to the passengers. This time she sensed something was decidedly wrong, and she was soon to find out her instincts were right on the mark.

The captain, in a monotone voice heaped in conviction, firmly stated, "We ask you to be sure your seat belts are properly fastened as we are approaching the airport in Dakar and will be landing soon. However," he continued, "we're having difficulty with one of the landing gears. We're waiting for data from the tower and ask that you carefully follow the instructions the attendant will issue at this time. Thank you."

Then came the bombshell that sent Gina into near hysteria, for an attendant promptly took over the loudspeaker and with distinct clarity issued an order which was none too reassuring. She gave instructions for fastening one's seat belt as well as those for crash landing positioning in case the gear wouldn't deploy. The attendant went on to say, "We'll be asking you to assume a crash landing position only if it's necessary, so please listen again as I repeat these instructions." In the meantime, two other attendants hurried down the aisles, scanning the cabin with a heightened look of purpose on their faces.

The next immediate order came from the captain as he advised all attendants to prepare for landing.

"Oh my God we're goin' to try and land in this storm!" Gina cried out. "We'll crash!"

"No we won't. Lots of aircraft land in stormy weather."

Gina's breathing was erratic as she rambled on. "But what about that landin' gear?"

Chapter 2

Friday

Kyle was aware of what most likely had happened. In her mind she ran through the steps a pilot takes during the process of landing, including checking the lights on the instrument panel to be sure all landing gears are ready to deploy. She knew that the SAA 340-600 must have at least three gears if not more, and in this case the instrument panel probably showed the crew that the front gear isn't functioning properly. It seemed highly unlikely to her that it would be the back gear, for in that case eight tires are involved and there would be no way the tower would allow a landing unless the fuel supply was at a critical point.

"Trust me," Kyle said. "The captain and crew want to land safely just as much as we do. They'll bring this baby in just fine."

The particular phrase about bending forward and placing your head between your hands in case of a crash landing was one that Kyle knew well. Therefore, in an effort to divert Gina's attention from a possible dire landing, she hurriedly explained, "Remember that charter flight I told you about? The one I flew to Dallas from Fort Myers when I had to issue that same warning. Even though the aircraft I was piloting at the time was merely a twelve passenger Learjet and not a four engine heavy like this one, I aced that landing like I owned the plane, and this crew will do the same. I'm sure of it!" She locked eyes with her friend. "We'll make it." She squeezed Gina's hand again, finding it clammy and cold.

Though Kyle issued those words with as much confidence as she could muster, she too felt her heartbeat pounding strongly within her chest and her own anxiety level peaked. This was not going to be a normal flight or a normal landing. She knew her upbeat message wouldn't erase Gina's fear, but there was nothing else she could do beyond praying that she was right.

Kyle turned her head to the left and looked out at the wing. The craft was in dense fog with rain still beating hard against the window. Though it was difficult to see through the rain and the fog, the plane's lights did allow her to notice that the pilot had put the flaps at thirty degrees for landing, and she felt the aircraft move into a descending mode. She deduced that the tower must have given them permission to land. That's a good sign, she thought, and she relayed that insight to Gina by stating, "See, all the attendants have taken their seats and have apparently buckled in. I'll bet the landing gear situation's been resolved."

Then, as she was feeling a bit less dubious about the flight's outcome, Kyle again looked out the window at the bruised sky only to see a blinding red and yellow flash of color streak out of the number two engine, the one closest to her window seat. Without thinking, she let out a slight gasp just as a lightning bolt struck so close to the aircraft that it lit up the sky. Within seconds the plane was weaving from one side to the other while the wings pitched up and down as intense crosswinds battered the craft in a never ending assault.

Gina was quick to pick up on Kyle's apparent concern, but all she could say was, "God, what's happenin'?"

This time it was Gina who squeezed Kyle's hand with a grip so strong it could have cracked walnuts. At the same time the tense voice of an attendant filled the cabin as she issued an order loud and clear, "We'll be landing in minutes. As we've instructed you and as the captain has just ordered . . . all passengers are to immediately assume crash position. I repeat . . . assume crash position." She again repeated the order with a solemn note. "Remember to keep your heads down."

Chapter 3

Friday

Kyle's view out the window confirmed that they were still in a dense cloud cover as the aircraft bounced about, its wings dipping from one side to the other.

Chanting the words like a mantra, Gina shouted out in sheer terror, "Dammit, dammit, dammit! We're goin' to crash."

Kyle's challenging retort, "No we're not!" startled Gina so much so that she bit down hard on her lower lip drawing blood.

"The pilot and crew aren't going to take any chances. Remember I said they don't want to crash any more than we do, and I'm sure they're very capable." Kyle quickly added, "So just follow the instructions. It'll be okay."

Gina hesitated for an unwary moment then leaned forward and placed her head in her hands.

"That's the way!" Kyle said encouragingly though concern knitted her brow. "You're doing just fine." While Kyle prepared to assume the same position, she could hear Gina reciting prayers under her breath.

Clasping her mouth shut, Kyle immediately followed suit and bent forward. Prayers, however, didn't come easily. Instead, a sense of melancholy hit her like a stone block. It was as if Ryan were sitting beside her. Even though the roar of the engines was enough to obliterate the sound of a screaming child, Kyle's mind couldn't let go of her fiancé's comment or the memory of their plans together. His words, "I'm so sorry, Kyle, but I can't marry you!" were enough to send any sane person to a psychiatrist's couch. They had come as such a complete surprise that they rendered Kyle speechless.

She did recall that Ryan had been unshaven that day, a rare occurrence for him since he always looked immaculate and clean shaven. Even his raven black hair looked disheveled and his sparkling blue-gray eyes appeared forlorn. That entire episode flashed before her and left her dazed. *Whatever could have happened that made him cancel the wedding?* One sorrowful tear teetered over the edge of her eyelashes and rolled down her cheek to splash on her hand and she sniffed in a sob.

Kyle's reverie was short lived, however, as the grinding sound of the landing gear under the fuselage dropped into place.

With panic in her voice Gina pressed, "What was that?"

In hopes of relieving some of Gina's stress, Kyle quickly clarified the situation by telling her friend that the sound was merely the main gear, namely the wheels, being lowered for landing. Thankfully she heard Gina issue a sigh of relief.

Being a pilot herself, Kyle envisioned the cockpit and the steps the crew were following in order to keep the craft on course. She lifted her head up and quickly glanced out the window to find the aircraft had penetrated the cloud cover and that the rain had subsided along with the massive lightning strikes. *A good sign!* She surmised the major problem that confronted the crew now would be harsh cross winds. She knew the crew would be busily trying to crab or side slip the plane into place in order to compensate for the velocity of those cross winds while aligning the craft with the runway. That certainly wouldn't be an easy task since the plane was being battered by tropical force winds and the wings were still dipping from side to side which, in a worst case scenario, could cause a wind strike if a lowered wing should hit the runway. Just then she felt the fuselage flare and the aircraft go into stall mode. Thankfully, that was another good sign, for she knew it meant they were close to reaching the runway and that the pilot had successfully leveled the craft.

Yet, when the aircraft finally touched down, its rear gear wheels apparently slammed onto the runway with such force that it jarred Kyle and Gina's bodies from their seats, as their seat belts strained to hold them in place. Kyle couldn't resist the temptation to peer out the window as the flaps dropped down and the spoilers popped up to slow the plane's speed. Then the thrusters kicked in with a deafening squeal that filled the cabin.

"Good grief. What now?" Gina yelled over the grueling sound.

"The pilot's just slowing down the plane that's all, Gina. I told you they'd bring this baby in without a mishap." Within seconds, though, Kyle could feel the nose gear bounce several times on the runway, followed by a tumultuous grinding noise that she clearly recognized as a broken front gear. The nose of the aircraft was obviously scraping along the runway on its undercarriage or belly and veering off course.

Although she couldn't see that portion of the plane, she knew sparks would be flying, and when she peered out the window again she saw ambulances, fire trucks and rescue vehicles trailing the craft as it finally came to rest in a grassy section near the end of the runway.

With the storm's temper spent, a roar of cheers along with a chorus of groans and screams erupted throughout the cabin. One glance told Kyle that Gina was undoubtedly shaken, for she was breathing hard and wringing her hands. Yet, within seconds she turned to Kyle and belted out, "That was a hell of a jolt." Her impish smile resurfaced and she savored a long swallow. "But, hallelujah, Kyle! We're going to be okay, right?"

"Sure we are," Kyle responded, trying to keep Gina's mood upbeat, although she knew full well the landing could have resulted in a far worse disaster. "Clearly," she said, "the crew held it all together. Good job."

Just then a flight attendant's voice quickly notified all that the front gear had collapsed, but that there was no danger of fire. She explained that they would be evacuating by chutes from the exits at the rear of the aircraft, and she asked that all passengers remain in their seats until they could take care of those in need. The crew was definitely worried about any casualties, though, for the announcement immediately included information regarding anyone who might need assistance. "Please notify the crew by pressing the appropriate button on the panel above your head," the attendant advised.

There was a good deal of scurrying about while the attendants helped some passengers to the chutes that had deployed upon impact. Since Kyle had been on many flights in the past in which passengers were anything but courteous to each other, she was amazed to find that this particular group, though some were more distraught than others, most were courteous and accommodating, a rare sight in such cases of calamity.

Gina couldn't get out of her seat fast enough when all were told to exit the plane. Fact is, she was like a coiled spring when she stood up.

However, her legs buckled beneath her. Though she tried to stand, her legs seemed as if they were made of Jell-O. Kyle quickly grabbed her by the arm until she felt strong enough to straighten up.

"I guess that trauma hit me harder than I thought," Gina confessed. "Wow!"

Kyle's voice registered concern as she asked, "Do you feel all right?"

"Yeah, I'm fine," Gina said, watching Kyle pull the luggage from the overhead bin. When the luggage was down and ready to haul away, Gina asked, "But how are we ever goin' to get to Johannesburg now?"

"I guess we'll just have to wait and see what they tell us," Kyle admitted. "I'm sure we'll know more once we get to the holding area. But hey, look out there. The storm seems to have let up."

With a decided rise of her eyebrows, Gina remarked, "At least that's one good thing, but all I can say is that this is a hell of a way to start a 'Getaway Vacation.'"

Kyle's restless gaze wearily scanned the area as she and all the other passengers filed into the small holding facility at the Leopold Sedar Senghor International Airport, named in honor of Senegal's first President. She had read that Senegal was building a new airport for the one million or more passengers that pass through the two terminals every day. It was easy to see why for she'd discovered this one was rated one of the worse airports in the world as far as waiting space is concerned. The reviews were right on target, for there was barely a seat to be had.

As Kyle and Gina looked about they could see that four passengers were being treated for non-life-threatening wounds, one of which looked like a woman had apparently dislocated her arm and another man must have bruised his leg. Sadly, though, it was reported that one gentleman apparently collapsed from a heart attack and had been rushed to the hospital. Surprisingly, there were comparatively few that were adversely affected by the rough landing.

"Aren't we lucky?" Kyle exclaimed as she watched the medical personnel helping another passenger into a wheel chair.

"I know," replied Gina. "Cripes, if I'd known we'd be in this mess, I hate to burst your bubble about gettin' away, but I would never have taken you up on your offer to pay my way on this safari. Nope, not even to an exclusive place." She ticked off eye contact with Kyle. An uneasy silence followed before she added, "You know I still care what happens in your life, but you've got to admit this's not what we planned."

Kyle agreed. "You've got me there. But look, Gina," she said, pointing ahead, "there's that guy that was sitting across from you, and the Federal Marshal's taking him into an office. He must really be in trouble."

"I guess you were right. He *was* a bad ass. But bad ass or not, how're we ever goin' to get to Johannesburg in time to catch that charter flight tomorrow?"

"I don't have a clue, but I'm sure they'll be announcing something soon. What say we try and find a seat before they're all gone?"

"Sounds good to me 'cause I'm still shakin' inside." Gina looked across the room at a counter where they were serving drinks and a minimal selection of sandwiches and fruits. "How about over there? I really need a stiff drink!"

In a rush to grab one of the remaining tables some distance away, Kyle scurried on ahead, but in her hurry to do so she bumped into a man who likewise had his eye on sitting in the same spot. Brushing aside a few strands of her auburn curls that had swept across her face in the commotion, Kyle apologized then offered a smile.

"I'm sorry, too," the man echoed, his words curved richly around his British accent and suave polish. With a gesture that was as smooth and exact as an expensive watch, he pulled up two chairs and sat down on one of them. Hesitating for no more than a heartbeat he spoke up saying, "Listen, I'm alone here, so why don't we just share this table? It doesn't look like there's anywhere else to sit."

"Fine with me," Kyle said, motioning to Gina who was battling her way through the crowd. "Where are you headed?" Kyle asked while at the same time grabbing a third chair and pulling it close to the table for Gina who was but a few feet away.

The man didn't respond, for he seemed too engrossed in gazing at Gina. "Better sit down in that chair fast," he jokingly called out to Kyle's friend, "or you'll end up sitting on the floor."

"I can see that," Gina gasped, quite out of breath. Even in that state of breathlessness her gaze feasted on the debonair man's silver-gray hair. "I sure hope we don't get stuck here for too long!"

"At least we didn't crash," he admitted. "I thought for a moment we'd be landing in the water off the coast."

"Well, I'm grateful that didn't happen, but where are you headed?" Kyle asked, repeating her question.

"Eventually the Kruger Park Lodge. Where are you two going?"

Kyle and Gina spoke in unison, "The Ingwe Private Game Reserve."

Kyle added, "They advertise that you can observe the Big 5 there and never miss seeing a leopard, more specifically a *Mauve Leopard*."

"I've never heard of such an animal," the Brit commented.

"Neither had I. The idea of seeing such an oddity really intrigues me. They say these leopards have a coat that looks like a muted lavender-gray color with no black rings like other leopards. Actually, that's why I chose the place." She shrugged as she looked at the stranger. "They stated in their brochures that this reserve is the only place they've been seen."

"Well, that should be fascinating."

"I think so. Besides some of reviews I read mentioned that a lot of times in the other reserves you never get a chance to see any leopards, let alone a uniquely colored one."

"My brother has said that's true. I don't know anything about the game reserve you mentioned, but I do know that even at the Kruger Park Lodge, some of the guests have gone out on a number of game runs and have never seen leopards. They seem to be the most elusive of the Big 5 and—"

Motioning toward Kyle, Gina interrupted. "Kyle here has some kind of a fascination for leopards."

"It's not a fascination," Kyle insisted. "It's just that I think they're gorgeous."

"That they are. By the way my name's Bradley Kingston."

With raised eyebrows Gina flashed a "come on" smile aimed directly at the Brit. "Are you down here on business, Mr. Kingston?"

"No, I'm here to see my brother who works at the Kruger Park Lodge, and you can call me Brad."

"Okay, Brad. And what does your brother do there?"

"He's a guide or what they call a game ranger. Been doing that for two years now and he likes it. He's always been interested in exotic animals."

"So have I," Kyle said. "By the way I'm Kyle Griffin and this is my friend Gina Austin."

Gina followed up with a witty comment about how she'd been coerced into coming along on this adventure. After receiving a grim, narrow-eyed look from Kyle, she tactfully omitted any mention of the fact that her friend had been abandoned by her fiancé just before the wedding. However, she did laughingly add, "So far this's been an adventure all right! I've gotta admit that!"

"Well I hope you have a great time there. Right now, though," Bradley said, "I'm going to the bar to get a drink. May I get you ladies something?"

"No," Kyle said, "we'll get ours when you get back. I'm not moving from this seat before then. I sure don't want to lose it."

No sooner had Bradley disappeared into the crowd, than Gina tipped her head and motioned toward him. "Hey, he's a handsome dude, and don't you just love the way the British pronounce the word, water? It sounds like wa-a-a . . . ta, and doesn't that accent just get 'ya? Not to mention the silver hair. But he doesn't look old." She rambled on as she watched Bradley make his way to the bar. "I think he's cool!"

"I don't know how old he is, but he *is* nice looking. Leave it to you to notice."

"Listen, I haven't had two husbands for nothin'. Besides it doesn't cost anythin' to look."

Gina waved her arms. "Look around you, Kyle. The world is full of men, and I'm goin' to catch a winner yet."

"You're too funny, but I'm glad you came along. You sure do brighten the day."

Gina paid no heed to Kyle's comment as she looked away. "Oh oh, here he comes. Listen up, Kyle. I'm goin' to find out more about this guy." She squared her jaw and cocked her head then declared, "Prime bait, right?"

Before Bradley could reach the table, an announcement blared over the loudspeaker stating that Flight 2011 to Johannesburg had been cancelled.

"Oh no!" Gina complained, a frown coloring her face.

"Well, you might have known that, Gina. That plane is in no condition to fly. Just roll with the punches," Kyle said as the two listened to the rest of the public notice which pointed out that another aircraft was being flown in and that the flight should be ready to leave in three hours. "At least we don't have to stay here overnight," Kyle stated.

Ignoring Kyle's words about staying overnight, Gina flashed an eager smile directed at Bradley when he returned to the table. A flirtatious grin blossomed on her lips as she questioned the Brit. "Did you hear that?"

"Yes," he said, willingly returning her smile. "I guess we'll just have to wait it out. Listen, I'll hold the table while you two go on to the bar." He took a sip of his martini, then swished his hand in a "go ahead" gesture. "Get yourselves a drink! I think we all need a few spirits."

Kyle watched as Gina's strong gaze never strayed far from Bradley, but when they were a few feet away from the table, Kyle gave Gina a harsh poke on the arm.

"What was that for?" Gina asked, puzzled at the severity of the punch.

"You've got your hooks out. I saw that big beaming smile you've been giving him. Remember, though, we'll most likely never see the guy again."

"Who knows? Doesn't hurt to find out a few things about him, right? You're gettin' your break away from Ryan. Maybe I can make somethin' out of this. Could be the guy's rich. Notice he's not wearin' a ring?"

"You're something else. I did notice, though, that he isn't wearing a ring. But the guy probably lives in England."

"We don't know that he lives in England. Maybe he's got villas all over the world."

Kyle shook her head and laughed. "You're really a hopeless romantic."

Gina beamed as they ordered their drinks and the two of them headed back to the table.

The next several hours passed like a blur for Kyle, who had downed too many Gin and tonics. The conversation around her seemed like a foreign language relayed through a faulty transmitter. Fact is, she often caught herself suppressing a yawn. She did take note, however, that a twinkle flirted in Gina's eye every time Bradley opened his mouth, and the girl seemed to be totally absorbed in every wordy comment he uttered.

Bradley, in response, appeared to have a runaway tongue, and it didn't take long for most anyone within hearing distance to know all about him from the work he did to the special underwear he wore. For Kyle that was a complete turnoff and her stomach tightened at each embarrassing sentence he spoke, yet Gina was transfixed.

When an announcement finally blared over the loudspeaker that the plane headed for Johannesburg had arrived, Kyle was elated until she heard the last phase regarding the passenger bookings.

"However," the male voice stated, "this aircraft will not accommodate the entire number of passengers booked on Flight 2011. Please check the scheduling board to see if your name is listed. We're sorry for the inconvenience, but those who are not listed are to be booked for the following flight that has been assigned an 8:00 P.M. departure."

"Oh my word!" Gina exclaimed, keeping her oaths to a minimum in order to impress Brad. "What else can go wrong?"

Kyle let out a yelp as she sprinted for the scheduling board, calling over her shoulder. "Sit tight and keep your fingers crossed. I'll check."

Chapter 4

Friday & Saturday

When Kyle checked the scheduling board at the Leopold International Airport, she found that Bradley's name was listed on the flight leaving shortly while she and Gina were not on the roster until the eight o'clock departure, a ten hour layover for the two of them. When she relayed the news to Gina, her friend was not happy.

"Oh, no!" Gina whined, offering a half-laugh of impatience. "You've gotta be kiddin'!"

All Kyle could do was to try and console her by mentioning that at least they wouldn't be stuck at the airport all night. "Look around," Kyle said, motioning specifically to Gina. "I'm just glad we've got a table and chairs. Pity those poor souls who are stretched out on the floor."

"I can surely see why this airport is rated the worse in the world," Gina said while the three of them munched on sandwiches and sipped drinks from the bar and the small deli. As exhausted as they were, time seemed to stand still.

Two hours later, at 11:15 A.M., Bradley wished them well as he went on his way to the gate for his departure. Gina couldn't resist giving him one of her beaming smiles with a wink attached, and Kyle noticed that Bradley returned the favor.

"Hey," Gina called after him, "maybe we'll see you again." Her bright blue eyes sparkled as she added, "After all we'll be in the same area."

Lifting a thin brow, Bradley grinned encouragingly. "Could be!" he said, the words rich with a British accent. That said, he waved and was on his way.

When Brad left, Gina turned to Kyle and, in her usual bubbly voice, relayed the fact that while Kyle was dozing off she'd discovered something about Brad. "Hey," she said, "even though he doesn't have villas all over the world, I found out that he's an art dealer in Tampa. Can you believe that?" She excitedly went on to tell Kyle that when she told Brad she had a degree in Art and Architecture, he seemed interested. "We've actually got something in common. Who knows? Maybe," she rambled on with her unique overzealous enthusiasm, "I can sell him some of my watercolors."

"That would be nice," Kyle said offering a long drawn out yawn. "Right now though, I just want to get out of here."

Gina grudgingly conceded that they would most likely never see the man again as they both tried to make the best of a miserable situation. Kyle took out her journal and proceeded to update it while Gina, on the other hand, finally slumped forward and fell asleep with her head cradled in her arms.

Journal Entry—2 *Storm cell encountered a half hour out of Leopold International Airport. A front landing gear collapse caused a near crash; however, the craft landed without serious incident. One man was taken to the hospital after suffering a heart attack. Only a few incurred minor injuries. Gina and I are fine. Relegated to waiting for a 10:00 P.M. departure. Gina, though traumatized, is holding up well. Met a Brit named Bradley Kingston. Gina just about climbed all over his bones like a puppy with a new owner. Fun to watch her interact with prospects for husband # 3. Hope the plane isn't late and that the flight to Johannesburg will go well.*

Surprisingly, the flight arrived early to the delight of Kyle and Gina as well as the remaining exhausted passengers who were more than eager to go aboard. Kyle did observe, however, that Gina was a bit skeptical when it came to getting onto another aircraft. As she passed the check-in desk before entering the ramp, she looked Kyle's way. The expression on her face turned from anticipation to uncertainty. With a decided emphasis she declared, "This better be uneventful or I'm taking the next freighter back to the States."

Kyle swallowed hard but agreed saying, "I sure hope it'll go well." As they proceeded down the ramp onto the plane she said, "I do want you to know you're a good sport. You know that?" Kyle grabbed Gina's arm as they got to the entrance of the aircraft and, in a voice fraught with emotion, she noted, "Where could I ever find such a good friend?"

Though the flight was a lengthy nine hours, it was, thankfully, uneventful. Because it was a night flight the cabin was dark and quiet, a perfect place for a long restful sleep. In fact, both were so refreshed when, after a picture book three-point landing according to Kyle, they finally reached Johannesburg at five-thirty the next morning, they were more inclined to want to hop on the charter flight and head for the game reserve than to be transferred to the Protea Hotel. But it did give them a chance to freshen up and enjoy a leisurely breakfast in the hotel's restaurant. When their driver announced that the van was waiting to take them to the charter craft, they were the first to board.

To Kyle's amazement Gina actually seemed to enjoy the charter flight in a twin-engine turbo prop that seated twenty passengers. She'd never been aboard a plane of that size, and it somehow appealed to her. She was constantly looking out the window, intent on viewing the land below to see what was ahead for the two adventurers. Though most likely annoying to the other travelers, she loudly shouted out sights that surprised her. Seemingly in a world of her own, Gina paid no heed.

"Maybe you're getting the 'traveling bug,'" Kyle suggested.

A smile lurked on Gina's lips and she glanced at Kyle. "Not really, but things do seem to be goin' along a little smoother. If this keeps up I may just be glad I took you up on the offer to follow you to the Dark Continent." With a brittle laugh, she added, "You gotta admit I'm tryin'"

Kyle shook her head. "I know and I appreciate it." She suddenly felt a breath jam in her throat as she thought of Ryan and the sadness that had overcome her. "I sure needed you here to help me get through this and I thank you for that!"

Within about thirty minutes the charter flight landed at the KMIA Airport in the vicinity of Nelspruit, the busiest rural airport in South Africa. All the passengers scattered, heading for locations beyond, but Kyle and Gina were escorted to a private air facility where they viewed a ten passenger de Havilland DHC-3 that would take them to their final destination, The Ingwe Private Game Reserve.

"Oh man, Kyle, the planes are gettin' smaller and smaller," Gina stated.

"Well, let's see how you like this one," Kyle responded as the two women walked out to where the plane was parked. "You're sure getting a chance to try 'em all."

The pilot, a sandy-haired man who looked like he might be in his late forties, greeted them with a hearty welcome, while at the same time reaching out his hand in order to grab the larger pieces of luggage that Kyle and Gina towed behind them.

"Glad to be here," Kyle remarked. She fingered a few windblown auburn curls out of her face and swept them behind her ear while covering her eyes to deflect the bright African sunlight. "It's been a heck of a long trip. I'm Kyle." Nodding her head toward her friend, she went on, "and this is Gina."

"Nice to see both of you. Sorry to hear about that rough landing in Dakar. It was mentioned on the news." As he loaded the rest of the women's luggage onto the jet, he turned and offered his hand. "By the way my name's Stephen Falkner. I'll be your pilot today as well as your wildlife game ranger while you're here at The Ingwe. You two must be seasoned adventurers to come through that rough landing in Senegal and still have a smile on your face."

"No, I wouldn't go that far. Seasoned adventurers we are not," Kyle jokingly emphasized. "We're just glad the pilot and crew held it all together and got us down safely."

Stephen assisted the women as they climbed the few steps onto the plane, both of them being pleased they had window seats.

Gina swiveled about watching Stephen circle the plane as he checked all the functions. Finally he removed the stairs, and she saw him checking the door on the passenger's side. "He's cute," she whispered to Kyle who merely offered a lop-sided grin.

"Are we the only ones going to the reserve?" Kyle asked when the pilot entered the plane.

After securing his door and settling into his seat, he quickly twisted about to respond. "You are," he said. "Fact is, I just returned another party of four to the airport yesterday afternoon. You're it for the next week. Though I think there's another party coming in on Friday." He paused. "But you're lucky 'cause you'll have the place to yourselves for awhile. That doesn't happen often. I don't like to brag, but this's one of the best reserves, and you two are the first to hopefully see the *Mauve Leopards*. In fact, late yesterday one of our reserve owners said he spotted two of them in the bush, as we call it."

"Your web site stated that they're a new breed to Africa, right?" Kyle piped up.

"That's true. I haven't had a chance to see them yet myself, but I'll do my best to find 'em for you. That's one of our guarantees. No guest ever leaves without spotting a leopard. Hopefully one of those rare ones."

Kyle leaned forward. "You must know the area well."

"I grew up in Limpopo Province just east of here and I know every inch of the land around this area. To me it's paradise on earth." He beamed so broadly when he phrased the last sentence that it was inevitable his dark eyes would glisten and highlight his infectious smile.

As he prepared the plane for takeoff, Gina abruptly hollered out, "Hey Stephen, Kyle's a pilot, too!"

"Really," he said while he manipulated several buttons on his instrument panel. "We'll have to talk about that later on." The "chit chat" ended abruptly, for one could tell by Stephen's intense demeanor that he was now strictly in "pilot" mode ready to seriously take on the task at hand. "Ladies," he stated firmly, "Please secure your seat belts will you?"

"Sure thing and I'd love to talk to you about flying in Africa," Kyle shouted back over the blare of the revved up engine. Happy to be on her way to what she hoped would block out the disappointment over Ryan's rejection, she took in a deep breath then glanced over at Gina. To her surprise her friend appeared to be quite content to be in place on this small aircraft. Amazing, she thought, for most people are more afraid of flying in small planes.

Without delay, they were taxiing down the runway. "Again," Stephen called out, "be sure your seat belts are securely fastened."

"Copy that, captain," Gina yelled back over the roar of the engines. Kyle couldn't help but laugh.

It took no more than thirty minutes to reach The Ingwe Private Game Reserve, but Kyle and Gina were fortunate enough to see some spectacular views along the way.

"Oh Kyle look . . . . look," Gina cried out. "Just below us. There's some elephants!"

Kyle already had her camera at the ready and was clicking the shutter in rapid succession. "I see them, Gina, and look to your right. See that herd of cape buffalo?"

"Is that what they are?" Gina hollered. "Wow! What a sight!"

Kyle was thrilled beyond belief, and she was equally pleased to see that Gina was enjoying the experience as much as she was. "This is going to be great fun isn't it?" she raved.

Gina didn't answer, for her head was turned and she was gawking out the window, straining to take in the sights that were, apparently, so unlike anything she'd ever seen.

Flying out of Nelspruit, Stephen purposely set up his flight pattern to skirt along the Panoramic Route which anyone driving from Johannesburg would take on the way to a game reserve. He swooped down over the deep and mysterious gorges, roaring rivers and cascading waterfalls.

"Just below us now is the Blyde River Canyon," he called over his shoulder. "And ahead is Bourke's Luck Potholes. You'll get to see these last two sites on a day's trip that's been scheduled for you."

"How exciting!" Kyle replied.

When the aircraft reached The Ingwe Private Game Reserve, Stephen made sure the women got a bird's eye view of the main lodge and the surrounding area before they landed. To Kyle it didn't look like a massive complex, but one that appeared to offer a uniquely different type of accommodation experience, far from such flashy cosmopolitan chains like the Hilton Hotel and others.

Kyle likewise strained to get a glimpse of the sprawling structure nestled in a wooded area of the reserve. "Gina, look at that giant watering hole in the back!"

"That's a natural watering hole and it's directly in the path of an elephant track. You'll see a lot of elephants coming down for a drink and—"

Gina quickly broke in, "What's an elephant track, Stephen?"

"It's like a migrating path," he said. "Sometimes those paths lead right through crop land, and that's when the farmers have difficulty."

"I bet they do," Kyle stated. Turning to Gina, she went on. "But I bet I'll get some great shots of elephants there?"

"Other animals, too!" Stephen confirmed.

Kyle grinned. "Wonderful!" she said. "Hey Gina, doesn't this whole setting have an *Out of Africa* look?" Before her friend could respond, Kyle leaned forward and yelled out, "I love the place already, Stephen."

"I had a feeling you would," he countered.

"Gosh," Gina said. "I never thought I'd be remotely interested in a trip like this, but hey, this is somethin' else. Wait 'til they hear about this at the spa. Totally awesome!"

As Stephen circled the outskirts of The Ingwe, it appeared that there was some sort of a large building at the far end of the expansive reserve. Kyle figured it housed something important for it had a high fence around it. The landing strip, which Kyle estimated to be 3500 feet in length, was quite a distance from the main lodge, and it ended at the gated entrance to the reserve.

Stephen's air tour took a good thirty minutes, and by the sounds of the "ooohs and aaahs" coming from the two excited women, he must have felt certain they enjoyed it. Finally, when Stephen landed the craft on the reserve's private runway, Kyle couldn't help but comment on the precision of his feather-like landing.

"I had to," he bantered. "Hey, you're a pilot. You'd know if I bombed."

Kyle laughed along with him. When the plane came to a stop in front of the main gate, Kyle noted that there was a SUV waiting for them. "Fabulous flight, Stephen," Kyle told him. She shook the pilot's hand and offered her thanks for allowing them an overview of the reserve. "I'm sure we're going to have a great time. Hope we can get together and talk about flying in Africa sometime. That's if you get a chance, of course."

"I'd like that," he said with another charming grin. "Once you two get settled maybe we can meet at the bar and talk. In the meantime let me get your bags."

While Stephen was taking care of the luggage detail, the woman who had driven down to the gate to meet the new guests introduced herself and welcomed the two. "I'm Carole Magona, the Office Manager," she said with an ambiguous smile, "and I want you to know I'm pleased you chose to visit our reserve, for we promise you an adventure you'll long remember." She cocked her head and proudly announced, "Personally, I think we're the best in the entire area. But then I guess I'm a little prejudiced."

"That's just what Stephen said," Gina chimed in.

"We do agree on that," Carole admitted. "Now, which one of you is Kyle and which one is Gina?"

As soon as they got the introductions out of the way, they all settled in for the ride into the facility in the SUV vehicle with advertising on the side panels. "I thought perhaps you'd be driving one of those Land Rovers that we see in all of the brochures," Kyle commented.

"No, we use them for all of our game drives, though." Pointing, she explained. "You'll notice all the advertising about the reserve."

"I see that," Kyle responded as she read aloud the words, "The Ingwe Private Game Reserve, giving our adventurous guests a thrill of a lifetime!"

"And that's true. We do try to pamper our guests. By the way, in some cases the Land Rovers are called Land Cruisers. I don't know why. Maybe some private reserves think it sounds more sophisticated. Here we refer to them simply as Land Rovers. At any rate, Kyle, why don't you sit in the front seat with me, for I see you've got your camera ready for action?"

Kyle beamed. "Great!" She stepped up into the passenger seat. "It seems so strange sitting on the left side."

"I suppose it'll take some getting used to, for we do drive on the other side of the road from the States. Hop in Gina and we'll be on our way."

Gina quickly pulled herself up into the seat behind Kyle. "I'm very willing to be back here. As Kyle knows, my idea of adventure is a lot different from hers."

"Well, I don't think you'll find any other reserve that packs such a fulfilling safari experience in such a short period of time." She paused for an instant as if she'd forgotten something . . . finally adding, "It's not for the weak of heart though. Just remember anything you want that you don't see provided just let me know, and I'll do my best to supply it, okay? Actually you two are really fortunate, for we usually have at least eight guests at a time, but the next group won't be coming here until Friday. So, for the week you're staying with us, you'll be our only priority. How lucky is that?"

"I could use some luck," Kyle replied, the words slipping from her lips before she realized the implications that statement might infer. For an instant she pondered whether or not to mention the fact that she could barely wait for this vacation. Yet, she hesitated, fearing Carole might ask why she felt that way. But she did inform the office manager that this vacation was definitely a much needed getaway.

Gina started to elaborate, but again seeing Kyle shake her head and frown, she decided to keep her mouth shut about the whole matter. Fortunately, Carole dropped the subject as they began the lengthy drive to the lodge proper.

Carole pointed out some of the unique spots along the way, namely the Kopjes. "That's the Dutch word for the small isolated hills with outcroppings of rock that you'll see all over the reserve. They act as a refuge for lion, baboon and hyrax as well as a variety of birds and reptiles." When Gina asked what a hyrax looked like, Carole detailed the animal as, in part, resembling a large rat.

"Yuck!" Gina replied, wrinkling her nose in distaste. "That sounds ugly."

"Well, let's put it this way. They're not what the average vacationer is looking for in Africa." Just as they rounded a bend in the road Carole pointed up ahead. "See, there on your right! That's a Kopje."

Kyle raised her Nikon. "Oh my gosh. I can see a lion up there." She clicked off several shots. With a voice filled with excitement, she called out, "Our first lion sighting, Gina!"

Carole smiled as she drove along Africa's vast Lowveld. She explained the term then interjected, "The word Lowvelt is another Dutch word. You may have heard of these areas as savannahs. They're like grasslands."

Kyle's eyes widened. "Now that's a spectacular sight. Look at the golden color of that tall grass. I've never seen anything like it."

Gina, too, appeared to be in awe of the surroundings, for her arms were waving from here to there as she pointed out the magnificent views all around them. "Wow!" she said. "This is turning out to be really wild, right Kyle?"

Kyle sat mute, mesmerized by the beauty of it all. "This is better than I'd ever dreamed it would be."

"I think you'll have a great time here. I've always loved the sunsets," Carole said rambling on. "Some of our guests tell me that they have never seen such vibrant colors of orange, red and gold anywhere in the world like here in Africa. I don't know, for I've never left this area, but I'd be interested in knowing if you feel the same."

"I'm sure looking forward to seeing everything including the sunsets, but especially the animals," Kyle countered.

"Oh, you'll definitely see all of the Big 5. We guarantee that as an incentive to come here and visit our private reserve. We're not as large as some of the other private reserves like Sabi Sand which is adjacent to us, but we do promise a unique experience. I think you'll enjoy your stay."

"What do you mean by the Big 5?" Gina questioned. "I don't get it?"

Before Carole could answer, Kyle interjected, "Aren't they the five animals that will come after you if you get in their way?"

"That's right. They will not necessarily run away like most animals will. They'll really hunt you down. The Big 5 actually include the elephant, the rhinoceros, the lion, the cape buffalo and the leopard. Some think that the hippo is one of those included in the Big 5, but that's not true even though they kill more people in Africa each year than any one of the others do. Of all of these, though, you're most likely see the leopard the least, for it's quite an elusive creature."

"I've always wondered what the difference is," Kyle asked, "between going to a private reserve and going to one of those places in Kruger National Park?"

"There's a vast difference. In Kruger Park the wildlife game rangers are not allowed to go, as they say, off trail. You'll find that Stephen will take you far off the beaten path into areas where you'll be able to experience the animals up close and personal. As I said, he's the best. I've been here for two years and all our guests rave about him."

Kyle's eyebrows arched thoughtfully. There was something compelling about the way Carole's voice choked up a bit when she talked about Stephen that made her wonder if the two might have a romantic connection. With that thought in mind, she eagerly told Carol about the off-course excursion Stephen took them on when they flew into the reserve. "He gave us an expansive view of the entire reserve as well as the lodge on our way in," Kyle said. "It was fabulous to see it from the air."

"I can't wait to see what the lodge is like inside," Gina chimed in. "It looked really nice from the plane, and how about those special colored leopards that Kyle keeps talking about?"

"Personally, I haven't been on a game run for awhile, but then I don't get in on many of those. I did hear, though, that Gideon Courtney, who's one of the owners of the reserve, says he's seen them. I don't know if Stephen's spotted one yet, but if one's out there, you can bet he'll find it. They're called *Mauve Leopards*, for their coat has a lavender-gray cast to it."

"How'd they get that color?" Kyle asked.

"You'll have to ask Stephen about that. I haven't a clue, and why we're the only reserve that has these leopards is a mystery to me. Actually in 2002 most of the fences between the various reserves were torn down and the animals are now able to migrate as they want. They say that's better when it comes to breeding."

Gina interrupted in a shrill yelp. "Quick, look over there Kyle . . . to your left! I see a whole bunch of giraffes."

"That's called a tower of giraffes," Carole noted.

Kyle cheered, a rapt excitement lighting her face. "I can see why. Can you stop for a minute again? I'd like to get some shots."

Carole did so as Kyle rolled down her window to get a clear view. She clicked off a half dozen or so photos while Carole went on to explain, "The name that always puzzles me is the reference they make to a group of zebra. They're commonly called a Zeal, but some call them a dazzle. Which is really not so strange."

Kyle set her camera aside. "Seriously," Kyle queried. "A dazzle?"

"That's what they say. Sounded odd to me at first. But to be honest when you see all of their stripes in a cluster, it does tend to dazzle you. Watch for some on your trip and see if I'm right." No sooner had Carole started the engine and had moved on down the road than she slammed on the breaks and cried out, "Oh my gosh. Look there! Impalas."

Gina and Kyle looked on in amazement as two antelope looking animals leaped onto the road and raced in front of them, jumping into the air, possibly as much as six or seven feet as they passed. "Oh, this is just perfect!" Kyle mumbled while snapping the camera shutter with as much speed as her Nikon would allow. "Sure wish I had my camcorder, but it's in my suitcase. I didn't think we'd see so many animals so soon."

"You'll need your camcorder for those action shots." Carole paused and glanced sideways at Kyle. "Strangely enough in the Zulu language the impalas are called gazelles."

"They're sure fast," Gina noted, watching Kyle while she leaned out the window in an attempt to catch a photo of them as they skirted off into the brush.

"Be sure to notice on your game drives that the gazelles don't have the black stripe on their rear ends like the impalas do and they can be smaller, too."

When Kyle stopped for an instant to refocus for a final photo of the graceful creatures as they headed for the tall grass, a huge bull elephant lumbered out of the dense brush to the right of their car not twenty yards in front of them. He suddenly turned and looked directly their way.

Hesitantly, but in a voice charged with emotion, Carole warned, "Sit perfectly still and don't make a sound!"

Chapter 5

Saturday Morning

Lynn Greene drove up to the entry of The Ingwe Private Game Reserve expecting the guard to immediately open the gate, for she knew the guards were well aware that she was the only one of the owners who drove a silver Porsche. Irritated when he didn't acknowledge her presence, she honked the horn three times then cursed, "Shit, get with it you imbecile!" Most were used to the foul language she'd frequently utter when things didn't progress as swiftly as she wished or when she didn't immediately get her way.

When the gates failed to open, she made a wide gesture of disapproval then pressed her hand on the horn again allowing it to blare in a steady stream that was loud enough to awaken the dead. "You damn idiot wake up!" she hollered out the window.

The guard, who'd been napping in his chair, sprang into action and the gates parted none too soon, for he knew that Lynn would most likely not hesitate to ram the wooden gate, leaving a trail of broken wood splinters. At least that's what he'd been told.

In this instance he got it open in time to watch her zoom past the gate, a cloud of dust from the roadway following in her wake.

Of course, Lynn wasn't in any mood to observe the scenic drive into the main lodge, for she had other things on her mind. But for any visitor to the area, the view offered a sheer visual delight because the curving road featured a host of unique sights, one of which is a good-sized watering hole that was aptly named "Hippo Brook" by Lynn's husband, Damon, and his partner Gideon Courtney. Another source of profound awe lay in this wonderland of vast savannahs or what the Afrikaans call a Lowveld or bushy grass plains. Waving in the wind, these golden fields of tall grass capture the essence of nature at its best. But again, Lynn had other things to think about and nothing, not even the beauty of Africa, could deter her from heading to her husband's office to speak her mind.

Actually, The Ingwe Private Game Reserve was not quite the facilities one would expect to find in the middle of the Big 5 territory, though the lodge was surrounded by a high fence placed about fifty yards out from the main structure including an equally secure tall gate. Both functioned to provide safety for their guests.

When Lynn reached the front gate, she pressed the button on her remote control unit. The gate was barely open before she barreled through it and hurriedly parked the car in her reserved parking space in front of the lodge. As she rushed through the lobby past the reservation desk, anyone who got a glimpse of the look on her face would know instantly that something wasn't going well. The intense frown, along with her rapid stride were signs of her displeasure. Carefully making her way around the reception desk toward the back of the building, she entered her husband's office, slamming the door behind her.

Startled, Damon looked up. "I see you made it back from Johannesburg."

She pounded her fist on his desk and blurted out in a voice laced with bitterness, "Yeah, I saw the Dean then I stopped at the bank and was told they won't extend our loan before seeing the profit and loss statements. You were supposed to take care of that last Friday! What happened?"

"I thought they wanted them by *next* Friday," he replied with a narrowing scowl. Pointing, he added, "See, I've got that date marked on my calendar, but don't worry I'll get the records to them this afternoon." He put his hand up to try and suppress her anger, telling her, "Just calm down!"

The spot on her cheek that always bulged out when she got angry was now ruby red as she shouted, "Don't you dare tell me to calm down. If it wasn't for me pushing you to get things done, we'd be in bankruptcy by now." Lynn slumped into a chair, her stomach roiling in angst. Pulling out her silver cigarette holder, she loaded it and lit up. After inhaling a deep lungful, she quickly explained that she was going in to town to see Gideon. "He says he's got news on that shipment from Jon Leatham. It better come in for I want out of here!"

She stopped for a second to catch her breath then pulled a long drag on her cigarette and exhaled through her nose. "The Dean says he's prepared to set me up as the head of the Toxic Research Center which is just what I had in mind, but he says he can't hold that position for me too much longer."

"Of course . . . toxic research. You're more fascinated with snakes than you are with me."

"It's not a fascination you fool," Lynn spat, her bulging orbs glared at him with frightening fury as anger burned away any other emotions. "The anti-coagulants from those snakes save lives, and you know that's what I was working on when you came up with the hair-brained scheme to buy this reserve three years ago. Well, I've had it, and I want to get back to my research in Johannesburg."

"Listen, there's no way I'm leaving this place. I want to expand it not sell it, and don't even talk about the divorce papers. You already know I won't sign 'em. Besides, you'll lose all of your Daddy's fortune if you even try to divorce me, for I've got those photos. You sure don't want your precious Daddy to see those, do you?" He rolled his hand over his balding head and squinted at her over his coke bottle glasses. "So, you'd better just settle down and make that Reptile Exhibit you set up on the premises your future with those snakes. That's the way it's going to be. Do I make myself clear?" Damon bellowed. His tone of voice sliced to the bone, silencing any excuses.

As her brow furrowed in concentration and her heart seemed to beat out of control, she blared, "We'll see about that. Remember Daddy said he won't give you any more funding."

"Well, he hasn't been informed of those scandalous photos I've got of you and you know who, and as far as funding goes, I've got the *Mauve Leopard* attraction coming to The Ingwe. Just wait and see. That's going to change everything."

"You're a bastard you know that?" Lynn barked, veins crosshatching her temples.

"Bastard or not, I'm running this show."

"You'd better keep in mind we've got two guests coming in today and that special attraction you keep talking about better be in place. You know what I mean. Besides the buyers will be here on Friday, and I want those two guests to be so enthused about seeing this new breed of leopard that they spread the word so the buyers will jump at the chance to sign the contract."

"That contract wasn't my idea. You and Gideon set that up, and I won't sign it as a sale. I told you I'll only sign a contract that offers the buyers a chance to purchase shares of The Ingwe, not take over the place."

Damon always seemed to rub Lynn's nerves like high-grade sand paper. So, in retaliation, she drew in another full breath then blew the smoke directly in Damon's direction, for she knew how he was bitterly against her smoking. Red faced and ready to explode, she attempted to change the subject. "Has Gideon contacted you at all?"

Damon leaned back in his chair, rested his elbow on the chair arm and tapped his fingers on his desk, knowing full well that doing so annoyed Lynn. "No," he said, "I haven't heard from him since he left for Tzaneen to get the shipment."

"Hell, you should be checking on him by now. He's only a partner, remember? You're holding the major shares in this venture, but it seems like he's the only one doing anything around here. They'll be plenty of complaints if those guests don't see those *Mauve Leopards*. We've advertised them everywhere. Whether this place sells or not, we can't keep charging exorbitant rates unless we can produce." Abruptly standing up she leaned forward, her face inches from his. With delight she forcefully snubbed out her cigarette in her husband's ceramic coffee tray then pointed her finger, with its meticulously manicured and polished nail, directly at him. "All I can say is that shipment better get here and soon!"

Damon stared at her with an unwavering sense of confidence that he knew would irritate her.

She started to leave then suddenly whipped about and glowered at him, her breath pumping hard. "You'll pay for this someday. I'd watch my back if I were you. And by the way, who is that idiot at the front entrance gate? I ended up honking and screaming out the car window at him before he opened it up."

Damon darted a quick glance at the ceiling before responding. "That would be Bapoto. He just started last week."

"Get the guy up to speed or fire him, you hear!" She said, issuing the request as a command. "Imagine if that happened to some of our guests. It's not a good sign of any kind of expedient customer service and you know it!"

Again Lynn slammed the door as she left her husband's office, anger rumbling through her like a jet at take off. It would have been difficult for Holly, the receptionist, to have missed hearing the curse Lynn uttered under her breath as she exited the office. Being quite familiar with Lynn's outbursts, however, Holly merely shrugged it off and continued typing as if nothing had happened.

Dropping his forehead into the palm of his hands, Damon sat for a moment, trying to calm down as the silence around him pooled deep. The marriage was in trouble, but he felt he had the upper hand. Still he was well aware of the fact that he needed her father's support if this whole venture were to succeed, for there were times when the receipts coming in were slow.

Damon knew their marriage had been built on greed. He'd married Lynn for one reason . . . her money. He had used her vulnerability at the time to get her to marry him. She, having just lost her mother to cancer, was so distraught that his purposely charming presence and his deceptive façade of caring had given her some peace. Now, however, things were coming to a head, and he realized he had to stand firm or he'd lose all he'd worked so hard to build.

Finally, after some thought, he lifted his head, then hesitantly pulled open the bottom drawer of his desk, whipped out a bottle of scotch and a shot glass and poured himself a drink. He'd tried all too often to give up his love of the stuff, but found it was the only way of relieving the pressure he felt running a competitive business such as a game reserve. For a second, after downing the drink, he closed his eyes and frowned. With a woeful sigh he reached out and punched a button on his phone. "Holly, see if you can contact Gideon before my wife meets him and tell him to call me on my cell. It's urgent. I've got to get to the bank, but I should be back by three."

Chapter 6

Saturday

Gideon answered his cell phone with a brisk, "Yeah! What is it?"

"It's me. You were supposed to be back by now. Where are you? I've been waiting at the restaurant for twenty minutes."

"I couldn't get the money from the bank, Lynn. I think Damon's screwed up again and my other contact hasn't come through yet. You know what that means."

"I know and you're right. Apparently Damon dropped the ball. He told me that he had the wrong date on his calendar. He's going in this afternoon. Can you get the shipment without the cash?"

"No. Jon won't bargain. He's backing off, or so he told me on the phone when I called him. I'm heading for his place now. No one knows about this under the radar deal but us, yet the guy has somehow found out that he can get more options in research trials from a group up north in Botswana. Apparently their options have no restrictions."

Lynn placed her hand over the receiver and whispered softly, "Well we've gotta get that delivery today. Our guests are already here. Do you really think Jon will be trouble?"

"I'm sure of it."

"Somehow you'll have to close that deal. Take care of it, okay?"

"I'd already planned on it. As I said I'm heading there now. I just talked to him on his cell, and he's expecting me though he sounds like crap, a cold or something." In his usual clear, forceful voice, Gideon added, "I'm going to do exactly what you and I talked about."

"Store them in the warehouse. I'll meet you there. How long will it take?"

"I should be back by two-thirty or three."

"I knew I could count on you!" Lynn said as she hung up. A grueling cramp pressed in on her stomach and she bent over in pain. Oh no, she thought. Not now. She knew her nerves were at a breaking point, and her husband Damon's attitude had only added to the stress she felt about their relationship. After heaving a sigh, she leaned back on the soft cushion in the restaurant booth and dialed Damon at his office.

"Damn it!" she said under her breath when she reached his voice mail. "Gideon told me Jon won't go for our deal anymore. We're going to have to close out that source. Too bad you botched the banking. Listen, I'll be in town for awhile. I'll see you at the Welcoming Dinner at seven, and you'd better be there!" She hurriedly closed the cover on the cell phone, gestured to a nearby waitress by snapping her fingers and, with a wry twist of her lips and a tone that signified urgency, she bellowed, "More coffee over here!"

Chapter 7

Saturday

It was raining when Gideon left for Jon Leatham's compound near Tzaneen, a city of approximately 650,000 and the largest municipality in the Limpopo Province He was careful to drive his unmarked truck within the speed limit so as not to make his visit to the region conspicuous in any way. He called Jon on his cell phone en route to be sure the old man would be waiting for him.

When Jon answered, Gideon could hardly recognize his voice. "What's the matter?" Gideon asked, "You still sound terrible."

Jon coughed into the receiver before replying that he thought he had the flu. "But that isn't a problem. I'll be here, Gideon. Just bring the money, okay? I've got your leopards waiting."

Gideon heard a distinct disconnect but not before he heard Jon utter another deep guttural cough into the receiver.

Gideon glanced to his right to be sure his crow bar was still on the seat. Unfortunately, he thought, I'll most likely have to use it to silence him, for it doesn't sound like he's in any mood to give us an extension of time to pay for the prize animals. With a stubbornly set jaw, he breathed in a great gulp of air knowing what he had to do would not be pretty, but it had to be done. Yet he rationalized that since no one else knew about this exchange, there would be no way anyone could trace the event back to him. As Gideon passed the Vervet Monkey Foundation which houses over 600 orphaned Vervet monkeys, he knew he was within five or so miles of the deserted road that would take him to the compound, a facility that no one would ever discover unless they were given specific directions because it was in a densely forested area east of Tzaneen. Since Jon was dealing in what some might refer to as a shady research project that could land him in trouble with the South African authorities, he needed the privacy this place offered plus a chance to garner unlimited resources. Gideon and Damon had given him that opportunity and he had willingly agreed.

Just shy of the gravel road leading to the front door of this secretive facility, Gideon stopped the truck, pulled a plastic raincoat from the seat beside him and stepped out of the cab door. The rain had intensified against a somber sky by now, so he quickly slipped into the raincoat and hurriedly scooted back into the cab, then checked to be sure the tranquilizer gun, that he'd loaded earlier, was in the cab door's side pocket and that the crowbar he'd placed on the passenger's seat of the truck was still in place. He quickly brushed a few rain-soaked strands of his brown hair from his eyes while scenarios of what might happen as he proceeded with the plan swirled through his mind.

Finally, after hesitantly grabbing the wheel, he started the engine and slowly made his way along the gravel road. His goal was to ease past the front entrance, drive to the back of the home and check to see if Jon was there. If Jon wasn't in, he planned to drive to the old barn in the rear of the property. Gideon knew there would be no one else around, for Jon was, if nothing else, a bona fide recluse who purposely lived by himself. Any stranger who encroached on his land would be met with a scowl, a curse and a twelve-gage, double barrel shotgun.

Gideon had known about Jon Leatham's work in research for many years. Fact is, even though the man was approaching his nineties, he was mentally as bright as a shiny new Krugerrand coin. So, Gideon and Damon had offered this unusually talented scientist the incredible opportunity to use his skill as a researcher, who had been banned from his last job for trying to create animal mutations, to develop a new breed of leopard that would enhance their game reserve and possibly encourage buyers to purchase the property. If not, then Gideon and Lynn hoped that Stephen would come through with a deal he was working on to purchase the property himself, for he'd always wanted to own The Ingwe. Anything Lynn and Gideon could do that would allow them to get rid of Damon and head for Johannesburg together would fit nicely into their plans.

Lynn had been adamant about selling the property as was Gideon; however, Damon was against any sale, for he loved the idea of running a private reserve. Therein lay the conflict in the partnership, a partnership that was slowly unraveling mostly due to Lynn's and Gideon's insistence on returning to a life in Johannesburg.

At any rate, Jon had jumped at the chance to work unfettered and the money he received took care of all the requirements needed to keep his efforts under the radar of the authorities. To Jon the money was only a necessity. His real pride came in stretching the limits of nature by amplifying his work on animal mutations.

Things had gone along well and both men assumed they would continue. Now that Jon had gone rogue, insinuating that he might be inclined to take his remarkable research to other interested parties who would let him carry on a more varied set of complex procedures, Gideon knew he had to take action. He couldn't allow that to happen. He and his partner, Damon, had too much invested in this latest venture, a scheme that would make their Ingwe Private Game Reserve the most unique and profitable in the entire region, and they, particularly Lynn, Damon's wife, didn't want anything to ruin that plan.

Gideon figured there were only two ways to settle this quandary about the animals. The first was to try and reason with Jon. The second was sinister, but perhaps the only way. He reckoned he'd play it by ear and hope for the best.

When Gideon finally stopped the truck at the rear door of Jon's dilapidated home, he leaned over, grabbed the crowbar and exited the truck. He carefully hooked the heavy metal bar over his belt and closed the flap on the front of his raincoat. It was still raining, but the downpour had turned into a light shower. Still, he was thankful for the moisture, for most any amount of water would help to eradicate foot or tire tracks or other evidence of his being there.

Gideon found the porch that stretched across the back of Jon's home hadn't changed. The screens were torn and the door handle was fragile, being barely attached to the door frame. Gideon was sure the house hadn't been painted in twenty years, for a good deal of the corrugated metal siding was rusting away. There were large gaps where the metal had fallen away from the basic structure and one could see inside.

He slipped out of his boots and set them under the roof overhang. Then, in stocking feet, he stepped into what any hoarder would consider a dream home. The porch, though exposed to the elements, was packed with junk of all sorts, much too overwhelming a sight for Gideon to comprehend. Although once before when he'd briefly stepped onto the porch, he'd noted the clutter of old cans, newspapers, crates of all kinds, and food containers filled with scraps of discarded meat and molding bread along with crawling cockroaches which were, most likely, delighted with the living conditions. Gideon hadn't seen the inside of Jon's home, for whenever Gideon visited the place, Jon always immediately took him to the barn. But this time when Gideon stepped into the kitchen which, like the porch area, was in shambles and a bed of filth, the stench was so overpowering it made him gag. *How can anyone live like this?*

Since Jon usually did all of his feeding chores in the barn during the morning and late afternoon hours, Gideon assumed the man would be inside the home. So, he shouted out Jon's name several times, but got no answer. Jon was nowhere in sight. That was a plus as far as Gideon was concerned, for he hurried back into Jon's crowded office then made his way through the clutter to Jon's desk. Surprisingly, though the home was in total disarray when it came to cleanliness and organization, everything within a three foot radius of Jon's desk was as clean and extraordinarily systematized as the records in a computer hard drive. It was amazing, and another plus for Gideon, who quickly scooped up all of the files he could find on Jon's recent research efforts on the part of The Ingwe Private Game Reserve.

Now, moving as swiftly as he could, he rushed to the porch door, put his boots on and hurried to his truck. Everything was going along just as he'd planned. Even the rain was cooperating, for it was still drizzling, thus covering his tracks. He opened the cab door and slipped into the driver's seat while at the same time placing Jon's research records on the seat beside him. He started the engine and, in low gear, drove down the gravel road to the old barn.

One of the double doors to the barn was ajar. Gideon had noted that Jon always left one side door open when he was performing his animal chores. Since Jon had been so adamant on the phone when Gideon told him he wouldn't have the cash at this time, Gideon wasn't expecting any cooperation. Basically though he was hopeful that something could be worked out, so he wouldn't have to follow through with the plan he and Lynn, excluding Damon, had agreed upon.

Gideon partially opened the other barn door and peered in. All was quiet until he called out to Jon. Then, through the semi-darkness of the barn's interior he could hear the underlying deep throaty grunts of the big cats, welcome sounds to Gideon's ears. He knew Jon was in poor health and hard of hearing so he called out again. Yet he received no answer. So, not knowing what to expect, he grabbed the crowbar from under his plastic raincoat and stepped into the barn. Seeing as how it was a rainy day, the barn's interior was darker than usual and it took his eyes a moment to adjust to the surroundings. He'd noted that Jon's home was nothing but clutter and filth, but he could tell the barn was cleaner than anyone would expect from someone who was raising African leopards. *But where is Jon?*

Apparently, the sound of Gideon's loud cry as he called out a third time caused several of the great beasts to growl and for a minute he stood so transfixed that he almost forgot his purpose in being there.

By now, however, he was quite able to see the many cages that lined the barn walls. He quickly observed there were eight of them. As he walked along viewing each cage, he noticed that six of the eight cages contained Jon's prize *Mauve Leopards*. The other two cages housed what Gideon knew were the two most recognizable leopards, those with spots of golden yellow and circles with black rosettes. He had been told by Jon that these black circles are not only on the fur but on the skin as well. Whatever the case, apparently Jon used these standard versions of a leopard in some kind of a process of mutation to produce the most spectacular creatures Gideon had ever seen. The coats on the *Mauve Leopards* possessed a muted lavender-gray coloring, and surprisingly the black rosettes were absent or so nondescript as to be almost invisible, leaving the fur with a velvety look. Gideon was awestruck, for these creatures were amazing, positively hypnotizing. Again, he stood transfixed.

Pulling himself together he looked ahead and observed that the door at the other end of the barn was partially open. So, figuring Jon might be out in the yard, he tightened his grip on the crowbar and the tranquilizing gun he'd brought with him then hurriedly moved toward the door, ready for any assault he'd encounter. But when he reached the last stall in the barn, he glanced to his right and gasped. Jon was slumped over one of the bales of hay. His face, pale and gaunt, was twisted in anguish.

Gideon felt his heartbeat quicken.

CHAPTER 8

SATURDAY

While Gideon stood in shock upon seeing Jon's lifeless body collapsed in the barn stall, Carole, Kyle and Gina likewise sat stunned as they viewed the huge male elephant who apparently had been startled by the presence of the vehicle on the road.

Carole's muted words, "Sit perfectly still and don't make a sound," didn't register easily with Gina, for as Kyle darted a glance behind her she spied her friend drop to the floor in the back seat, her face alarmingly ashen and her mouth set in a grimace.

"Oh jeez!" Gina mumbled under her breath, her voice shaken. "What next?" she added in a strangled whisper.

Though Kyle was shocked, she couldn't take her eyes off the giant beast. She sat totally motionless, fascinated by the animal's behavior as he suddenly began to shake his head. Kyle was mesmerized despite her fear. She felt her flesh stir. Her heart beat so hard that she could feel the vibrations in her temples.

The elephant's huge ears flapped fiercely against his sides. He raised his trunk and trumpeted an earth-shattering bellow that shook the road bed as well as the SUV. Kyle, though as stunned as either one of the women, raised her camera and, forgetting all else around her, began clicking the shutter in an attempt to capture a scene she never would have imagined she'd ever encounter.

Then all was quiet for an instant. Kyle thought the episode was over, when suddenly the beast swung his trunk down between his tusks and lowered his head while his ears continued to flap in the wind.

Carole caught herself just short of a scream as she clapped her hand over her mouth. Gina reached up and tried to grasp Kyle's arm. "Damn, what's happenin'?" she blurted out.

Before anyone could reply, the elephant let out another frightful high-pitched screech. Kyle watched as his front leg clawed at the gravel road shooting a cloud of dust far into the sky. Then, with a huff, he charged forward toward the car at an alarming clip.

CHAPTER 9

SATURDAY

Even though adrenaline was rushing through her body and her heart beat frantically, Kyle continued to click the shutter on her Nikon, unabashed by the concept that she might be the victim of a death charge. It was a thrill she'd never known before, and she wasn't about to give up a chance to capture the images on film. If I only had my camcorder, she thought.

As Gina said later, it seemed like the charge lasted an eternity as she lay quivering on the floor of the SUV, but the episode likely persisted no more than a few seconds before the huge animal stopped short, perhaps as few as ten feet from the SUV. He raised his trunk, uttered another high-pitched cry in which Kyle actually could see inside the beast's mouth. Then, as disruptively as the frightful charge had begun, the huge elephant turned and lumbered across the road into the dense brush.

Kyle blew out a lungful of air in a labored gasp that caught the tightening of her jaw. She hurriedly twisted about and poked Gina who still lay huddled on the bed of the vehicle. "He's gone," she exclaimed her voice beset with emotion as her shoulders sagged and her heartbeat began to slow down a bit. Then, quickly turning to Carole, who had her hands clamped on the steering wheel and a frozen look on her face, Kyle excitedly added, "I got it all on film. Wow! That was a real thrill."

"My God, girl! Are you crazy?" Gina wailed in anguish, pulling herself up onto the back seat. "That was a thrill? That was a death wish for cripes sake. I've aged ten years, and you can be sure I need a change of pants." She leaned forward and dropped her head into her hands, hands that were shaking so badly that one would think the poor woman had palsy. "Oh no! What else can happen?"

Fine lines etched the corners of Kyle's eyes and she blew out a lung full of air. "I don't know," she confessed, "but the trip has certainly started out with a thrill."

Carole gave her head a toss and, in a voice filled with emotion, she blurted out, "Whew! To be honest that was not the kind of thrill we advertise. In all my time here I have never, and I really mean *never*, seen an elephant attack a car like that."

Kyle could tell the woman was not the "assured" person who met them at the gate. It was obvious the event had affected Carole as she went on to say, "I've heard about elephant attacks on film, but I've never been in the middle of one, and I've got to admit that shocked me, too, Gina." She rested her head on the seat rest for a moment before revving the engine. "Let's get out of here and on to the lodge, oka—"

"It can't be fast enough," Gina interrupted. "I'm shaking like a leaf and I need a shower. I'm sure you know why."

Disengaged from the two women's interaction, Kyle sat, head down, reviewing the photos she'd just taken of a charging male beast. "Oh Gina, these shots are fantastic. Prize winners for sure."

An exhausted Gina bit down on a finger nail she'd broken off during the encounter. "Great!" she offered with a hand gesture. "Now can we get on to the lodge? My head's splittin'."

"Of course," Carole said regaining her composure. "We'll be there in no time."

Kyle again paid no heed to the verbal exchange. With a continued burst of enthusiasm, she went ahead photographing in an effort to capture all she could of the scenery and whatever animal sightings she saw along the way. Fortunately, at least as far as Gina was concerned, the women didn't encounter any other extreme confrontations and the ride was long enough to allow her time to let her nerves settle down.

Gina's cry, "Is that the lodge?" was an outburst of transparent pleasure.

"That's it," Carole responded, happy to see her guest relay a feeling of joy and not fright.

Both Gina and Kyle strained to see out the windows at the formidable structure nestled in a lush tree-lined area on a slight hill overlooking an enormous natural waterhole.

"We'll be inside in no time," Carole advised as she tapped her finger on her remote control unit, allowing the tall gates to swing open.

The lodge up ahead was enough to make Kyle's heart beat a bit faster from sheer delight. She was certain she'd chosen a true wildlife experience in Africa, the Land of Contrasts. The two-story structure was formidable looking with a massive thatched roof. Of note, the second floor was built like all stilt buildings, high above the ground with an encircling railed balcony. The building was reddish brown in color and rich in the warm tones of the surrounding area, a refreshing change from modern city buildings made of steel and glass.

Carole pointed ahead as she described the building in detail. "It's two stories high as you can see and it's all made out of African Mahogany that's termite resistant. I think you're going to be amazed at the lobby."

"Why?" Kyle asked.

"You'll see 'cause we're coming up on it now."

Gina nudged Kyle. "Hey look. It has no walls around the first floor!"

Both women marveled at the front entrance that was, indeed, open to the elements. "I can't believe they'd have anythin' like this on a safari trip," Gina said. "Aren't they worried about animals comin' into the place?"

"No, the fencing keeps them away and we do have guards." Carol stopped short and offered a humorous giggle. "I must say though, that occasionally we do have a Vervet or a Malbrouck monkey pop in for a visit. But the guards are right on their tails if they do manage to sneak in." Carole smiled. "It's fun to watch them being chased. They squeal a lot and they're speedy little devils."

"Well, I can't wait to see the place," Kyle said while Carole parked the car. "This is going to be so much fun!"

"Don't worry," Carole advised, "we'll have you in your suite in no time. You can settle in and have lunch by the pool. How's that sound?"

Kyle was so lost in thought about what was ahead for the two of them as she gazed in wonderment at the open-air lobby that she ignored Carole's comment, but Gina was quick to speak up. "Now this's more like it. Come on, Kyle. Let's get settled in and go to the pool for lunch. I'm starvin'."

A porter was there at the entrance and ready to scoop up the women's luggage and take it into the immense lobby which had a high vaulted ceiling and huge wooden beams that seemed to stretch to the sky. The furnishings were rich in colorful African textures and large animal carvings were scattered throughout. A massive stone fireplace stood tall against the far wall along with a winding stairway of polished wood that soared up to the second floor. In Kyle's mind the sight was enough to take one's breath away.

"Here we are," Carole stated with a decided hint of pride in her voice. "We'll get your keys and, as I said, have you in your suite before you know it."

After getting their keys from Holly at the reception desk, Carole escorted the two women through the lobby, the bar and the restaurant into the poolside area. "Lunch will be served here in about half an hour," she stated. "So you can come right on down after you get settled in. The luggage will be in your suite when we get there. Just follow me."

Gina sprinted ahead exclaiming, "You bet." Her enthusiasm was contagious, for the other two quickly followed. Turning back to Kyle, Gina whispered, "I really need a shower and that pool looks great. Just so we don't have any more thrills. I'm thrilled out!"

A smile touched Kyle's lips. "You know you're a good sport. Who else would make it through an elephant attack and not hate me for dragging you here?"

Carole finally forged ahead and led them back through the restaurant, the bar and into the lobby where Kyle spied Stephen at the far end of the massive room. She noted how Carole was quick to raise her hand in a wave as well as a cheery greeting, "See you later Stephen?" she hollered.

"Yeah," he yelled back. "I'll be poolside for lunch first. You two are going to meet me there, right?"

"We'll be there," Kyle responded as she turned to Carol. "He said he wanted to talk shop since we're both pilots."

It was obvious to Kyle when she relayed that information to Carole that the woman was more than a little annoyed at her for showing an interest in the pilot/game ranger. *Perhaps I'm stepping too close to the fire on this one*, Kyle contemplated. *Then again, the guy is good looking and personable.* Yet, when she recalled Ryan's rejection, she grabbed the threads of that unraveling trauma and thought better of getting involved with any guy. *Not now. Maybe not ever!*

Carol's demeanor seemed to change after that verbal exchange between Kyle and Stephen. Kyle noticed how the woman appeared less eager to please or, Kyle reasoned, *I could be reading her wrong.*

While the three women crossed the room, Carole asked, in a portentous tone, "Do you want to take the stairs or the elevator? The elevator's down that corridor." She pointed to her right.

Kyle shrugged. "The stairs are fine."

"Sure. I don't care. Just get me to a shower," Gina chimed in.

Then, as the women passed the reception desk, Holly rushed up from behind them. "Hey, Carole," she called out. All three stopped in their tracks. "I'm sorry to bother you, but I forgot to tell you when the guests checked in. I've got a notice here for a Kyle Griffin."

"I'm Kyle, what is it?"

"I don't know. It came in by FAX and one of the other clerks put it in a sealed envelope." The clerk handed the envelope to Kyle and smiled. "I'm sorry. I guess I was confused by the name. With the name Kyle I was expecting a man."

Kyle grinned back. "Don't worry about it. That was my mother's doing. I get a lot of mail trying to recruit me into the army."

"What's that all about?" Gina asked inquisitively as Carole looked on.

"Huh," Kyle noted as she glanced at the sender's name on the envelope. "It's from Ryan."

Gina pressed arguably, "What in the world does he want? And how did he find out you were here?"

"I've no idea."

"Good grief, aren't you going to open it?" Gina insisted. She raised an eyebrow and glared at Kyle. "Hey girl, "I'd want to kick his ass!"

"Whoa," Carole said with a dubious look on her face. "That sounds ominous."

Kyle downplayed the scene by casually stating, "It's nothing to worry about. Just a little bit of trouble in paradise, right Gina?" As the three of them made their way up the stairs, Gina dropped the matter, for she evidently caught on to the fact that Kyle didn't want to talk about Ryan in front of Carole.

Their suite was a short distance from the stairway and when they walked in, a broad smile lit Kyle's face. "Wow! This is beyond belief, far more than I expected."

The women's luggage was neatly stowed in one corner of the spacious suite while two beds with end posts, draped with sheer netting, accommodated one wall. Overhead fans whirled about the glass-enclosed room with its wall of windows that opened onto a large wooden sundeck, offering the guests a glorious view of the natural waterhole not too far away.

Kyle was awestruck. "This is delightful," she told Carole.

"I knew you'd be impressed," Carole said while she abruptly turned and headed toward the door. "But listen, I'll leave you two to get settled in." Glancing back over her shoulder she hollered, "If you need anything that isn't here, just let me know and don't forget lunch at poolside in thirty minutes. By the way, don't be alarmed if you hear a drum beat around dinner time. That's an indication that dinner's being served in the restaurant and that's usually after six, though tonight there's a Welcome Dinner at seven."

"Sounds great and you can bet we'll be there!" Gina called out.

After Carole had gone, Kyle gloated, "Well, what do you think of the place?"

Gina let out a loud, "Hallelujah! How in the world can you afford this? It must have cost a fortune."

"Hey, all of the money I'd saved for the wedding went into this trip. We've only got a week here. So enjoy it, okay?"

"Oh, I plan to." That said Gina flopped down on the bed while Kyle opened the glass doors and stepped out onto the deck. "Look out here, Gina. We can see everything for miles and that waterhole is huge. There's a fence out a ways from this building," she added, "but I can see right down below to where the animals come for water." All of a sudden she cried out, "Oh, my God!"

"What is it?"

"You'll never believe this."

Gina hopped off the bed and stepped onto the deck. "Believe what?"

"See!" Kyle pointed, then wasted no time before hurriedly dashing back into the suite. She grabbed her camera and started photographing one shot after the other.

"They look like they're in a fight. What's that little animal?" Gina asked excitedly.

"I think it's a warthog. The other's some kind of a buffalo and look . . . the buffalo's backing off." Kyle laughed aloud. "Imagine that. I've got to get my camcorder out of the suitcase. I'd love to get these action shots."

"Well, thank goodness we're in a secure building. At least I don't have to worry about animals in a fight. Right now I'm goin' to take a shower and get down to that poolside lunch." She paused for an instant. "Hey, what did Ryan want and how'd he find you? You don't have any family, and I know full well my Mom wouldn't have told him. She thought what he did to you was despicable."

Kyle's brows arched. "Wait a minute. I remember you told Barbara where we were going."

"My sister? But why would she tell him?"

"I don't know."

"Damn her. I'll kill her when I see her."

"Maybe it's not her fault. Maybe it just slipped out," Kyle suggested. "Let's give her the benefit of the doubt until we know what's going on."

"Well, what'd Ryan say?"

"I don't know I haven't opened the envelope."

"I'd trash it if I were you. What a scum bag!" Gina let out a sigh then headed for the bathroom. "Listen, I don't care what happens next. I'm goin' to take a shower."

"Go ahead. I'll sit on the deck for awhile. Meet you at the pool."

After a quick shower, Gina headed out. "I'm gone," she yelled as she opened the glass door and peeked in on Kyle. "Don't wait too long now, or you may miss lunch, and for Pete's sake let me know what's in that envelope. You know I'm nosey."

Kyle flashed a smile. "Yeah, yeah. See you later."

After Gina left Kyle pulled the envelope out of her pocket and stared at it. *What could Ryan ever say to me that would make up for the hurt I feel? Maybe Gina's right. I guess I should just throw this away and forget it.* Kyle's mind wanted to do so, but her heart wouldn't let her, so with shaky hands she ripped open the flap and gazed at the folded sheet of paper.

Chapter 10

Saturday

Damon's trip to the bank didn't go well at all. In fact, the associate who spoke with him told Damon that unless The Ingwe Game Reserve could show a profit within the next week, or even a promise of some good returns, their line of credit would be closed. This was a blow that Damon wasn't prepared for, since the bank had always gone along with his assessment of the potential outlined in Damon and Gideon's original business plan. To Damon it seemed as if everything was dependent on the outcome of the special attraction of *Mauve Leopards* to the reserve, an attraction that no one else had to offer at that time.

Several attempts to reach Gideon on his cell phone failed. All Damon received was his partner's voice mail. Frustrated at what he considered obstinate behavior on the part of the associate at the bank, Damon sat for some time in his car, considering his options which were few to say the least. He'd tried his utmost to make The Ingwe Game Reserve the best ever, but being a small venture compared to the expansive Sabi Sand Game Reserve, a property next to The Ingwe, he knew the competition was fierce. However, he was not about to give up. *The new attraction will cause a stir and a rush of guests to see this new breed of leopard. I know it will.* On that positive note he headed back to his office.

All was going well on the drive until Damon passed by his favorite "long time" hangout where he, along with Gideon, had planned the entire Ingwe Project. The bar sign beckoned him as he drove by, and though he knew he shouldn't stop, he did. Just one drink, he reasoned.

That one drink turned into "who knows how many" refills of scotch and water. When he left the place he was walking upright so to speak, but his senses were dimmed and he was feeling no pain. This will all blow over and we'll be on top of the world again was his mind set as he entered his car and continued on the way to his office.

All afternoon Gideon had been receiving cell phone calls from Damon, but he'd ignored them, choosing instead to concentrate on getting his precious cargo to the warehouse at The Ingwe Reserve. As he left Jon's barn after loading the leopards into the truck, he observed that the old man still remained lifeless. He checked again, but heard no pulse. It had been a chore to tranquilize all of the cats and move the cages to his truck and he was exhausted.

Before leaving, he quickly gathered up some meat from the freezer in the barn stall where Jon lay. After doing so, he carefully looked over the scene to be sure he'd left no trace of his being there. Gideon knew this encounter was most likely going to be nerve wracking, but he never dreamed the outcome would be such that he hadn't needed to use the crowbar to kill Jon, and he was grateful for that. It was obvious that the man's age and poor health had taken care of the job for him. Nevertheless, Gideon's nerves were rattled and his heart beat hard against his chest, harder than he'd ever noticed before. Now, the task was to get the leopards to the warehouse without being detected.

Again, he drove carefully being sure he broke no roadway rules that would alarm the authorities thus ruining the prospect of using the cats to attract patrons to The Ingwe. For after all, he knew he'd done nothing other than steal the big cats from Jon's compound. He definitely hadn't killed anyone. So, to be sure no one would ever find out about the truck delivery, he entered the reserve from the west where there was no entrance gate and go guards on duty.

As soon as he pulled the truck up to the warehouse gate he was quick to see that Lynn's car was in place. He was certain she'd be there, and he was anxious to show her the special cargo.

Lynn was, indeed, waiting for him. He parked directly in front of the double doors where he spied her leaning against the door frame.

"Where in the world have you been? I've been worried sick," she hollered, her voice loud enough to let Gideon know she was upset about the long wait. "What happened with Jon?"

"Listen Lynn, this's been a harrowing day. Let's leave it at that for the moment. I'll tell you about it later." He started for the door then turned back and waved at her. "Come look at our catch. I think you'll be pleased."

She quickly followed his lead as he opened the truck's back doors.

The big cats were still drowsy from the tranquilizer, but a few of them did utter low growls as Gideon stepped onto the bed of the truck. He stretched out his hand and pulled Lynn up beside him.

Lynn's hand flew to her mouth, then a smile lit up her face. "Oh, they're beautiful! I've never seen anything like this."

"And no one else has either. Just think of it . . . we're the only ones in South Africa that can make that claim, Lynn. This should make the difference in selling the place if that other deal to sign over the title to Stephen doesn't work out."

For a few moments Lynn walked past the row of cages and continued to marvel at the leopards' spectacular coats of velvety lavender-gray. "They'll shock the world," she said, turning to Gideon. "But I don't like the fact that Stephen knows all about how you handled the deal with Jon and how you got the leopards here in the first place."

"Don't worry about it. He knows when to keep his mouth shut. He's not going to say a word, for he wants this place. Besides he's got too much riding on having everyone know we've got a new breed of leopard on the reserve."

"I'm still skeptical. I think you're too trusting."

"It'll be okay. Right now let's get these beauties into the warehouse and close up the place. We've got a lot to do to get them into the field ready to be viewed by those guests. They did arrive today, didn't they?"

Lynn nodded. "I talked to Carole and they got here. You're right, though," she said as her gaze snapped back to Gideon, "we'd better get them into the warehouse and get back to the lodge."

Fortunately the animal cages with the drowsy cats stretched out inside were not too heavy, so it didn't take too long to get the cages lined up in the warehouse behind some of the heavy equipment stored there. "It's a good thing you're young," Lynn said, huffing a bit after the last cage was in place. "You've got the strength of a giant."

"You're no slouch either, love," Gideon said, planting a kiss on her ripe lips.

Lynn settled down on one of the tracker seats and looked up. "I hesitate to ask, but do you want to tell me now about what happened to Jon? Did you have to go through with our plan?"

"No, I didn't have to kill him. He was dead when I got there," Gideon explained.

The frown that captured Lynn's face showed sudden doubt. "Dead . . . how?"

"The old guy must have died of a heart attack because when I found him he was out like a light and hunched over a bale of hay."

Lynn scowled and spat out the words, "Maybe he just fainted or something."

"Hell, I checked the pulse in his neck *and* his wrist several times. There wasn't a sound, and he sure wasn't breathing. Besides when I talked to him on the phone before I got there he was coughing up a storm. He told me he had a cold or the flu. That coupled with his heart problems most likely got to him."

"You're sure now?"

Gideon hissed through his teeth then jeered, "Yeah I'm sure. He was dead all right!"

Lynn got off the seat and paced the floor of the warehouse. "Yeah," she added, her jaw locked in anger, "but what if he wasn't?"

Before Gideon could respond, they heard a car pull up in front of the warehouse. Both rushed to the open doors to see Damon's car approaching. He didn't look too steady on his feet when he stepped out of the car and Lynn immediately frowned. "Oh no. He's at it again."

As soon as Damon exited the car it was easy to tell he'd had one too many, for this step was uncertain and he slurred the words, "Did you get the leopards?"

"You've been at it again," Lynn raved. "Of all the times to get drunk. You could have another seizure."

"Well get yourself in here and look at the leopards," Gideon grumbled, his tone harboring as much or more disdain than Lynn's. "And you'd better be ready to get out in the field by early morning. We've gotta get the cats into the trees ready for the game drive. Those guests better see *Mauve Leopards* on their first drive, or I'll swear I'll kill you myself." Gideon shook his fist at Damon. "I didn't go through all this for nothing, you hear?"

"Don't you shake your fist at me! I know what you're doing behind my back, but maybe when the buyers get here we can get this all straightened out and hopefully I can get you out of my hair. I'll buy you out if I have to."

"With what?" Lynn shouted, her voice raw and ragged. "Shut your mouth and take a look, then get back to the house and get some sleep. It's obvious you'll never make it to this evening's Welcome Dinner."

Low growls of discontent emanated from all around the room as Damon passed by each cage. "They look good from here, but don't you worry I'll be at that damn dinner or whatever you call it, and I'll be just fine by early morning. See you both later." Without another word Damon stomped out as both Gideon and Lynn stood wide-eyed.

"What a loser," Lynn said with a sigh. For an instant she sat perfectly still and stared into space mumbling softly, "Too bad he doesn't have . . ." Her words trailed off.

"What'd you say?" Gideon asked.

"Oh nothing. I was just assessing the situation," Lynn replied thoughtfully.

"I sure can't see why you ever married him."

"It was one of my weak moments all right," Lynn admitted, gazing directly into Gideon's eyes. She rolled her fingers down his cheek and shook her head. "A regrettable mistake."

As she turned toward the door, Gideon spun her around, reached out and pulled her toward him. "Hey, come here, you cougar you. If you hadn't married him, I never would have met you, and that's been the best thing that's ever happened to me." Gideon pressed Lynn close and hugged her. Then with the tip on his finger, he lifted her chin and kissed her, a warm kiss that made Lynn stir with emotion. "Damon's never seen your soft side has he? He doesn't know what he's missing."

She kissed him back. "Are you kidding? I wouldn't even want a kiss from him even if he offered one."

Lynn exhaled a deep breath, and planted another kiss on his lips. "I hate to leave you, though I think I'd better get back to the lodge."

"You're right, but I do need to see you later on," Gideon said. "About eleven thirty, okay?"

"Fine. See you in my room."

"I'll be there, love," he said, patting her cheek. He gave his hand a swish in the air. "Go on now. I'll feed the cats and be right over."

Lynn walked toward the warehouse door. As she turned to look back at him her face lit up and she threw him a kiss. "I sure need you."

Gideon's cell phone rang immediately after Lynn left the building. Noting the name of the ID caller, Gideon answered with an abrupt, "What?" After listening for an instant, he blurted out, "But you *are* going to get that payment to us, aren't you Stephen? Otherwise we can't transfer the title to you. You know that, right?" He shook his head with displeasure. "Well," he said, pausing to listen. "You'd better come through fast or you know we'll find another buyer even if Damon's against it."

Still holding the envelope from Ryan in her hand, Kyle sat for a few more moments on the deck watching the animals as they wandered down to the waterhole seeking a refreshing drink. She pondered what Ryan could possibly say to her now after such a devastating climax to what she thought would be a perfect wedding. Finally her need to know far outweighed the hurt she felt inside, so with trembling hands and a heart beat that seemed uncontrollably erratic, Kyle opened the sheet of paper and read two simple words, "Call me."

Her head dropped back against the chair and she stared up at the blue sky as loose memories played through her mind. Her eyes clouded over and she could feel her pulse pounding hard. Nerves distraught, her whole body shook as she gasped for air. *What does he think I am? After that crushing announcement that he couldn't marry me, he wants me to call him?*

Kyle sat stunned, unable to comprehend what in the world could have caused Ryan to change his mind so quickly. In a burst of tears that streaked down her cheeks, she bent over sobbing. She pulled a tissue from her pocket, blew her nose then brushed away the tears. *I won't let him do this to me,* she thought, crushing the sheet of paper and tearing it up into little pieces. *No way!* She pulled in another hesitant sob, got up and threw the bits of paper into the waste basket. Her face registered a determined look when she left the suite on her way to the pool to meet Gina. *I'm not going to let anything ruin this trip.*

* * *

In the meantime, Gina hurriedly made her way to the pool where she was surprised to find Stephen already stretched out on one of the lounge chairs with a drink in his hand.

"Now this is really livin'," she explained, glancing about. The kidney shaped pool was designed so that a Jacuzzi fit snuggly into an outlet on one side and an amazing rock mound constructed of various colored rocks of all sizes highlighted by an assortment of native plants and a cascading waterfall covered the far end of the pool, a gorgeous sight indeed. It appeared to be a jungle setting.

"Hey Karen!" Stephen called out when he saw one of the women from the kitchen approaching. He sat up in his lounge chair and added, "Will you get Gina a drink?"

"Sure," Karen said cheerfully. "There's lemonade and some cokes over here." She pointed to a table with an assortment of beverages.

Gina grinned, "I had bourbon straight up in mind. Any chance of gettin' one? If you knew what we went through with that elephant attack on the way here, you'd know why I need a stiff drink."

Both Karen and Stephen's eyes widened in shock. "What do you mean an elephant attack?" Stephen asked in alarm.

"I never would have believed it, but that's what it was," Gina insisted. Stephen and Karen listened intently as Gina humorously detailed the whole incident and the fright she felt. "I've had enough excitement on this trip already to age me ten years." Fact is, her facial expressions and accompanying gestures were so hilarious that both Karen and Stephen couldn't help but laugh.

"I'll be right back with that drink. Sounds like you really need it," Karen said as she walked away snickering at Gina's comical description of the episode.

Stephen slipped off the lounge chair and motioned to Gina. "Why don't we sit over there at a table? By the way, where's Kyle?"

"She's comin'. But I can tell you I'm not goin' to wait for her. I'm starvin'." An impish smile surfaced. "Care if I load up and dive in?" Gina said, moving toward the buffet table.

"No, go ahead. I think I'll get something, too. It's way past my lunch time." As they were choosing from a selection of sliced meats, various bread choices, fruits and condiments, Stephen gave Gina a sideways glance. "Hey, you made quite an impression on Bradley. Did you know that?"

Gina snapped her head to the right to see a smile on Stephen's face. "What do you mean?" she asked, not realizing that her face was like an open book and that anyone could tell when she was delighted.

While Stephen continued scooping up some of the assortment displayed at the buffet table, he grinned. "Well, Bradley's brother, Patrick, who I know works at the Kruger Park Lodge as a game ranger, called me and said that Bradley spoke well of you, and he explained that he'd like to go with us when we take the Panoramic Tour on Wednesday." Stephen raised an eyebrow. "What do you think?"

Gina hesitated no more than a second before she enthusiastically responded in her usual upbeat manner. "Sure why not. He seems like a nice guy." S*ounds promisin'. Wait 'til I tell Kyle.*

Chapter 11

Saturday Afternoon

"We're over here, Kyle," Gina hollered when she saw Kyle enter the pool area. "Come on the food's great."

Kyle waved and headed to the far end of the deck. "The pool looks fabulous. How's the food?"

"Super! I was starvin' so I went ahead," Gina piped up. "I didn't want to waste any time, 'cause I'm goin' to get my suit and have a swim. Just look at that water. Boy, this is my kind of life."

Kyle grinned and her voice dropped an octave or two. "That's Gina, Stephen. She does like the good life."

"Well, I don't blame her," Stephen commented as he munched on an apple. "As I've told other guests, this game reserve's the best." He paused for an instant; however, his ardent zeal must have gotten the best of him, for he eagerly exclaimed, "I plan to own The Ingwe some day." Those words slipped from his lips before he had time to contemplate their impact and he instantly regretted saying them.

"Really," Kyle commented. "That's quite an ambitious goal. You must really love it here."

"I do," Stephen said shifting in his seat, for he realized that wasn't necessarily a message he should be projecting. The deal was too fragile to jinx it now, but it was too late to retract his words. All he could do was try and cover his inadvertent blunder by changing the subject.

But Kyle wasn't about to let such a noble endeavor pass by without some response, so she quickly encouraged him by stating, "Hey, I wish you well. One should always follow their heart and most particularly a dream." That said, she stepped to the buffet table and grabbed a plate. "I can see why you love the place, though," she rambled on. "I had no idea what to expect, but so far it's more than we could ask for. Right, Gina?"

Gina gulped down a swallow of bourbon before agreeing, "Other than a charging elephant, it sure is."

Kyle laughed and absentmindedly added, "I guess you're right. Gosh, there's really a great assortment here." After selecting some salad items and freshly baked bread, she squeezed into the only other seat at the table, one that was situated close to a row of deck chairs.

When Stephen got up and went back to the buffet table for some luncheon refills, Gina whispered to Kyle, "If he plans to buy The Ingwe he must have a rich uncle or whatever. Maybe I should be trying to charm him rather than Bradley." She giggled, waved her arms in a flamboyant manner then downed another large gulp of her bourbon.

Kyle just about choked on that last comment, the one about using her charm on Stephen rather than Brad. "You're really a character all right, but I don't think that'd work, Gina. It seems Carole has her claws into him. Haven't you noticed that already?"

Gina lifted one eyebrow and grinned. "I don't know about Carole, but it sure looks like he thinks you're something else."

Kyle's face flushed. "Get out. Believe me I've no interest in any man right now, definitely not him." She raised her voice in obvious annoyance. "Forget about it!"

"Forget about what?" Stephen said as he seated himself back at the table.

"Oh, nothing. Gina was just clowning around."

For the next half hour while the three ate, Stephen told them about the different types of activities they'd be engaging in while at the reserve, namely a trip to a Silk Farm, a night game drive, a morning game drive, a walking tour or a bush camp experience, as well as an all day Panoramic Tour of the Bourke's Luck Potholes, the Blyde River Canyon, God's window and Pilgrims Rest which, he detailed, is an historical site. He paused as if to check their reactions. "Oh, and I don't want to leave out the balloon ride over the reserve with champagne cocktails waiting when we land. That's the best part as far as I'm concerned," he explained while displaying a brilliant smile. "How does that sound?"

Gina rolled her gaze upward and gasped at the thought of a balloon ride. "The champagne sounds fabulous, but," and she looked directly at Kyle, "there's no way I'm goin' up in a balloon . . . not after that incident with the elephant."

"Don't worry, Gina. You don't have to go anywhere you don't want to. How about you, Kyle?"

"I'm game for all of it, Stephen. But I have to admit that elephant encounter was something I hadn't expected."

Gina was quick to add, "Well, it sure did scare the hell out of me. Tell me we won't get into anymore situations like that again, Stephen."

"Hopefully not," he told Gina, "but I do take you into some out of the way places all right."

Gina scrunched her lips together, cocked her head, and put on a comic face. "Jeez, I know that won't bother Kyle 'cause she's the adventurous one, but as far as I'm concerned, I prefer to see scenes like that in a movie."

Frowning, Stephen took a sip of his drink. "Then I'm curious, Gina," he asked looking her way. "Why did you come on this trip?"

"It's a long story." When she saw Kyle shake her head, she knew better than to explain the traumatic cancellation of Kyle's wedding plans and the reason they embarked on this adventurous sojourn to the far end of the earth which, in their minds, was Africa. "I think that's up to Kyle to say. I'm only being a friend."

Stephen shrugged and laughed. "Well, I won't press the issue, but let me reassure you that I'll try to keep you from falling into a river filled with crocodiles. How's that, Gina?"

Gina gulped down a full breath and turned pale.

"Are you okay," he questioned seriously.

"Oh, yeah," she said with a bite of sarcasm. "Your idea of savin' me from the crocodiles makes me feel a whole lot better." She paused then glanced at the two of them. "Hey, do you mind if I leave you and run up and get my suit? I wanna get into that pool. There aren't any crocodiles in there, and I can easily abstain from hearing any more horror stories about animals right now."

"No, go on ahead," Kyle casually remarked. "You know, on second thought I think I'll go with you." She twisted around to try and get out of her chair, since it was in such an awkward position. With a quick glance she turned back to Stephen. "Can we talk about flying some other time?"

"Sure, I've got to get going anyway. I've got work to do this afternoon." He reached out and, in an attempt to move Kyle's chair so she could get up, he accidentally brushed his hand across her back. Kyle hadn't been expecting the contact and she smiled, for it felt good to feel his warm hand pressed against her.

At that very moment Carole strode across the deck. Kyle looked up and immediately noted a reluctant nod and a deep frown on her face. She surmised that apparently Stephen's rather intimate hand gesture displeased her. Though Carole went on to exhibit a cheerful demeanor when she looked at Stephen, her voice carried a touch of angst as she said to him, "I *will* see you later, right?" It was obvious to Kyle that there was something serious going on between the two.

Not skipping a beat, Stephen huffed out a breath and looked at her, his face as impassive as granite. "Yeah!" he responded. He immediately got up and waved as he left, while Carole proceeded to tell Kyle and Gina that she wanted to take them on a brief tour of the lodge before the Welcome Dinner where they would meet the owners of The Ingwe.

"Fine," Kyle told Carole. "I'd love to see the rest of the place. So far it's delightful. What say, Gina? We can go for a swim afterwards."

Gina nodded. "Okay. I'm good with that."

After Stephen left, Carole seemed to revert to being more like the pleasing office manager they first encountered upon landing on the airstrip. To Kyle the change in behavior was, for the most part, easily detected. However, it wasn't obvious to her if Gina noticed the change or not. As they left the pool area Kyle couldn't help but wonder about relationships and how they get bogged down with complications, her own included. With Carole showing that amount of jealousy, she reasoned that the woman definitely had designs on Stephen.

Quickening her step, Carole crossed the lodge's massive lobby and took the two down a corridor to show them several rooms. "The first room here is for the devoted exercise buff," she explained. "As you can see you'll find most everything you need to keep fit."

Both Kyle and Gina stuck their heads in to get a look. "Nice," Kyle said. "I can pop in here after our swim."

Gina giggled, "Yeah, while I'm nappin'."

"To each his own," Carole said with a shrug. "Personally, I never seem to find the time to get enough exercise. Now this next room on our right," she went on, "is the library, where you'll find quite a few American authors' works. Feel free to go in and browse any time and," she said pointing ahead, "in the room to your left you'll find Dr. Lynn Greene's Herpetology Exhibit. She's actually the wife of one of the owners. She's also a zoologist who did research in Johannesburg. She was involved in extracting the venom from snakes like the Puff Adder that you'll find displayed here. Fact is, that snake, along with the Black Mamba, are probably the most dangerous in Africa. Here's the room." She stopped and opened the door. "You can see the hours when the exhibit is open posted here. I think you'll find the place fascinating, though I sure wouldn't want to be on the receiving end of either one of those snakes."

As they entered the large room, a woman looked up from her desk located near the entrance. Carole was quick to introduce her as the person responsible for overseeing the library, the exercise room and Dr. Greene's Herpetology Exhibit. "This's Marian Cummings," Carole stated. "She's here to answer any questions you may have about the exhibit or to sign out a book you wish to read from the library next door." Without skipping a beat, Carole went on introducing Kyle and Gina as the current guests.

"Nice meeting you, Marian," Kyle said offering a smile. "This is quite a treat, something you'd expect to see in a museum."

Marian returned the smile with a bright show of teeth. "It is a treat. As you'll see the exhibit features reptiles and amphibians such as frogs, toads and salamanders which differ from snakes becaus—"

Kyle cut in. "Because they lack scales and can live in the water or on land, but they return to the water to breed, right?"

"Not only is she a pilot," Gina stated, "but she's a walking encyclopedia. It amazes me, though I can do without the snakes. Yuk!"

"I guess a lot of people do feel that way, but I can tell you're really interested in science Kyle, and I think you'll enjoy talking with Dr. Greene, for she's very enthusiastic about her exhibit. I don't know how long you're staying at The Ingwe, but feel free to come in when you get a chance. This particular room is open from one to two."

"Only for an hour?" Kyle questioned.

"Well, we find that most of our guests aren't overly interested in snakes and amphibians, and we open just long enough so we don't interfere with the morning and afternoon attractions like the game drives. Now if you'd like to come in at some special time, I'll check and see if we can schedule that. No problem."

Kyle tipped her head. "No . . . no, that's okay. I'm sure I can find the time. I'd love to go through it, for it *does* fascinate me."

"Great. I'll look forward to seeing you then. You may also want to check out the gym and the library." She quickly continued, "And if you can't find me check with the Front Desk."

Before Marian could add any more specifics, Carole interjected, "Believe it or not Marian, they're our only guests this week."

"That's a change. We usually have at least eight at a time. You'll have the whole place to yourselves," she said with another smile. "I'll look forward to seeing you."

"You'll both probably hear a lot more about this place from Professor Greene at the Welcome Dinner," Carole said while they headed for the door. "Well," she said, stopping short, "I'd say that about covers it, ladies." She turned back. "Oh, I forgot one of the best features of The Ingwe. We have a spa at the far end of lodge. There you can get a *ranga* massage."

Gina eyes brightened. "That's for me! When's it open?"

Carole responded, "Just ask at the desk and they'll see that you get a schedule."

"I'm not into massages," Kyle stated. "What's a *ranga* massa—"

This time Gina was quick to interrupt. "Now you're talkin' my ballgame, Kyle. A *ranga* is a massage given in an outside settin'."

"That's right, Gina. In fact, ours overlooks the waterhole so you have a good view of all the animals while you relax. It's great."

Gina smiled at Kyle. "I don't know if you're goin' to go, but you can bet I'll be there."

"I hope you do," Carole added. "I should ask before you leave, have you found everything you need in your suite?"

"Everything's great," Kyle replied, "and I look forward to meeting Dr. Greene." As they left the room she glanced at Gina. "Want to get your suit now and have a swim?"

"Do I ever!"

"Don't forget the dinner's at seven in the dining room," Carole said. "I won't be there, but I hope you have a good time. See you two later."

"I'm sure we will and thanks," Kyle yelled out as Carole crossed the lobby and headed for the Front Desk.

"Come on, let's go," Gina suggested as she bounded up the stairs. "Hurry up! Hey, I'll race you to the suite. But when we get there you've got to tell me what was in that note from Ryan."

Kyle shook her head and darted up the stairs in an effort to beat her friend, who had often admitted that, in the last few months, she had packed on a few more pounds on that five foot two frame of hers than she'd care to admit. Kyle won the race, had the key card already inserted in the door and was entering the suite when Gina caught up with her.

"Hold it!" Gina cried out, her breathing as labored as a runner who had just completed a marathon. "That wasn't fair 'cause you've got longer legs." When she rushed into the suite, she immediately bent over, hands on her knees, and stopped for an instant to take some deep breaths. "Now," she said, blowing out a puff of air. "I really do need to get into that pool."

The two changed into their suits, grabbed two towels and headed downstairs again. "Let's not run this time," Gina joked. "But I'm goin' to keep askin' until you tell me what Ryan had to say in that note. 'Ya hear?"

Half way down the stairs Kyle stopped, heaved a deep sigh and, in a subdued tone, confided, "All he wrote Gina was, 'Call me.'"

"Who in the hell does he think he is?" Gina snapped back. "And why would he think you'd ever want to talk to him again?"

"I've no idea," Kyle said, her voice stalling in mid-sentence. Even though she was heartbroken, in some strange way she knew down deep she still loved him. Yet, I can't let him do this to me, she thought. Holding back tears, she looked at Gina. "If he's changed his mind, that's just too bad, for I'd never be able to trust him again, would I? Or if he's got some other girl on the string and he wants to let me know about it, then good luck ever seeing or hearing from me again." The words spewed from her mouth as tears wells in her eyes. "No. I'm not going to run back and forget what he did."

"That's the attitude, Kyle. As I told you I'd want to kill him, and you're perfectly right in ignorin' the scum bag. Don't you dare crawl back as if nothin' happened! I think you've done well so far." In an effort to try to ease Kyle's bout with despair, Gina patted her friend on the shoulder. "Come on, let's get down there and enjoy that gorgeous pool. We've got the rest of the day ahead of us and we don't wanna waste a minute. You paid too much for this trip. What do 'ya say?"

Kyle sniffed in a sob and followed as the two went on to have a delightful swim in water warmed by the hot African sun. "This is fabulous," Kyle shouted as she swam directly under the waterfall, coming out the other side with her head of auburn curls clinging to her flawlessly tanned skin.

Gina stepped out of the pool with not a drop of water on her short blond hair and grabbed a towel to wrap around her waist. "Heavens, if I dunked my head under the water like you do, I'd look like a drowned rat. Somehow you look like a top model in one of those ads selling a skin product."

Kyle ignored her friend and continued swimming laps in the pool. In contrast Gina plopped down on one of the many deck chairs, put on her sun glasses then rested her head against the back of the lounge, absorbing the bright rays of the sun.

For an hour the two enjoyed the comforts of the pool and the beverages left there in a cooler for them. "Man, that was refreshing!" Kyle said while she prepared to leave. "I'm going to sit on our deck and see if any elephants are at the waterhole this afternoon. Maybe even another warthog."

"Do that," Gina replied as she put her watch on and prepared to get up. "As for me I'm goin' to take a nap. We've got several hours before dinner. Just get me up in time to get dressed."

Back in their suite while Gina stretched out for a nap, Kyle picked up her journal and headed for the suite's spacious deck. There were no animals anywhere near the waterhole that afternoon. She reasoned that the sun's intense heat discouraged any trips out of the shade of the trees. Yet, this quiet time allowed her to document the last few days of their adventure into the Dark Continent of Africa.

Journal Entry—3 *While waiting for a flight out of Dakar, Senegal after our unfortunate crash landing, we met a British gentleman at the Senegal Airport. Gina took a liking to him and watching her approach to hooking husband # 3 was hilarious. Our flight out of Dakar was delayed, but thankfully uneventful. Stayed a few hours in Johannesburg before boarding the shuttle flight to Nelspruit. Stephen Falkner, pilot/game ranger for The Ingwe Game Reserve, met us in Nelspruit and flew us in a ten passenger de Havilland DHC-3 to the private airstrip at the reserve. Met there by manager Carole Magona who drove us to The Ingwe Lodge. Got some good shots of animals* and even encountered an elephant attack on the drive into the lodge, but the big fellow veered off before any damage was done to us or to the car. Got great photos, but the episode scared Gina to death. Suite at the lodge is fabulous with a spacious sun deck overlooking a waterhole where, on the first day, I saw a warthog and a buffalo facing off like a battle might ensue, but the buffalo backed away. The lodge has no outer walls on the first floor. Guards are there for security and there is a fence all around the lodge itself. Carole gave us a tour of the facilities. Lodge has a massive lobby, a pool, an exercise room and much more to offer besides an unbelievable collection of snakes, some poisonous, and a number of amphibians. Lunch by the pool with Stephen and Gina followed by a delightful swim. Looking forward to the Welcome Dinner tonight, the Silk Farm tour on Monday and all the other excursions.

The melting hot tropical sun finally took its toll on Kyle. The pen slipped from her hand and she dozed off, awaked suddenly by the sound of the dinner drums. "Come on, Gina," Kyle hollered, "I guess that's the call to the Welcome Dinner."

Both questioned each other as to what to wear to such an event, but they chose to stay with a casual look, preferring safari slacks and tops they had purchased for the trip.

"How can you look so ravishing after a swim that left your hair drenched?" Gina asked, gazing at Kyle's auburn hair that was now a mass of shoulder-length curls.

"Ah, it's a curse. I'd love to have that California look with the straight long hair, but that's not a possibility for me unless I have this mop straightened, and it's too much trouble. But, who cares anyway, let's just have fun."

Gina ran her fingers through her short blond hair and grudgingly released a small smile of envy. "I should be so lucky, but it sure makes me jealous."

"Come on. You've got enough curves to make any guy's eyes pop! Let's get to that dinner."

As the two were entering the corridor that led to the dining room, they passed a room with a name plaque on the door which read "Gideon Courtney." They wouldn't have noticed it at all, but for the fact that they heard a man and a woman arguing, their voices streaming into the hallway. Kyle stopped and grabbed Gina by the sleeve. "Wait a minute," she whispered, bringing her finger up to her lips as a signal to be still. "Listen!"

As the voices in the room rose in pitch, Kyle noted that it was, indeed, a man and a women arguing over something. Though it was difficult to distinctly hear all the words, some came thorough as clear as the sound of a harsh fog horn.

Kyle heard the woman say, "I checked and there's no way he can do it tonight!" She strained to hear the man's response which was raspy to say the least, but she couldn't understand him. Even though Gina had grabbed her arm and, with a head motion, was trying to get Kyle to leave, she didn't. Instead Kyle moved closer to the door while loud voices sliced the air at the far end of the corridor.

Gina pulled at Kyle's arm again. "Hurry up. Can't you tell people are comin' this way?"

Kyle huffed out a breath and looked at Gina sideways as if she didn't hear a word her friend said. "You know I've got a nagging feeling things aren't as they seem here at the lodge."

Chapter 12

Saturday Evening

When Kyle and Gina entered the dining room, Karen greeted them with a cheery, "Nice to see you again. Did you two have a good swim?"

"It was great!" Gina and Kyle said in unison.

"Are we too early?" Kyle asked.

"No, not at all. The owners will be here in a few minutes I'm sure. Let's get you seated and you can take a look at the menu before they arrive. I've got a place right by the window where you can see the grounds. It's a pretty place isn't it?"

"It sure is," Kyle commented while the two followed Karen to a large round table by a bay window overlooking the landscape which featured huge carved African statues.

"Look at those figures. They're amazing," Kyle said, watching Gina choose seats that gave them the best view of the gardens. "I've got to take some of their artwork home."

Gina pulled in a tight scowl. "I hope you're not thinkin' of tryin' to ship one of those gigantic statues. Then again," she said jokingly, looking up at Karen. "But I wouldn't put it past her."

Karen grinned and passed out the menus then took the order for drinks. "You may order anything you'd like since this is all inclusive. There's some special dining choices as well as the standard serving of chicken and steak. The chefs here are fabulous. They really are! You'll find that they specialize in International cuisine, particularly South African dishes. But, whatever you order I'm sure you'll be pleased, and do take your time in choosing your entrées. There's no rush. In case you're interested, the national favorite of South Africans is lamb, though there are many different choices on the menu. I'll be back in a minute with your drinks."

"Oh my gosh!" Kyle raved. "Look at this. There are all kinds of things here I've never tasted before. See," she said, reading aloud. "There's Zebra Steak with garlic butter, potato wedges and salad; Springbok Fillet served with vegetables and corn fritters; Kudu Steak with mushroom sauce and finally Bushman Sosatie, a kabob of Ostrich, Crocodile, Zebra, Kudu served with corn fritters and a salad."

"Don't count on me for any experimenting. I'm not into any of that even though I am starvin'," Gina snapped back.

"Hey, where's your adventurous spirit?" Kyle teased. "I hope I can get one of their scrumptious recipes before we leave. I'd love to try one."

Just then Kyle glanced up to see a man and a women coming toward them. "Welcome to The Ingwe!" the woman said with a hand wave as they approached. "We're delighted to see you. I'm Dr. Greene but you can call me Lynn. I'm the wife of one of the owners and this is Gideon Courtney the other owner. My husband's off at a business meeting, so I'm taking his place. Perhaps we can fill you in on some of the attractions we have to offer."

As the two sat down across the table from Kyle and Gina, Gideon Courtney smiled then told them he hoped they would enjoy their stay at The Ingwe.

The woman was shorter and, though attractive, she appeared much older than Mr. Courtney, who was dressed in a tan sport shirt and brown casual slacks. In contrast, she wore a cocktail dress. Their attire seemed to be quite a dichotomy. Gideon Courtney towered over the doctor. As Kyle estimated he was most likely in his mid-forties and at least six foot five inches tall. He had a full head of hair and a dark brown goatee. Her hair was tightly pulled back from her face emphasizing her high cheek bones. In some ways, at least in Kyle's mind, she displayed a stern aura about her that seemed to dissuade any reference to her by her first name. Strange, but to Kyle it seemed that Dr. Lynn Greene's face was a mood ring, and her smile posed a distinct detachment.

"What I heard from Stephen," Dr. Greene said, looking directly at Kyle, "is that you're a pilot."

Kyle was going to reply using the doctor's first name, but couldn't quite do so, preferring instead to refrain from using any titles when addressing her. "Yes," she responded. "I fly charter flights for business clients. And this is my friend Gina Austin, who has been kind enough to accompany me on this African adventure. So far it's been a wonderful experience."

Gideon Courtney spread his napkin on his lap at the same time commenting, "I'm glad all is going well so far, Kyle."

As they chattered on, Karen arrived with the drinks for Kyle and Gina then asked the doctor and Mr. Courtney for their orders.

"We'll have our usual drinks," Dr. Greene stated, "and I'll have the Shrimp Salad, no rolls."

"Fine, Dr. Green," Karen replied shyly. Somehow it seemed to Kyle that Karen was hesitant when addressing the doctor as if she'd been reprimanded at one time and didn't want a repeat performance.

"And what would you like Mr. Courtney?" Karen asked.

"Give me the Prime Rib . . . no potatoes but I do want a Caesar Salad."

Gina hesitated for no more than an instant before ordering the chicken parmesan with an order of fries. Kyle followed with a request for the Bushman Sosatie, saying, "I want to try all of these different flavors. This should be fun."

Karen smiled. "Surely. We'll have your entrées out in no time."

Gushing charm Gideon Courtney addressed Kyle and Gina. "Is this your first trip to Africa?"

Gina didn't hold back on describing their adventure so far. "Oh yes!" she answered, her face contorted in a uniquely comical twist. "In fact, it may be my last if we have any more run-ins with elephants like we had on the drive into the reserve." For a few minutes she rambled on about the attack.

"Gina was scared to death, but I got a lot of great photos. I guess I was so busy clicking the camera shutter I didn't have time to be afraid. Fortunately," Kyle explained with a grin, "it all turned out just fine. I think the big bull decided we weren't worth the run."

Mr. Courtney smiled but Dr. Greene's face showed only a bitter joviality that was as fragile as a filament and there was a distinct wooden look behind her eyes that appeared to Kyle to be cold and calculating.

"That's certainly unusual," the doctor said, "for we've never had such an episode as long as we've been here. Let's hope the rest of your visit is less hectic."

The verbal exchanges continued on in an uncomfortable vein and the rise and fall of the conversation was disturbing; therefore, Kyle was delighted to see Karen arrive with the tray of drinks for Dr. Greene and Mr. Courtney. One would think a Welcome Dinner would be just that . . . a cordial affair where all felt welcome, she thought. But it was just the opposite.

"This is really an experience of a lifetime," Kyle said breaking the silence. "Stephen was nice enough to tell us about some of the side trips that we'll be able to enjoy. He told us that we had a choice of taking the game walk or staying in a tent out on the reserve for one night, and we've decided to try the camp site adventure."

"It was Kyle who thought that would be fun. The vote is still out as far as I'm concerned," Gina quipped. "She's slept in a tent before in national parks, but—"

Cocking her head to one side, Kyle interrupted. "But I've done so in the safety of our national parks, not on safari, still it's got to be exhilarating."

"We think it is," Mr. Courtney confided. "And neither one of you have to worry about security. We have guards there and an electrified fence all around the camp. I think you'll find it quite a thrill."

"Well," Gina responded with a degree of skepticism, "I'm willin' to try."

"Good. I hope you find all of the side trips worthwhile especially seeing our *Mauve Leopards.*" That said Gideon Courtney added enthusiastically, "Apparently we're the only reserve in Africa in which they've been spotted." Though willingly lying, he covered any hint of deception with a smile as his piercing gaze locked on Kyle and then Gina. "I saw one of them yesterday and it was quite a sight."

"Your fascinating ads were very compelling. That's the reason I chose The Ingwe Reserve," Kyle said looking directly at Gideon Courtney. "And I'm really looking forward to those game drives and seeing Africa's share of the world's animals particularly that new breed of leopard you mentioned. Are they really purplish in color?"

"They're more of a lavender-gray," Dr. Greene cut in. "Isn't that what you told me Gideon?"

"That's true, and they don't have the small dark rings or rosettes as they call them on their fur like other leopards. I've no idea how this mutation occurred, although they are quite something to see!" Another necessary lie.

Dr. Greene willing perpetuated the hoax as she went on and on about how their reserve was the only one to have seen the new breed. "Then again," she continued, "I'm sure you'll also enjoy the dinner on Friday when the next group of guests arrive. That evening we'll have a *Boma* buffet with a delightful native demonstration by some of the local Shangana Tribe."

Kyle cocked her head. "What's a *Boma* buffet?"

"I'm so glad you asked, for Carole said she didn't get a chance to show you our *Boma* enclosure on her tour. It's on the far end of the lodge. In fact, I brought along some brochures for you. Perhaps you can check out the location sometime this week."

Then, as if lecturing to a group, she explained, "*Boma,* also known as a kraal, means a livestock enclosure or a kind of fort such as a fortified village or camp whereby the people inside can feel safe from any marauding animals. Out on the savannahs such structures are made up for the people within a fort or village."

Dr. Greene stopped for a moment while Karen returned and asked if anyone wanted additional cocktails. After receiving a negative response, she left stating that the entrées would be ready soon.

Dr. Greene smiled vacantly then turned back to Kyle and Gina. "To get back to your question about *Bomas,*" she continued on, "as I said, some are constructed out of thorny bushes that keep the animals from encroaching and they're a wind shield as well. Now, we use the term in a different light, though we've kept the concept of the tall enclosure partly in place." She paused for an instant while she pulled several pieces of literature from a case she had with her and passed one each to Kyle and Gina.

"As you can see it's a circular structure more akin to a wall than a fence. Tables for the guests are lined up in a half circle against the curved wall. On the other side they'll be a row of tables with a variety of delicious *Braai,* which are barbequed dishes including exotic venison and vintage South African wines." She stopped to take a sip of her drink. "The interior of the *Boma* is lighted with lanterns and a central fire. After the guests have made their selections from the buffet, members of the Shangana Tribe, who are referred to as Shangaan warriors, perform a native dance to entertain our guests. They're quite delightful. I think you'll find it a fascinating evening. Do take a look at the place when you get a chance."

Kyle spoke up. "We'll definitely do tha—"

Just then Karen approached with a large tray carrying the entrées. "Enjoy!" she said when she had placed the last of the plates on the table. Looking specifically at Dr. Greene she added, "If there's anything else you need just let me know."

Kyle smiled as she moved her drink aside so she could set her salad closer to her plate. As they ate Kyle mentioned how much she liked the kabob, especially the crocodile which was a flakey white meat she stated tasted like chicken. "The Ostrich," she explained, "is my second choice. By the way, that *Boma* buffet sounds wonderful," Kyle went on. "Without a doubt you've got some good chefs. I should mention, too, that Stephen not only told us about the upcoming excursions we can take, but he gave us an overview by air of the reserve. It's pretty large isn't it?"

"Well, it's 420 square kilometers all told which is about 160 square miles. Actually, we're a fairly small reserve," Gideon stated, while slicing into a juicy section of prime rib. "Now Kruger National Park and the Sabi Sand Reserves just east of us are much larger, but they don't offer 'off-road' game drives, and you'll find that Stephen's a wonderful game ranger. He'll take you into places where you'll get up close to the animals. For example, at Kruger Park the game rangers stay on the main roads, missing some of the personal experiences you'll fin—"

"As Mr. Courtney was saying, The Ingwe Private Game Reserve and the other game reserves make up what they call the Greater Kruger National Park. So far Sabi Sand right next to us has grown to over ten game reserves within its borders."

Gideon Courtney followed up with, "Kruger National Park covers over 758 miles in the Province of Limpopo and Mpumalanga. You might also find it interesting to note that the first tourist car came into Kruger Park in 1926 well before you two were born."

"Well, I'm happy we're getting a chance to see it all. Interestingly enough Carole took us on a tour of the lodge and we saw the Herpetology Exhibit. It looks fascinating," Kyle said while freeing a piece of meat from the kabob skewer. "We'll definitely get there to see it before we leave." She glanced at the doctor. "I hear you had a hand in extracting the venom from some of Africa's deadliest snakes. That must be a challenging task."

At the very mention of the exhibit, Dr. Greene's eyes lit up and she was quick to detail her part in the work of producing antivenom. "It was, but it was also very rewarding. By taking the venom, which in technical terms is called antivenins, from the snakes we make antivenom, a biological product called anti-ophidic serum. That's referred to as a vaccine process developed by Louis Pasteur."

Gina seemed bored by the details of the doctor's work and appeared more interested in relishing her meal. Kyle, on the other hand, while savoring the dessert served, which contained a delightful combination of flavors that melted on her tongue like candy, listened intently to what the doctor had to say. She could tell Dr. Greene was devoted to her work in the field of biology. "It sounds like you really loved the work," Kyle pointed out, "and, as you say, it must have been rewarding."

"Yes it was," Dr. Greene said while catching a side glance from Gideon. "Why don't you two tell us a little about how you pass your time in the States."

Kyle and Gina both described their chosen careers in two diverse fields. "But," as Kyle said when they all got up to leave, "I'd say that I think we enjoy our work as much as you do. I don't know how you came to own this reserve, but we're both glad we're here, and so far we find everything just perfect. We couldn't ask for anything better." Flashing a quick glance at Gideon Courtney, Kyle added, "And we're certainly looking forward to seeing those *Mauve Leopards*."

"It's been a pleasure meeting both of you," the doctor said showing no sense of feeling though Gideon Courtney displayed a congenial attitude more akin to that offered customers whom one wishes to impress.

Kyle gave a nod saying, "Thanks again for a delightful meal, and we hope to see you again before we leave."

After they were far enough away from Gideon Courtney and Dr. Greene to be out of hearing range, Kyle's dark eyes flashed as she stopped and looked at Gina. "Did you notice that woman's voice?"

Gina's brows narrowed in thought. "What about it?"

"I'd swear those are the same voices we heard arguing in that office, particularly the doctor's, and remember the name on the door was Gideon Courtney. Now I'm really curious as to what's going on around here."

"Lighten up, Kyle! You're suckin' the oxygen out of the room," Gina complained. "Here I was enjoyin' a great meal and now you're knee deep in other peoples' problems." Her expression warmed. "Come on girl! Have some fun! Let them worry about whatever it is that's botherin' 'em. You've got enough on your plate. Let's get to the bar."

With obvious reluctance, Kyle frowned, curling words in her mind. *Something's not right. I just know it.*

It turned out to be an interesting evening, for several other parties came into the bar from other reserves, perhaps in an attempt to check out The Ingwe, and Stephen showed up as well. At any rate, The Ingwe had several musicians on site to entertain the guests, and Kyle and Gina had a great time dancing with a few of the men in the party. Stephen asked Kyle to dance with him during one of the slower numbers and, as Kyle told Gina on their way back to the suite, "He's a good dancer. Fun, too!" All in all it was a surprise they didn't anticipate, and it proved to be an unexpected pleasure.

Although both Kyle and Gina enjoyed the efforts of the chefs to prepare a delicious meal, they were tired from the long flight, the trauma of a near plane crash and the elephant attack not to mention the boredom and strain of the frosty Welcome Dinner. Therefore, they left the bar at about eleven and headed for their suite, grateful that there was no pressure on them to get up and meet an early morning schedule.

Gina, in her own comical way, blurted out, "Hey girl, I saw the way Stephen looked at 'ya and I'd say he's got the hots all right!"

"Oh get out!" Kyle chided, her face flushed. "You're imagining things."

Chapter 13

Sunday

A guided tour was on the agenda for Sunday. The van, sent over from the Silk Farm, didn't arrive until ten o'clock, so Kyle and Gina had plenty of time to enjoy a leisurely breakfast. Apparently the Silk Farm offered tours to neighboring private game reserves on a daily basis. That particular excursion was included in the package Kyle had designated when she signed the contract for their stay at The Ingwe.

The van was packed with guests from other resorts and both Kyle and Gina found it fun to talk to a few of them about their experiences so far. One woman commented about how she loved the game drives. "I'd never been to Africa, but I talked my husband into coming back next year and bringing our granddaughter with us. She's in college studying International Trade."

"That sounds like a great idea to me, and I'm sure your granddaughter will love it. Have you taken her on trips before?" Kyle asked.

The woman smiled with the pride only a grandmother can display. "Oh, yes. We've taken her to several places already. You know they grow up so fast, it's best not to wait to do things, for sometimes it's too late."

"You're certainly right there," Gina conceded. "My nieces are all grown up, and I never see them anymore. They're too busy with their friends."

The woman nodded. "That's what happens."

The Silk Farm was way beyond what either Kyle or Gina expected, for it was an actual factory setting where tourists, by way of a guide, can learn the process of how silk is made as well as visit the showrooms that display and sell the beautiful rough textured silks that are unique to Africa. Kyle and Gina were wide-eyed while they watched the tour guide explain all about the process of producing silk.

"First of all," the guide said, "you might be interested in knowing a bit of history about silk itself. Stories persist that for thousands of years the royal families of China had silk, but they kept the process of making the product a secret for 2500 years. The penalty in China for revealing the source of how silk was made was death. A cruel beginning, right? At any rate, we now know the process, and it's been a successful product ever since." She went on. "To begin with, the baby worms or, as they are technically called, *Mulberry Tree Caterpillars,* hatch in this egg house." The woman showed us large tables that were filled with baby worms. "They must all be scooped up and moved to the next room."

Gina whispered to Kyle, "Yuk, I wouldn't want that job." Kyle's eyes rolled upward and she nodded in agreement.

From the egg room the guide took the group to another location also equipped with long tables filled with leaves. "Here," she said, "we gently place the worms onto the Mulberry leaves using feathers so we don't injure the babies."

Gina grinned, whispering again, "It sounds like they're referring to the worms as people."

Kyle managed a resigned smile as she shook her head suggesting to Gina that she keep still during the presentation. But to both Kyle and Gina it wasn't difficult to see the worms were eating away at the leaves, and that is exactly what the guide pointed out. "The baby worms will eat these Mulberry leaves for some time."

She proceeded from table to table talking as she walked. "Actually the worms go through several stages, namely the egg, the larva, the pupa and then the adult stage which in reality is a moth. The first stage takes three days. The second also takes three days, and the days increase until the last stage which is eight days. Between each stage the worms go into molt or in the case of worms it means they shed their skin like a snake. During this molting period the worms don't eat at all."

In another building the guide stated, "Here we have the worms that are ready to spin their cocoons. We'll scoop them up and carefully attach them to these branches that stick upright as you can see right over here." She led us to another entire room devoted to worms that were spinning cocoons. This cocoon process can take from 48 to 72 hours." She stopped for a moment and turned to explain that, "It takes ten days for a moth to emerge from the cocoon. One can tell the females from the male moths by their size. The females are larger. The male moth at that time mates with many females over a five day period and then it dies. Neither the female nor the male moth can eat, drink or fly, so they all eventually die. The female, however, before doing so, produces the eggs from which, as you most likely guessed, we get another batch of baby silkworms."

Finally, she explained pointing ahead. "This is the facility where the pupa is being disposed of by boiling. The pupa is actually the remains from what's left over when the moth emerges. "From there," she concluded, "our weavers produce the fine silk textiles and duvets you'll see in our storefront."

After answering a number of questions from the group, we all stepped into the storefront in order to view the richly woven and colorful silks on display.

Gina again whispered to Kyle, "Nasty business, but the silk is gorgeous, and I can see several pieces I want already." She babbled on. "I'll take some back to Barbara. She'll be delighted."

Kyle was overwhelmed with the choices, for each one was more opulent than the next and she, too, couldn't resist the temptation to buy a number of yards of several different fabrics. In fact, Gina almost bought a bolt, but when she asked for the price, she backed off and settled on a mere ten yards instead.

"I know you sew, Gina, so you'll be in seventh heaven making whatever it is you're going to make with all that silk."

"I might as well, Kyle, for I'm sure I won't get back here any time soon, if ever."

The tour was topped off with a treat at the attached small outdoor café where everyone who wished could freely sample their cold homemade ginger beer, a drink that neither Kyle nor Gina had ever tried before. Gina, of course, was delighted . . . Kyle not so much. In any event, they both thanked the guide and the store owner and hopped into the van with the others who were equally loaded with purchases and all were escorted back to the various reserves on the route.

"Wonderful!" Kyle said softly as she slipped several American dollars into the hand of the driver who gave her a broad grin.

"Now that was a fun day," Gina announced when they walked into the lobby where they both spied Stephen heading for the back of the building.

He quickly hollered, "Hey, did you two have a good day?"

"What does it look like?" Gina called out, holding up her packages.

Before Kyle could offer her opinion, she looked to see if Carole was behind the Front Desk, for from what she'd seen previously the woman didn't seem to appreciate her having any contact with Stephen. When she saw that Carole was nowhere in sight, she called out to Stephen, "Gina's going to need to hire a private jet to get all this home."

Stephen gestured. "Don't forget the game drive's at four."

"I'd never forget that!" Kyle reassured him. "We'll see you in the lobby."

Stephen beamed. "You'll find me outside waiting."

"Okay," Kyle responded.

"Did 'ya notice the way he looked at you, Kyle? I still think he likes 'ya."

Kyle gave her a perplexed glance.

"I know I'm right. I saw the two of you dancin'. That was no standoffish approach if I ever saw one. He was up close and tight. You can't fool me."

"Get out of here! You're way off base."

Chapter 14

Sunday Evening

Kyle and Gina sorted their "Loot" as Gina called it, and placed it in the closet before grabbing a late lunch in the dining room. Then they returned to the suite and changed into apparel more appropriate for a game drive, namely beige garb which included a jacket with a number of pockets. Before leaving the suite, Kyle grabbed a can of bug spray and her camcorder. With care she pulled the strap on her Nikon over her head letting the camera hang down on her chest ready for use. "I'm going to narrate the scenes on the cam from now on," she told Gina. "I don't want to miss those action shots. I've already missed some good ones . . . like that elephant charge." She paused. "Though I did get some good stills."

"Jeez, why did you have to remind me of that elephant," Gina complained, her face showing more than a little skepticism. "I'm already scared out of my wits about a game drive this late."

"Ah, come on. We'll be fine."

Gina's expression remained leery as they made their way to the lobby and out to the front of the building in time to find Stephen leaning against the hood of the Land Rover. Kyle hadn't paid much attention to him before, but he looked particularly striking that afternoon. His sandy hair was tossed about in the wind, and one might easily say his jeans told more about his manhood than he likely expected.

"Are you all ready for some animal sightings?" he shouted. That unmistakable smile of his revealed a bright set of teeth.

"I sure am," Kyle replied returning an eager grin before glancing at her friend. "This is going to be so much fun Gina!"

"I hope so." The slight frown that lined Gina's face still reflected a case of uncertainty. And when she looked at the vehicle the frown deepened substantially. "But this doesn't have a top?"

"We only put that on during the heat of the day," Stephen replied. "We don't need it now since the sun's going to set soon. In fact, it gets a little cool on occasion, though tonight should be nice." He turned abruptly and waved. "Here comes our tracker. He's from the Shangana Tribe. His name's Mankhelu, but he prefers to be called Million."

Kyle questioned, "Why the name Million?"

Jokingly Stephen went on to explain that his father always wanted to make a million, but he knew he wouldn't be able to do so; therefore, he nicknamed his first born son by that name."

"How clever," Kyle said when the black tracker reached them, nodded and hopped up to the seat on the front of the Land Rover.

After formally introducing the women to Million, Stephen motioned for the two to get into the vehicle. "Hope you remembered to bring along some spray. You may need it."

Kyle pulled the can from her jacket pocket, saying, "We did."

"Good. I think you should put some on before we get going."

"Okay," Kyle agreed as the two coated themselves as suggested.

"We're using the smaller Land Rover tonight so one of you can sit up front with me if you like. Next week, when the group comes in, I'll have to use the bleacher seating Rover, but for now this'll do just fine."

Kyle didn't hesitate for an instant before exclaiming, "I'll sit in front."

Gina pulled herself up into the back seat. "That's more than okay with me," she exclaimed, settling in. "The farther away from the animals I get the better, and by the way how late do we stay out there?"

By then Kyle had seated herself in the passenger's seat on the left side of the vehicle next to Stephen who grinned and jokingly answered, "We'll be out about two and a half hours or so, Gina." He shot Kyle a steady look. "She's being dragged into this, isn't she?"

Kyle grinned, twisted around and darted a look at her friend. "Oh, you're going to love this. Just wait and see."

"Time'll tell," Gina fired back just as Stephen started the engine.

Kyle was too busy to notice Gina's displeasure, for she was getting her cameras ready for what lay ahead. "I'm loving every moment of this," she told Stephen who seemed to be delighted at her enthusiastic approach to an activity that likewise apparently brought him much joy.

"Oh, before we get started I don't want to forget this, so I'll ask you now if it's all right for Bradley Kingston to go along tomorrow on the Panoramic Tour. Gina said she didn't mind. How do you feel, Kyle?"

"Gina's already mentioned that and it's fine with me," Kyle replied.

"Good." He pulled out his cell phone, dialed Carole and asked her to call Bradley Kingston at the Kruger Park Lodge and tell him that he's included on the tour. "And Carole, be sure to tell him to be here at ten o'clock tomorrow, okay?"

Kyle looked directly at Stephen. "I think Gina made quite an impression on Bradley. I wasn't surprised he asked to go along."

Stephen shrugged his shoulders, smiled then darted a look back at Gina. "I guess so."

It was a pleasant night with the air comfortable enough to allow one to set a jacket aside as they enjoyed the last remnants of summer's warmth. They quickly made their way out to the front gate, taking a back road away from the lodge and skirting the South section of the Sand River.

"With this fairly moderate breeze tonight," Stephen noted, "the animals should be out and about, and even though the moon won't be full I think we'll get some good viewing opportunities. I'm going to try and find those *Mauve Leopards* Gideon Courtney's raving about. I haven't seen them, but you can bet I'll try to find 'em, though there's plenty out there to see anyway."

As they bumped along on the rough road, Gina was quiet. Kyle guessed her friend was either bored or was simply afraid they might encounter another elephant on a rampage. Kyle did notice that Stephen had a .458 Magnum Winchester rifle resting across the dashboard of the Land Rover and she commented on it. Stephen's reply was simple. "Oh, yes." he said. "Actually most of our guests don't know what it is."

Gina piped up, "I certainly didn't, but it sure makes me feel better to know you've got a gun."

"So you know what this Winchester is, Kyle? Are you into guns?" he asked in earnest.

"I do some range shooting, not with a .458 though. I've targeted with a .454 raging bull but not that rifle." She grinned at him. "We don't usually encounter any roaming elephants in Florida."

Stephen returned the grin. "Probably not," he said jokingly. "But you seem to be adventurous, Kyle."

Gina cleared her throat. "Oh, yeah she is and prickly independent, too. I've told her she does like to go out on a limb."

Stephen's stare locked on Kyle for a moment. "That's something to find in a woman." He continued on commenting on his sense of admiration for women, especially those who were knowledgeable about guns.

Kyle quickly shifted her gaze away from Stephen. Strange, she thought as she sensed a glimmer of frustration at her apparent interest in the game ranger who, before this evening, aroused no feelings of caring whatsoever. Now, however, she felt a sudden flush engulf her. *Huh, perhaps I haven't lost my need for intimacy. Yet, this is crazy.* With that thought in mind, she switched her attention to exploring the sights around her.

Once again Stephen brought up the subject of his admiration for women, but the statement fell flat. So he backed off and resorted to describing details of the area in general. "We're in Mpumalanga Province," he mentioned, "which in Swazi means Paradise Country." He was about to elaborate about Swazi and Paradise Country when Million motioned to their right and softly called out, "Over there!"

Stephen veered off the beaten path and into the low grass. "I see," he replied in a whisper. He eased the Land Rover over some rough ground. Stopping, he pointed ahead. "Look up on that clearing."

"Unbelievable," Kyle murmured softly.

"What is that animal?" Gina asked, leaning forward in her seat.

"Sh-h-h," Kyle responded. "I think it's a badger, right Stephen?"

"You're right. It's a honey badger."

On a mound in front of them the ferocious badger was actually chasing a cheetah. No one spoke as Kyle filmed, quietly narrating the scene before her. "Got it," she blurted out just before the cheetah disappeared over the ridge and the badger let out a loud squawk and shuffled off into the brush.

Kyle beamed. "Wow! How lucky we are to have seen that. I can't believe the cheetah would run away. That was priceless!"

Stephen nodded. "Show me that later on, will you, Kyle? I'd like to see it. Even though the cheetah can run a hundred kilometers or about 62 miles an hour, they can be frightened off by a badger. Not many animals want to get in the way of a honey badger. They're vicious, but they keep down the rat and the scorpion population."

"I can see why," Gina said.

"Yeah, and they'll even take on poisonous snakes. It's good to see you enjoyed that Kyle." He paused to glance back at Gina. "Are you okay back there?"

"Uh-huh. That *was* pretty neat . . . as long as they're headin' in the other direction," she confided.

"Good call, Million! Let's see what else we can find." Stephen eased the Land Rover back onto the dusty road. It wasn't long before they spotted another member of the antelope family. "Those are impalas. They're all over the place here as well as gazelles." he explained. "Both are favorites when it comes to food for the lions. See the black markings of a large letter 'M' on their back sides?" Laughingly he added, "Some people call them McDonald's like the hamburger chain."

"I can see the M," Gina said with a degree of excitement. Kyle didn't respond for she was too busy filming and narrating the scene at hand.

When Kyle finally stopped filming and looked up, she was quick to say, "We saw some impalas on the way into the lodge didn't we Gina? They were leaping across the road. I didn't have the cam out at the time, but I did get some good shots." Totally exhilarated she rambled on. "Hopefully I'll have a treasure of photos when we get home 'cause this's better than I ever dreamed it would be."

By now they were driving on a ridge overlooking an incline where Million spotted a herd of elephants.

"Jeez," Gina snapped "I'm glad they're down there."

Fortunately the incline was on the left hand side of the Land Rover, giving Kyle a perfect chance to film, which she did while at the same time commenting on a little one who was nursing or at least trying.

"Oh, Gina. Isn't that something? How lucky can I get to be able to film this?" Kyle continued narrating the scene into the speaker on her camcorder while Stephen maneuvered the Land Rover over a narrow bridge with a low railing. Sitting proudly on the bridge's railing was a baboon with one leg propped up on the railing and the other indiscreetly dangling over the side. Apparently the creature wasn't at all concerned about the passing vehicle, for he merely looked up, his piercing eyes glaring at Gina. Stephen stopped just as Gina gestured and cheered boisterously, "He's got a 'hard on'!"

Her cry must have scared the baboon, for he darted away. "Gina!" Kyle shouted. She quickly turned off her camcorder and loudly protested over a series of giggles. "Do you realize that comment's on my recording?"

The knee jerk reaction from Stephen and Million was hilarious, both laughing uncontrollably, and Gina, who attempted to apologize, made it worse by cracking up herself. "Hell," she raved, "I guess that's one way you'll always remember me."

Stephen questioned as he motioned toward the back seat. "Is she always like this?"

Kyle merely shook her head. "Pretty much," Kyle explained. "What you see is what you get."

"This's going to be fun," Stephen concluded. He offered Kyle a sideways glance and a wink that was definitely meant to provoke a response. "At least I won't have to hold back with you two. I like that."

Kyle couldn't help but notice the gleam in Stephen's eyes. Darn it, she thought, I don't want to get involved but I can surely see what Carole finds appealing in this man. He's a fun guy to be with. This may turn out to be a winning trip after all. Then again . . . .

Gina interrupted Kyle's train of thought. "Hey Kyle, we haven't seen any rhino yet have we?"

"No," Stephen quickly responded, "but they're a prize for poachers. I'll tell you some shocking statistics," he said. He abruptly stopped the Land Rover, twisted around and placed his arm on the seat back. "Kruger Park actually has drones to check on the poachers. Fact is, they've set up automatic movement sensors along the borders to relay any intrusion. I bet you two didn't know that a rhino's horn can bring in thirty thousand dollars a pound on the black market."

Gina gasped. "Wow, that's a lot of money."

"Do the drones help to stop the slaughter?" Kyle asked.

"Sometimes. But, in 2009 a selected group of rhinos had invisible tracing devices inserted into their bodies to enable the wardens to at least locate the carcasses. This way they reasoned they could hopefully track down the smugglers by satellite."

With his left arm still resting on the seat back, Stephen went on to explain that the fences between the various private game reserves were taken down in 2002 because they found that the fences interfered with breeding and caused frustration among the animals. "You'd be shocked at the number of rhinos we're losing in Africa each year."

"I've heard about that," Kyle stated. "But we never know if what they say is true or not."

"I don't know what you've heard, but the future's bleak for those animals. Someday, if they don't halt the killings, we may only find rhinos in zoos."

Kyle's frowned. "How sad."

"It is. Fact is, Africa's home to about 80% of the world's remaining rhino population, which totals just over 20,000. But that figure's dwindling. Between 2000 and 2007 an average of 15 rhinos were lost to poaching. That number has increased every year. In 2013 there were 1000 slaughtered. If that keeps up it wouldn't be long before, as I said, you'll only see rhinos in zoos or the like."

"Well, I hope they can stop all that," Kyle said with a degree of skepticism. "But it doesn't sound good."

"No, and most of this is caused by the desire on the part of the Far East to get the horns which they use for aphrodisiacs, hangover remedies and what they consider cures for cancer. None of which are true. We can only hope they'll wake up and see what they're doing, for I love the animals. They're so unique and worth saving." He swung around in his seat and revved the engine, then moved on.

Kyle could tell that talking about the rhino slaughter had affected Stephen, and it was easy to see how he loved the land and its animals. She hesitated saying anything, but to brighten the situation and to break up the silence, Kyle finally spoke up. "Hey, I hope we get to see those *Mauve Leopards* before they decide to move on to some other reserve."

"Well then, let's get going and find those elusive creatures," Stephen said enthusiastically as he quickly pulled back onto the road.

Kyle's eyes brightened. "That'd really top off the night!"

Stephen grinned. "It sure would."

They had no sooner rounded a bend when Kyle called out. "Over there! Aren't those wildebeests?"

"Yeah, that's exactly what they are. You've been studying up on the animals haven't you?"

"I try," Kyle said while she raised her camcorder and started recording. "That's a really big herd, and aren't they magnificent, Gina?"

"Personally," Gina whispered, not wanting to interrupt Kyle's recording, "they look like all the other antelopes to me."

Kyle merely snickered as she watched Stephen smile out of the corner of his mouth.

"I told you. What you see is what you get. But she's always good for a laugh."

Gina stretched her hand up, grasped the front seat and pulled herself forward. "Are you two pickin' on me?"

Kyle turned off her camcorder and looked at Gina. "Of course not. You're so much fun to be with, that's all."

Stephen was silent for a moment, intent on surveying the area ahead. "Hey Million, I think this is a perfect time for a Sundowner."

Gina questioned, "A what?"

"It's my surprise for the night. Since it's still light enough, how'd you like to stop up ahead on that hill and have what we call a Sundowner which involves cocktails and a few snacks."

"Oh, that'd be perfect," Kyle said, her voice charged with eagerness. "It's so beautiful here."

Gina let out an exhaustive breath. "If we don't see any elephants then it's okay with me."

"Good, then let's go." Stephen drove the Land Rover up to the top of a crest of the hill and put the vehicle in park. "Gina, check under your seat and pull out those two baskets will you? The drinks and the rest are in there."

"Well I sure missed that." She grinned as she pulled the baskets out and handed them to Stephen. "Damn!" she said jokingly. "Here I could have had a few drinks along the way."

Both Kyle and Stephen smiled. In no time, though, Stephen had the drinks and the snack dish set up on the hood of the Rover. While Million kept tabs on the surrounding area, all enjoyed a cold drink and a selection of native fruit, cheeses and tasty crackers as they gazed out at the vast golden savannah below, which now glistened from the radiance of the fading yellow sun. In the quiet of those few moments Kyle couldn't help but notice the sounds of the awakening nocturnal wildlife, both from the call of the birds to the strange animal noises coming from the far reaches of the plains.

She looked at Stephen and breathed in a deep sigh. "This sight is beyond belief," she said, looking at the setting sun which was now tipping ever so slightly below the tree line. The sky was ablaze with color. Yellows, varying shades of red, blues and gold all streaked across the horizon forming a rainbow so unique to Africa.

"There is nowhere in the world one can see such beauty as our African sunsets. "They're a sight to behold, and I'm glad you got a chance to see one," Stephen went on.

Kyle nodded. "I can see why you love the place."

Stephen's eyes met Kyle's and he passionately responded with, "I really feel part of this land. I can't tell you why. It's just a feeling."

Kyle paused for a moment. "I feel it, too, Stephen. It's like the wild and the tame are interwoven into a basket that keeps the whole continent together."

"I've never heard it said so well," Stephen remarked as he stared out over the waving golden grass.

Gina, who was standing on the front of the vehicle, broke the serene spell that seemed to be engulfing Kyle and Stephen by mumbling. "Are we going to get back before it's really dark?"

"Yes, I guess we'd better get going. It's getting late," Stephen answered. "Although, it's nice to be out here when Million can highlight the sights with his spotlight."

When both women got back into the Land Rover, Gina said nothing. However, Kyle knew that her friend most likely didn't appreciate the reference to being out in the reserve at night.

"Look over there," Kyle said as they started out again. "What a never ending thrill." She grabbed her Nikon as Stephen stopped the vehicle to let her get some photos of Zebras acting up.

"I've never seen Zebras that playful," Kyle blurted out. "They're never like that in a zoo." As Stephen drove, she rambled on about what she'd seen of zebras in the zoos she'd visited. "They always seem quite blasé."

"Hey, they've got a reputation for being the comedians on the savannahs down here. I guess they wanted to give you a good show."

"Well, they sure did. That was great. I can't believe we're really here, Gina." She looked about to see that her friend had fallen asleep with her head resting on the seat. "Huh," Kyle said to Stephen. "She's out like a light. I swear she could fall asleep in the middle of a hurricane."

"I guess Africa isn't her thing," Stephen remarked. "But you seem to be enjoying the place."

Kyle heaved a sigh. "Oh, I couldn't be happier. This's a trip I've dreamed of for years." As she peered about, blinking against the buttery light that filtered through the brush, she felt a tinge of sadness realizing that she had always hoped she would visit this magnificent spot on earth with Ryan.

Just before the sun made a last ditch effort to stay afloat above the trees, Million called back to Stephen. "There's a lion off in the bushes. Right side."

"See him," Stephen whispered euphorically to Kyle.

"I see him. Gosh, he looks like he's bathed in the evening glow of the setting sun. What a beautiful sight."

As the Land Rover bumped along the rough road, Stephen mentioned that it was most likely time they headed back to the lodge. "We'll have to try and find those *Mauve Leopards* on our next trek." He had no sooner moved the vehicle into some low grass, when he spotted what he thought was a leopard in one of the trees.

"Flash your light over there," he told Million. And sure enough, it was easy to see a leopard's eyes shining in the spotlight's beam before he looked away. "It's a leopard all right," Stephen exclaimed, "but it's not one of the *Mauve Leopards*. Though we're lucky to see any leopards at all. They're hard to find."

Surprised, Kyle grasped the strap of her Nikon and pulled her camera into place just in time to click off one shot before the great cat disappeared into the tree branches. "I don't know if I got anything, Stephen. Can we sit here for a minute while I try and pull it up?"

"Sure, go ahead!"

Kyle bent over, opened the Nikon's viewer screen, hit two buttons and "Voila" there was the leopard just before it darted away. "Oh, my gosh, Stephen. I got it!" Kyle cried out. That one shot did it! See here." She leaned sideways and gave Stephen a look.

"Great. It's not one of the *Mauve Leopards*, but it sure is an elusive leopard all right. You're a good photographer. I told you that." He gave her a thumbs-up gesture. "Hopefully we'll get to see one of the special breed and you can capture that one on film as well. In the meantime, I guess we should head back."

"Sure, that's fine, and I think I can speak for Gina. If she wakes up and it's pitch dark all around her she'll probably freak out."

Million nodded. Stephen pulled forward and headed down the road toward the lodge. The sun had now dipped below the tree line and Stephen had turned on his headlights. Though the road was bumpy causing a bit of a rumble as they moved along, all was quiet in the brush around them until a loud thump sounded near the back of the vehicle and the Land Rover began to shake.

That thump was enough to awaken Gina who sat up and yelled, "What's going on?"

Stephen knew immediately what had happened. He slowed down and pulled over to the side of the road, stopping just short of the main road leading back to the lodge. "Well, believe it or not I think we've got a flat tire."

"Oh no!" Gina's words dying in a hiccupping gasp. "Not out here at night."

Stephen slid out of his seat and Million hopped off the front of the Land Rover. "No problem here. Sit back and we'll be on our way in no time."

Though to Kyle this was merely another thrill to enjoy, she could tell that Gina was more than a bit concerned for she was nervously nibbling on her fingernails again. Off and on Kyle also witnessed that twitch in Gina's cheek that only occurred when she was anxious. She tried to assure her friend that all would be well, but Gina admitted it didn't help.

"Don't worry, Gina," Stephen pointed out. "The animals don't want any confrontation with bright lights and we'll be out of here soon." While Stephen was getting the spare tire and the jack out from the back of the vehicle, Kyle got out and watched as he prepared to change the tire. "Does this happen often?" she questioned stooping down beside him.

While he twisted off the lugs and pulled the rim and the old tire from its mount, he told her that the rough roads sometimes do cause a flat tire. "But we're prepared for whatever happens. So don't worry."

"Oh, I'm not," Kyle said. She stood up, leaned forward and looked into the darkness of the surrounding savannah. It appeared that the shadows moved like silent gray wolves in the forest, but it didn't frighten her at all. "As far as I'm concerned this is another thrill I hadn't anticipated. It's great!" But when she looked at Gina, she knew her friend didn't share that opinion, for she was wide-eyed.

"You would say that," Gina piped up. "Just get us back to the lodge."

Stephen was about to place the last of the lugs on the hub cap when a loud snort sounded from off to the right. Million aimed his spotlight toward the guttural sound. A tunnel of light emphasized the features of a massive rhino, and he wasn't more than fifteen or so feet from the Land Rover.

Gina's eyes darted about as if she were expecting danger in every shadow. She bit her lip, crying out, "Now what?"

Duck down, Gina, and Kyle," Stephen whispered. "Kyle, get into the Rover but keep low and don't stand up. I'll tell you why later."

Chapter 15

Sunday Night

Situated at the far end of The Ingwe Reserve, a short distance from the Lodge stood a thatched roof structure that was the home of Dr. Greene and her husband. It was a discreet living arrangement in which the center of the building had a large room with a vaulted ceiling, a fireplace and a mini kitchen with a bar. On one side of the structure was Dr. Lynn Greene's bedroom and on the opposite side was Damon's Greene's bedroom. Each had their own side entrance so anyone could enter without disturbing the other. Apparently they found this arrangement met the needs of their symbiotic relationship and, since they rarely had guests in the home, not too many were privy to the details of their marriage.

Gideon, who lived in a suite on the second floor of the lodge, was well aware of the conflict in the Greene's marriage and on this particular Saturday night at 11:30 P. M. he made his way to the side entrance of Lynn Greene's bedroom and knocked three times, a signal they had devised long before their affair had taken on real meaning.

Standing in a sheer negligee with the light from the lamp on her bedside table highlighting her shapely form, she motioned for Gideon to come in while at the same time commenting, "He's not going to make it tonight."

Gideon brushed past her shaking his head. "No, I knew he'd be out cold. He'll have to sleep it off." Lynn closed the door and swung around to look up at him, for he was very tall and she a mere five foot five. The exasperated look on her face told worlds about her state of mind, and the frustration only deepened as she sat down on the side of the bed. Gideon sat down beside her and placed his arm snugly around her waist. She exhaled an exhaustive sigh then gazed up at him. "I checked on him earlier and it's a wonder he didn't have another seizure after that one last week. I told him to stay away from the scotch, but he never listens." Lynn placed her hand on Gideon's thigh and gave his leg a squeeze. "Is there any way you can get those leopards into the field tonight?"

"No Lynn. I can't do it myself. Even with Damon helping it's going to be a chore." He looked down for an instant then went on to explain that they'd have to take the cats out in the late afternoon the next day while the guests were on the Panoramic Mountain Tour.

"He better be ready then," Lynn said bitterly. "That's our only hope for getting those clients who're coming in on Friday to buy this place, and we need the two guests that are here now to attest to the fact that they've seen the mutants."

"Well, we've still got that deal with Stephen pending. That is if he comes through with the cash. Maybe we can get the divorce settled after that."

"But," she said, hesitating, "are you sure Stephen can get that much money in time?"

Gideon leaned over, stretched his right arm across the width of Lynn's upper back, gently pressed his left hand on her waist, then pushed her back onto the soft bed sheets, his face hovering over hers. He gently ran his fingers through her dark brown hair, hair that was no longer tied up in a tight chignon, but was flowing about her shoulders. "He says he's been planning this for three years and I don't know if he can pull off the deal, but all I want right now is a part of you. You look gorgeous tonight. Do you know that?" His lips met hers, first with a moist touch, then with the desire that was meant to elicit an emotional response. It did and Lynn melted into his arms.

"Oh Gideon," she moaned, her voice filled with the passion of the moment. "I wish we were back in Johannesburg together. I want to be out in the open about all this." She stroked his cheek and gently rolled her fingers over his lips. "Dealing with Damon is enough to drive anyone mad."

"I know," Gideon agreed while he slipped one of the straps of her gown over her shoulder. "Let's not worry about anything tonight. Just hold me, will you? That's all I ask."

"You know you don't have to ask," Lynn whispered into his ear. She stood up and let her gown fall to the floor. After dimming the light, she lay down on the bed, her body ripe for the taking. That's all the invitation Gideon needed to ignite the lust he felt for this women who, in his heart, he knew no one fully understood but him.

Gideon quickly undressed and crawled into bed beside her, pressing his warm flesh next to Lynn in a mating ritual that's as old as time. For the next few hours they nursed each other's need for love like only two souls devoted to each other can do, both wishing that these precious moments could last forever.

Well before Gideon met Lynn in her bedroom, Stephen, Kyle, Gina and Million found themselves stranded in the midst of The Ingwe Game Reserve, stuck there with a flat tire on the Land Rover while on a night game drive that happened to fall on an evening when there was no trace of a moon in sight. The all encompassing darkness was enough to scare anyone, much less those who weren't expecting that much of a thrill, and they found themselves confronted with the piercing eyes of a very skittish rhinoceros that stood nearby. Fortunately Stephen had finished placing the new tire on the vehicle just before they heard the loud, gruff grunt of the animal off in the bushes. The rhino was obviously letting the intruders know that they were encroaching into his space.

Million had immediately flashed the flood light to highlight the beast while Stephen picked up his tools and returned them to the Rover.

Fortunately, with Stephen's guidance and without invading the rhino's domain they all skillfully slipped back into the vehicle. The engine hummed to life and they moved slowly away from the scene. Million sat in place flashing the spotlight from side to side as they headed back to the lodge until the moon finally punched a hole in the darkness. As he drove Stephen was on his cell calling in to report the mishap. "We'll be there shortly," he told Carole who admitted she was getting anxious.

When Stephen parked the Rover in front of the lodge, they all heaved a sigh of relief. Kyle noticed that his face showed the strain he was under as he tried to keep his guests safe. "Hope that didn't discourage you two from future game drives. We haven't had a tire blow out for quite some time," he stated. "But you never know about these roads. Did you enjoy the rest of the drive?"

"I sure did," Kyle responded as she shook Stephen's hand. "This trip's proving to be a thrill a minute and I like that." Strangely, he squeezed her hand and held on to it a little longer than she expected. For an instant it made her feel a little uneasy. Wonder what he meant to imply by that, she thought to herself. *But then I'm probably reading more into it than I should.*

Gina noted the handshake and gave Kyle a curious smile as they left to go back into the lobby.

"Have you got all of your things, you two?" Stephen asked, following a step or so behind the women.

"I've got everything," Kyle responded. "How about you, Gina?"

"I'm fine. I just want to settle down for a minute," she said. "I don't know about you but I'm goin' to the bar and get a drink. Wanna come?"

"No, I'm going to the suite and update my journal before our late dinner. Remember they said it would be at eight because of the game drive." She paused for an instant. "Oh, by the way Stephen, when are we to be down here in the morning for the tour?"

He was already heading for the Front Desk, but he quickly turned about. "Ten o'clock will be fine, and wear good sturdy shoes, for there'll be some hiking involved."

When Stephen was out of sight, Gina stated emphatically, "Well, I'm goin' to wear those shoes you told me to buy, but I can't promise I'll do any hikin'. Maybe I'll hike to the coffee stand. There's got to be one or two of them on the tour."

Kyle shook her head and called out while heading for the stairs. "I'll be down for dinner at eight."

On the way back to move the vehicle Stephen bumped into Gideon and told him about the mishap with the Land Rover. "Hey," Stephen explained, "we did see a leopard out there tonight, but we didn't see any *Mauve Leopards* anywhere."

"I hope you find 'em soon," Gideon said knowing full well that it was up to Damon and himself to see to it that the *Mauve Leopards* get into the field before the Friday deadline. "I'm counting on you to find 'em on your next game drive, Stephen. Keep a good eye out. Stay alert!"

"I'll do my best."

"I'm sure you will!"

Gideon had told Stephen about the prospect of getting the leopards, but not the specifics of where he got them, and he certainly hadn't informed Stephen of the fact that he would be responsible for keeping the cats fed so that they'd stay on the reserve. Hoping to cap the lid on the details of this ruse, he and Lynn felt it best to keep some things to themselves until the proper time.

Kyle hurried to their suite and quickly pulled out her camera to check the shots she's taken that day. She was pleased. She cleaned her camera equipment, a necessity when dealing with the dust one picks up on the lenses on the African savannah, then packed all of it for the next day's tour and set out her clothes for the trip. The excitement of it all was getting to her, so she quickly picked up her journal and headed for the deck. She entered data she thought would be descriptive of the whirlwind day they'd just encountered on the grounds of The Ingwe Reserve. However, periodically she'd stop and look out at the waterhole and the spotlight that highlighted the animals that were there for a refreshing drink. It was fascinating to listen to the awakening of Africa's big game animals on their night hunt and feel the fragrance of sweet wind all about her, even noting the flight of a flock of cranes against the Technicolor sky. All was so peaceful.

Journal Entry—4 *This was truly a fast-paced Saturday and Sunday. First on the trip into The Ingwe Reserve we met Carole Magone, the office manager and had an exciting ride into the lodge, for we saw a few animals, but the one that caused the stir was the elephant that charged our car. Thankfully the big guy decided we weren't worth the effort and lumbered off. Carole took us on a tour of the lodge. Lots to see including a Herpetology Exhibit which is the pride of Dr. Lynn Greene, the wife of one of the owners. Had a refreshing swim in the pool, but a disappointing Welcome Dinner. Gideon Courtney and Dr. Greene attended. The doctor said that her husband was busy and couldn't make it. Then it was on to an evening at the bar where Gina and I met some tourists from other reserves. We danced and had a ball. The next day, Sunday, we visited a Silk Farm and learned how* *silkworms produce the gorgeous silks available for purchase around the world. That evening we went on a late afternoon and evening game drive. Enjoyed what the Afrikaans refer to as a Sundowner (cocktails and a snack out on the savannah). The evening was great. Though we saw a bevy of animals we were cursed with a another mishap, that being the Land Rover had a flat tire on a pitch dark road with a angry looking rhino standing off in the bush just yards from us. Stephan had told us to slowly get back into the Rover but that we shouldn't stand up in the vehicle. He told us later the reason one should never stand up in a touring car like a Land Rover when near a wild animal has to do with the outline of the vehicle itself. The animals are used to seeing the tourists in vehicles of one shape where all are seated, but when they see that configuration change they are aroused and could attack thinking the vehicle is a threat. Interesting! Gina is holding up well considering, and I was somewhat intrigued by Stephen's handshake when we arrived back at the lodge. He is a fascinating man who has a passion for Africa and most particularly The Ingwe Reserve.*

Chapter 16

Monday

Bradley Kingston drove his car into The Ingwe Private Game Reserve at 9:45 Monday morning in order to be sure he wouldn't be excluded from the Panoramic Mountain Tour. He scanned the lobby and started walking toward the Front Desk when all of a sudden he heard his name being called out. Bringing his head around, he saw a sandy-haired man approaching him and he hollered back, "Yes," I'm Brad Kingston. "I'm here about the Panoramic Tour."

"Glad you signed on, Brad. I'm Stephen Falkner. I've known your brother Patrick for a few years, and he called and said you'd like to be included. We've only got two other guests going out today."

"I know. I met them on the plane coming from the States. We had a near crash in Dakar. Did you hear about that?"

"Oh yeah. They told me all about it. What a shame the trip had to start out like that, but I hope you're enjoying it down here."

"I am. Actually it's the first time I've had a chance to come down to see my brother. It's quite a place, and I'm looking forward to seeing some of the sight—"

Brad was interrupted by Gina's bubbly voice as she called out from the far end of the lobby, "Hey, Bradley!"

Both men turned to see two women hurrying toward them. "Are we late?" Kyle asked, shoving her fanny pack to one side to accommodate her camera bag.

"No no," Stephen responded. "Brad just got here. Are you two ready for a great day on the tour? You look like you're dressed for it."

Looking down at her feet, Gina gestured. "If you're talking about these hiking shoes, Kyle's the one who suggested them."

"They're perfect," Stephen responded. "You'll be doing some hiking if you want to see it all."

"I'm not much of a hiker," Gina said humorously. "I may be the one you meet on the way *back* from the hike."

Kyle burst out with, "Hey, I want to see it all. How many chances does one get to see this place?"

"We'll play it by ear and do whatever you want to do. How's that?" Stephen said with a definite degree of confidence.

"Fine," Brad agreed, looking toward Gina who was gazing admiringly on him.

Kyle, displaying a raised eyebrow, couldn't help noticing the apparent connection between Brad and her friend. *Coming with me on this safari may be a trip Gina will never forget for more than one reason.*

"Then let's get moving," Stephen announced. He picked up his backpack. "The car's out in front."

"Are we taking that same Land Rover?" Gina asked.

"No we're got the SUV today. Better for long hauls." He looked back at the group as they stepped out of the lobby. "Are you going to be filming, Brad? And how about you, Gina?"

"No," was the replied from the two.

"I'll leave that to Kyle," Gina countered. "She's the enthusiast."

"And I didn't bring a camera," Brad said. "I'm an art dealer who does acquire prize photographs, but I'll leave the filming to the experts."

"You deal in art works. That's interesting," Stephen replied nonchalantly. "Gina's told me she dabbles in art."

Gina was still beaming like a young schoolgirl and, by the look of it, Brad seemed to be quite smitten with the attention she was giving him.

Kyle and Stephen merely glanced at one another and smiled, for it was obvious Brad and Gina were determined to set their own agenda. "Well," Stephen called out while looking at Gina then at Brad, "since neither one of you are doing any camera work, what say Kyle sits up front with me so she can get those moving shots along the way."

Brad offered a nod and Gina didn't have to respond, for her actions spoke louder than words as she hustled herself into the back seat faster than a flea scurrying across a slate floor. Again, Kyle knew full well that her friend couldn't be happier. A ride with a distinguished Brit was most definitely to her liking.

"Okay, hop in Kyle and we'll be off to see the sights." When they were all seated, he pulled out a folder from his backpack. "Here's a few maps of the area. It'll give you an idea of where we're going." He placed his left arm on the seat back and handed two of the maps to Brad and Gina then gave Kyle a copy. Quickly retrieving a set of brochures, he handed one to each of the group as well, saying, "You may want to look these over, too, for they're a preview of the amazing sights we'll see."

That said, he twisted around in his seat, put the key into the ignition and started the engine. "And listen, if you have any questions just speak up. I'll be glad to tell you all I know about these fabulous sites."

Gina and Brad spent the next few minutes looking over the maps and the literature, but Kyle was more interested in getting her camera gear ready for whatever was ahead, and it wasn't long before she got her first shot. About a half mile from the lodge she cried out, "Look there, Stephen. Can you stop for a minute?"

"Sure," he said agreeably. He pulled over to the side of the road where two huge cape buffalo were standing off in the grass. "If you remember cape buffalo are on the list of the Big 5, and they're referred to as the 'Black Death' for they can be as dangerous as ever if you provoke 'em."

No one said a word as Kyle proceeded to take a few shots. When Stephen pulled away, the smile on Kyle's face could have brightened the darkest of days. "Stephen," she enthusiastically exclaimed, "they looked like they were actually posing for me. They're such intense looking creatures. Yet so stately. And those massive horns look like they could cause a lot of havoc."

"How true," Stephen remarked making his way out of the main entrance gate. "Now if you all want to look at your maps, I'll tell you where we're going first and that would be the Bourke Luck Potholes."

Brad called out, "I see the place and I presume we're going north."

"You're right. It's a bit northeast really, for we're on that major route north. The map isn't as specific as it could be. Actually the Potholes lead to the Blyde River Canyon which we'll see later on. Both sites are spectacular. Take a look at the brochures and you can see a few of the features before we get there. At the Potholes there's an Information Center that shows some of the socio-historic factors of the 700 mile walk through the Potholes."

Leave it to Gina to let out a hearty gasp. "Seven hundred miles! Give me a break!"

Kyle immediately responded. "I knew she'd say that."

Stephen laughed. "I had a feeling that would get someone's attention, but we'll leave the whole expanse of the total mileage to the explorers, and we'll do whatever you want, for there are several different pathways you can take."

Gina nudged Brad. "Well, I'm for exploring the Information Center. How about you?"

"We'll see," he said, while he quietly continued to peruse the maps and brochures.

Kyle was too busy observing the surrounding area and listening to Stephen's comments about sites along the route to pay too much attention to Brad and Gina, but she did hear disjointed bits of conversation about their careers and what they wanted to get out of life. They certainly seem compatible, she thought. In retrospect that eased Kyle's mind, for she was the one who had convinced Gina to accompany her on this trip even though her friend was anything but a safari type. So, maybe all would turn out well for her best friend.

Brad could be heard telling Gina that he was pleased to see her again. That was a comment Gina seemed delighted to hear, and with her "appealing charm" she didn't hesitate to make the most of the situation. First, she asked him to detail some of the works he has in his gallery in Tampa, then she proceeded to tell him that she has done a good deal of painting herself. "Watercolors mainly," she went on. "I don't like working in oils. They take forever to complete."

"I can tell you're a woman of action," Brad stated in response to her mentioning the time involved in painting in oils. "Are you working professionally in the art field?"

"No, I own a Day Spa in Fort Myers and its thriving quite well. I only paint as a hobby." She laughed aloud, "Funny, Brad, but I still love the smell of paint."

"Well, I admire your tenacity."

That last verbal exchange between the two perked Kyle's interest and she turned just in time to observe Gina as she pressed her head on Brad's shoulder. "Oh, you're only trying to flatter me," Gina said in her own coy way. "Keep it up though. I like it."

Kyle couldn't help chuckling, for it seemed Gina was acting like a school girl on a first date, crawling all over him like a rash on a hot summer night.

Stephen must have heard the exchange as well for he immediately glanced Kyle's way and she noted that he also had a smile on his face. This could turn out to be a very interesting trip, Kyle thought.

Within minutes Stephen pulled into the parking lot at Bourke's Luck Potholes. "Here we are," he said, cutting the motor and palming the keys. "Get ready for a thrill." While they walked to the Information Center, Stephen gave them an overview of what they might see including a picnic area where they sell souvenirs. "And," he went on, "it's interesting to note that these Potholes are named after a gold digger named Tom Bourke who staked out a claim that, unfortunately, didn't produce a single speck of gold." He stopped for an instant at the entrance to the Center, stepped back and opened the door. "But believe it or not, later on others did find gold here. You may want to mull around and read whatever you wish about the place. I'll just wait and when you're ready we can walk down and view the site. Oh, and by the way, the wash rooms are on your right." He grinned, "Everybody seems to ask that question first."

"Thanks," Kyle said as the group scattering about. "I'm really looking forward to viewing this place."

While the group glanced at the signs and inspected the large wall map, Stephen talked with the clerks at the Information Desk and asked if there had been any changes that he, as a game ranger who takes clients on tours, should know about. They chatted on for a time until he saw first Gina and Brad, then Kyle move toward the front entrance. "I guess you're ready to go, eh?"

"Let's get to it," Brad spoke up.

"Well, as you probably read in there," Stephen explained as he elbowed the door open, "these varying colored Potholes are odd shaped holes that were carved into the red sand bedrock by swirling water pools over eons. Some of the Potholes are almost surreal shapes like something an artist would create. Be sure to notice how the craggy cliffs drop down into cylindrical Potholes." He stopped as they started down the path. "In some areas you'll see waterfall after waterfall, but that's a bit into the walk which I said can be lengthy."

They all looked on awestruck. "They're magnificent!" Kyle solemnly stated, her camera at the ready. "The sun's hitting the rocks just right. I should be getting some great photos." While Gina and Brad stood gazing down at the deep crevasses, Kyle continued to click away, determined to get a "prize" shot if at all possible.

"See those odd shaped holes in the rock?" Stephen said. "They stand out best over on the right side of the river." With an outstretched finger he motioned ahead. "You'll see many more of these when you walk across that bridge over there."

Without missing a beat, Gina quipped, "We're goin' to do what?"

"We can cross the bridge," Stephen clarified. "There's a beautiful view of more Potholes when you get to the other side of that curve in the river over the bridge. Actually that's the meeting place of two rivers. The Truer River tumbles into the Blyde River. It's an outstanding view. Who's game to try?"

Gina raised both hands, palms up. "I'll pass," she responded emphatically. "You guys go ahead. I'll look for souvenirs."

"Anyone else?" Stephen asked.

Kyle was quick to respond. "I wouldn't miss this for the world."

Stephen glanced at Brad. "How about you?'

"I'll forgo the walk over the bridge, but I will take a short stroll down a bit." He turned to Gina, "See you later at the gift shop."

"Fine," Stephen replied. "Let's go, Kyle. Brad you can follow 'til we get to the curve that leads to the bridge. We'll meet you two later at the Information Center. Count on about forty-five minutes all told, okay?"

Brad agreed and they all started off on their separate journeys. Brad walked along the route admiring the view then headed back to meet Gina who was in her glory buying hand-designed jewelry made by the native women of the Shangana and the Thonga Tribes. Brad, on the other hand, was fascinated by the artwork unique to the area. In fact, he purchased some fine pieces. "I'll ship these home from Kruger," he told Gina.

As for Kyle, crossing the bridge couldn't have made her happier, for she was used to being high above the clouds, and the structure, though as secure as any bridge could be, was still a chance to feel out in the open with nothing by sky above and the good earth below.

Stephen appeared amazed at her capacity to be so absorbed by all she saw around her. "You surprise me, for you do like adventure, don't you?" he again commented admiringly. "Many I take on these tours are hesitant when stepping out over the canyon."

Kyle went on to detail her love of flying and how that changes one's perspective of heights. "It makes you feel like you're closer to Heaven," she said aiming her lens at some of the craggy Potholes below. "You can see a lot more of them over here. Too bad, Brad and Gina can't see this."

"Hey, keep shooting like you're doing and Brad and Gina will be able to see the whole place without even being here."

"I hope so. I take so many photos." She stopped for a moment, looked at him and grinned. "Someone once told me that if I'd been shooting the enemy in World War II like I shoot scenes, the war would have been over in no time."

Stephen nodded while his beaming smile lit up his face, an attraction Kyle couldn't help noticing.

"They're probably right, but with the digital format one can take hundreds of photos on one film clip and the cost is minimal, right?"

Stephen nodded as he ambled along the path. Kyle found the sights spectacular, and she commented that someday her photos will make a perfect power point presentation. Strangely, whenever Kyle looked toward Stephen she found him gazing at her and she questioned him about it.

"Oh, I didn't mean to stare," he said his eyes flashing, "but I've never met anyone like you. You get so engrossed in what you're doing."

"That must be the pilot virtue in me, but I must say that I've always wanted to go on safari and this adventure is the high point of my life so far. It's obvious that you love Africa so much."

"I'm glad you find the land fascinating. It's been my life." He turned and glanced down at the rock bed below. "I can't see myself anywhere else on earth." He choked up a bit as he uttered those words. Then quickly realizing he was not alone but a game ranger responsible for a group on tour, he immediately added, "I guess we should turn back. I said we'd meet the others in forty or so minutes."

"Okay," Kyle answered. "It's been great, Stephen. "I'm glad you suggested the walk over the bridge. It was fabulous!"

Soon they were waving to Gina and Brad who had managed to accumulate a stack of souvenirs. While they all stopped for coffee at the Information Center, Kyle slipped out and bought a few souvenirs herself, and before long they were on their way to the next attraction, The Blyde River Canyon.

"Well here we are," Stephen reported as soon as they parked the SUV in the parking lot.

"The Canyon's actually a nature reserve," he clarified when they walked up to the rim. "It's situated in the escarpment region of eastern Mpumalanga, which—"

"Sorry to interrupt, but that's the oddest name. I love the sound of the word," Kyle noted, while proceeding to repeat it with emphasis. "Mpumalanga."

"It probably does sound weird to you, but we're so used to it," Stephen replied jokingly. "Though I guess it does have a certain ring to it. At any rate, the Blyde River Canyon Reserve protects the area from the flow of the two rivers I mentioned earlier. Fact is, it's the third largest canyon in the world after the Grand Canyon and the Fish River Canyon in Nambia." Following a brief stop to view one scene, Stephen continued his narration. "The canyon includes the geological formations around Bourke's Luck Potholes and, believe it or not, it's sixteen miles long."

Kyle took photos of the canyon from the viewing point, but agreed with the others that they should forfeit the walk down the many steps to the base, for it was quite a distance.

"Then let's get on to see our next site which is God's Window," Stephen announced. "But how about stopping along the way to get a bite to eat? It's after one and I'll bet you're starving."

There was no indecision on anyone's part. All were more than happy for a much needed break.

"Good," Stephen said. "Check your maps if you want to, for we're going to take the scenic route so you can observe the fascinating sights along the way and I'm sure we can find a good spot to stop for lunch."

They did stop at a small roadside diner that offered a variety of sandwiches, salads and other selections that were welcome treats for a group that was eager to find some refreshments and a cool drink.

In no time they were back on the road, headed for God's Window. "You won't believe the view from the vantage point at God's Window where you can see Africa at its best," Stephen contended. "In my mind I think Africa is a Land of Contrasts, but I'll leave it up to you to decide."

The group found his words to be so very true. When they reached the peak and Stephen parked the vehicle, they had to walk down a steep footpath along the escarpment to reach the actual viewing platform overlooking the gorge and the Lowvelt plains below. Each remarked on the beauty of the view.

"This high plateau," Stephen lectured, "is inhabited by mountain reedbuck, baboon troops and rock hyraxes."

"Oh," Gina exclaimed. "Are those the animals that look like rats?"

"Yeah! They do look like rats."

Kyle's Nikon was working overtime as she clicked off one shot after another all the while Stephen was narrating. When she finally took a break, she mentioned that Carole had told them that the hyrax hide in the Kopjes.

"They're really anywhere there's vegetation," Stephen replied. "That's for sure. Also in the Lowvelt below you'll find hippo and crocodile. You'll find them in places around the dam where you'll also see Kudu, blue wildebeest and waterbuck. Even zebra roam the wooded areas. It's really unique down there."

"What's that mass of rock at the bottom that looks like it juts out of the ground?" Kyle asked.

"That's called the Pinnacle. It's a huge formation all right, and as you can see it reaches almost to the height of where we're standing. Notice how the sides are jagged but yet the cliffs are sheer and the top is covered with foliage. It most likely took that mass of rock centuries to erode into its present state."

"Beautiful," Kyle said raising her camera again.

Turning to an area close by, Stephen pointed to some of the fauna. See those orchids over there on the hill. You'll also find lilies as well as all kinds of tree ferns. In fact, there are one thousand varieties of plants recorded in this area. It's a grand view isn't it? I guess that's why they call it God's Window."

While other tourists actively moved around the viewing platform, Kyle, Gina and Brad merely stood silently taking a last look at the scene.

"A wonder to see," Kyle said. "I feel so lucky to be able to come here."

"I can see why my brother loves the place so much," Brad admitted. "The entire area is spectacular. We have one more site to see, right Stephen?"

"Oh yes. We still have Pilgrims Rest. Come on. Let's head there now."

"Hey," Kyle spoke up, "that's the historical town I saw in one of the brochures?"

"It sure is."

Pilgrims Rest turned out to be a fun place to visit, for it had a Victorian charm about it with a touch of Dutch architectural design almost everywhere one looked.

"This is an old mining town," Stephen explained as they walked the streets with the wooden sidewalks and old fashioned storefronts. "It dates back to the gold rush days of 1873. It's like a living museum."

The group spent more than two hours taking in all that the town had to offer and, of course, picking up some of the souvenirs that Gina determined she just couldn't do without, and her list went on . . . and on. It wasn't until about four o'clock that they all decided they'd had enough for the day. On the way back to the lodge they drove into Hazyview. Brad and Gina, almost in unison, called out, "Let's stop here for coffee."

Kyle was quick to agree, "Great idea!"

Stephen didn't hesitate for a moment as he switched lanes and pulled into Perry's Bridge Trading Post, a unique small store that offered plenty of souvenirs and a coffee shop setting that seemed perfect for the end of an adventurous day of sightseeing.

On their drive back to The Ingwe Reserve they stopped twice so Gina and Kyle could rummage through all kinds of wood carvings and trinkets that vendors were selling along the highway. They both ended up with two bags each of souvenirs. Brad seemed happy to stay in the SUV and talk about Africa in general and his visit with his brother Patrick.

Fortunately they made it back to the reserve in time to have a few drinks at the bar. Notably Brad stayed on to recapture the excitement of the day. Of course, anyone viewing the scene couldn't miss noting that Brad's interest was definitely aimed at Gina and she let it be known she relished the attention as she listened to him in thick contentment.

After a leisurely dinner, Kyle's journal entries were brief. The late afternoon game drive the night before and the expansive tour that day had left both Gina and Kyle ready for a full night's sleep after dinner. Gina slipped off to sleep before ten while Kyle spent a few minutes on the deck drafting phrases that would hopefully preserve her memories of a wonderful day seeing the glorious sights of her newfound Africa.

Journal Entry—5 *While we left The Ingwe for our Panoramic Tour, I was lucky enough to spot two cape buffalo in the bush. Stephen stopped the car and I took some photos that are exceptional. It was as if those big fellows were actually posing for me. The Panoramic Tour turned out to be more than I'd ever expected. We saw the magnificence of Bourke's Luck Potholes, a place that certainly bridges time. In fact, I crossed the bridge there that connects one side of the river canyon to the other and leads to a place where the Blyde River and the Truer River merge into one. The Potholes are even more spectacular on the far side of the bridge.*

The Blyde Canyon, the third largest canyon in the world, stretches for 900 miles and is enough to take your breath away.

God's Window lived up to its title, for it offered a magnificent view of the world below. It surely was an expanse that seemed to stretch out forever. "The Pinnacle," a massive rugged stone structure that looked like it jutted out from the bedrock in an effort to reach the sky, dominates the center of the valley.

Pilgrims Rest was a unique old time historical town, most akin to our old west. We had fun shopping and walking the wooden sidewalks. All in all I had a delightful time, and it appeared that Bradley, who signed on for the tour, and Gina hit it off quite well. It will be interesting to see what happens with those two. I must say that Stephen was very accommodating. I found him charismatic and an interesting individual with a strong passion for his work and for the land he loves. All good qualities.

Kyle put away her journal and slipped into bed feeling comfortable in this, as Stephen calls it, Land of Contrasts. For awhile she tossed and turned, for she couldn't help but wonder what the morning's balloon ride over the reserve would be like. Another adventure to be met head on, she thought and maybe another thrill. *Who knows?*

Chapter 17

Monday Afternoon & Evening

Gideon met Damon in Damon's office about four o'clock knowing that they had but a few hours to get the job of moving the cats into the reserve before dark. Fortunately Damon had recovered from his hangover and was prepared to get the job done.

"Come on. We'd better get going. This isn't going to be easy, but we've got to get the cats in place—"

"I know," Damon interrupted. "Lynn's been harping at me since last night."

"Well, you did put a crimp in our plans you know," Gideon badgered critically. "If the guests don't spot those *Mauve Leopards* when they go out on their game drive on Wednesday afternoon, we're in trouble, for the buyers are coming in Friday for the *Boma,* and we need those guests to be overjoyed at the fact that they spotted a new breed of leopard."

Damon winced. "I know that, but don't talk so loud. My head's splitting and your voice's killing me."

"And whose fault is that?" Gideon barked, savoring every moment he could allude to his partner's inadequacies.

Damon said nothing else but merely grabbed his coat and a pair of heavy gloves. "You do know, though, that I'm not going to be a part of selling this place. I want those prospective buyers to sign on as part owners or at least buy shares. That'll keep the bank off our backs."

"We'll see about that," Gideon mumbled under his breath. He and Lynn had devised a plan for selling the place, but Damon's version about selling was far different from theirs and, in their minds, it was not even a consideration. Gideon realized he'd have to wait and see how it all worked out. In the meantime, he still hoped the secret deal he'd setup to sign over the place for the 9,504,000 ZAR, meaning Krugerrands, or a large six figure amount in U. S. dollars that had been agreed upon with Stephen, would work out and that somehow Damon would be out of the picture. That way he and Lynn could escape from the "Hell Hole" they considered The Ingwe, to live their lives in Johannesburg.

So, while Stephen and the guests at The Ingwe Reserve along with Brad were winding down a day of sightseeing, Gideon and Damon drove to their warehouse and prepared to spend the next few hours moving the big cats into the trees deep in a forested area of The Ingwe Reserve.

Gideon parked the truck off to one side of the warehouse so there would be plenty of room to open the huge double doors that allowed for removing some of the large equipment stored there. "I'll drive," Gideon offered and Damon didn't argue. He did, however, comment as they pulled one of the doors aside, "I don't know how you managed to move them in the first place."

"It wasn't easy," Gideon replied with a degree of disgust as he shoved open the other door. He had never liked Damon, and having to take the responsibility for all the rough jobs was trying his patience.

When the two men entered the warehouse it was easy to tell the cats were aggravated, for their growls and low tone hisses could be heard with clarity. They were, indeed, frustrated. A few of them were moving their heads back and forth in an effort to pace within their cages which were much too small for such activity.

"By the way, since you were too boozed up to care," Gideon said sarcastically, "I did feed the cats yesterday. They haven't had anything today, so we'd better take some meat with us and use it to entice them out into the trees. I'll get the cages into the truck. Why don't you get the meat out of the containers I brought in. They're over there in the corner."

Damon was silent, for he knew he could arouse Lynn's anger with his tough talk, but Gideon was another story. He backed away when Gideon spoke, for not only was the man stronger, taller and built like an athlete, but he was at least twenty years younger. So, Damon stepped over to the containers and filled one of the bags nearby with the meat supply as instructed. Then, after storing the meat in the truck, he helped Gideon load the rest of the cats aboard.

They left via the back entrance to the reserve, for there were no fences with guards there. They made their way several miles to the east into the forested area that offered a good deal of tree cover for the leopards.

The sun was barely tipping the tree tops when Gideon stopped the truck next to a wooded area within a mile or so of The Ingwe Reserve's private tenting facilities. As Gideon had explained to Kyle and Gina at the Welcoming Dinner, "These facilities include six canvas tents that are meant to allow the guests, who wish to experience the adventure of sleeping out in the bush with the animals, a chance to do so. For security there's a fence surrounding the area that offers protection for all those in the camp, and the place is monitored daily by one of The Ingwe's guards; therefore, it's ready for use at all times."

"We'd better leave the cats off here where Stephen is bound to go when trying to spot those leopards on Wednesday," Gideon determined.

Damon said nothing in opposition to that decision, so with care Gideon backed the truck up as close as he could to the thickest point of the tree trunk, leaving just enough room to open the roll-down door at the back of the truck. Both men got out and surveyed the area after opening the door of the truck. As they did so it was apparent the big cats were displeased with the state of their confinement and with their capture in general, for an undercurrent of growls could be heard from every direction.

Gideon climbed back into the truck bed followed by Damon. First they allowed the cats to smell the contents of the container that held the raw meat. Then Gideon climbed up onto some of the higher hanging branches and placed the meat in spots where it would be secure and in line with attracting the leopards. He figured the cats would rush for the food. At least that was the thought he had in mind. He was careful to leave at least two pounds of meat in each spot for that's the daily consumption of these particular animals.

Both men decided it would be best to release the *Mauve Leopards* first, since they were the attraction everyone needed to see at The Ingwe in order to make sure that the place was financially stable. Luckily each cat clawed to get out when the men moved their cages as close as possible to the tree branch. In fact, when Gideon dropped the cage door onto one of the low branches in order to release the first *Mauve Leopard*, the cat couldn't have scrambled out any faster. He immediately leaped high into the tree to capture what he undoubtedly presumed to be prey.

After they'd let two of the *Mauve Leopards* go free, Damon rolled down the truck door at Gideon's direction while at the same time Gideon slipped onto the driver's seat and the two drove off to another tree location nearby where they proceeded to follow the same routine which, surprisingly, had proven very successful.

It was already getting dark when they reached a tree on the outskirts of the grove. So far all had gone well and, of the eight caged animals, only two cats remained to be released. Again, moving along rapidly Gideon backed the truck up to tree trunk, perhaps too rapidly this time, for he failed to note some glaring eyes that were watching from the surrounding oil black darkness.

Gideon planted the raw meat in a top tree branch as he had done before, then he opened the cage door. Again one of the cats sprang out and up the tree like a bullet in flight. They watched as he kept climbing until he finally reached the raw meat Gideon had left for him. Without hesitation the leopard began to gnaw away at it. One thing about these cats, they can smell meat from a good distance away, no mistaking that.

Gideon pulled the last cage forward. This cage contained a female, one of the original cats that Jon had used in his mutation experiment. She seemed skittish when Gideon opened the cage door and she made no move to escape. He prodded her with a long pole, but that proved to be of no use. It didn't faze her.

"Tip the cage," Gideon called out, "and shove it forward." They both heaved until the cage door was dangling a foot from the branch. The leopard rushed out, but instead of climbing onto the branch she jumped to the ground then hesitated for an instant before attempting to dart off. The move may not have been fast enough, though, for within seconds Gideon smelled the stink of something foul just as a pack of hyenas rushed in, seemingly from nowhere, and appeared to attack her from all angles. Unfortunately, Gideon and Damon were trapped in the back of the truck with no way to get into the cab. They had no idea if the cat made an escape or not for the darkness was thick about them. That said, however, it took Gideon only a second to react to the men's plight.

Chapter 18

Monday Evening

Gideon pulled his cell phone from his jacket pocket when he heard the familiar ring and answered with a startled, "Yeah."

"I couldn't help but wonder how you're getting along. Why haven't you called?"

"Why haven't I called?" Gideon yelled, in a manner that implied he had been through an ordeal that left him exhausted. "Well, Lynn, Damon and I barely escaped from a vicious pack of hyenas if you want to know."

"Hyenas?" Lynn questioned. "What do you mean?"

"One of the cats didn't jump into the tree like all the others. No way. Instead she decided to jump down, and believe it or not, a pack of killer hyenas surrounded us trying to get to her. I had a hell of a time getting from the back of the truck to the cab. Fact is, one of 'em got me by my pant leg just before I jumped onto the seat. Damn it I could even hear his maniacal laugh as I drove away."

"So you're all right?" she asked with concern.

"I'm fine though Damon's still in the truck bed. I knew he'd never be able to make it to the front, so I slammed the door down and headed for the cab. Good thing too, for those foul smelling marauders were out for blood."

"Did you get the job done?"

"Yeah. Luckily that last one we released wasn't one of the *Mauve Leopards*. She was one of the breeders. Stephen should be able to spot one of the new breed when they're camping on Wednesday."

"Did the leopard get away from the hyenas?"

"I think so. She was dashing off as fast as I was when I beat it out of there. At any rate, we'll leave the truck at the warehouse and be back to the lodge shortly. I hope all this is worth it, for it's the attraction that may entice those buyers to consider signing that contract we've had made up." He paused for a moment. "Unless that money deal with Stephen works out and we can pay off the bank by late Friday."

"Let's hope one of these deals comes through. Anyway, I'm cleaning the tanks in the lab now, but I'll call you in the morning."

"Lynn, watch what you're doing. Those snakes are dangerous."

"They are, but you know I don't take any chances. The tanks have to be cleaned and I've got to get the brood fed."

"Be careful! I worry about you, love."

"I'm fine. Good job out there, Gideon. I knew I could count on you. You're the glue that's holding this whole place together." She closed her cell phone cover and proceeded to finish the job of feeding the snakes and the amphibians in her collection. Not an easy task, but one she did with passion. To her, working with these creatures was a pleasure that most would find disgusting if not disturbing to say the least. None of the snakes were shedding at the time, so it made cleaning the tanks much easier. She had already used the pressure hose and the solution to clean each tank, one at a time, of course. Such as it was, she did have to move a snake or an amphibian into a holding tank in the meantime. The Black Mamba, a young snake, was probably the most difficult to handle since, in general, mambas are highly aggressive snakes and will strike at the slightest provocation. She had purposely purchased a young mamba because adults can reach at least eight feet in length, and since a snake tank should be two-thirds larger than the snake, it would take up too much space in her Herpetology Exhibit. This young one was no more than fifteen inches in length.

At any rate, she finished cleaning the last tank, that of the Black Mamba, and proceeded to use her snake fork with her left hand to hold its head pressed onto the bottom of the holding tank while she picked it up by its narrow head with her right hand. Using a heavy canvas bag that she'd already prepared for the transport, she clamped her right hand over the snake's mouth, painstakingly careful to keep its mouth securely closed. Then she gently shoved the snake into the narrow opening in the bag, being extremely watchful that the head stayed firmly secured between her fingers. The bag itself had been set up beforehand so that the rim of the bag was pulled back leaving a hole just large enough for the snake's head to be inserted. This is a tricky maneuver, for one slip of the hand and the snake's fangs, though small, could inflict a deadly blow. In the case of a Black Mamba the mortality rate is 100%. One direct strike can kill a dozen men even though the snake may be young.

Most other snakes, the ones that are not as poisonous as the Black Mamba can be inserted into a burlap bag by merely dropping the head in first with the tail following. Not so with the Mamba. One can't take any chances that it might strike when let go. The trick of pulling that portion of the rim back over the top edge of the bag, then slipping one's hand out as one grabs the top of the closed bag is the secret to a successful transfer.

In the long run Lynn was, if nothing else, an expert in the process, for she was used to milking the toxins from the snakes in her laboratory in Johannesburg, toxins that were used for their antivenom by hospitals and snake bite victims. Yet she treated each transport with proper reverence. Soon she was gently depositing the Black Mamba into the tank. After that she continued on with the feeding routine which included offering the different foods needed by each particular breed. Her favorite, the Black Mamba, got its share of the thawed out mice and rats. She always used frozen pre-killed food, for in this way her precious lot weren't exposed to the parasites that live on all wild game.

With the task of cleaning and feeding complete, Lynn washed up, confident that each one of his prize showcase creatures were secure for the night. Of course she didn't have to clean the tanks every night, but on the days she did, it was a lengthy ordeal which required strict attention to the task.

After locking the laboratory door, she went back to their private residence and poured herself a double martini. She had just sat down on one of the lounge chairs in the living area when Damon walked in. He looked as if he'd been through a full day of work as a mechanic, for his clothes were covered with dust. It appeared he had been sitting on a bed of dirt, which was true, since he found himself being jostled about in the truck bed on the way back to the warehouse. Every time Gideon made a turn or hit a bump in the old road within the reserve, Damon was tossed from one side of the truck bed to the other.

Lynn didn't have to ask him what happened, for she already knew the story of the hyena attack. But, she couldn't resist ridiculing him for his part in the escape from the smelly creatures. "I hear that you couldn't make it out of the truck bed fast enough," she said tasting the words of sarcasm as they burned in her throat.

Damon was in no mood for such talk. He quietly walked up to the bar and poured himself a drink. With a menacing scowl on his face and nerves as tight as an archer's bow, he shot back. "You should talk. I didn't see you doing the job."

That last statement set Lynn's overheated mind on fire. "Someone's going to twist in the wind if this all fails, and it's not going to be me!" Her words snapped like a bull who ruled the meadow without bellowing.

The argument went viral from that point on with Lynn getting more and more peeved as she spouted off, mouthing a bevy of oaths. Damon didn't hold back, either. The curses were flying in both directions. It wasn't a pretty scene.

He's going to have another seizure if he keeps drinking. Huh . . . maybe that's my way out. At any rate, I'm glad I don't have to sleep with the bastard. Abruptly turning, she headed for her bedroom. She slammed the door and pressed her back against it as she looked up and heaved a deep-seated sigh that, without a doubt, defined her state of frustration. *Hopefully I can find a way out of this marriage and it better be soon.*

Chapter 19

Tuesday Morning

Gina rolled over in bed and groaned when Kyle poked her and explained, "Hey, I'm going, but I'll be back before lunch. At least that's what Stephen said. Have fun at the pool."

All Kyle got in response was a grunt. Gina had decided to skip the Balloon Ride that morning, preferring instead to settle in and enjoy the benefits the lodge offered. Not so for Kyle, though. She'd tossed and turned all night and had even set her alarm clock for 5:30 A. M. She was well aware that it's best to fly balloons right after sunrise when the winds are the calmest due to the fact that the sun is low in the sky. Therefore, she was up and dressed when the savannah was still clothed in darkness. Fact is, she stepped out onto the deck just in time to see the sun pop over the horizon.

She'd worn her boots and jeans as Stephen had recommended, but since she had been on similar balloon rides to North Port, Florida from her apartment miles south in Fort Myers, she already knew the need for protection in case the basket landed on a rough patch of land.

Generally speaking, balloons simply float with the wind. The pilot has little control over the specific destination like an airline pilot does. While the hot air balloon pilot can control the altitude by finding a wind flow that's going in the direction he or she wishes, it's impossible to fly into a crosswind or an upwind draft. In essence, hot air ballooning is the oldest successful "Human flight carrying technology" and it's part of a class of aircraft known as balloon aircraft.

With the excitement children show when receiving a gift they'd dreamed of having, Kyle grabbed her Nikon camera and hurried to the lobby. Halfway down the stairs she realized she'd forgotten her camcorder and had to backtrack to her suite to get it. There she found Gina still fast asleep. "You're missing out on some real fun!" she called out as she closed the door and hurried to meet Stephen who was waiting near the front entrance.

"Hey, glad you could make it," Stephen said when Kyle reached him. "The chase crew is already outside. I take it Gina's not going?"

"I knew I wouldn't be able to talk her into it, but I told her she's missing a great ride."

As they walked outside, Stephen asked her if she'd had any hot air ballooning experience.

Kyle nodded. "Yeah, not a lot, but I've been up a few times and I loved it."

"Great! Sometimes our guests freak out when they get up there. With a day as good as this one we should have an easy flight."

Lanny, the air balloon pilot, along with his four man crew were checking the contents of the truck when Stephen and Kyle reached them. "We're set if you two are," Lanny said, offering his hand to Stephen and Kyle, a handshake that Kyle could tell was obviously strong. These guys know what hard work is, she thought, for he's got a firm grip.

Within minutes Carole came strolling out of the lodge. "Sorry I'm late, but we had a call-in to check on the *Boma* celebration on Friday. Are we all set to go?"

"We are," Stephen confirmed, getting into the passenger side of The Ingwe's SUV. "Let's move out. The clock's ticking."

Carole was relegated to driving since she was planning to go along with the chase crew and eventually take Kyle and Stephen back to the lodge after the flight. Kyle settled into the back with all of her camera equipment. Since Stephen didn't have to drive, he found it convenient to swivel about in order to ask Kyle if she had any questions about the balloon ride and the "Champagne Toast" they were about to enjoy after the flight. Kyle mentioned that she'd read a bit about the history of ballooning, but certainly not as much as she knew about flying aircraft. Stephen seemed eager to fill her in on many of the details. "Did you know," he exclaimed "that the first hot air balloons were developed as a signaling mechanism by the Chinese military strategist Zhuge Lian around 220 AD, and that they were called Kongming Lanterns?"

"I wasn't aware they go back that far," Kyle replied. "I do recall reading once, though, that the first recorded *manned* hot air balloon flight was made on November 21st. I think it was in 1783."

"Some say October 19th, but others say it was that November date," Stephen stated. "Actually the first time anyone took a balloon into the air was in June of that year. That flight only lasted ten minutes, though. The first manned flight of any consequence was completed by a scientist named Jean-Francois Pilatra de Rozier and a manufacturer named Francois Laurent d' Ariandes They were the first humans to take a balloon up for any length of time. The particular balloon they flew was created by the Mongolfier brothers."

"Fascinating. You certainly are a bastion of knowledge all right. Thanks Stephen."

Carole, having been relegated to driving, couldn't get a word in edgeways, for Kyle and Stephen were exchanging data way too fast, and the expression on Carol's face when they reached the departure site was one of displeasure. Again, it was apparent to Kyle that this woman was most certainly jealous of her relationship with Stephen and she wasn't about to let anyone intervene.

Funny, Kyle thought. If she only knew that right now my interest in men is at an all time low, and that I have absolutely no desire to get involved with Stephen or any other man for that matter. Not after what Ryan did.

The tension between the two women eased up a bit when Kyle and Stephen went off to observe the chase crew as they prepared to inflate the envelope which is actually the bag or body of the craft constructed of a strong, light-weight synthetic fabric such as rip stop nylon or Dacron. At the throat of the envelope the manufacturers use a fire resistant coating to protect the base of the envelope from the burner blasts. Hanging just below the envelope is the burner used to fire the propane fuel into the envelope. All this data was explained by Lanny who wanted his passengers to be well informed about all the features of a hot air balloon. It was easy to tell this pilot loved his work and that he took each flight as a serious venture.

While Kyle and Stephen were observing the team at work, Carole merely sat in the SUV and watched from a distance. Kyle supposed she was still a bit peeved at Stephen for his lack of attention to her. Wow, Kyle thought. I'd hate to be in Stephen's shoes.

"It'll take about fifteen minutes to inflate and get this baby into the air," Lanny remarked as he removed the inflator fan from the neck of the balloon and attached it first to the burner then to the basket. "Why don't you get whatever gear you need and be ready to move out. We've got a perfect day for a flight," Lanny added with a smile.

Kyle and Stephen had already brought all their essentials close-by, so they had sufficient time to observe the crew at work. Kyle watched carefully as Lanny and his team used a gasoline-operated fan to blow cold (outside) air into the envelope. He told Kyle, who was eager to see the entire process, that the cold air partially inflates the balloon to establish its basic shape before he opens the burner flame valve, sometimes referred to as the blast valve and aims it into the mouth of the envelope.

"This burner flame heats the air inside," he said while he prepared to open the valve. He maneuvered his hand into place adding, "The burner unit gasifies the liquid propane, mixes it with air, then ignites the mixture so I can direct the flame and exhaust into the mouth of the envelope 'til the balloon inflates all the way and lifts off the ground. It won't be long. I don't know whether you know this or not, but hot air is less dense than cold, so it rises." Both Kyle and Stephen were well aware of that fact, but Kyle told Lanny that she appreciated his explaining the process so thoroughly. "Nice to know the facts," she acknowledged.

When Lanny finally opened the burner valve, the flame burst into the mouth of the envelope just as he had described, thus creating an earth-shattering blast. He immediately shouted out an order to a crew member called a crown-man who was holding the crown-line. "Keep her steady, Harry!"

In essence the "crown-line" is the tethering rope that's attached to the apex or the crown of the envelope. It's the duty of this "crown-man" to see that the envelope doesn't sway and that it doesn't lift off before it's sufficiently buoyant.

When Lanny decided the balloon was ready to launch, he walked around the craft checking to be sure all was ready for lift off. Both Kyle and Stephen, being pilots themselves, knew the importance of such a flight check. When he completed his inspection, Lanny told Kyle and Stephen to get their gear aboard and then to climb into the basket themselves. They immediately did as instructed.

Among other things, Kyle had noticed that this basket was made of woven wicker, but she knew that some hot air balloon pilots prefer rattan or aluminum. Also inside, strapped to the sides of the basket, were two propane tanks connected to the burner valve via piping. And, of course, by opening the valve, the pilot is able to force the propane and air mixture through the burner into the envelope causing that earth-shattering blast which gives the craft its ability to stay aloft. Along the top rim of the basket were handles and a rope line for the safety of the passengers, for sometimes the landings can be rough.

Lanny placed his radio receiver, a rolled-up blanket and his navigation gear into the basket then got in himself. "Release the line," he shouted to one of the chase team crew. As the balloon began to rise into the sky, it was all waves and smiles coming from the team as well as from Kyle and Stephen who both seemed delighted to be on their way. It appeared that the wave Carol offered was anything but enthusiastic. Nevertheless, they were going up into the bright blue heavens and Kyle couldn't have been more exhilarated.

From then on it was the duty of the ground crew, who are referred to as the chase team, to follow the balloon and recover it upon landing. Their own precious cargo was, of course, the cooler that contained the liquor for the "Champagne Toast" when the balloon landed, a highlight of any balloon flight even in the States.

Lanny, who was the pilot and the owner of this particular hot air balloon flight company, had chosen to have his chase team use the company's pick-up truck instead of a trailer which is used primarily because it can haul all of the equipment as well as the passengers on the return trip. However, since Carol had driven to the site in the SUV and was willing to follow the chase team to the landing site and take the passengers back with her when the balloon landed, there was no need for the huge trailer.

The basket they were in that day was one designed for four passengers. Fact is, some baskets used in commercial hot air ballooning carry as many as two dozen passengers. However with this smaller version, Kyle and Stephen didn't have to position themselves in any particular strategic manner in order to keep the basket balanced. It was small enough for each to have enough space to enjoy the ride without much concern.

"It's like we're floating on air," Kyle commented, though she knew why the balloon was able to float, and it was all do to the

Archimedes' principle which in physics states that the amount of lift (buoyancy) provided by the hot air balloon depends primarily upon the difference between the temperature of the air inside the envelope and the temperature of the air outside the envelope. However, technicalities aside, hot air ballooning offers a serene feeling of weightlessness which is beyond the realm of science.

"It's so beautiful up here. And look at that view below," Kyle raved as she pointed to a huge herd of wildebeests grazing on the savannah. "I've dreamed of this for years."

"Well, I don't know what made you plan this trip, but I'm glad you're enjoying it, and for me it's like heaven up here," Stephen responded.

"I see you're not afraid of heights," Lanny told Kyle as he prepared to open the valve and accelerate their climb.

Kyle grinned. "Not one bit."

After Lanny had finished working the valve to get a sufficient blast and had turned the valve off, Stephen remarked, "She's a pilot, too. She flies commercially."

"Hey, and you fly too, Stephen. We've got three pilots on board. That doesn't happen often."

Kyle barely heard the conversation between the two men, for she was content to scan the land that stretched out for miles and miles. For a moment she wondered what it would have been like if Ryan had been with her. That thought was soon discarded when she remembered his hurtful words. Never again, she thought.

For the most part Lanny let his passengers enjoy the sights without any commentary as he continued to focus on being sure the valve was opened at just the proper time and kept open but a few seconds so the balloon slowly drifted along up and down at the desired altitude. Since there is no way to steer a balloon like most aircraft, one is relegated to climb or descend into wind currents, sometimes going in different directions.

When Kyle asked Lanny if he flies at night he responded with, "Rarely. Most of my passengers prefer to see the landscape."

After Lanny had opened the valve, let the flame blast for a few seconds then closed it, Kyle went on to inquire about the temperature inside the balloon.

Lanny was quick to offer an answer. "It heats up to about 212 degrees Fahrenheit or a 100 degrees Celsius." Since he knew that Kyle was a pilot and would understand the details of flight he added, "To lift a thousand feet into the air you need 65,000 cubic feet of hot air. A lot of heat, right?"

"You bet," Kyle admitted. "I've never taken the time to inquire, but is there a record of the longest hot air balloon flight?"

Without skipping a beat, Lanny responded, "Yes, there is. The distance record was shattered in March. I think it was March the 21st back in 1999 when the *Breitling Orbiter 3* touched down in Egypt. Bernard Piccard and Brian Jones circumnavigated the globe and set records for 19 days, 21 hours and 55 minutes, over 46,759 kilometers or about 29,000 miles. They started out in Chateau-d'Oex, Switzerland and landed in the Egyptian desert on a nonstop flight. Quite a feat."

"That's unbelievable." Kyle shook her head. "I can't imagine being in the air that many days. That blasting sound would drive me crazy," she said with a grin.

"I guess I'm so used to it that I hardly even notice."

Just then a down draft caused the balloon to dip a bit lower, giving Kyle and the others a spectacular view along the banks of the Sand River and a group, or what Carole had called a "crash of hippos", some in the water and some on the banks.

"Oh great!" Kyle said as she leaned on the edge of the basket and pulled her camera into position. Without wasting any time, she began to click away in hopes of capturing the scene on film. "Perfect Lanny! I hope I got a clear shot." The smile on Kyle's was one of sheer delight when she glanced at the pilot and added, "You couldn't have timed that better if you'd planned it. Without a doubt this is the best trip I've ever taken in a hot air balloon. I'll never forget it!"

"I feel that same way every time I go out on a game drive," Stephen volunteered. In the excitement of the moment he blurted out, "I've got high hopes of owning The Ingwe someday." Oh no, he thought. I've already slipped and mentioned that to Kyle before. He immediately regretted saying anything about his desire to purchase The Ingwe Reserve, for he knew it was best to keep the details of the sale under wraps in case something fell through. He tried to cover his faux pas by diverting Kyle's attention to the landscape and saying, "We'll be landing soon, right Lanny?"

"Yeah, I'm already looking for a spot, but so far no luck. It's too dense. Hopefully there will be something up ahead. We'll see."

Kyle paid no heed to Stephen's apparent slip of the tongue. She was too busy watching Lanny maneuver the craft. She noted that periodically he radioed his chase crew to check on their position in relation to the balloon's heading. He had mentioned that the team was having trouble tracking, for the balloon was heading into an area that had no roads. When he radioed the last time the crew was quite a distance from them. It wasn't long after he had relayed the data about the chase crew's difficulties that he spotted a clearing that looked like it would suffice for a landing site.

"I'm going to try and take her down in that area ahead, so hold on. Sometimes these landings can be rough and it looks like the wind's picking up,"

Kyle and Stephen both braced themselves as Lanny opened the burner blast vent in order to let some of the hot air escape thus decreasing the temperature inside the envelope and causing the balloon to descend. It wasn't long before they were a few yards from the ground then a few feet and finally the basket touched down and bumped along three or four times. Kyle couldn't keep count as it was anything but a smooth landing. Eventually, though, the basket tipped over on one side and came to a complete stop. Kyle ended up with Stephen lying on top of her, his cheek pressed tightly against hers and his hand on her breast. The position seemed awkward for a moment until they both began to laugh in an effort to ease their apparent embarrassment.

"Are you both okay?" Lanny asked, slipping out of the basket first. "Sorry, but I think we've got at least a five mile an hour wind and it's hard to ease her down with that amount of wind."

With a jovial grin, Stephen crawled out of the basket and held out his hand to Kyle. "I'm okay, Lanny. You all right, Kyle?"

Kyle couldn't help chuckling. "I'm fine. What's a few bumps along the way when you're having fun." She checked her cameras and they were still intact. "All's great here." Her giddy laughter masked a feeling she had when Stephen lay beside her. How she longed for that sensation of closeness, a feeling of intimacy she greatly missed. She quickly brushed those thoughts aside hoping the "Champagne Toast" would help relieve any heartbreak she felt deep inside.

As Kyle, Stephen and Lanny surveyed the scene, they all agreed that at least they had landed on a good open spot, void of trees and underbrush. Lanny was quick to radio his chase team to see where they were. On most hot air balloon landings the chase team tries to get to the landing site in time to either help with the landing or to pack up the gear while the passengers enjoy the "Champagne Toast." This time they'd have to wait for the chase team, for they were carrying all the supplies and apparently they were having a difficult time locating a route into the site. There were no roads, so they had to cut across the savannah.

In the meantime, all being able-bodied individuals, Kyle and Stephen helped Lanny deflate the envelope then detach the burner. While their balloon pilot continued to pack up what he could before the team arrived, Kyle and Stephen leaned against the basket and talked about something they had in common . . . flying.

Stephen said he'd been anxious to discuss the topic with her ever since she arrived, but there had been little time to do so. Now, he fired off one question after another. It was obvious to Kyle that he was sincere about his desire to get to know her better and that, interestingly enough, sparked a thirst on her part to get to know him better as well.

"Been flying long, Kyle?" Stephen asked.

Kyle leaned her head to one side and glanced up for a second. She thoughtfully replied, "Well, I'd say it's been about fourteen years. Started as soon as I got out of college." She looked down and hesitated before she went on to explain, "My dad was a pilot." Her voice quavered a bit when she said those words.

Stephen must have picked up on the emotion of the moment and the strain in her voice, for he was quick to ask, "Do you mind my asking? Is he still flying?"

'No," she said looking away, sadness again evident in her demeanor. When she finally looked toward Stephen she found that his eyes were intensely focused on her. "My father was killed in a plane crash," she said. "He wasn't flying at the time, for he and my Mom were on their fortieth wedding anniversary." She paused for a second before replying. "But neither one of them made it."

"Oh, I'm sorry. Where were they going?"

"Right here, Stephen. They had their heart set on seeing South Africa. The plane went down near the Verde Islands."

Stephen heaved a deep sigh. "Again, I'm sorry. That's a painful thing to have happen."

"I guess the flights from Miami to Johannesburg aren't landing in the Verdes anymore. We got here via Senegal."

"You're right. That's happened since the new airport was built in Dakar. But I'm curious about what caused you to come to South Africa. Was it personal? Didn't I hear you say that you wanted to get away?"

Kyle didn't want to get into a discussion about Ryan's rejection, but somehow Stephen offered such a compelling and sympathetic attitude, she felt comfortable talking about the marriage cancellation with him and she did just that. "Frankly," she confided, "I've no idea what caused Ryan's refusal to go ahead with the wedding, and that's the hardest part to accept. Not knowing really hurts."

Stephen reached out his hand and placed it over hers. "If you ever need a shoulder to lean on, I'm here. Personally, with a woman as smart as you and good looking as well, I think the guy must be an idiot."

He gave her hand a squeeze then released the grip. "Anyway, I'm glad you're here. You're the first guest we've had at The Ingwe who's shown so much enthusiasm for all that Africa has to offer, and to me that means everything." Stephen apparently could see the sadness in her eyes, and he immediately tried to brighten the situation by initiating further questions on flying. "What's your rating anyway?" he asked, obviously trying to cheer her up.

Kyle blinked and brushed her hand across her forehead in an effort to dispel thoughts of Ryan and get back on track. "I'm okayed for props and jets up to the Lears, but not for the heavies yet. How about you?"

"I flew commercially at one time out of Johannesburg, mainly the Airbus 340 and the 747's, but I really like the smaller craft, probably because I often like to fly alone. It's great up there all by yourself with just the sky and the clouds around you."

Kyle was well aware of that feeling of solitude and peace one gets when you're flying alone with no distractions. "Strangely enough," she explained, "I know exactly what you mean. It's a joy that most don't understand."

"You're amazing you know that? You said you fly for a private company. What planes have you flown?"

"The company has two Cessna Citation Mustangs that we frequently use when we're going into airports with short runways, and we do have a lot of business customers that prefer to use us rather than deal with the hassle of larger airports."

"I can see why. Do you have a partner?"

"No one in particular. Sometimes on the smaller planes I'm the captain, but there are times when large jets are involved I'm second officer. It makes no difference to me. I love flying."

"You're quite a woman. Adventurous and good looking at the same time." He gave her a wink. "Keep up the good work. You're one of a kind, Kyle, and I admire you."

Kyle couldn't recall the last time she felt a flush course through her body, but Stephen seemed to have a way about him that brightened her day and caused that stir deep inside that told her he could charm most anyone. "You're too flattering, Stephen. I'm no better than any other pilot."

"Wanna bet?"

Stephen had no sooner responded to Kyle's last comment when they all heard the roar of car engines. Looking up they could see the chase car along with The Ingwe Reserve's SUV off in the distance, leaving dust in their wake as they crossed a patch of dry ground.

"'Hey, you did have a hard time finding us, didn't you?" Lanny called out to the driver when he reached the site. The man nodded and proceeded to bring the cooler over to the where the balloon basket landed. Then all four of the crew got to work bagging the envelope and loading the contents into the truck.

Meanwhile Carole pulled up and greeted Kyle and Stephen. "How was the landing?" she asked.

"Not one for the books," Lanny claimed as he shouted out instructions to his team. "At least we got a good open spot."

"Well," Carole said, "let's get the champagne out and celebrate. I heard you say back there in the SUV that you've done a little ballooning, Kyle."

"A couple of times, and I've yet to land without a bump or two. It's not an easy craft to maneuver for sure." She stopped for a moment as she watched Carole go back to the SUV and get a small table and a cloth and bring them closer to the basket.

"Can I help with anything?"

"No Kyle," Carole said, "I've got it covered." Glancing at Stephen she asked, "How'd you enjoy the ride?"

"It was fantastic!" Motioning toward Kyle he added, "Am I right?"

"It certainly was. The savannah's beautiful and we saw wildebeest and some hippo on the banks of the Sand River. I think I got some good shots from up there. In fact, I'll check them now. Do you want to see 'em, Stephen?"

"Yeah I do," he responded sidling close to Kyle as she raised the camera by its strap and pulled open the viewer. "Oh look!" she pointed, "here's one!"

"That's a great shot!" Stephen exclaimed, calling out to Carole to come and take a look.

"I haven't time now," she countered in a tone as cool as shaved ice.

Kyle immediately turned off her camera and closed the viewing cover, for she could sense that Stephen's attention to her was annoying Carole. "Well, let's have that toast," Kyle said to the group. "I could use a drink right now."

Carole had already set up the table and had put the glasses in place. "Will you open the bottle, Stephen?" she asked. He did so and she promptly poured the champagne.

Lanny called the chase team and they all picked up a glass of bubbly.

As Kyle raised her glass, she offered a toast to Lanny and the crew. "Although the landing was a bit bumpy," she stated, "it was still a safe one, and we thank all of you for what you've done to make this day so special!"

"Thanks, Kyle," Lanny replied. Then he raised his glass again and recited one of the balloonist's popular toasts. "Here's to 'Soft winds and gentle landings!' Though this one was less than gentle, as you said, at least we're all safe."

Shortly after they toasted the flight and the chase team finished what work they had to do to get ready to head back to the lodge, Kyle and Stephen helped Carole put the table and the glasses, etc. into the SUV. When they were set to leave the site, Carole told Lanny to meet her at the lodge's Front Desk. "Mr. Greene's supposed to have signed off on the check this morning. We can pick it up when we get there."

"Sure," Lanny acknowledged, "see you there."

Kyle declined the suggestion from Stephen that she sit up front with Carole on the ride back, for she could see the decided frown on Carole's face at the proposal. Her excuse for not doing so was one of convenience as she stated, "Seeing as how I can film from both sides of the SUV if I see animals along the way, I'll sit in the back, okay?"

Carole agreed. Stephen said nothing. Kyle's instincts were right, for it was a strained ride back to the lodge. There was very little communication between the three, though Kyle did brighten the trip a bit when, just before they reached the lodge, she cried out. "Over there! I see cheetah." She was right, and Carole did accommodate her request to stop the SUV while she took a few photos.

"Look at those cute little ones!" Kyle announced, her voice relaying her overwhelming excitement. Neither Carole nor Stephen said a word, but Kyle could feel the tension building between the two of them, and she was especially happy to see the lodge entrance looming ahead.

Chapter 20

Tuesday Afternoon

Lynn opened the door to Damon's office and poked her head in to see him sitting at his desk. "Gideon's been bombarded by calls from the bank," she said glaring at him. "They keep asking if we're going to meet that Friday deadline, and he claims you're not answering your phone. He's furious."

Wearily, taking off his glasses and running his hand over his balding head, Damon grudgingly replied, "Let him handle it. He thinks he's such a big shot."

"Oh, that's just great!" Lynn raved. "And you're the one who got drunk and couldn't help him get the cats into the field so that the guests would see them on their first game drive. Fact is, they have only a few more chances to do so before the buyers arrive on Friday. For all we know those *Mauve Leopards* have moved on by now. You'd better get to Stephen and tell him he's got to come through. The buyers simply have to hear about the new breed from our guests and not just from us. Our advertising the fact won't mean a thing, and it surely won't get us a sale. They'll think we're lying." She was confident her unassailable remarks held weight.

"Stephen knows full well he's got to find those leopards. Do you think he's a fool?"

"No, he's no fool, but you surely are. I've had it with all your antics. I'm sick of hearing about your precious game reserve!" She sat down on one of the seats opposite her husband's desk, pulled out her cigarette holder, slipped a cigarette into place and lit up. When she exhaled she blew the smoke directly his way. It was a purposeful act, for she knew her smoking irritated him.

Damon held his hand up and coughed heartily. "Put that damn thing out, Lynn. You're killing me with the smoke." He coughed then cleared his throat.

"I don't intend to change. Get used to it," was her spirited reply. "I know you don't want to sell this place, but we're going to lose it entirely unless we get some financing soon and you certainly haven't helped any. You know my father said that last loan was the end of the road. He's not about to open his wallet anymore."

"You've made that perfectly clear before, Lynn," Damon said sharply. He cleared his throat again. "And I don't want to hear about your father and his money. Stephen said he's got a deal going to get the cash to buy this place, and I'm hoping that if the buyers don't come through with a bid to purchase stock in The Ingwe, then Stephen will get the cash." Damon swiveled around in his chair and, for a moment, stared out of the window at the lush reserve grounds. "You know how much he wants to own this place. I'd stay on with Stephen if he takes over, but not with a group that'd boot me out in a heartbeat." He turned back to Lynn. "You know I don't want to leave," the words dying on his lips.

"Well *I* do!" Lynn pressed while giving him a cutting glance. "I don't care how we get out of here, whether it's via the buyers or Stephen's initiative, it's going to be one way or another." She got up to leave saying bluntly, "I'm going into town for supplies."

Although Damon's face looked impassive when she closed the door behind her, he was seething inside. He knew the entire situation was affecting his health. His doctor had told him so. But there were only two ways things could work out in his favor. Stephen or the buyers would bring in the needed funds or, if need be, he'd have to go through with his plan to, in essence, blackmail Lynn by telling her that he'll expose the explicit photos he had of her to her precious Daddy, photos she'd never want the man to see, for he'd surely disown her. In such a case she'd lose out on his fortune worth an estimated 4,306,000.00 ZAR, the currency symbol for the South African Rand, and in U. S. dollars that's a cool four million.

The more Damon anguished over his dilemma the more his right hand began to shake. "Oh no," he said aloud. Rushing from the room, he crossed the hall that led to the back entrance. From there he hurried to his residence and pulled his medication from the medicine cabinet. He'd forgotten to take his Lamotrigine that morning. Most likely the anxiety regarding his current financial situation and Lynn's aggressive behavior were preying on his mind, and the medicine did help to calm his nerves.

For a good half hour he sat on one of his lounge chairs and tried to settle down. Eventually his hand stopped shaking and his breathing returned to normal. Those focal seizures were coming more and more frequently now, though he thought he'd been good at hiding them from anyone including Lynn and Gideon. He'd have to be sure and carry some pills with him, he reasoned. However, in the long run, he knew that somehow his bottle of scotch was all he could rely on to close off the world around him.

Chapter 21

Tuesday Afternoon

When the chase team reached the front of the lodge they saw Carole parking the SUV in the side lot. Lanny slid out of the truck bed and waited for Carole, Kyle and Stephen to reach the front entrance where he followed Carole to the Front Desk. Stephen and Kyle waved goodbye and headed for the bar, for it was well before lunch time and they said they needed a cold drink. On their way across the lobby, Kyle glanced up and saw Gina descending the stairway that curved down from the second floor. To her surprise, she spied Brad no more than a few steps behind Gina.

"Hey," her friend shouted. "Did you guys have a good flight?"

"It was outstanding!" Kyle called back. Then she looked up at Brad. "And how are you two doing?"

Apparently Gina spotted Kyle's bobbing eyebrows when they finally met, and she immediately offered an explanation for Brad's being there even before Brad could elaborate. "I was showin' him our suite, Kyle. He thinks it's really phenomenal. We've planned a day out for a change. Wanna come along?"

"Where are you two going?"

Brad announced, "To Hazyview and then, if you like, on to the Shangana Cultural Village just minutes away where my brother said there's a Marula Craft Market. I thought you two women would like something like that. They'll be plenty of chances to get some souvenirs."

"Sounds perfect," Kyle said. "First though, I'm going to the bar. I need a coke or something cold and then some lunch. Do you want to do that first, then go out this afternoon?"

Gina turned to Brad. "How about it?"

Brad nodded in agreement and suggested that Stephen come along.

"I've got some work to do this afternoon, but I'm okay with lunch."

On the way to the bar, Gina continued to probe into the details of the flight and wasn't at all shocked when Kyle grinned and explained, "The flight was great. The landing . . . not so much. You'd probably have freaked out."

"See Brad," Gina beamed, "I was right. I knew I shouldn't go up in a balloon. We had a lot more fun lounging at the pool, didn't we?"

"We did, and your friend's quite a lot of fun, Kyle."

Kyle snickered. "Now that's something everyone can agree on."

After they'd all seated themselves at a table with a spectacular view of the grounds, Stephen and Brad asked the women what they'd like to drink. Kyle requested a coke while Gina couldn't wait to down a Martini. When the two men left to get the drinks, Kyle quickly prodded Gina on the arm. "And you say you were only upstairs showing Brad the suite."

A smirk curled the corners of Gina's mouth. "You think I'd lie about somethin' like that?"

"Huh," Kyle snorted a laugh, "are you kidding?"

"Well, believe it or not it's the truth. I'm playin' this one really cool. I think this guy's a keeper, and I don't want to do anythin' to scare him away."

Kyle's brows pulled into a tight frown. "You're really serious?"

The men returned with the drinks just in time to save Gina from having to answer, so all Kyle got in response was the mischievous glimmer in her friend's spaniel eyes and a suspicious grin.

"You know," Brad said, taking a sip of his cocktail, "I've been thinking of going on your Bush Camp outing on Wednesday. May I sign on, Stephen, and what do you say, Kyle?"

Gina shrugged. "He's already asked if I objected, and I told him it's okay with me."

"I don't see why not," Kyle agreed.

"Fine," Stephen said. "I'll stop at the desk and tell Carole. She'll take care of it for you, and I think you'll enjoy it. We've got a good set up out there in the reserve. It gives one the illusion you're separated from the world."

They talked on for another hour while they had lunch. Kyle and Stephen described the sights they saw and all about balloon flying in general. Stephen could be heard laughing aloud at Kyle's description of the balloon landing, and one could easily tell his attention was on Kyle. There was admiration in his eyes when he told Brad about her job of flying commercially.

"Oh, go on Stephen," Kyle could be heard saying. "It's just a job."

"Well, it takes a special kind of woman to do it," Stephen stressed.

"I sure know I couldn't," Gina said jokingly poking Stephen's elbow. "You deserve a lot of credit, Kyle." For fun she raised her glass in a toast to Kyle. Brad and Stephen quickly joined in.

Kyle blushed. "Cool it you guys. You're embarrassing me."

Stephen smiled. "On that light note, I'm going to leave you. I've got a lot of work to do, but I'll see you tomorrow for the afternoon game drive."

He took one more sip of his coke and got up just as Gina exclaimed, "You do know I'm not going, right? I already told Kyle I want to enjoy a leisurely massage and get some sun."

"Yeah, I know," Stephen confirmed. "She told me, and that's fine with me, Gina. I hope you have a great time." He gave the group a wave as he started out, telling them all to enjoy themselves on their outing that day. Purposely glancing at Kyle again, he added, "I'll see you tomorrow at three o'clock here in the lobby?"

"You bet!" she responded. "Hope we can find those *Mauve Leopards*."

He turned about and shouted as he crossed the room. "So do I Kyle." Perhaps she was wrong but she could have sworn he extended her a wink. Not so, she thought. He most likely had something in his eye.

After lunch, Bradley drove around Hazyview to get a feel for the small town, then they headed north until they reached the Shangana Cultural Village, which was a fascinating representation of how the natives lived. Within the village itself one could see the structures in which the natives lived and the garments they wore. An intriguing place.

Inside each thatched roof hut were many items that each particular family had for sale, anything from beautiful hand woven garments to hand carvings and tribal headwear used during their celebrations.

The Marula Market was a wealth of gift items as well, all made specifically for the tourists by the Shangana people. Their talent was unsurpassed, and the merchandise was uniquely creative. In fact, Kyle actually mentioned that she felt guilty buying such magnificent merchandise that was worth much more. As the group entered the market proper, one of the warriors greeted the visitors wearing a typical garment worn at their festivals.

Kyle and Gina commented on the garments saying that they'd seen photos in magazines, but there was nothing that could compare to seeing the actual sight of a warrior in native costume. Notably, when Kyle bought some of the souvenirs she claimed she couldn't resist, she actually gave the merchant more than the asking price, for she knew how much time likely had gone into the making of the item. In essence, she felt guilty about paying so little for such worthy crafts. Most of the natives, although they were used to bargaining for the sale price, couldn't believe anyone would want to pay more. In some cases they refused her offer to add a few Rand to the sale. What a shame, Kyle thought, for the products are worth so much more. She reasoned that they hadn't yet discovered the concept of greed.

As they were getting ready to leave, Kyle called out when she spotted a few wood carvings she said were too perfect to pass up. "I think I'm going to need another suitcase when we're finished here."

"So am I, but it's worth it. How many times am I goin' to get a chance like this," Gina enthusiastically explained while stuffing her third bag with a gorgeous hand woven shawl. "Like I said, I'm sure I'll never get back here again."

A good hearted Brad purchased a few items himself, but he couldn't match the women's untiring and ambitious nature when it came to shopping and he, good naturedly, ended up carrying many of the shopping bags. When they finally got back to the car and had loaded all of the contents aboard, Gina bubbled over with joy giving Brad a quick peck on the cheek.

"Well then," Brad said, squeezing Gina's hand, "I guess that was all worth it!"

On the drive back to the lodge Kyle sat in the back seat, preferring to have Gina sit beside Brad. She didn't say a word, but she did listen to the two of them banter back and forth, Gina giggling a good deal between a smattering of laughter. Her friend didn't seem to be losing any time "reeling in" Brad if that was her goal. Perhaps Brad isn't the jerk I thought he was, Kyle thought. Whatever the case, her wish for Gina was that she had finally met someone who would make a good team partner in marriage, and in doing so make both of them happy. Even though thinking about marriage was disheartening, Kyle again attempted to close off thoughts of Ryan. *Old loves die hard. But somehow I've got to move on.*

Fortunately it didn't take too long to get back to the lodge, and when she saw the gates open up, she heaved a sigh of relief. A night of just plain loafing was in order. This entire trip so far had been such a whirlwind of activity. However, even though she didn't want to miss a minute of the adventure, she relished a respite.

Brad helped the women by carrying some of their bags into their suite, but excused himself saying that he was having dinner with his brother since Patrick had a night off duty. As he departed the suite, Kyle tried to ignore the romance that apparently was brewing between the two of them, so she proceeded to empty the contents of her shopping bags onto her bed. However, she did notice that Gina planted a more than casual kiss on Brad's lips, a kiss that lasted quite some time, and Brad certainly didn't seem to be inclined to push her away or decline the contact.

After he'd left, Kyle couldn't resist the opportunity to tease Gina about their blooming romance. "And you said you'd never get serious with anyone again. All you said you wanted was a little fun. Yeah sure!" Catching Gina's surprised look, Kyle brushed her auburn curls behind one ear. "That kiss looked like more than an offer of a one night's stand. What's goin' on?"

Gina's normal giddly tone changed. She stood at the door of the suite looking dead serious. "I truly can't tell you Kyle, 'cause I've never felt like this before. At first I thought of Brad as just a fling, but now . . . I don't know, and it really scares me."

Kyle sat down on her bed and looked up at Gina whose forehead had fused into a deep frown. "Maybe I'm not ready to commit again. You know he *was* married before."

For a second or two Kyle said nothing, finally confiding, "Gina, we've been best friends for years, and I certainly am not one to give advice, but this time I think I'm right."

When Gina sat down next to her, Kyle saw another side of her friend, a serious side that she'd never seen before. "Some things are just meant to be," Kyle said. A loaded silence followed as if she were trying to think of a way to explain her feelings. Finally, she said, "Like meeting Brad on the plane and his staying at the Kruger Park Lodge. It can't all be coincidence. And if this is what it looks like to me, Brad may be your best hope for the future. I can see he has some strong feelings for you. Let it work itself out, but let your heart tell you whether or not he's the right man for you." Kyle put her hand on Gina's shoulder. "My advice is to follow your heart."

Sensing that the mood was getting too intense, Kyle immediately changed the subject. "Why don't you go down and take a swim or get a massage while I update my journal before the drums start beating for dinner." Kyle grinned. "Hey look on the bright side. You're a lot better off than I am." She slipped off the bed, grabbed her journal and headed for the deck. "Get going and enjoy that gorgeous pool, we've only got a few days left."

"You're right," Gina said, getting up. "Hell, I'm going to the pool and chill out." She retrieved her bathing suit and The Ingwe pool towel and headed to the bathroom to change. "I'll be back before the drums beat." She stopped for a second and chuckled. "That sounds so weird."

Kyle shook her head and nodded. "Have fun," she called out. Quickly opening the sliding door she stepped out onto the deck and flopped down on a lounge chair, her journal and pen in hand. For a few moments she sat there and stared out at the waterhole, where some warthogs, a few huge elephants and one young gazelle were enjoying a refreshing drink.

It was a warm day with a whispering breeze that touched her cheeks like a soft brush. The sun was high in the sky and the light rays shimmered over the surface of the waterhole, leaving ripples along the water's edge. *What a glorious sight! Man and nature as one. Too bad not everyone recognizes the beauty of it all.* She opened her journal and with pen in hand began her next entry.

Journal Entry—6 *Hot Air Balloon Ride. Gina didn't go on the ride with Stephen, Lanny and me. She missed out on a spectacular flight. Lanny, the pilot, was very knowledgeable and told us many details about flying data I hadn't heard about before. I could see for miles along the savannahs with herds of wildebeests or as some say wildebai. I also spotted a parade of elephants moving along in a stately procession. Kopjes dotted the landscape with lions partially hidden within the rocks. Near the landing site I got a shot of hippos or what they call a "crash" of hippopotamuses on the banks of the Sand River. An amazing collection of the great beasts. The landing was bumpy but we finally came to rest with the basket tipped on its side. Stephen ended up on top of me. To tell the truth it felt good. We had a great talk about flying and strangely we got into a conversation about my parents' death. He showed so much empathy that I poured my guts out to him regarding the marriage plans that went by the wayside. I shouldn't have been so forthcoming, but he's a great listener, and he seemed genuinely concerned. Hope I didn't sound like a victim.*

On the way back into the lodge I saw Brad and Gina coming down from the second floor. She claims she was just showing Brad our suite. Sure she was! Brad took us on an afternoon tour of Hazyview, the Shangana Cutltural Village and the Marula Market. Bought more souvenirs. My suitcases are overflowing. Brad is going to help Gina and me pack up some of these treasures and ship them home ahead of our flight. Good idea! The Shangana tribal members will be the ones entertaining us at the Boma on Friday. Looking forward to that treat. On the way home from our brief tour, Brad and Gina had a great time. Strange, but I felt like a third wheel.

Chapter 22

Tuesday Afternoon

After Stephen left the bar following the balloon ride and the visit to the bar for drinks with Kyle, Gina and Brad, he immediately went to the Front Desk to see Carole and get her to include Brad in the Overnight Camp experience scheduled for Wednesday.

Carole already knew Brad's telephone number from her last call to him, so she agreed to contact him again and tell him the cost, etc. "I'll see that it's taken care of," Carole said. "By the way, have you got a minute?"

"Sure, but I do have some work to do this afternoon," Stephen replied. "What's up?"

"Hold on," she added as she hurriedly turned toward Holly, a staff member who was on the computer at the far end of the counter. "Holly, can you take over for awhile? I've got to show Stephen something."

Holly agreed and Carole motioned for Stephen to follow her outside. She skirted the building to an open portion of the parking lot out of view of the lodge entrance.

"What's out here?" Stephen said his expression showing a bit of surprise. "What's this all about?"

"It's about you."

He cocked his head to one side. "What do 'ya mean it's about me?"

She crossed her arms and stared at him with a critical look of discontent. "I saw the way you've been making up to Kyle."

"You've got to be kidding," Stephen scoffed. "What do you mean?"

"Hell, I saw you and Kyle clowning around at the bar and then at lunch. Don't try to fool me. I could tell that you seemed to be *really* interested in what she had to say."

"We were just having a good time. She's a pilot so we've got a lot in common, and how did you know all that, anyway? Were you spying on me?" Stephen asked, his stance along with the perturbed look on his face left no guessing about his state of mind.

"I was at the pool, and I could see and hear what was going on. So don't give me that garbage about just having fun. Besides I watched you put your arm around her on Saturday when she first got here."

"Are you kiddin'."

"No, but it was when you were all getting up to leave after lunch at the pool," Carol said, offering a glance of seething contempt.

"Hell, I don't even remember that," Stephen cajoled. His head tipped boyishly while an irresistible smile lingered on his face.

"Well I do, and to me it looked like you were getting a *little too familiar* with her. Speaking of being familiar . . . when I asked Lanny about the balloon landing 'cause you know we've got to be sure we don't get any lawsuits from guests claiming injury, he told me that it was a rough one and that the balloon landed on its side with you on top of Kyle. Talk about getting familiar. How did that feel?"

"What do you mean how did it feel? It felt uncomfortable."

"Huh!" Carole protested with a scowl. "I've been thinking about this a lot lately. Fact is, I don't know whether or not to believe you when you say you're going to buy The Ingwe and marry me. How are 'ya goin' to get the money?" Anyone observing the scene could tell that Carole was a wild card, obviously distraught. It seemed that nothing short of a marriage license was going to calm her shattered nerves.

Stephen stood there with his mouth wide open not knowing what to say. Thinking he had to do something to quiet her down, he tried to explain that he'd accumulated a bundle over the past three years and that he was getting the rest of the money he needed on Friday. "Then," he went on, "we can be married as we planned."

"You mean we can get married right then?"

"Sure, as soon as we can," Stephen replied though thoughts of Carole's possessiveness were becoming ever more vivid in his mind. Anger was pulsating as a rapid heartbeat. *I guess asking her to move in with me was a bad idea, and telling her we'd get married was another mistake. I should have left things as they were.*

Kyle, he thought, was another story. He knew he could fall in love with her. She was everything he wanted in a woman . . . smart and gorgeous. Besides, she was on the rebound from a disastrous wedding cancellation. Surely when he got the deed to The Ingwe he could get her attention, romantically that is.

"Well," Carole snapped, pointing her outstretched finger directly at Stephen. "Is there going to be a wedding? Yes or No?"

"Just as soon as I can pay Gideon and get my signature on the deed to The Ingwe we can talk about getting hitched. How's that?"

Carole's eyes narrowed and she frowned as the muscles of her face corded up. She was no dummy. She'd worked her way up to manager at the reserve, and the way Stephen said the words "getting hitched" didn't sound like a lover's way of letting her know she was the only one in his life. Then again she didn't want to forfeit a chance to be married to the owner of The Ingwe and all the perks that would go along with that status. And, just maybe Kyle would have nothing to do with Stephen. Then she'd have lost everything she'd set out to accomplish. *I'll play it safe and just go along with his plan. Hopefully I'll come out a winner.*

With that thought in mind, Carole decided to change her tactics from one of hostility and accusation to that of intimacy and compatibility. *If this is a game for him, she could play the game, too.* However, she still wanted to know a few things about the money situation. "And where are you getting the cash to buy The Ingwe?" she blatantly asked throwing the words like daggers.

"I've got that covered. As I told you, I've been stashing it away for quite awhile and the last payment comes in on Friday morning. The appointment's at ten, for Gideon has to get the cash to the bank by three. They're pressing him for it and, from what I've heard, they won't give the business any further financing." He paused as if contemplating her response. "You know very well that Gideon wants to get out of the contract with Damon and I want The Ingwe."

Stephen went on to tell her where he was going to meet the lender and how much he'd always wanted to own the reserve. With a hungry expression on his face, he reiterated what he'd often told her. "Owning The Ingwe has been my dream for years."

Carole softened her tone and her demeanor. She could see the passion in his eyes. "But don't you have a morning game drive on Friday?"

"No, I've got nothing on my agenda that day. Friday's *Boma* day, remember?"

Carole reached out and gave Stephen a hug. "You're right. I sounded like such a bitch. I get overzealous I know. But I've been wondering where you go in the afternoons when you don't have anything on the schedule here at the lodge."

"I've got lots to do to get the money for this place, and frankly that's none of your business."

Carole could see Stephen was perturbed, so she backed off again. "I'm sorry," she exclaimed, giving him a kiss on the cheek. "Do you still love me?"

"Yeah I do, and stop worrying. Things'll work out just fine. Trust me," he said promptly returning the kiss, the kind of kiss a woman remembers. "You'd better get back or Holly's going to wonder what you're up to."

"You're right. Forgive me for being so jealous, but I love you and I want to be a part of your life."

"You will be," Stephen replied nonchalantly. "I'll see you later at home."

"Yeah." Carole nodded then turned and waved, calling out, "Love 'ya!"

As soon as Carole returned to the Front Desk, she immediately sent Holly on an errand while she dialed an outside line, but no one answered her call. "Damn!" she mumbled aloud. "He doesn't have his answering machine on." *I've got to remember to call him later.*

Chapter 23

Wednesday

Lynn stopped by Gideon's office early that Wednesday to check and be sure Stephen knew the importance of finding those *Mauve Leopards* on their afternoon's game drive. Suspiciously obvious to Gideon, when he looked up from the desk, was the fact that she locked the door behind her.

"You missed me last night didn't you?"

"You bet I did. Why didn't you stop by?" Lynn asked.

"I didn't get back from Johannesburg until after two. But I did get data on some places we can move to if things go well here." He got up, skirted the desk and embraced her with a gentle hug, his arm pressing tightly around her waist. With another delicate touch he raised her chin and kissed her passionately, a warm kiss, one of those kisses that is meant to linger in one's mind for some time. But then that's the man Lynn had fallen in love with. It wasn't something they'd planned; it just happened. "I needed you last night," Gideon said. "Needed more than a kiss, love."

"I know. How much longer can we go on with this farce? I can barely look at Damon. He makes me sick." Glancing up at Gideon she skimmed her fingers down his cheek and tweaked his goatee. "Did you remind Stephen to be sure and find those *Mauve Leopards* on his game drive this afternoon?"

"I didn't need to remind him. He knows how important it is, for we've only got 'til Friday. He's well aware that if he doesn't find 'em, then we'll most likely lose the place, for who wants a game reserve that's deep in debt? Certainly in no way am I going along with Damon's idea of offering the buyers shares in The Ingwe. I want out!"

"No more than I do," Lynn responded. She gave Gideon a push that landed him back in his chair. Teasingly she pulled up her skirt and straddled his hips while she started to unbutton his shirt. Gideon, being the man he was, quickly planted another kiss on her soft lips and began to loosen his tie. "Can't wait, eh?"

Lynn gave him a sly glance and proceeded to slip out of her blouse and unbutton her bra strap while offering a devious smile. "What do you think?"

Chapter 24

Wednesday Afternoon

Kyle and Gina got up late that Wednesday morning. Fortunately there was no rush to meet a deadline that day. Kyle slipped into her jeans and pulled a light sweater over her head then ran her fingers through her curls. "Whew!" she exclaimed, shouting across the room to Gina who had grabbed her clothes from the chair and was making her way to the bathroom. "I'm sure glad we've got some free time. I love the tours and seeing the sights, but I'm bushed."

"So 'um I," Gina responded. "It's been great though, and I'm glad you asked me to come along. Besides, this Brad deal might just turn out to be the real thing. I can't believe how we met him. It sure seems like fate to me."

"Funny you should say that for I've kinda got a good feeling about Stephen, too."

"Hey I'm all ears," Gina said, peeking around the corner of the bathroom door. "Whatcha mean a feelin'?"

"Oh, I don't know. Like I told you, he was so empathetic when I told him I'd been—"

Gina interrupted her, yelling from the bathroom. "I know what you were goin' to say, but don't you ever say it. You were *not* rejected. It was Ryan who made the mistake, and I know he's goin' to be really sorry some day. He's a jerk! You deserve better, girl."

"Well, it's too late to moan over it now. Let's get some breakfast." Kyle quickly ran a comb through her mop of curls and grabbed her camera case. When she didn't hear a reply, she called out again. "Are you ready yet?"

"Yeah," Gina said strolling across the room. "Let's go. I'm starvin'."

After they'd finished a good *All American* breakfast of eggs, sausage, hash browns and countless refills coffee, Kyle announced that she was going to stop by the Herpetology Exhibit until Gina reminded her that it wasn't open until one o'clock.

Kyle puffed out a lungful of air. "Oh, you're right, and I sure can't eat lunch before one, so I'll just check it out tomorrow. What are your plans for the day?"

"I know exactly what I'm going to do . . . get a *ranga* massage. Wanna come along?"

"Gosh no, I hate massages. I can't understand how anyone can relax lying on that table for so long. It beats me."

"Hell, I fall asleep. You gotta learn to relax." Gina glanced at her watch. "It's already eleven. What say I meet you for lunch at the restaurant at one o'clock?"

"One's okay. I think I'll just walk around the grounds, and if I'm not in the restaurant look for me in the library or the gym. By the way what are you going to do this afternoon since you decided you don't want to go on another game drive?"

"I'll be at the pool. Don't worry about me. I'm just as happy to relax, and I sure don't want to be stuck out on the road with another flat tire, even if it's in the day time," Gina said with a scowl. "No thanks."

"Okay, see you at one!" Kyle spent an hour in the gym working out. Then she went to their suite and took a shower before strolling the grounds and watching the animals through the fenced off area as they converged on the waterhole.

Gina, on the other hand, relaxed and enjoyed a soothing *ranga* massage. In the case of The Ingwe, the massage table was situated on a raised porch that had no walls, so one could enjoy the fresh African air as well as gaze out on the grounds that offered views of native sculpture and colorful foliage. To Gina it was a heavenly experience and she dozed off several times.

At one o'clock they met at the restaurant and had a leisurely lunch. "This has been a perfect day as far as I'm concerned," Gina said. "The massage was great, and I love the idea of havin' it done outside. I'll have to see if I can't arrange somethin' like that at my spa."

"That's a good idea. Bet your clients would love it." As they both took one more gulp of coffee, Kyle furtively slipped a spoon into her purse.

Wide-eyed, Gina frowned and swiftly looked about to see if anyone was watching them. "What are you doin'?" she whispered.

"What do you mean?"

Gina leaned forward and questioned Kyle again. "I mean what are you doin' takin' that spoon?"

"Sh-h-h," Kyle said. "I'll tell you later."

They both got up from the table and left, but Gina couldn't help shaking her head. "I don't get it," she said when they reached the lobby.

"I've got a plan and I'll tell you later. Right now I'm going for a walk on the grounds. See you later. Where are *you* going?"

"Most likely to take a nap," Gina replied.

Kyle waved as she left. "Then I'll see you later back in the suite. I've got that three o'clock game drive you know."

"You're actin' strange. You okay?"

"Sure, I'm fine. See you later!" That said Kyle was gone.

Gina gave her head a toss and headed upstairs. *What's she got on her mind now? With Kyle no one ever knows.*

Chapter 25

Wednesday Afternoon

Kyle strode out onto the grounds and walked as far as she could from the building until she reached a cluster of jasmine bushes in front of the compound fence line. Crystal beads of morning dew hung heavy on the foliage that occupied the area around the flowering jacaranda trees with their colorful lavender blossoms. It was a beautiful place. She looked around to see if anyone was watching, but saw no one in sight. This will be a perfect spot, Kyle said aloud. Once again she glanced about. The place was deserted. On the pretense of inspecting the flowering plants in that area, she walked far enough into the bushes so that no one could see her. There she removed the spoon from her purse as well as a double bagged, double sealed packet that was made of heavy plastic. She quickly dug a hole, at least seven inches deep, along the fence line and placed the packet into the bottom of the hole. Then working as swiftly as possible she covered the opening with dirt, packed the earth down as tightly as she could and sprinkled some leaves and branches over the entire area. Finally, she slipped the spoon back into her purse and slowly made her way out of the cluster of fauna and immediately returned to their suite.

Gina wasn't there. Assuming she was still at the pool, Kyle went into the bathroom and scrubbed the spoon until it shone. She was just about to place it back into her purse when Gina walked into the bathroom, an Ingwe Lodge towel wrapped around her wet bathing suit. She must have been instantly taken aback when she saw the spoon in Kyle's hand, for she immediately asked, "What in the world are you doin' with that spoon from the restaurant? Are you keepin' it as a souvenir or somethin'?"

"No, I didn't want a souvenir, and I'm not keeping the spoon." She reached into her purse. "See, I'm putting it back into my purse, and I'm going to return it when we have dinner."

"You're what?" Gina said totally puzzled. "Why did 'ya take it in the first place? That's not like you at all, girl. What's goin' on?"

"To tell the truth, I used it to dig a hole out on th—"

"You what?" Gina cut in.

"You may think this is crazy, but I dug a deep hole and put a time capsule in it."

"What do 'ya mean a time capsule and what for?"

"Well," she said reverently as she gazed at Gina, "before we left on the trip I made up a reinforced plastic packet and put my Dad's and Mom's picture in it along with their funeral notice." Her voice was unraveling as she spoke. "They never made it to Africa, and I wanted them to come along with me." Kyle clamped her mouth shut while tears flowed down her cheeks and her heart beat hard within her chest as she paused for a moment before pulling in a sob.

Gina stood silent. She walked over to Kyle and gave her a hug. Instantly regretting her words, she said softly, "That's the most sentimental thing I've ever heard of. I'm so sorry for questionin' you. I should have known it would be somethin' important." She cried along with Kyle. "You never do anythin' frivolous like me and I'm so sorry. I didn't mean to be out of line." She hesitated while brushing her hand over her mouth. "That's a wonderful tribute, and I'm sure they'd be so proud of you."

Kyle stood wiping her eyes with her fingers, while Gina broke down and ran to grab some tissues. When she finished blowing her nose and wiping the tears from her cheeks, Gina asked, "Why didn't you tell me you were goin' to do that?"

"I couldn't talk about it, for I knew I'd break down and cry. I just wish they could have been here with us or at least seen Africa for themselves."

"I know, but you've done a wonderful thing. What daughter would have even thought of doin' anythin' like that? I sure wouldn't have. Is that the reason you chose South Africa when it came to gettin' away from Ryan?"

"Yeah, it was. I wanted them to be in the place they'd always dreamed of seeing." Kyle stiffened her back and cleared her throat. "Now," she murmured, "they can really rest in peace."

Gina pulled some slacks from the hanger in the closet. "You're amazin'. You know that? It's a pleasure bein' your friend. I know you'll always come through in a crisis. That's for sure."

Gina proceeded to get dressed and Kyle changed into her safari wear, including boots and gear for the game drive.

"I better get down to the lobby," Kyle stated. "I told Stephen I'd be there on time. Sorry you're not going. It should be fun. Whatcha going to do the rest of the afternoon?"

"I think I'll go to the library and get a good book and sit by the pool. Doesn't that sound great? In fact, I'm goin' to try that local beer called *chibuku*. They say it's strong with some kind of a distinctive taste."

"I've got to admit it sounds relaxing, but," she added jokingly, "just think of me out there fighting off the hordes of beasts that may storm the lodge. Stephen and I'll keep them at bay."

"Oh sure you will! Get out of here and have fun. This is your playground. Enjoy it."

Chapter 26

Wednesday Afternoon

Kyle met Stephen right on the dot of 3:00 P. M. at the entrance to the lobby. However, just as Stephen started to pick up some of Kyle's gear to help her take it to the Land Rover, Carole, who was at the Front Desk, called out Kyle's name.

Startled, Kyle looked over her shoulder to see Carole waving to her. "Wonder what she wants," Kyle remarked. She set her camcorder and her backpack down and headed for the other side of the lobby.

"What is it, Carole?"

"I hate to bother you since you're on your way to the game drive, but I thought this might be important. You received another message. Holly said it was a FAX, so she put it in an envelope. She tried to get you, but you weren't in your room." Carole reached under the desk. "Do you want to take it now or pick it up later?"

"I'll take it with me now, Carole. Thanks." Kyle stuffed the envelope into her pocket and hurriedly walked back to where Stephen was waiting. "Let's go," she stated.

Frowning Stephen asked, "Everything all right?"

Kyle smiled and gave a nod. "Sure." She started to pick up her gear, but Stephen reached out and grabbed it. "Here," he offered, "I'll take those to the Rover." He immediately scooped up her backpack and hoisted the strap on her camcorder over his shoulder.

As Kyle and Stephen left the lobby, she happened to look toward the Front Desk. What she noticed was alarming, for Carole was scowling at her with a stare that was as cold as liquid ice. *There's something going on with that woman, I can sense it.* Brushing the thought aside, she stepped up her pace in order to catch up to Stephen.

Million, their tracker, was already waiting for them at the Land Rover with a broad grin framing his face. "Good afternoon Miss," he said, putting his own native spin on the words.

Kyle returned the grin while Stephen placed her gear on the passenger seat.

"Hey Million! Good to see you again," Kyle called out. "I'm all ready for the animal show. You track 'em; I'll photograph 'em. How's that?"

Million beamed again at Kyle's comment. He always seemed to take such pleasure in the way Kyle teased him.

He certainly is accommodating, Kyle thought and a perfect representative of his Shangana Tribe. She watched him take his place on the seat attached to the hood of the Land Rover. *But he'd really be in trouble if we were suddenly attacked from the front. Yet he appears fearless.*

"Let's head out!" Stephen said, starting the engine.

"I'm ready for action," Kyle responded slipping into the passenger seat beside Stephen. "I hope we see a lot of animals today. I'm really going to miss this place."

"We'll miss you, too. It's fun to see how much you enjoy the game drives. Let's hope we find those *Mauve Leopards* this time."

"Me too, for I haven't got many more days here." As they drove out of the enclosure and away from the lodge, Kyle's curiosity got the best of her, and she slipped the envelope out of her pocket. In an attempt to be as discreet as possible she held the paper by her side and out of Stephen's view. She inhaled a ragged breath and her hands shook as she read the words.

Stephen was apparently aware of her uneasiness and, though he didn't turn his head to look at her, he did ask if all was okay.

There was a noticeable tremor in Kyle's voice when she replied, "No no, it's nothing of any importance."

Chapter 27

Wednesday Afternoon

Masking her frustration over the contents of the FAX she'd received, Kyle enthusiastically blurted out, "We've got a gorgeous day for a game drive. Let's get out there and find those *Mauve Leopards,* Stephen. I know you can do it," she declared while covertly stuffing the envelope back into her pocket. She turned her head to the left to avoid any eye contact with Stephen and closed her eyes for an instant. *I'm not going to let anything ruin my last few days here. No way!*

The first thirty minutes of the drive were unexceptional as far as seeing any animals was concerned, but the view of the open savannah and the rocky Kopjes kept Kyle hypnotized, for the grandeur of the landscape seemed to be the most beautiful place on earth. In her mind . . . Africa crouched low on the horizon like a lion in ambush, tawny and gold. "You know, Stephen, I can't get over how much I feel at peace here. I hate to think of leaving."

He gazed her way. "And I can't imagine you not being here. You make the excursions so much fun, and as you say, this *is* the most beautiful place on ear—"

Million interrupted, "There!" he said quietly, pointing up ahead at one of the outcroppings.

Stephen quickly stopped for he knew Kyle would want a photo. "See him, Kyle?"

"Good grief he looks like he's a sentry guarding the place," Kyle exclaimed, raising her Nikon and focusing on the baboon. "And he's not moving a muscle. Good shot! It looks like he's posing for us like the cape buffalos did."

"It's great to see them at a distance, but don't get too close. I've seen them jump up on cars and threaten the people inside," Stephen warned. "They can be vicious."

"I guess so, but they look so regal, and it's fun to see 'em outside of a zoo." Kyle bubbled over with happiness as she clicked off several shots. Again, she was as delighted as a child who had just received a new toy at Christmas. Apparently her exuberance was contagious, for when she looked at Stephen he was beaming. "You probably think I'm nuts for getting so excited," Kyle said.

"I sure don't. In fact, it's fun to watch you enjoying the sights so much. Many of our guests get bored after awhile. They don't necessarily like the inconvenience of going off road and all the bumping around one has to do to get close to the animals. You seem to love it."

"Oh I do, and I can't imagine anything more thrilling. You're a good guide you know that, Stephen? I bet some guides get bored just doing this every day."

"Perhaps they do, but to me it's not even a job. It's a pleasure."

Kyle kept her gaze focused on Stephen as he drove on. *He really does love this place, and I can see why.*

"Speaking of 'off road' let's see what we can find over there." Stephen announced motioned to his left. "I see some trees, and if we're ever going to spot those elusive leopards, we've got to move out of these open plains 'cause leopards like dense brush and forest." He abruptly drove down into a shallow ravine and up the other side to reach a secluded valley of low grass and thickets.

"I see what you mean by 'Hold on!'" Kyle shouted as her curls went flying. She swallowed hard, grabbed her camcorder and clasped the Land Rover's door handle with her left hand. "This is as much fun as a roller coaster."

Stephen headed toward some dense brush where, as he explained, the Knobthorn and Marula trees dominate the area. The ground was full of potholes and patches of small rocks that made the ride anything but smooth. "Is this too rough for you, Kyle?" Stephen shouted out over the sound of the motor.

"No, I love it. If this leads to the *Mauve Leopards* then I'm all for it."

Finally the ground leveled off just as Stephen jokingly called out, "You can let go of the handle now."

"When you say 'off road' you really do mean it, don't 'ya? It's still thrilling though." While they headed for the trees, Kyle settled back and took time to look over the landscape. Noting that some beautiful bushes had red flowers with white centers, she asked about them. "I've never seen anything like 'em."

"They're Impala Lilies. They're not really lilies, but they do look like 'em don't they? Not a good choice to munch on though, particularly if you're an antelope, for the sap can be deadly. In fact," Stephen went on, "the San people, or as they call them the bushmen, use the sap for their poison arrows. They also use the larvae from a special white speckled beetle as poison for their arrows. They mix the beetle larvae with some scrub substance and produce the most venomous toxin ever known to man."

"Really? That's interesting. We've got plants in the States that are just as pretty and they're lethal, too. Though I don't know about beetles."

Stephen nodded but was too busy driving to acknowledge her any further as he spun the wheel to avoid a huge rock that was yards from the tree line, then drove up a gulley wall and into a shallow ravine. "Keep a sharp eye out, Million!" he pressed as he drove between two trees.

Kyle could tell Million was already searching, for his head was bobbing about like a cartoon character.

"It's going to be hard to drive in here. I'll have to make some sharp turns to avoid the trees, but maybe we'll be lucky."

Since Million was in the tracker seat he could see much farther ahead than either Kyle or Stephen, but it was obvious to Kyle that Stephen and Million worked as a good team. Though they rarely spoke to each other, Stephen followed each signal Million offered. Unfortunately, however, after about thirty minutes, Stephen decided to head back.

"I think I've got another spot we can try," he suggested, disappointment evident in his voice. He had just circled around a large Marula tree in an attempt to make his way through the trees and underbrush, when Million put his hand up, offering a signal. Stephen put his foot on the brake and slowed to a stop.

Kyle leaned over to Stephen. "What is it?" she whispered.

Stephen put his finger up to his lips, then pointed to his right.

Totally surprised by the sight, Kyle gasped. Up ahead was a jaw-dropping beauty of a *Mauve Leopard* sitting on what looked like a log. The fingers of sunlight that filtered through the trees illuminated the cat's delicate lavender coat, a spectacular sight.

Stephen reached for his camera that he'd stowed under the front seat of the Rover, but the strap caught on one of the seat bars and the strap wouldn't release. Kyle, however, raised her Nikon and began to click the shutter as if it were a matter of life or death. She must have gotten off five or more shots before the stunning creature uttered a low muffled growl, darted for a tree, climbed a low hanging branch and disappeared among the thick leaves on the branches above.

Kyle's face lit up. "Stephen," she cried, "you found one."

All sat stunned, hoping to get another sighting, but after some time Stephen decided it was useless.

"I could barely believe my eyes," Kyle said, her heart beating like a pounding drum.

"Gideon Courtney was right!" Stephen reacted with pride. "There *is* such an animal as a *Mauve Leopard*. He shook his head and squared his shoulders. "We can all be witnesses to that, but it would be great if you captured the big cat on film, Kyle."

Kyle leaned over and patted Stephen on the shoulder. "I hope I did." Million swiveled around in his seat and gave Kyle a broad smile, one that revealed his missing front tooth. Kyle knew the tracker must have been overjoyed for he never, at least as long as she'd known him, ever opened his mouth when he smiled.

Stephen put the Land Rover in gear and started back out of the maze of trees. "That was so worth it," he confided.

Kyle was already working the Nikon in order to pull up the shots she took, hoping beyond hope that at least one of them was clear enough to have recorded the sighting.

When they finally reached the outskirts of the tree line, Stephen stopped the Rover and enthusiastically asked, "Did you get him?"

Her face aglow, Kyle twisted her right shoulder to one side and leaned sideways so she could get as close to Stephen as possible in order to expose the viewing screen. "See!" she gloated. "I got him, Stephen!" She bubbled over. It seemed momentarily unreal. "This shot's the best. He's moving in some of the others."

After he took one look at the screen, Stephen's face absolutely lit up. "You're amazing," he told Kyle. "The lighting's perfect with that beam shining down from the top of the canopy."

The color in the photo was startling, for it defined the lavender-gray tint with clarity. Stephen pointed at the screen. "See Kyle," he said, his face inches from hers, "just like Gideon said, the black rosette rings are completely missing from this leopard and his fur looks like soft down. Gideon says he thinks this is some kind of a mutation and that the cat may have a little known genetic condition that causes either the overproduction of red or blue pigment or an underproduction of dark pigment." He paused before adding, "Looked like a young female to me. Just wait 'til they see this at The Ingwe." Anyone could tell that Stephen was overjoyed, and apparently he couldn't resist the temptation to let Kyle know how he felt. Perhaps without thinking he gave her a light kiss on her cheek, saying, "I'm so glad you were here to record this."

Kyle's face flushed as she quietly moved back into her seat, not knowing what to say. Stephen seemed uncomfortable as well. "Sorry, I got a little carried away. Didn't mean to do that." He cleared his throat and revved the engine.

When Kyle looked up she could see that Million was chuckling.

Other than the sound of the Land Rover moving back onto the dirt road, little conversation went on between the two for awhile. For Kyle it seemed like an awkward time, but that soon ended when Million motioned again with the hand sign that Kyle recognized as a signal for Stephen to stop. Up ahead, Kyle spotted a sight that she felt was so very unique, one that most people would never see. Stephen had already stopped when Kyle started shooting the scene of two lions and a cub casually strolling along the road.

"Oh, this is priceless," Kyle whispered as she took both stills and cam shots. Apparently the lions didn't take note of the vehicle until they were yards from the Land Rover. When they finally realized what was ahead, they all hurried for the rocks and the brush beyond, the young one running beside one of the females.

Kyle turned to Stephen. "Can you believe that?"

"I've run into sights like that, but never one in which the cub is walking along with the females." He nodded in Kyle's direction. "You should work for National Geographic."

"I'd have loved that, but remember you're the one who got us to this point. Without you and Million, I'd never be privy to such scenes."

"Well, I hope I didn't ruin it for you back there. I know you're going through a bad time right now, and I really didn't mean to be so forward. Got caught up in the moment I guess."

"Forget it, Stephen. I was overly excited, too, and seeing that *Mauve Leopard*, as they call them, was the highlight of the day."

"I'm just glad you were here to record it. I couldn't get my camera out in time." He offered a nod. "You know, you're a great photographer."

"That was my minor in college, but I'm no professional. Although when it comes to photographing animals, I'm more determined than ever to get the best shot."

The sun was deep in the afternoon sky when Stephen announced that it was about time they stopped for a Sundowner.

"Oh, that'd be wonderful," Kyle cheered. "I could use a cold drink."

"Good! I talked Karen into having the chef pack something special, one of Africa's vintage wines. Hope you like it."

"I'm not a wine connoisseur, so whatever it is I'm sure it's great."

"Okay then. And I know just the place to stop. It's off road, but not quite in such an out of the way place as that Marula and Knobthorn forest." Stephen turned sharply and headed across a field. "See that Baobab tree in front of us?"

"I've seen pictures of those trees." To Kyle the mighty tree up ahead looked as if it reached 50 feet into the sky with branches resembling the roots of a tree stuck upside down in the rich red African soil.

"Looks perfect to me. Let's stop there! It's out in the open, a good place for a sundowner."

As soon as Stephen parked the Rover close to the tree, Million hopped off his seat on the front of the vehicle and offered to help, but Stephen told him to relax, for he had already gotten the basket from under the back seat. "Great spot don't you think, Kyle?"

Kyle agreed and Million nodded his approval as well. "It's perfect!" she said. For a moment or two she ignored the two men as she gazed about at the expanse of tall grass that stretched out before them like a waving sheet of shimmering gold. "What a magnificent sight this is, Stephen. It looks so peaceful here."

Notwithstanding the beauty all around, Stephen explained that one must always be vigilant when out in the bush no matter how peaceful the area appears, especially when you're alone or with a small group. Having said that, he grabbed the rifle that he had positioned across the dash board and placed it on the hood of the Land Rover. Eventually the two leaned against the hood of the Rover and prepared to enjoy the wine and an assortment of hard cheeses. Meanwhile Million sat on the top of the back seat and kept his eyes focused on the view from the rear. He said he didn't want any of the cheese, but he did accept a glass of the vintage wine.

"How do you like the wine, Kyle?" Stephen asked. "It's a Veenwouden Merlot. 1997 I believe."

"I don't really know one wine from another, but I like it. It's not too sweet," Kyle replied absentmindedly as if in a state of euphoria. "I can't get over how comfortable I feel here. I love it." She took another sip of the wine. "You know Stephen, I've noticed something about the animals in Africa, the ones out in the bush."

"What about 'em?"

"Compared to the ones in the zoo, and I've been to a lot of zoos, they seem more alive, more sensitive to what's going on around them. Their eyes have a sparkle that is definitely lacking in those you see in a zoo."

"I hadn't thought of it that way, but you're right. They do have an urgency about them, but I guess that's not unusual. When your life's at stake, I'd say you'd be pretty alert, too."

"Funny, but I like that sense of danger lurking about." With a wayward grin she glanced at Stephen. "You probably think I'm crazy."

"I'd say it's the reason you're a pilot and not a spa owner like Gina. You've got to admit there's a bit of danger every time to take to the air."

"I guess you're right. What you need though, is courage, and that reminds me of what Amelia Earhart once said. Fact is, I loved the quote so much I memorized it."

"What'd she say?"

She stated that, "'Courage is the price that life extracts for finding peace. The soul that knows it not, knows no release from little things; knows not the vivid loneness of fear, nor mountain heights where bitter joy can hear the sound of wings.' That's the feeling I get when I'm flying. It's like being in heaven."

"That's a beautiful quote, and I get that feeling, too."

"Speaking of flying, have you flown the Enbreer Phenon 100?"

"No, but I've heard of it. It's a new plane, right?"

"Yeah. I just checked out on it. It's a great one to fly."

"What's the range?" Stephen asked.

"A thousand miles. We use it on flights to the Caribbean and Mexico. It's a nine passenger craft counting the two man crew and it travels at 350 to 400 miles an hour. Bet you'd like it."

"Sounds good. I'd love to give it a try." He picked up another slice of cheese. "Now see, that's what I mentioned about your liking to live on the edge. You wouldn't be satisfied with a desk job would you?"

"Hell no," Kyle reacted. "I'd be bored to tears."

He gazed admiringly at Kyle. "You're something else. Neither would I."

Stephen took a sip of his wine. "How could someone like you, who appears to enjoy daring encounters be best friends with Gina, who seems to avoid any mention of danger or uncertainty?"

A frown crinkled Kyle's forehead. "I've no idea, but we've been best friends for years. Must be the Yin and the Yang effect. You know . . . like opposites. I do know that she's a lot of fun to be around."

"So I've heard from Brad. He seems to think a lot of her." Stephen shifted his weight to lean on one elbow. "Do you want some more wine and cheese, Million? We've got plenty over here."

Million shook his head indicating that he was fine. To Kyle this capable tracker seemed content to relax with his arms stretched out at his sides as he leaned back on the seat.

"Hey, Stephen. You once mentioned that you wanted to own The Ingwe. That'd be a big undertaking wouldn't it?"

Stephen took in a deep breath. "Yeah, but I've wanted that ever since I started working here three years ago. It's a dream I've had for a long time. I'm sure trying."

"Well, I hope you can make that dream come true," Kyle echoed even though her voice carried a hint of melancholy. She didn't mean to sound so disillusioned, but all she could think of was how her dream of becoming Ryan's wife had been shattered by one shocking sentence. For a moment her mind drifted off to faraway places and sad memories of her own dreams that still lingered like an overwhelming fragrance.

Kyle looked at Stephen then glanced away. *How can anyone who looks so young afford to buy The Ingwe? Yet Brad already told Gina that Stephen was forty-eight. So he really isn't that young. Then again anyone with sandy hair seems to age well. Maybe he has wealthy friends or parents, or he could have saved his money over the years to buy the place. Who knows?*

"You okay?" Stephen asked. "I thought I heard a bit of sadness in your voice."

"Oh, it's nothing. But I do hope all goes well with your plans. The Ingwe's a great reserve."

"Actually, I don't know if the owners told you this or not at the Welcome Dinner, but The Ingwe and all the other private game reserves make up the Greater Kruger National Park, and believe it or not with all of them put together they're the size of your state of Connecticut."

"No, they didn't mention that. I've seen maps of the place, but unless you're standing on the ground here, it doesn't register. I *have* seen old movies of people coming into the park a long time ago though," Kyle said. "Is that true?"

"It is. Fact is, even though the park was established in 1899, the first tourist car didn't come through 'til 1926, and the whole place has boomed since then. However, if the poaching doesn't stop we may not have these animals around anymore."

"How sad! That's why I had to come here. I can't imagine there being a world without them."

Stephen took a final sip of wine, saying, "Let's not dwell on the negative, and right now I think we'd better pack up, for I want to show you one more of my special places before it gets dark, all right."

Kyle straightened up. "You bet! Let's move on captain. I'll help get this back into the Rover and we'll be off."

In no time they were back on the road heading for what Stephen called a surprise.

"Is that the surprise?" Kyle cheered, her voice once more exuding rapt excitement.

"That's it!"

Ahead of them was a huge pond about the size of four football fields. The banks of the pond were sloped so Stephen couldn't get close to the edge, but he did stop on an incline and park the Land Rover. "I'm glad we got here before the sun went down. You can get a good view of the hippos. See 'em Kyle?"

"I do, and it's great to be this close. Remember the ones we saw along the banks of the Sand River when we were up in the balloon? This view's a lot better."

She raised her camera to capture a few shots of the hippo when all of a sudden she was distracted by a giraffe she spied across the way. Stephen mentioned that it presumably was a male, for it was large and he stood but a few feet from the tree line. For some time he waited there gazing about as if he were surveying the area before making a move. Apparently that's exactly what he was doing, for a few minutes later he started down the bank to the water's edge. When he reached the pond he, again, stood there and looked around before attempting to drink. While Stephen and Million sat quietly by, Kyle grabbed her camcorder to capture the action as she narrated the scene. Then she pulled on the strap of her Nikon and got the camera into position to take some stills. She expected the giraffe to merely bend his neck down to reach the water, but she was wrong. Instead he bent his front legs forward at an angle then dropped his long neck to reach the water.

It wasn't until he began to drink that two younger giraffes emerged from the exact spot that the elder giraffe had been standing. They, too, lumbered down to the water line. It was amazing to see them lined up all drinking at one time.

"Imagine that," Kyle whispered. "He was actually checking the area out to see if it was safe."

The hippos that were at the far end of the pond must have spotted the movement of the giraffes, for one of them promptly moved closer to where Stephen had parked the Land Rover.

Kyle had stopped filming with her camcorder and was in the process of taking some stills of the giraffe, when suddenly a hippo's massive head emerged from the water not too far from the vehicle. Kyle had no sooner taken a few photos when the hippo opened his mouth and uttered some earth-shattering vocalizations of snorts, grunts and wheeze-honkings as well as a few subsonic hisses that whipped up a whirlpool of waves all around him.

Stephen's face revealed his concern. "We'd better get out of here," he stated calmly though it was obvious to Kyle that he was more than a bit uneasy. However, when Stephen turned the key in the ignition and the diesel wouldn't start, fear pinched the words in her throat as he said, "Oh no!" Then . . . before Stephen had time to try and restart the vehicle again, the colossal beast burst from the water and headed right for the Land Rover.

Photo courtesy of Kyle M. Neven

Chapter 28

Wednesday Evening

Carole had attempted at least a dozen times to use an outside line to reach her brother, but with no success. He wasn't answering his phone nor was she able to leave a message on his voice mail. Even the text messages were going unanswered.

Dusk was beginning to set in, and she knew she had several errands to do after leaving the lodge and going home for the night. Yet, as frustrated as she was, she decided to try and call him one more time. The phone rang for at least six long rings before her brother finally picked up.

"Where've you been?" she barked. "I've been trying to get you all day?"

"Went over to Nelspruit to get some tires for my car. Two of 'em are shot." He paused for an instant. "I was just getting set to leave to meet Michael. What's so important?"

Carole hadn't gotten a word out her mouth in response to her brother's question when Holly, the desk clerk, strolled in from the back room holding an armful of files. She proceeded to pull out a cabinet drawer right beside where Carole was standing. Not wanting Holly to hear her conversation, Carole abruptly told her brother that she would text him the data. "And, you'd better read it, for it's crucial. You know what I mean. It's about that job we were discussing."

"Oh yeah. I know what 'ya mean. I'll watch for the text and let 'ya know when I get it. Is this job comin' up soon?"

"It sure is," she replied. "I'll talk to you later." She put the receiver back into place and smiled at Holly. "I'm leaving now, for I've got some things to do before the stores close."

While Carole proceeded to pull her purse from the bottom drawer of the counter, Holly called out, "Since we haven't got anyone coming in tonight and Ben will be here for the night shift. I'm going to leave in about a half hour. Is that all right?"

Carole rounded the corner of the Front Desk then answered with, "That's fine. Have a good one." She gave a hat-tipping salute to one of the guards and walked to her car which was parked in the lot on the far side of the lodge. She immediately sat down on the car seat and began texting her brother. *He'd better follow up on this!*

Seconds after Carole reached her car and was in the process of texting her brother, Stephen, Kyle and Million drove up in the Land Rover and Stephen parked in front of the lodge. The sun had just dipped below the horizon, leaving a patchwork of colorful red, blues and gold sweeping across the sky in a rainbow pattern.

"Another Technicolor sunset," Kyle proclaimed. "And the far end of a long but perfect day."

"Got a little tricky, though. Hope that didn't scare you too much," Stephen said as he quieted the engine.

Kyle leaned back in her seat, twisted her head to her right and smiled at Stephen. "Are you kidding." she said. "I loved it. That, plus seeing the *Mauve Leopard,* was a great thrill. I was sure that hippo was going to hit us before you pulled out. I never thought you'd ever get the Rover started." She straightened up in the seat, leaned forward then grabbed her camcorder from the floor of the Land Rover. "I haven't a clue as to how you remained so calm."

"I've had close calls like that before, but the secret's not to panic. Hippos are notorious for charging then turning around and going the other way." Stephen stepped out of the Rover, reached into the back seat and grasped the handle of the container that held the contents of their Sundowner.

Million had already hoisted himself out of his tracker seat and was standing by, ready to help if needed when Kyle slipped out of the vehicle and reached for her backpack. "I was so surprised to see the big guy veer off and lumber down the bank. Wow! He was a massive hippo wasn't he?"

"He was a big male all right and there's no doubt they can be dangerous. More people are killed by hippos in Africa than any other animal, but I think I've mentioned that before."

"You did, but it's a lot different when you see them up close in the wild, particularly one who is bent on attacking you. That's for sure."

Stephen grinned in that boyish way he had about him, "More exciting isn't it?"

"Gosh yes. I wouldn't have missed that for the world, and I want to thank you for all you've done to make this a really memorable trip. You're a great guide."

"Thanks, Kyle. That's why I want to own The Ingwe. I want to give all of our guests a treat they'll never forget." Turning to Million he handed him the container that held the contents for the Sundowner. "Will you help with this Million and take it back to Karen?"

Million agreed as always. He took hold of the container and smiled as all three of them started up the walkway to the lodge. Stephen must have noticed that Kyle was having trouble carrying all her gear, so he promptly nudged Kyle with his arm and grabbed her backpack then slipped it over his shoulder. "There, that's one less thing to carry."

Kyle found herself staring into his intense eyes which to her seemed dark and unreadable. Actually her skin felt a bit flushed and warm when he touched her and she found it difficult to slow her steadily racing heart. Brushing off the sudden arousal, she quietly said, "The load was getting a bit heavy. I've got to learn to take less gear."

Carole, who had been sitting in her car in clear view of the front of the building texting her brother, took note of Stephen's arrival back at the lodge. She watched eagerly to see how Stephen interacted with Kyle, and she quickly observed what she thought was more than friendly behavior when Stephen edged up close to Kyle. Carole couldn't quite make out what he was doing, but to her it looked like Stephen was getting a *little too friendly* again. *Son of a bitch. He's definitely attracted to her, and I know he's going to dump me for Kyle, if not for her then for someone else.* Carole's insides were seething as she started the car and drove out of the parking lot and through The

Ingwe's gate. "You bastard!" she said aloud, "I'll show you a thing or two and you'll pay."

Even before she did the shopping that had to be done, she went immediately to the apartment she shared with Stephen, packed her suitcases, then literally threw the cases into the back of the car and drove away.

"I'm leaving that damn roving-eyed, two-timer," she raved, dropping the bags on the floor in her sister's hallway.

"What happened," her sister asked, stunned at Carole's actions.

"It's Stephen. I'm sure he's going to dump me," Carole announced. As she continued to rant and rave, tears rolled down her cheeks. Ragged emotion reared its ugly head and Carole burst out with, "I'm so damn mad. But, I'll make him pay. Just watch me."

Knowing that Carole was bipolar and that she was most likely not taking her medicine, her sister tried to calm her down by offering to fix her dinner. "Come on in. You can stay here," she said, grabbing Carole's arm, "and we can talk about it. Everything's going to be okay, you hear?"

While Million went off to return the Sundowner container to the kitchen, Stephen helped Kyle carry her gear up to her suite. When Kyle opened the door she expected to see Gina, but Gina wasn't there. "I bet she's still at the pool, for I don't think it's quite dinner time," Kyle said. She dropped her gear on her bed and turned to Stephen. "Hey, let me take that backpack and thanks for carrying it."

"No problem," Stephen replied. "Here you go." He handed it to her then turned to leave. If I see Gina at the pool do you want me to tell her you're back?"

"That'd be great. By the way, I had a super time today, and seeing that *Mauve Leopard* and then the hippo charge really topped it all off, believe me."

"I'm glad," Stephen said. "I enjoyed your company." As Stephen stepped out the door the drum beat announcing dinner sounded throughout the building.

"Oh oh!" Kyle exclaimed. "Gosh it's time to eat. I'd better get cleaned up."

Stephen called out from down the hallway. "Don't forget to check your itinerary, for we've got the overnight bush camp tomorrow. We'll be leaving here about four o'clock."

Kyle shouted back, "Don't worry I'll be there. I've even talked Gina into going." Humorously, she added, "I think that's because Brad's coming along."

Chapter 29

Wednesday Evening

Stephen hurried into the lobby and on to Gideon's office in hopes of catching him before he left for the day so he could tell them about seeing the *Mauve Leopard* on the game drive. He had no sooner rounded the corner of the Front Desk when Gideon appeared at the other end of the lobby. "Hey Gideon!" Stephen called out. "I've got good news."

"Great!" Gideon shouted back.

When they finally got together in the center of the lobby, Stephen could barely wait to tell Gideon his good fortune. "We only saw one *Mauve Leopard*, a female I think, but she was beautiful, just like you described."

"Where'd you find her?"

"In that grove of Marula trees not far from The Ingwe's tenting facility."

"'Perfect," Gideon replied. "Maybe when you take the guests out tomorrow you can find that one or others. Did you get her on film?"

"I had my camera with me, but I couldn't get it out in time. Kyle though, got several fine shots before the cat dashed for the trees. We've got the proof you need now, and I think it'll bring more guests here. I want to own this place, now more than ever, Gideon."

"Just bring in the cash and it's yours. You know I want out, and I'm sure we can work something out so that Damon signs off on the deal. Just keep tracking those leopards, for I don't want them to wonder off to Sabi Sand or some other reserve."

"I know, Gideon," Stephen said, "but the best way is to be sure there's food there, and I'll see to that. They won't want to leave if they've got fresh kill."

"Good job, Stephen. I'll tell Damon and Lynn, and let me know what happens tomorrow, for the buyers will be here on Friday."

"Just remember I've got your ear on first bid, if I can get the cash, right?"

Gideon patted Stephen on the shoulder. "Right!" Gideon tried calling Lynn on her cell phone, but he got no answer so he proceeded to Damon's office and gave him the good news. "Things are looking up and Stephen said he'll keep fresh kill in the grove where he found her so they'll stick around. I'm sure the buyers will be impressed."

"Thank God, he found one. But I'm still not going to sign this place over to any buyer unless Stephen comes up with the money and I can stay on in some capacity," Damon replied firmly.

Gideon moved to leave then turned back and announced, "We'll see about that!" After he left Damon's office he called Lynn on her cell phone, but she still didn't pick up. He left a message that he'd be in his office sorting out the papers for the deed to the property to be sure all is ready for a sale. He held back the information about Stephen finding the *Mauve Leopard* for he wanted to surprise her. Wait 'til she hears the good news, he thought. Hopefully we'll be living in Johannesburg soon instead of this isolated back country.

Lynn, who had been away from the lodge when Gideon called, finally responded by telling him that she was on her way back and that she'd see him in his office.

Gideon was sitting on the leather couch in his office with papers spread all over his glass coffee table trying to sort through the ones he'd need for a sale of The Ingwe when Lynn burst into the room. As usual she locked the door behind her before excitedly asking, "Have you heard anything from Stephen yet?"

There was a decided glint in his eyes when Gideon responded. "I sure have, love." He patted the seat beside him and told her to come on and sit down beside him. "I think you'll like what I've got to say,"

Lynn couldn't reach the couch fast enough. "Come on," she coaxed. "Don't tease me. What happened?"

Like someone who'd just discovered gold in a cookie jar, Gideon beamed. "Stephen found a *Mauve Leopard*. And you'll never believe where he found her."

"Where?" Lynn said grabbing Gideon's hand.

"Close to our tenting facilities."

"That's perfect," she said peppering him with a number of kisses on his cheeks. "Now it's just a matter of getting rid of Damon."

"You don't think we can talk him into signing these papers for a sale?"

Lynn shook her head. "No way. He'll never sign. I know how stubborn he is."

Gideon shifted in his seat and faced her. "Then what've you got planned?"

"Don't worry about it. I know how to handle him, but it's gotta be the right time. Now though I've gotta take the supplies I just bought to the lab. " She stood up, then leaned over and planted a soft kiss on Gideon's lips and slyly added, "If you want more than that you'd better stop by tonight."

Gideon lips curled at the corners. He abruptly grabbed her by the arm and pulled her down onto the couch. "That's the best offer I've had all day. You can bet I'll be there."

Kyle was in the process of getting dressed for dinner, when Gina returned to the suite. "Hey girl," she stated. "I just met Stephen in the lobby and he said you had a thrilling time out there today. He didn't elaborate for I think he was on his way home. What was the thrill all about?"

Kyle slipped her bag over her shoulder and started for the door. "Are you ready for dinner?"

"Sure, I got dressed earlier and I'm ready to go. Spit it out! What happened?"

"I'll tell you on the way. Come on! That drum beat awhile ago so they'll be closing up shop without us if we don't hurry."

"Okay, okay!" Gina replied, "but I'm not gonna let up. I wanna know what happened."

"Boy, do I know that," Kyle teased as she started to close the door to the suite.

"Hold it," Gina countered as she elbowed her way past Kyle and grabbed a book from her bedside table. "Let's go," she added, running to catch up to her friend.

They must have sat at the dinner table for over an hour while Kyle relayed all of the day's adventures. "That *Mauve Leopard* was just amazing. The color's striking, too. And believe me Gina, that was the biggest hippo I've ever seen. For a second or two when it didn't look like Stephen was going to get the Rover started, I nearly panicked. Of course I didn't let him know that, and don't you dare tell him."

"I won't, but am I ever glad I wasn't there."

"You'd never believe how calm he was. It didn't seem to faze him." She gazed out the window of the restaurant. Her eyes ricocheted back to Gina. "You know, he's quite a guy. Totally unflappable."

"Do I hear a spark there somewhere?"

"I don't know. Maybe. Right now I've had enough excitement for the day. I think I'm going upstairs and sit on the deck. You coming?"

"No, I'm goin' to return this book to the library then stop for a drink at the bar. See you upstairs."

"Sure. I'll be on the deck." Kyle's intention was to update her journal, but that goal fell by the wayside when she actually collapsed onto a lounge chair, leaned back and focused on the waterhole now highlighted by the floodlights. The view of the animals drifting down for a late drink and listening to the nocturnal sounds of Africa awakening from a day of rest was too tempting. So, she merely sat there quietly taking in the unsurpassed beauty of this unique place.

"Hey," Gina called out. "Wake up, Kyle. It's already after ten. Let's hit the sack."

A sleepy-eyed Kyle shook her head. "After ten? Have I been sleeping that long?"

"Apparently, for Brad drove over and we sat by the pool until a few minutes ago when he left."

"Gosh, I guess I must have been tired," she mumbled as she followed Gina back into the suite and closed the sliding doors behind her. "And we've got that camping tomorrow. I guess you're right I'd better get to bed. By the way, Brad's going isn't he?"

"Yeah, he says he's game."

Kyle snickered. "That ought to be interesting. You're sleeping in *our* tent aren't you?"

"Well of course."

Kyle face lit up with a sly smile and she joked, "Yeah sure!"

Chapter 30

Thursday Morning

At 8:45 A. M., as Dr. Adendorff left Room 355 on the fifth floor of the Tzaneen Medical Center, an announcement paging the doctor rang through the halls, "Doctor Adendorff to ICU, STAT . . . Dr. Adendorff to ICU, STAT." Rather than reporting in on his cell, as he passed the nursing station he told Nurse Brewer, who happened to be on the desk at the time, to call and tell them he was on his way.

The ICU nurse was busily attending an elderly man when Dr. Adendorff entered the room. The patient, who had been admitted late Saturday apparently suffering from what was diagnosed at the time to be complications from pneumonia, had been unable to speak up to that point. However, as the nurse told the doctor, "He coded on Monday, but we got him back and he's on oxygen. He seems to have come out of the delirium and is somewhat alert now, but he's showing several signs of neuropathy, complaining that he can't move his legs, and he's also been raving on about some kind of leopards."

"Leopards?" the doctor said as he picked up the man's chart.

"I can't make out all the words, but it sounds like the word 'leopards' to me."

Dr. Adendorff performed the usual stethoscope routine, then checked the man's neuromuscular functions. As the man continued to bluster on about leopards, the doctor suggested they keep the patient on oxygen. "The raving about leopards may be a delusional effect, but this paralysis is something else. Check with the medics who brought him in. See what they say, and get a spinal tap, an electromyography and a nerve conduction velocity test done STAT. Let me know the results immediately."

* * *

While the doctors at the Tzaneen Center are attempting to solve a medical crisis that had afflicted an elderly man in Tzaneen, South Africa, Kyle and Gina are awakening to a bright new day that offered a once in a lifetime experience of sleeping in a tent in the wild which the Afrikaans's refer to as a bush camp.

"When's Brad going to get here?" Kyle asked Gina who was stuffing her bag with items she thought she might need for the overnight tenting experience in The Ingwe Reserve's bush camp.

"He's goin' on some outing with his brother this mornin', but he said he'd be here early, about two I think."

"I can't believe you talked him into going. Then again I can't believe that you're even considering it. But, I'm glad you'll be there. We'll have fun."

Gina straightened up and, after an unwary moment, glared at Kyle. "So, you don't think I can do it, eh? You just wait, girl. I'll show you." She set her bag aside and slumped down on the bed. "Then again, to be honest, the only reason I said I'd go is because Brad'll be there, but I guess you knew that."

Kyle grinned. "I figured that all along. You can't fool me!"

"Anyway, are you ready for breakfast? I've got my stuff packed and I'm starvin'."

"What do you mean ready? I've been all set to go for an hour. Been on the deck watching some elephants at the waterhole." Kyle started for the door. "So let's go!"

As the two women walked down the stairs, Kyle mentioned that, since they have only a few days left on the trip and that she hadn't yet had a chance to see the Herpetology Exhibit, she planned to go there at one o'clock. "I can make it today 'cause we don't have to be ready for the camping deal 'til four, and as far as lunch goes I'm going to skip it and pack on a big breakfast. You okay with that?"

"Sure. Go ahead. I'll lounge by the pool and grab somethin' if I get hungry. I don't think I'll need much though, for Karen told me that we're goin' to get a big treat at the camp site." Gina opened the door into the restaurant and slipped in before Kyle. "Besides," she said turning to Kyle as the two made their way to a table. "Brad'll be here early." Then with a devious look including that one-sided raised eyebrow, a look that was strictly Gina's alone, she added, "Maybe we'll lounge together at the pool or elsewhere."

Kyle smiled and shook her head from side to side. "I pity the poor devil. He doesn't know it yet, but he's a goner."

"Ya think?" Gina chided as she sat down.

After their late breakfast, that rightfully could have been designated a brunch, Kyle and Gina parted, Kyle spending a few moments in the library before going to the Herpetology Exhibit, and Gina returning to their suite to change into her bathing suit before hightailing it to the pool.

Kyle was waiting at the Herpetology Exhibit's door when Marian appeared with key in hand. "I was wondering if you'd get around to checking out the room."

"It's just been such a whirlwind of a trip, Marian, I haven't had a chance to get here, but I sure didn't want to miss out. It's so fascinating that the doctor has such an exhibit on site here at the lodge."

"Personally, I think Dr. Greene's done a fantastic job." Marian unlocked the door and held it open for Kyle. She put her purse in a desk drawer and offered to give Kyle a tour of the amphibians and snakes that Dr. Green had accumulated over the three years The Ingwe had been in operation.

"What would you like to see first Kyle, the snakes or the amphibians?"

"I've got to say the snakes," Kyle said. "They fascinate me."

"That's what most people say, for they sure are scary looking, particularly when you know they're venomous."

"You're right there," Kyle replied. "Kinda gives you the creeps. I saw one TV show where they were trying to trap a Black Mamba that had gotten into someone's kitchen in South Africa. When they finally caught it, it was eight feet long. Talk about scary."

"Well, here's Dr. Greene's Black Mamba." She pointed ahead. "This one's a young male, only seventeen or so inches long. The tanks here aren't big enough to hold a full grown Mamba that can grow to eight feet. Notice, Kyle, that the Black Mamba isn't black at all."

"I see, "Kyle responded, "It looks like an olive brown."

"Right. Only the inside of the mouth is black. Tiny snake though, isn't it?"

"It sure is compared to that Puff Adder over there," Kyle commented.

"I've been told that the Puff adder is the deadliest snake in Africa because it causes the most fatalities. See how the Adder's body is so much larger than that of the Black Mamba." She paused while Kyle bent over and observed both snakes. "But the Mamba is exceptionally vicious and more easily provoked." Marian went on to say, "And apparently the venom is more rapid acting, for while it takes usually five vials to treat a patient who's been bitten by most venomous African snakes, in the case of a Mamba bite one needs ten to twelve vials of antivenom."

Kyle straightened up and flinched. "Keep the lid on that tank, right?"

"You bet!" Marian agreed. "And see how all of the tanks are in the direct sunlight."

"I'm sure that's for a reason."

"It is," Marian affirmed. "They need to recharge their system, just like a battery needs to be recharged. That's why you'll see them sunning themselves by lying out on rocks or warm patches of ground. You do know they're cold blooded, right?"

"Yeah, I know that. In fact, our Florida alligators do the same thing. They lay on the warm banks of the rivers."

Marian nodded. "Here Kyle, take a look at the different species of snakes we've got in the exhibit." Marian moved about showing Kyle tanks containing a Puff Adder, a Boomslang, a Gaboon viper and an Egyptian Cobra. "All of these are poisonous. Fact is," she went on, "Africa has the most poisonous snakes in the world, although Australia isn't far behind. How many different antivenins do you think there are?" Marian asked.

Kyle frowned, "I don't have a clue."

"There are twenty-two."

"Unbelievable."

"It was to me too. Many get confused when they hear the word *antivenin*. They think the word should be *antivenom*—"

Kyle interrupted. "I bet I know what you mean. I read about that. It's really that venomous snakes produce what is called antivenin . . . with an 'in' That antivenin is made into antivenom . . . with an 'om' and that antivenom is what they inject into people with such snake bites."

"You got it. A bit confusing. Dr. Greene periodically gives a great lecture on how they catch or what they refer to as 'parking' a snake then they milk it in a laboratory. She was the head of a laboratory in Johannesburg for some time. She was very good at the job from what I've heard."

Marian continued on for the rest of the hour explaining many more details about each particular snake and the many amphibians. Lots of people get confused about the difference between a frog and a toad.

I don't know much about the differences," Kyle commented, "but I do know that a frog has a smooth slimy skin and a toad has more of a warty dry skin. Am I right?"

"True. And frogs tend to lay eggs in clusters while the toad lays eggs in a long chain. Also the frog likes to leap and swim but the toad prefers to walk instead of hop of leap. Interesting, huh?"

"It sure is. I can't imagine understanding all there is to know about all these species."

"Well Dr. Greene seems to have devoted her life to it." As Marian began to wind up the tour, she added, "Though I enjoy the job of showing others the different exhibits, I'm not sure I'd would want to devote my life to it like the doctor does."

Kyle nodded and thanked Marian for taking the time to clue her in on some vital statistics regarding snakes and amphibians although she couldn't help but agree with her. "It's a wonderful exhibit," Kyle said chuckling "but I wouldn't want to make it a life's work, either."

Holly rushed into Damon's office Thursday morning with an urgent message that had just come in. "Someone from the Magistrate's Department called and said they'd like a call back immediately. I didn't know if you were in or not or I would have held them on the line and come and notified you. I'm sorry, Mr. Greene, but it seemed like it was important so I thought—"

"Never mind all the details, but did they say what it was about?"

"No. The man just said to call this number immediately." She hesitantly handed a piece of paper to Damon.

"Okay okay, you can go," he motioned with a swift imperious gesture of dismissal. "I'll give them a call."

Holly quickly left, for she knew that Mr. Greene had a temper just like his wife, and she thought it wise to get as far away from him as possible.

What in the world can they want now? Damon thought. The wardens were out just last month to check the place. He sat for a few minutes wringing his hands before picking up the phone and calling the number Holly had given him.

The Magistrate's clerk was exacting in his message to Damon and it left the part owner of The Ingwe with an unsettling feeling. "We've received a referral regarding The Ingwe Reserve and, per the Magistrate's request, we're sending out two of our District Wardens to inspect the reserve. It will be early morning tomorrow and, according to our records, you're one of the owners. Is that correct?"

"Yes, I'm one of the owners. I—"

The clerk interrupted. "Will you be there in the early morning?"

Damon could sense his anxiety level building as a chill washed over him. It felt like the inside of his body was actually quivering, but he did manage to say, "Yes, but why another inspection? You were here last month doing the same thing."

The clerk wouldn't give Damon any details, but he did stress that it was an important matter, and again he asked, "I take it that you'll be there in the early morning."

"Of course. I'll be on site at eight."

"Good, I'll relay the message." The clerk abruptly hung up leaving Damon completely shaken. He reached out to hang up the phone, but he encountered another spasm in this right hand. It was so agonizing and uncontrollable he had to use his left hand to steady it in order to drop the receiver back into the cradle. He quickly opened his lap drawer, pulled out a bottle of medication and popped a pill into his mouth. Then he grabbed his bottle of scotch from the bottom drawer of his desk and took a swig. Leaning back he pressed his fingers along his temples and tried to calm the migraine that was swiftly coming on.

It took him more than a half hour to settle down enough to confront Gideon, who was enraged when he got the news. "Couldn't you get any information out of the guy?" Gideon demanded.

"No," Damon countered. "The man merely said it would be an inspection."

"Well we'd better get out to the warehouse and be sure there's no evidence that we had the leopards in there. I know we cleaned the place before, but we should go over it again. You know full well they better not find a trace of those leopards." Gideon grabbed his jacket and had his hand on the doorknob when Lynn showed up.

"I came here to get some data on the *Boma* tomorrow," she said, looking puzzled. "Where are you two going?"

Damon knew an explosion was about to occur when Lynn found out about the call from the Magistrate's Office, so he quickly slipped out the door and headed back to his own office, calling over his shoulder. "I'll see you later Gideon."

Lynn stood rigid with a perplexed look clouding her face. "What's going on?"

Gideon dreaded telling Lynn about the scheduled inspection, for he knew she'd want specifics, and he had nothing to tell her.

As usual she couldn't keep her voice down, and she blasted out with her usual curses. "Why in the hell didn't he tell them to hold off until the *Boma's* over? You both know I've got so many details still unresolved for that dinner, and we've got to have things perfect for those buyers."

"Sh-h-h," Gideon shot back. "Keep your voice down. Someone might hear you."

"I don't give a damn if they do. Those wardens don't come out two months in a row. Something's wrong. I know it!" She drew in a shuddering breath. "Well, this is a damn box of trouble, and you and I both know Damon won't be able to keep his mouth shut. The least little thing and he'll crumble. He's as weak as a newborn."

Gideon reached out to comfort her, but she pushed him away. "Don't give me any of that now," she scowled. "We've got to get busy and think fast. In fact," Lynn went on, "I think *you* should meet these wardens not Damon. I don't want Damon anywhere around them. If this has anything to do with Jon—"

Gideon cut in. "How could it. He was dead and no one else knew about the leopards but Stephen, and he's not about to tell anybody, for he's as knee deep in this deal as we are."

Lynn shook her head. "I still think it's got something to do with Jon."

"Listen, if this has something to do with Jon, and we're still not sure that's the case, you know I'll never confess to anything. Besides no one knew I was anywhere near Jon's barn." He paused and slumped down in his office chair. "Let's not panic. Damon and I'll go out to the warehouse tonight and make sure that there is no sign of any leopards being there. The wardens won't be able to prove a thing."

Lynn sat down on the chair in front of Gideon's desk, leaned forward and dropped her head into her hands. When she finally straightened up, she let Gideon know in no uncertain terms that the two of them better do a good job in the warehouse cleanup or else.

"I know, and we will. Don't worry. I'll see that it's taken care of."

"It better be done. But hear this . . . if Damon looks like he's going to crack, I *will* do something about it."

"What can you do?"

"I've always had a plan for Damon." She looked away then gave Gideon a side glance. "Been waiting for the right time. That's all." She started for the door. "You meet those wardens and let me know exactly what they're after. I'm counting on you to smooth this mess over just like you always do." She glared at him. "Don't you let me down 'ya hear?"

Chapter 31

Thursday Afternoon

Four o'clock rolled around way too fast, for Kyle had taken a nap on the deck and had to be awakened by a call from Stephen who was already in the lobby with Brad and Gina who were all set to get going on their camping excursion.

"Sorry guys," Kyle said as she rushed down the stairs, totally out of breath. "It was so darn peaceful on that deck I fell asleep. Hope I didn't hold you up too long."

"No no," Stephen said. "We're not on that much of a schedule and since you're the only ones in this party, it's your call anyway. Have you got everything . . . like bug spray, medicines if you need them or whatever. You did get the list of recommended items, didn't you?"

Everyone nodded, so Stephen raised his hand like the lead man on a military hike and called out, "Let's go! We're taking the larger Land Rover today because we've got a cook and two guards with us plus Million, of course. One of the guards is already there, and he brought all of the necessary supplies. So, let's move out!"

Gina walked beside Kyle on the way to the Rover explaining all along that she was going to give Kyle a call in the suite, but time got away from her, too. "In fact, Brad and I just got to the lobby ourselves. How was the exhibit?"

"It was great," Kyle responded turning to Brad. "It's swell that you could make it. This should be a fun night. By the way how was your trip to the Art Gallery with Patrick? You said you were going this morning."

"It was an outstanding show. I wish you two could have been there. I purchased two fine paintings that I'm sure will be easily sold in one of my next auctions."

"Oh, I'd love to see 'em," Gina said.

"Well you'll have to wait until we get home. I had them shipped just like I had all those souvenirs sent home for you two." He paused and gave Gina a wink. "Now you've got another excuse to come up and see me."

Gina's responded with a bright grin, an obvious clue that it would be a grand night for those two.

Impulsively Gina rushed ahead asking, "Are we going in one of those bigger cars, Stephen, the ones I've seen that have different levels?"

Apparently Gina hadn't been listening when Stephen mentioned the "tier level" vehicle before. Kyle noted it, though, and reasoned that her friend was most likely too intrigued with Brad to be paying any attention.

"Yeah Gina. We're going in that large Rover over there," Stephen said pointing to the parking lot on the side of the building.

"Hey Kyle," Gina stressed, "now we can say we rode in both types of cars out in the bush."

Kyle glanced at Stephen then at Brad. They both had wide smiles on their faces. She slyly leaned over to Stephen and whispered, "She wants to be able to brag to her clients at the spa."

When they got there, the cook, the two guards and Million were already seated in the three-tier Land Rover. Stephen recommended that Kyle sit up front with him so she could photograph if she wished, and she readily agreed. Gina and Brad sat in the second row while the cook and the guards occupied the back tier.

Kyle was totally preoccupied with photographing the countryside and Gina had been relatively quiet until suddenly she leaned forward and poked Stephen on the shoulder. "I probably should have asked this before I agreed to go on the camping trip, Stephen," she questioned, her voice stalling as she spoke, "and I hate to bring this up now, but I'm having second thoughts."

"What?" Stephen pressed while Kyle looked over her shoulder and frowned.

"Is this tent we're going to be sleeping in out in the open where animals can get to us?"

"No Gina," Stephen said calmly. "There's an electrified fence surrounding the camp, and there will be a guard on duty all night to be sure we're safe." He stopped the Rover and twisted around in his seat. "But listen, if you don't want to go it's all right." With an exceptional degree of patience, he added, "We'll all understand."

Gina sat back, heaved a deep sigh and squeezed Brad's hand. "I'll be fine as long as I know they can't get to us." She looked at Brad. "I'm sorry. I guess I panicked there for a minute."

His eyes still on Gina, Stephen went on to say, "It's obvious that you've got people here that care about you Gina, and I'm not going to let anything happen to anyone on this camping venture. That's for sure." He turned and patted his .458 Magnum that lay across the dashboard. "And the guards are all highly-trained in fire arms as well, so we'll be fine." When he turned back to Gina, she was wearing a reluctant smile. "Still want to go?"

Gina looked at Kyle then at Brad. "Yep," she said, "I said I'd do this, and I'm damn well going to do it. So let's go, Stephen. Full speed ahead."

Stephen started the engine and gave Kyle a side glance. "You okay with going, Kyle?"

"You bet!" She tipped her head to one side and gestured, signaling her approval. "I'm with Gina. Full speed ahead."

"I'm going to drive by that grove of Marula trees where Kyle and I spotted the *Mauve Leopards* yesterday and—"

Kyle broke in. "I've got some shots of one of them, Brad. I've already shown them to Gina, but remind me to show you when we're in camp."

"Fine," Brad responded. "That'd be great."

"Kyle got several good shots yesterday Brad, and the grove I'm talking about isn't too far from the campsite. Maybe we can get another glimpse of the cat. Everybody okay with taking a detour?"

Since there were no objections, Stephen veered off onto a side road and across a patch of grasslands and that deep ravine until he reached the grove. Million, who was again sitting on his tracker seat on the hood of the Land Rover, pointed the way into the maze of trees to about where they had seen the illusive cat before. Stephen stopped the Rover and they sat there in silence, all looking up into the trees, hoping to get a glimpse of the prize leopard.

"There!" Kyle whispered while signaling to her left. "I saw some movement in that tree." She was right. Leaping from one branch to another one could easily spot the lavender-gray color of the *Mauve Leopard* climbing up into the top branches and out of sight.

"Shoot! We must have scared him or her or whatever," Kyle said looking at Stephen.

Brad piped up. "But at least we know there is such a creature. I'll have to tell Patrick, he'll want to come to The Ingwe and take a look."

Stephen knew full well why at least one of the prize leopards would still be in the grove, for he was leaving raw meat in the tree branches. Yet he never let on. His show of enthusiasm could have rivaled any test of honesty. Maybe he could have passed a lie detector test. Who knows? At any rate, he went so far as to state, "Well I guess The Ingwe will soon be on the map, right, Brad?"

While Stephen started the Rover and began to wind his way out of the grove, Brad tapped him on his shoulder. "I'd say you'll most likely get a lot of new clients once the advertising breaks on this news. Nice job of finding them."

"Well, it was Gideon who spotted them first. We were just lucky that day, right Kyle?"

"I'd say so. How many times does one get to see a unique species of cat like that?" Kyle concluded.

"Okay, let's head for the camp," Stephen announced. "The cooks have got a superb meal to get ready for us. I think you'll be surprised. Two of them are already there working on the menu."

Kyle looked back and the cook they'd brought along was smiling. They must enjoy getting away from the lodge and serving a meal outdoors for a change, she thought.

The road paralleled the banks of the Sand River at one point and up ahead Million motioned to Stephen for there were two male elephants in the river and from the look of it they weren't happy.

"Oh, Stephen, stop here!" Kyle called out. "Oh my gosh! They're fighting." As Stephen slowed down and stopped, Kyle raised her camera and clicked off several photos of the two sparring.

"What a trip," Kyle said beaming. "We've seen so much in such a short time." She glanced at Stephen. "You really know how to show a girl a good time and, to me, this is a *really* a good time!"

Gina giggled and glanced at Brad. "That's our Kyle! She's something else."

Stephen said nothing, but Kyle could tell when she looked his way he was pleased.

Within ten minutes they were at the campsite. Stephen got out and opened the gate, then closed and locked it behind him. When he got back into the Rover he commented about what a wonderful night it would be out in the bush. "And we're supposed to have a full moon tonight, too!"

"What does that mean?" Gina asked.

"Well," Stephen answered. "You'll be able to see any animals that are in our neighborhood."

Gina blew out a puff of air. "You're kiddin'. And that's a good thing?"

"Sure it is. But don't fret Gina, we'll have a huge fire going all night and a fence around us with guards on duty, too. Besides, with Brad here what do you have to worry about?"

Brad shrugged and gave Gina a hug. "No worries when I'm around."

Oh man, Kyle thought. This is going to be some party.

Stephen parked the Land Rover and the cook left to begin helping prepare the meal in the makeshift kitchen attached to the outdoor eating area while the two guards stood by waiting for orders from Stephen.

As the rest exited the Rover, Kyle breathed in the delicious aromas coming from the kitchen. She couldn't help but ask, "What's cooking? It smells so good."

"Oh, the cooks are whipping up a surprise on the grill. You'll love it. But in the meantime, let me show you the tenting area," Stephen said, motioning toward six tents placed randomly on the camping site. I think you'll be very comfortable for the night. Kyle and Gina agreed, for the tents were definitely more than they expected. Although they were constructed of canvas they had a wooden frame. Both women were equally amazed to find the tents were equipped with a bathroom. Stephen referred to that part of the tent as an "ensuite."

"Nice," Gina said. "I thought we'd be sleeping on the ground in a sleeping bag."

"No way," Stephen teased. "We treat out guests to the best. Now you've got a choice of which tent you want. Some are closer to the outdoor eating area over there, and some are nearer the fence line."

Kyle burst out with, "I know where I wanna be." She quickly pointed. "Over there."

Gina gulped. "You mean by that fence?"

"You bet. I want to hear the lions roaring."

Gina started to ask Brad which tent he was going to take, when Stephen cut in. "I'll let you all make your choices and you can get your gear from the Rover into your tents if you'd like. I'm going to check on the cooks, and I'll meet you over there at the eating area where we'll have a late afternoon spread and then dinner later on." He pointed to a thatched roof enclosure with an elephant skull at the entrance. "But hey, take your time and look around. There's no hurry."

The tent that Kyle chose had twin beds like all the rest and it was within six or seven feet of the fence. But it offered a wonderful view of whatever might be outside the enclosure and that's what she wanted . . . . to be as close to nature as possible. *After all, how many more chances will I have to be here in the heart of Africa?*

Gina, although she did bring her bag into the tent that Kyle had selected, remained skeptical.

CHAPTER 32

THURSDAY EVENING

When they all met at the open-air eating facility, the cooks had cocktails waiting for them. "That's called a "Dawa" in Swazi or Swati as the natives call it in their language," Stephen stated. "Loosely translated it means Magic Potion. It's a mixture of Vodka, honey, lime juice and crushed ice. Hope you like it. There's also an assortment of fruity harvest wines there for you as well."

Brad tipped his head acknowledging that he was pleased. "Good taste," he said sipping one of the Africa wines. "And whatever's grilling in that kitchen is making me ravenous. When's dinner?"

"About six-thirty," Stephen responded. "Until then enjoy the afternoon refreshments."

Kyle and Gina couldn't get over how festive the thatched roof facility was for being located in a campsite. Glowing lanterns hung all around and flickering candles adorned the long table that was covered with a white linen table cloth. At one end of the table the cooks had placed an array of platters containing cold meats, fruits, and cheeses as well as freshly baked quiches. "This is fantastic," Kyle noted, seating herself in one of the canvas chairs. "I love it here, Stephen."

All remarked on how wonderful it was to be able to enjoy Africa's wild country with all the comforts of home. "You seem to have thought of everything, Stephen," Brad said, leaning back in his chair. "Hasn't he, Gina?"

Even Gina agreed the day had been perfect so far. "The weather's phenomenal," she elaborated, "and you've sure succeeded in makin' me feel at home here. It's so peaceful."

"I'm glad you're enjoying yourselves. After dinner we'll light the open fire and sit around it as if we were out in the wilderness."

Gina joked, all the while reaching for a drink. "You could have forgotten the part about the wilderness."

As long as you can joke about it Gina, all will be fine," Stephen chided as he nibbled on a piece of fruit.

Before everyone dispersed in order to return to their tents and get organized for the night, Stephen asked Kyle if she would like a photograph of Million standing beside a skull of a cape buffalo. Kyle couldn't get to her camera fast enough.

"Wonderful!" she called out to Million as she took the photo. "You look great!" She immediately pulled up the shot on her viewer and let Million take a look. Normally Million didn't smile with an open mouth for as she had noticed before, he had a missing front tooth. However, this time Million beamed broadly apparently pleased that he was getting his picture taken. Fortunately Million's missing tooth wasn't noticeable and he was pleased.

When she asked him if he'd like her to send him a copy when she got home, he nodded and answered politely, "Yes Miss." Before Kyle went to her tent, she commented to Stephen on what a fine man Million seemed to be. It must be a pleasure to have him on your staff here."

"It is, and he's the best tracker around. I'm lucky to have him."

Exotic Escape

When Kyle and Gina finally got to their tent they sorted their clothes and all their gear so they'd have everything ready for bed. While Gina returned to the thatched roof eating facility to meet Brad, Kyle picked up her journal, but immediately put it back in place. It was getting dark, and merely listening to the sound of the wind and the chatter of the birds was too tempting to miss, she thought. So she stretched out on the bed and quietly closed her eyes, enjoying every second of being on safari in a bush camp so far from home. *This is the most peaceful place on earth. I really don't want to leave.*

Before long, however, she heard Gina calling her for dinner. "Come on, Kyle. You'll never believe the spread." Gina was right. The place looked like a photo layout in some sleek cuisine magazine. Shiny chafing dishes lined the table along with silver utensils. The formal menu which lay across each plate offered an assortment of entrées.

"Oh my," Gina said, "what's this 'Surprise' entrée, Stephen?"

"That's for you to guess and to try if you wish. For those who don't want to give it a try then there is the roast leg of lamb or the grilled bush chicken."

"Well," Kyle said, speaking up first, "I'll try that surprise. I had ostrich at the restaurant and it was delicious. I hope this is another treat like that was."

"Oh, I think you'll be pleased," Stephen said. "And by the way, the word 'Welkom' on your menu isn't a typo as some of our guests think. It's the Dutch word for Welcome."

Gina looked over the menu which was beautifully formatted. It read:

MENU
Welkom to Ingwe Bush Camp Dining
Peppermint Liqueur or Watermelon Lemonade

Hors d'oeuvres: Baked Brie with toasted pecans and maple syrup

Entrée:
　—Surprise Offering
　—Grilled Bush Chicken stuffed with herbs, celery, onions and feta.
　—Roast Leg of Lamb

Served with . . . Crunchy Baked Potatoes and sour cream
　　. . . Butternut Squash
　　. . . Basmati Rice and Braised onions

Dessert: Light Lemon Mousse and Mombasa coffee
After Dinner Drink: Cape Brandy

"Are you responsible for all this at the bush camp, Stephen?" Brad asked.

"Yes, I am, and I can't believe I get paid for doing it. It's a passion for me."

Noticeably impressed, Brad commented, "This is going well beyond the ordinary. I've eaten in some significant restaurants, but this menu is, as I said, way beyond what anyone would expect in the bush. I've got to applaud you for that." Then, in his pronounced British accent he continued to laud Stephen's efforts. "It's a night of gustatory splendor."

Gina jabbed him on the arm. "A night of what?" she teased.

"It means a sense of good taste," Brad explained.

"Brad," Gina snickered, "you're so smart."

"Well, anyway," Brad went on, gesturing toward Kyle. "I think I'll choose the 'Surprise Offering', too. I'm sure it's something I've never tasted and that's good."

"Go for it, Brad, but I'm goin' with the chicken," Gina spoke up.

"Fine," Stephen acknowledged. "I'll tell the cooks. They'll be serving in a few minutes. For now sit back and enjoy the wonderful weather and the bright stars above. It's a grand evening."

Finally when the dinner was served Kyle was the first to comment. "This is exceptionally tasty," she said as she bit into the 'Surprise' entrée. What is it, Stephen?"

"Oh, I'll tell you when we're sitting around the fire."

"Oh come on," Brad protested.

"I've got a reason for holding back. I'll tell you later."

"Okay," Brad said. "We'll let you off the hook off until then, but it certainly is delicious."

"And," Kyle spoke up, "I can't get over those Hors d' oeuvres. The menu said it's called Baked Brie. I hope they let me have copy of the recipe for those. They're delicious."

"I'll see if I can make that happen," Stephen responded.

The group must have sat at the table for an hour enjoying the relaxing setting with its flickering lanterns and candles and comfortable canvas chairs. The experience of enjoying a bush camp dinner under the stars is a quintessential component of any Africa safari and, as Kyle explained to all during the meal, "This particular experience has got to be the best it can be. I'm amazed at the cooks' mastery of culinary arts in such a primitive setting and the entire ambiance of this whole camp is beyond belief, Stephen," Kyle said. Raising her drink she offered a toast. "You've given us a treat we'll never forget, and I want to thank you." All raised their glasses and joined with a loud, "Hey, Hey!"

"This's heavenly," Gina added.

"It's perfect," Kyle said in agreement. "We've got a full moon and bright stars tonight, Stephen. It's like you planned that, too."

"Yes, it is perfect," he replied as they all settled around the open fire the guards had started while the guests were eating.

For the next several hours Stephen told tales of animal life on the savannahs including the fact that elephants in the wild eat almost five hundred pounds of vegetable matter and thirty gallons of water every day while at the same time often losing their teeth from many years of stripping the bark off the trees. "They can deplete an area in no time," he explained, and when asked about the poachers, Stephen detailed how the park wardens use drones to locate the culprits. "They also use automated motion sensors that relay any intrusions along the borders to a central center where the wardens go out with specialized dog units."

"How about the rhinos?" Kyle asked. "We hear a lot about them being killed for their horns."

"That's another poaching situation," Stephen said. "Actually since 2009 some Kruger Park rhinos have been fitted with invisible tracking devices implanted in their horns which enable the officials to locate carcasses and trace the smuggled horns by satellite. But it still remains a huge problem that I mentioned to Kyle before."

"I hope they solve it soon, or future generations won't be able to see those creatures in the wild, and as far as I'm concerned that'd be tragic," Kyle stated. She paused for a moment then burst out with, "Okay Stephen, you promised to tell us what the 'Surprise Offering' was. Now fess up!"

Brad smiled. "Let's hear it, because it was most certainly delicious."

Stephen confessed the reason he doesn't reveal the specifics is that many guests are repulsed by the thought of eating wild boar. "But, cooked over an open flame for hours and hours it is good, isn't it?"

Kyle admitted. "I never would have guessed that."

"Neither would I," Brad agreed.

Gina, on the other hand joked, "Well, I'm glad I stuck with the chicken. You guys are a lot braver than I am."

Eagerly wanting to relay facts about his beloved Africa, Stephen continued to detail specifics. "One more statistic you've probably never read about is the fact that a lot of this land was owned by the Makuleke Tribe. They gave it back to the government on the condition that they be allowed to invest in the private sector of tourism which turned out to be profitable for them and actually promoted many more private reserves to be opened." He topped short. "A case of good business sense I guess. All parties made out well. And then there's the story of the *Lion King*."

"I had no idea about the tribe's purchase, but what about the *Lion King*?" Kyle asked. "That was a movie, right?"

"It was," Stephen acknowledged. "Are you sure you all want to hear this? Some find it scary." He sat wringing his hands and grinning.

Frowning, Gina said hesitantly, "What do 'ya mean scary?"

"Well, it's a true story that happened in a bush camp. The tale hit the headlines in most all the newspapers in South Africa and," he said looking at Gina, "I don't want you to have nightmares."

Kyle looked squarely at Gina. "We can take it, can't we?"

Gina grabbed Brad's hand and looked up at him. "Sure, as long as he's here."

"Okay," Stephen said setting the scene by describing that this all occurred, as he'd mentioned, in a bush camp in South Africa a number of years ago. This particular bush camp did not have a fence around it. In other words it was accessible to any animal that might track by. And apparently there had been some evidence of elephants in the camp, for one of the guests spotted elephant dung near their tent.

Gina put her hand up to her mouth, grimaced then raised her shoulders in disgust.

"At any rate," Stephen continued, "a very wealthy woman who was married to a prominent lawyer apparently wanted to take her only son on an African Safari. However, her husband couldn't get the time away from the office, so she booked a trip for her son and herself.

"They arrived at the bush camp and were immediately shown to the tent that had been assigned to them. It so happened, though, that the young boy's mother and father had spoiled the youth to the point that he most often got what he wanted and, in this case, he didn't want to sleep in the tent with his mother. He wanted his *own* tent.

"Now even though the owners insisted that he should not sleep alone, the mother finally relented after the boy caused such a stir that it disrupted the entire camp. One stipulation made by the owners was that a guard would have to be posted outside the youth's tent. However, the boy would not accept that decision either, and he firmly complained about wanting to sleep in the tent with no guides around him.

"Eventually the mother reluctantly backed down and so did the perturbed owners who, of course, were thinking of their bottom line. After all they had been paid a premium by this particular wealthy guest.

"It so happened, too, that the boy had always been a fan of the movie *The Lion King* and, as you know if you saw the movie, the hyenas were very friendly little creatures in that flick. Most presume the boy wanted to get closer to the hyenas by opening the tent flap so he could see them . . . a crucial mistake on his part." Stephen hesitated, watching his guests as they sat awestruck and wide-eyed in anticipation.

They were all dancing with impatience when Stephen said, "W-e-l-l," drawing out the word to create more suspense, "as the newspapers stated, hyenas did come into the bush camp that night, and with the tent zipper open and the flap pulled aside, it was an easy invitation for a kill.

"When his mother awoke in the morning and entered the boy's tent, she let out a spine curdling scream that they say could be heard for miles. The boy was nowhere to be found. The only evidence the authorities could find to identify the attacker or attackers was the putrid scent that only a hyena can emit and one of the boy's shoes covered in blood. The boy had totally vanished into the night."

Stephen noted that everyone was sitting on the edge of their seats. "So, what did they do?" Gina questioned.

"They could do nothing, and the mother was so distraught that she wouldn't go home. In fact, I believe she still lives somewhere around here. She stated she couldn't leave her son, and most think she actually lost her mind. That's a true tale."

Kyle struck Stephen playfully on the shoulder. "Wow! That's enough to make us all glad you've got an electric fence around this place."

"You bet," Gina said as she sidled up to Brad.

"You've left us with something to think about," Brad remarked. "I'll be sure to zip up my tent. In fact, I think I'll call it a day. How about you, Gina?"

"I'm willing," she said as the two got up and strode away.

"Thanks for a good time," Brad called out. "I'll never forget *this* night."

Gina, who had already latched onto his arm and was gleefully looking up at him, said, "I may be wide-awake all night."

Kyle smiled. *I'd bet the bank on the outcome for those two.*

Stephen who had a mischievous grin on his face, remarked, "The guards will be walking the perimeter all night and remember the fence is electrified. Besides we keep the fire going out here all night, too. So, don't worry, Gina."

After Brad and Gina were out of sight, Kyle pulled her chair closer to Stephen's. "You know I could sit by the fire all night. This's my idea of heaven." She leaned back in her chair and stared at the glowing fire. "It's been a wonderful evening, Stephen. I appreciate all you've done to make it so special. Thanks again."

"This is my idea of heaven, too," he said as they sat there quietly together. "Want a glass of wine?"

"That'd be great."

Stephen nodded. "Good. I'll check on the guards then I'll bring us some wine."

Kyle was still leaning back in her chair gazing at the stars when Stephen returned. "Here," he said. "This is the best in the house."

"Thanks," Kyle said heaving a deep sigh. "I think you were extremely patient with Gina back there when she suddenly couldn't decide whether or not she wanted to go on this venture. I've got to admit that was nice of you. I bet most guides would have been angry."

"Well, some people think they're going to like an outing, but get cold feet when they get started. I didn't want her to think she's the only one who had those feelings. I've had others change their minds in midstream as well. It's no big deal."

"It shows character Stephen, and that's what counts."

Kyle settled back in her chair and looked about at the campsite. The moon had reached its zenith in the dark velvet sky and the night began to wane. The silence was heavy and unbroken.

"This's wonderful. It's like there's a sense of the beginning of time here," she said softly. "I love the sounds of the animals, the lions roaring or bellowing or whatever you call it, and the owls hooting. Everything seems to come alive at night." Kyle paused and took a deep breath. "No one can ever know exactly what it's like until they're experienced this. It's a dream I've had for years."

Stephen leaned forward, his eyes trained on her. "I'm glad you finally made it, and I've got to say, you're the most—" He stopped short as his voice caught in his throat.

"The most what?"

"I probably shouldn't say this, but." he went on hesitantly, "you're a great person to be around. You seem to celebrate every experience with such eagerness. It's exhilarating, but I suppose that sounds far out."

Kyle glanced at his ruddy completion and his sandy-colored hair as the light from the fire highlighted streaks of varying shades of blond. "No Stephen, it's not. That's a feeling of being alive, and I've missed feeling that way."

For the next few moments they sat quietly both staring at the fire while the wind softly blew the flames in circles of red and gold. Then, as if it were planned, they both gazed at each other at the same time and the conversation again turned to relationships, a stream of talk that seemed to pull them close.

"You know, Kyle, I've got to tell you that I felt a sense of guilt when we talked during that game drive where we stopped for a Sundowner."

"Why did 'ya feel guilty?"

"I guess I was torn between wanting to know you and thinking I shouldn't persist."

Kyle frowned. "I don't understand."

Stephen shook his head. "I've no idea why I felt like that. Maybe it was because you told me about your cancelled wedding plans, and I didn't want to seem like I was taking advantage of your feeling lonely."

"That was *my* fault Stephen. I shouldn't have burdened you with my problems." With a nod and a flick of her hand she gestured, "I'm sorry."

"No need to be sorry. We all have difficulties. But I'd still like to get to know you better."

With raised eyebrows Kyle mentioned to Stephen that she thought he and Carole were, in a manner of speaking, a couple.

"Actually we were at one time," Stephen acknowledged. "We've dated and have been living together for awhile, but that's over. In fact, there's a deep void in my life right now . . . to the point of loneliness."

"Sorry."

"Don't be. I won't go into any details, but it'll all work out. My thoughts right now are elsewhere."

Kyle flicked a glance at him. "What do you mean?" She asked, gingerly taking a sip of wine.

"I know I told you about this, but I haven't confided in many that my goal now is to own The Ingwe."

"I remember your saying that. I really hope your dream comes true."

Stephen gazed at Kyle, his voice solemn and his eyes intense. "And I sure hope you find the happiness you deserve, for there's a fire inside you that's irresistible."

Kyle's heartbeat quickened as he leaned into her space, their faces inches apart. There was something haunting in his eyes that reminded her of lost love.

Stephen reached out to stay her hand and Kyle willingly grasped it. He pulled her up and into his arms. "May I?" he asked, the words heated the air as he spoke.

She quickly pressed her fingers on his lips and smiled. It wasn't long before his tongue slyly circled her lips, moistening them, preparing them for an eager entry.

Kyle felt her body quiver in anticipation and she held her breath against a whimper of passion. A hot flush raged through her as he teased her lips and kissed them softly then quickly surrendered to the deep need inside. At fever pitch she kissed him like an orphan starved for love. The more they were together the more she felt that this man had captured her heart. His kiss was proof enough to her that they were meant to be together on this starry night in the heart of Africa. Within seconds she burst out with, "I want you, Stephen."

In that silent moment that followed she felt a surge of passion race though her body as she watched his eyes caress her. Hand in hand they walked to Stephen's tent where she stood watching as he closed the tent flap, turned on, then dimmed the bedside lantern and carefully pulled back the bed cover. He moved around behind her and nuzzled her neck and chin. Then he slipped her jacket off while Kyle unbuttoned her blouse, his nimble fingers grazing her shoulders with a feather touch.

With a rush of emotion, Stephen turned her around to face him. In the embrace of darkness he reached down and gently raised her chin and kissed her. Kyle's eyes watched his every move as he stepped out of his jeans and pulled his shirt over his head. She followed suit and quickly removed her jeans and shirt as well. When she lay down on the bed, he quickly slipped in beside her. Kyle closed her eyes as thoughts flashed through her mind. *Is Stephen the love I'm looking for?*

Chapter 33

Thursday Late Evening

Carol called her brother from her sister's house and reminded him of the meeting on Friday at 10:00 A. M. "Whatever you do *don't let anyone see you!*" she emphasized. "He can't know who did this, you hear?"

"I know. I got it. I get a chunk of this, right, 'cause I gotta split with Michael."

"You will, and tell Michael to keep his mouth shut. He could ruin everything if he tells a soul. Just do what I told you and you'll get your share. It should be worth a lot to both of you."

"Okay Sis. I'll call you when it's over."

At the same time Carole was making the late night call to her brother, Kyle was in Stephen's tent in the bush camp romantically running her fingers through Stephen's sandy silk hair while he covered her face and neck with soft, tender kisses then gently stroked her breasts.

Suddenly tears welled in Kyle's eyes and she bit down on her lip crying, "I can't do this!" She sat up, placed both hands over her face and gasped for breath.

Stephen fell back and blew out a lung full of air. "What is it, Kyle?"

She slipped out of bed and ran her fingers through her disheveled auburn curls. "This isn't right, Stephen."

Straining to get his breath, he leaned up on one elbow. "What's not right?"

"My being here," she exclaimed. She rambled on about being sorry as she buttoned her blouse then put on her jeans and jacket. "I can't do this. I've still got feelings for Ryan, and I can't deceive you like this. I'm sorry!" She quickly slipped into her boots, unzipped the tent flap and hurried out into the night.

Feeling strongly that the supposed tryst was nothing but animal heat, she warily made her way back to her tent, passing one of the guards who was standing by the gate. She waved to him, but she made no attempt to communicate, for she was tearing up and her nose was giving her fits in light of the fact that she couldn't stop sniffling. When she unzipped her tent flap, she was actually relieved to see that neither Gina nor her travel bag were there. She surmised that her friend must be with Brad and that was essentially a good thing, for Kyle was in no mood to talk. Within minutes she had secured the tent. Too distraught to bother to change, she fell into bed with her clothes on. For a time she lay listening to the whisper of the wind and gazed at a stream of moonlight that was exposed through an opening in the canvas window flap. *Why did I let my emotions get the best of me? I can't believe I did that. Oh Ryan, what have you done to my life?*

She lay there wide-eyed, her heart pounding, her head throbbing, her stomach twisting like two hard fists battling within. Disjointed thoughts shot through her mind like shrapnel as emotional rigor mortis set in.

She must have dozed off, but was awakened by an intermittent deep-throated melodic growling sound coming from somewhere close by. Startled, she sat upright and looked about. Nothing was stirring in her tent. Then she heard the growl again, so she leaned over and with care pulled a corner of the window flap back just enough so she could see out. Since she was merely a few feet from the fence and the moonlight shone brightly that night, it was fairly easy to see a silhouette moving about. She squinted and peered out again. Oh, my God, she said with a gasp, her breath catching in her throat. In front of her was a white lion, moving back and forth along the fence line. If her heart was pounding hard before, now it was hammering, and she fought off the wild urge to scream.

Mesmerized, she couldn't take her eyes off the big cat. Eventually, though, she grabbed her camera hoping the light would be sufficient to allow a shot. Fortunately she was able to click off but one photo. However, the flash must have scared him off for within seconds he was gone.

Kyle dropped back onto her pillow and inhaled deeply, hoping beyond hope that she had captured a view of the cat. It was, without a doubt, a once in a lifetime opportunity. Though exhausted, she pulled the film up on her viewer. She was stunned for she had, indeed, gotten one clear photo image of the white lion. She sat staring at it unable to believe that in one instant, just that one second, she'd actually captured what most people are never privy to see . . . a white lion in the bush. She set her camera aside and dropped back onto the pillow totally spent. The next thing she heard was the zipper of her tent being opened and Gina's voice calling out, "What happened to you?"

Chapter 34

Thursday Evening

After his discussion with Gideon about the clerk's call from the Magistrate's Office regarding an inspection of the reserve, Damon hurried back to his own office on the other side of the lodge. By the time he got there his right hand was shaking so that he couldn't hide the tremors. Feeling more than a bit dizzy, he immediately took another pill and headed for his residence where he collapsed across his bed as another focal seizure took hold of him.

Meanwhile, Lynn had left Gideon's office, giving him specific instructions to get things in order for the inspection. She had made it clear to Gideon that nothing can go wrong . . . nothing! Gideon was well aware of that fact, and he reassured her there would be "No stink of failure." He'd see to it that there was no evidence of any leopards in the warehouse and that he would get Damon to help him with the cleanup.

Gideon's hope that Damon would assist him in the warehouse cleanup didn't pan out, of course, for when he tried to reach Damon in his office, the man was nowhere to be found. So he called Lynn who knew immediately what had happened. "He's most likely hiding out in the residence," she stated. "I'll get over there and see."

"Call me back."

"I will." It was already dark when Lynn got to their residence that Thursday night. As she suspected Damon was in the bedroom, but he was in no shape to help Gideon in any cleanup effort at the warehouse.

"You loser!" she shouted when she saw him stretched out on the bed. "You're the weakest man I've ever known. I can't count on you for anything." She could tell he'd most likely had another seizure, but she couldn't have cared less. With a decided huff, she left the room and slammed the door. Quickly dialing Gideon on her cell phone she told him that he'd have to do the work himself. "I think he's had another seizure and he's not going to be worth a damn if you're looking for help from him. He'll be out for hours."

"Don't worry. I'll get out there right now, but calm down. This'll be over soon."

Gideon drove immediately to the warehouse and spent the next three hours sweeping away any evidence that there had ever been *Mauve Leopards* in the place. He was careful to make certain that none of their soft fur coating was left behind. Then he stacked the cages in an empty corner of the warehouse and gave the floor one more inspection. When he left he felt confident that he'd done all he could do in order to pass the District Warden's inspection, and he relayed that message to Lynn even though it was after one in the morning.

"Thanks, Gideon. I knew I could count on you. Get some sleep and be sure that you're the one who greets those wardens in the morning."

"I will and you get some sleep, love."

Chapter 35

Early Friday Morning

Back in the bush camp Kyle was bubbling over with enthusiasm while showing the group her image of the white lion she'd taken the night before. By a stroke of luck the photo had come out well considering it was shot through a fence. Stephen admitted he was astounded to see the film, for he had no idea there was a white lion in the area.

There was an unquestionable tension evident between Stephen and Kyle that was easily recognized by Gina if not the others. In fact, Gina commented to Kyle later on that Stephen's personality had taken a decided turn away from his usual cheery attitude to one of indifference.

The next morning after an early breakfast, that decided change in attitude that Gina noticed was especially obvious as Stephen quite nonchalantly announced that the group was going to return to the lodge earlier than expected. His explanation included the fact that the *Boma* was scheduled for six o'clock and the cooks were needed in the kitchen.

On the way back to their tent to get things organized to leave the camp, Kyle explained what had happened with Stephen. "I did go to his tent last night, Gina, but I walked out on him," she said. "I told him I still have feelings for Ryan."

A frustrated look lingered on Gina's face as she asked, "What's wrong with you, Kyle? How can you possibly say that you still have feelings for Ryan? I can understand not necessarily wanting to sleep with Stephen, even though I think he's a great guy," she rambled on, "but to even mention that you were still thinking about that jerk is crazy. Are you out of your mind?"

"Okay, okay! Let it go, Gina. I can't explain it, but I still can't believe that Ryan did that, and somehow I still love him."

"Oh girl, I don't want to press this anymore believe me, but you're just prolonging the agony by constantly thinking about him. You're gorgeous and there are plenty of other good guys around."

Kyle stopped in her tracks and looked directly at her friend. "Let's forget it for now. We've got that *Boma* to celebrate tonight. That should be fun, and besides we've only a short time before we head home." She raised her hands in a gesture of aggravation. "Frankly Gina, I don't have time for any complicated affair right now especially way down here in South Africa." A network of wrinkles lined her face and she uttered a deep sigh then started toward the tent. "Come on. Let's get our things ready."

"All right, but I hate to see you hurtin'."

"I know you do and you're a good friend, but I'll have to work this out for myself. That's all there is to it."

Just before Kyle and the group returned to the lodge from their overnight bush camp excursion, two officers in beige uniforms arrived at The Ingwe Private Game Reserve just after nine-thirty in the morning and, as he promised, Gideon was there to greet them. They showed their badges and announced, "We're the Wildlife Officers that are here to inspect the reserve. I'm Officer Du Preez and this is Rouz. Are you Damon Greene?"

"No, I'm his partner Gideon Courtney. We don't quite understand why you're coming out here today since you completed an inspection just last month, but how can I help you?"

"We'd like to go out into the reserve and check out the property. Is your game ranger available to show us around?"

"No, I don't think he's back from an overnight bush camp with a group of guests, but I can show you the area."

"Good, but before we go we'd like to talk to your partner as well. Is he in and if so we'd like to see him before we head out?"

"I'll call and check," Gideon said as he dialed Damon's extension. He hadn't counted on the officers asking to speak to Damon, for if he had he would have seen to it that Lynn kept her husband out of his office, but that didn't happen. Damon, to Gideon's dismay, answered the phone in his office. "We've got the two wildlife game officers here Damon. They want to talk to you. Can you see them now?"

There wasn't much Damon could do but to agree to see them.

"I'll show you his office," Gideon replied. "When you're ready let me know and I'll take you out into the reserve." He knew that was a tragic mistake, letting them talk to Damon, but there wasn't anything he could do about it. However, when he ushered the two men into Damon's office he decided to stay and observe how Damon reacted. That turned out to be a good idea, for his partner was, if anything, evasive and he acted as guilty as sin.

"I really don't know anything other than we're not having any trouble on the property and no poachers that we know of," Damon commented. Although his words painted a favorable picture of the reserve, it was the actions that Damon exhibited that were evidently on the minds of the officers, for Gideon saw one of the men quickly glance at the other.

Damon, obviously nervous, kept brushing his fingers across his mustache in an impulsive manner that was a sure give away that he was, in fact, holding back details. However, since there was nothing outright alarming about what Damon had to say, the officers looked at Gideon and stated that they were ready to go out for the inspection.

"How long do you think we'll be gone?" Gideon asked. "I'll tell the desk clerk."

"You've got a lot of property to cover, but if all's well it shouldn't be more than two hours or so," Officer Du Preez responded.

"Fine. Let me get my jacket from my office and notify the clerk. I'll meet you in the lobby in a few minutes."

As Gideon was walking away from the officers and heading for the Front Desk, he heard one of them say, "This is that deal about the Tzaneen Medical Center referral, isn't it?"

When Gideon heard the words "Tzaneen Medical Center" his shoulders sagged and his heart raced, knowing full well that evidently they suspected The Ingwe was involved.

He stopped at the desk and told Holly that he would be out in the reserve with the wildlife officers and that he could be reached on his cell. Then, on the way to his office, he hurriedly dialed Lynn. "The officers are here and I'm going out into the field with them since

Stephen isn't back yet from the overnight camp. I can't talk long, for they're waiting for me, but Lynn," he paused for an instant, "I heard one of them mention the 'Tzaneen Medical Center.'"

"Oh God, then this must have something to do with Jon. How can that be? You told me he was dead."

"I don't know, though I was sure of it. And Lynn, they insisted on talking to Damon. I could tell by the way he answered their questions, he's going to crack."

"Don't worry. I'll take care of him."

"Why don't you give me a call in about forty minutes or so while we're out in the reserve. That way I can let you know if all is going well or not."

"Will do. Be careful" she said. Shortly after that conversation with Lynn, Gideon met the officers and they were on their way.

As soon as Stephen's camping group returned to the lodge and he had expressed his hope that they all enjoy the *Boma* buffet that evening, he left them. Kyle and Gina promptly returned to their suite to drop off their bags while Brad went to the pool and planned to meet them later.

Stephen had hurried away for a reason. He had plans. It was already after nine-forty in the morning and he had an appointment at ten. No way was he going to miss out on that meeting. It was the last meeting with his contact and the start of his owning The Ingwe. He was sure of it.

When he reached the parking lot at the Perry's Bridge Trading Post in Hazyview, there were no cars on the side of the building, so he parked along the back fence beside a group of bushes that were out of view from the front entrance and the street as well. He arrived at exactly ten o'clock, but since his contact wasn't there, he turned off his car engine, opened the windows and sat and waited.

The pressure must have gotten to him, for he closed his eyes for an instant, at least he thought it was an instant, but in the minutes to follow he would regret that lapse of judgment. One moment he was peacefully resting and waiting for the contact to arrive. In the next few seconds Stephen gasped as he felt the cold steel touch of a gun barrel pressed tightly against his neck. He couldn't get a glimpse of the person at all, for he couldn't turn his head. Then he heard a man's deep voice warning, "Don't move or I'll kill 'ya. Where are the drugs?"

Another man opened the passenger side door and stuck his head in. Stephen, in a state of shock, abruptly shifted his gaze to the left and saw the man, but he had no idea who he was, though he did see the glistening blade of a knife in the man's hand.

When Stephen tried to look to his right to see who was holding the gun, he was lucky enough to get a swift glimpse of a man wearing a scarf around his mouth and chin. As he squinted trying to figure out who it was, he thought he recognized the blond hair. Then suddenly he felt the gun barrel dig deeper into the skin on his neck.

"I don't have any drugs," Stephen answered sharply.

"Yeah, well we know you do. Hand 'em over and no one'll get hurt."

"Who said I had drugs?"

"Never mind, but I know you do," the man countered.

Totally confused Stephen asked, "You're not the contact who met me before."

"No, we took that guy out. He's over there in the bushes, so don't expect to see him today or ever." The man stopped, took in a deep breath and scowled. "I'll say this one more time. Where are the drugs?"

Stephen knew he couldn't take on both of the men at one time, but if he could grab hold of the gun he'd have a better chance of getting out of this alive. So he took a chance and declared, "They're in the trunk." He said that purposely, determining that if he opened the driver's door he could slam it against the man's body and hopefully knock him down with just enough time to get the gun.

"Give me your keys," the man demanded.

Stephen knew that if he gave him the keys, they'd never let him out of the car and that'd ruin his plan. So he refused saying, "No, but you let me out of the car and I'll open the trunk and you can take the drugs."

"Okay, but no tricks," the man said, "or I'll blow your head off. Now open the car door real slow and get out."

All Stephen could do was to follow orders. He opened the car door and slowly stepped out. That's when he decided to stand his ground. It's here or never, he thought. So with one fast move he reached out and tried to grab the gun barrel. *If I can just wrestle it out of his hand.*

It was a gamble, but one he felt he had to take. He'd worked three years to accumulate the money to buy The Ingwe and the last payload of bags of Dagga were in the trunk of his car, and he wasn't about to let that dream of owning the reserve go unfulfilled.

As the two fought, the gun fell out of the hand of the masked attacker. Stephen tried to bend down and grab it, but the other man stepped in and, during the shuffle that followed, the gun was kicked to one side. Both men began to punch Stephen with blows to his face, chest and back. Stephen tried to avoid the onslaught, but he was outnumbered. Now bloody and weak he tried to inhale but the air seemed to ignite a spark in his lungs. In the struggle his heart raced and his skin burned as if scorched by an open flame. A foul tang of hot breath spewed from one of his attackers.

Stephen moaned and tried to cry out, but fear pinched his throat. All he could manage was a strangled whisper as he grasped the scarf that covered the attacker's face and pulled it down. Stunned, Stephen said, "Not you?" It was then he felt a hard blow on the back of his head. Stephen gave one last frenzied shudder, one final breath. Then a fizz of lights like bubbles in seltzer exploded in his head and all went black.

Chapter 36

Friday Morning

While Stephen is fighting for his life, Kyle, Gina and Brad were enjoying themselves at The Ingwe pool on a glorious sun-filled African morning. "I can't believe this trip is almost over, but I'm really looking forward to the *Boma* tonight," Kyle said as she sipped a tall glass of pink lemonade. "It's been an adventure of a lifetime, and I'm glad you came along Gina."

Brad sat upright, his legs straddling the lounge chair, as he slyly said with a wink and a nod toward Gina, "Hey Kyle, I'm glad Gina came along as well."

"Oh you two!" Kyle raised her eyebrows and her glass at the same time. "I think you've got something good going on and I'm glad. Here's to a fantastic future for both of you." As Kyle said those words she felt a surge of sadness rush through her, for those would have been the words spoken at her wedding. Tears filled her eyes, but she quickly turned her head to avoid Gina and Brad's gaze. "I'm going to stop at the restroom. Be back in a minute." That said she promptly left the two and hurried off.

Her leaving so abruptly must have startled Brad, for he immediately asked, "Is there something wrong with her, Gina?"

"No, it's just that she's havin' regrets about the weddin'. I think she's still in love with Ryan. I feel so sorry for her, but it's one of those things that maybe only time'll heal. Shame, too, 'cause she's such a great gal besides bein' 'knock out' gorgeous as well."

Brad eased back in his lounge chair. "She'll find somebody else. I wasn't looking for anyone and I found you."

"Nicely said," Gina teased. She leaned over and gave him a quick kiss. "You're pretty special you know that."

He grinned. "Keep talking. I like what you're saying. By the way, I've told Patrick that I'll be at the *Boma* tonight. I'm going to stay and enjoy the evening with you two, and I hear there are others coming in today."

"Yeah, I was talking to Holly at the desk and she said they've got a group arrivin' late this afternoon. They'll be just in time for the big dinner." She turned and glanced at Brad. "Hey, I'm wondering about lunch. What time is it?"

Brad checked his watch. "I've got eleven o'clock. When do they start serving?"

I think they're going to put a spread out here on the pool deck. I love that." She looked around at the greenery and the rocky waterfall at the end of the swimming pool. "This place is phenomenal. I can't get over the fact that I almost backed out of coming here." She breathed a sigh. "I never dreamed they'd have such luxury in South Africa not mentioning the fact that I found you."

"The Kruger Park Lodge is just as nice. Patrick says there are a number of great private reserves in this area, but when the news gets out that The Ingwe has a new breed of leopards on their reserve, this place will be packed."

"It probably will, though I like it now with just the few of us here. It's like we own the place," Gina said as she reached over and tickled Brad on his stomach.

Brad didn't respond. He merely leaned back and smiled. "You make life fun. You know that?"

"Don't I though!" Gina replied, batting her neon blue eyes.

While Gina and Brad continued to massage each other's egos, Kyle made her way to the restroom and hurried into a stall. There she stood with tears rolling down her cheeks, a nose that wouldn't stop dripping and thoughts that wouldn't let go of Ryan. *Why can't I just forget him?* She grabbed some tissue and brushed the tears from her cheeks, trying to push the memory of her former fiancé into some far corner of her mind where it could be lost forever. Then perhaps I can move on, she thought.

When she returned to where Gina and Brad were lounging by the pool, she was pretty well cried out, so to speak. At least the tearing had stopped and she'd regained her composure. "When are they going to open the restaurant?" she asked Gina when she sat down on a lounge chair.

"I just told Brad that I heard they were goin' to have a spread out here at poolside. Somethin' to do with the big bash tonight, but I don't know when. I suppose they're pretty busy in the kitchen."

At that same moment Karen entered the pool deck with two other members of the kitchen staff. The two men were carrying the table and Karen had the table cloth and a large tray in her hand. "Hi everybody," she said cheerfully. "We'll have this all set up and ready for you in no time. They decided to serve out here, for we're really busy in the kitchen with all that's going on for the *Boma* tonight."

"That's great Karen. I think I can speak for Gina and Brad when I say don't rush. We're not in any hurry. It's so wonderful out here. I never want to leave."

Karen smiled. "That's good to hear. We'll be right back with the rest of the menu."

Within the next fifteen minutes the table was set and the luncheon was ready for the guests. "Enjoy!" Karen called out.

Kyle hollered back, "Thanks. I know we will. It looks scrumptious."

They enjoyed every morsel. The trays were filled with a variety of drinks, lunch meats, homemade breads, cheeses and fruits. Oh, and the pastries were so tempting that Gina, of course, had to try a few of the desserts first, and she stated they were out of this world.

"This is heavenly," Gina said to Kyle. "And I was telling Brad that I almost declined the offer to come with you, remember?"

"Yeah, I do. Aren't you glad you changed your mind?"

"Am I ever, not only was the trip great, but look who I found en route?" She gave Brad a side glance. For the next thirty minutes they sat comfortably beside the fabulous pool with an outstanding view of the reserve grounds while munching on a delicious luncheon that they didn't have to prepare.

Kyle noted, "What more can one ask?"

Chapter 37

Late Friday Morning

The field trip into the reserve proceeded along well for a time. The officers found no evidence of poachers or any stray animal kills that looked suspicious. On that note, Gideon surmised that the female leopard that had been bombarded by the pack of hyenas had made it out alive, and he was pleased to see that the officers seemed to find no irregularities on the reserve grounds. However, the warehouse proved to be problematic. When the officers spied the cages, Officer Du Preez was quick to ask, "Why would you need eight of these?"

Gideon had prepared himself well, for he immediately countered, "We do have to capture some animals and report them to the Magistrate's office on occasion, animals that have been wounded and need care, and we feel it best to have a good supply of cages on hand for such occasions. Why do you ask?"

"Because the report we got in was that eight animals have been stolen from someone, and it seems strange to me that you just happen to have eight cages."

"That must be a coincidence, for I've not heard of any such theft."

"Well, when we get back to the lodge we'll check around and ask your staff if they know of any such thievery in the area. As far as I'm concerned—"

Just then Gideon's cell phone rang, and he excused himself for he said it was most likely a problem relating to the *Boma* they were having that night at the reserve. "I'm sorry I'll have to take this, but I'll only be a moment." That said, he walked a distance away and answered with, "Lynn, we've got problems. I can't talk long so just listen. The officers are questioning the number of cages in the warehouse. Apparently they have received a report of a theft of leopards and the number of the cages taken was eight, the exact number in our warehouse. When they get back to the lodge they're going to question everyone. Damon will break. I know it. He's going to ruin everything."

"Damn it," Lynn said grudgingly, "and you told me the man was dead." She paused for an instant as if thinking. "Listen, I'll take care of Damon. I've been waiting for the right time and it's now. You keep those officers occupied for forty minutes and I'll have it done." With that she hurriedly hung up.

Gideon slapped the cell phone lid in place and walked back to where the officers stood. "There," he said, "that's all taken care of. I've just got the south quarter to show you and we can get back to the lodge." At that point his heart was pounding hard against his chest and he only hoped his voice was steady enough to mask his frustration.

When he heard Office Du Preez say that he was willing to finish up seeing the south section of the reserve and then get back to the lodge, Gideon let out a slight sigh of relief. *If I can distract them for forty minutes like Lynn said, maybe we'll come out of this just fine.*

Chapter 38

Late Friday Morning

Lynn wasted no time. Since it was only eleven-twenty she knew that her Herpetology Lab, as she called it, would be closed. Hopefully if Gideon's plays his cards right and keeps the officers away from the lodge for forty minutes, I can see to it that Damon's not a problem, she reasoned. "Good thing Gideon told me to make that call to him," she mumbled to herself as she grabbed her briefcase and left by the back entrance. From there she skirted the building and re-entered into the corridor that led to the Herpetology Lab. She carefully locked the door behind her so that no one would be able to enter unexpectedly without her knowing it. She quickly placed her briefcase on the table and opened it.

Then, with all her training and experience supporting her every move, she carefully removed the Black Mamba from its tank. She did so as cautiously as she had done in cleaning the tank, but again with an urgency that went far beyond any routine cleaning effort.

Knowing that every moment counted, she placed the Black Mamba, now safely secured in the sack, into the briefcase and closed the lid. She hid the snake hook under her jacket and made her way out the back entrance again, into the building and down the corridor that led to Damon's office. She knew he wouldn't be there, for he always went back to the residence at about eleven-thirty then on to lunch at noon. If nothing else he was a man of habit.

Once she entered Damon's office she quickly closed and locked the door, another precaution. She rested the briefcase on his large glass topped desk, and in doing so scraped the bottom of her briefcase on a ragged edge of the glass on the left-hand portion of this desk. With a shake of her head she uttered a curse for Damon's inattention to details. *He should have had this fixed!*

Hurriedly opening his left-hand top drawer, she reached into her briefcase and removed the sack that held the Black Mamba then carefully deposited the top of the bag into the drawer and let the snake slip out. With precision-like timing she closed the drawer. Lastly, she set her briefcase and the snake hook behind a plant near the office door so she could take them with her when she left and so Damon wouldn't see them when he entered the room.

At one point she thought perhaps she'd use the Puff Adder for her deadly deed, but she changed her mind because the Puff Adder, although equally capable of delivering a lethal bite, has a wide girth and her specimen was much older than the Black Mamba. Therefore, she reasoned, because of its size it might cause problems when trying to position it in the drawer.

At any rate, the stage had been set. At that moment she found herself gritting her teeth as her stomach knotted and her nerves gave a belated tremor when she picked up the receiver to call Damon. He was surprised by her call, but was delighted when she told him that the bank had called and that somehow they had arranged an interim loan that would hold off payment for a few days. Lynn explained that she'd picked up the papers, but that he must sign them immediately and get them back to the bank. "I put the papers in the top left-hand drawer of your desk thinking that you'd be back soon, for I didn't know where you were at the time. But listen, I'm in the kitchen now trying to get the *Boma* dinner organized. You'd better get over to your office before you go to lunch and sign those papers right away." She paused to take a quick breath, for her voice was getting weak from the strain of setting her devilish plan into motion. "I'll swing by and take the papers back to the bank while you're having lunch. Are you listening to me?" she questioned.

"I am and I'll go there now. Let me know what they say when you get back, for if we can hold off the bank for another few days maybe we can get those buyers who are coming in today to sign on as shareholders in the reserve as I originally wanted."

"Of course. That'd be great," Lynn said abruptly. It was a lie, but necessary. She had systematically planned this course of action well ahead of time and was waiting for the right moment. Strangely, though

Damon rarely listened to her, this time he seemed willing to take her at her word. *But why now?* She deduced that he seriously wanted to believe that the bank was going to give him a few more days to keep his beloved reserve.

CHAPTER 39

EARLY FRIDAY AFTERNOON

Lynn stood around the corner of the corridor watching for Damon, and when he strode down the hall, she met him as if she'd just come from the kitchen. "Good," she said. "Get in there and sign. They're in your top left-hand drawer. I'll hurry and get them to the bank."

Damon opened his office door, moved across the room and sat down at his desk, pulled his pen out of his jacket pocket and opened the top left-hand drawer with his left hand.

Within seconds he cried out as the Black Mamba, known for being aggressive, struck out at him, then recoiled for another strike.

Damon's hands went flying, scrapping along the desk top leaving a stream of blood running down his hand and arm. The shock must have sent him into another focal seizure, for his right hand began to shake. His arms thrashed about and he looked dazed.

Lynn rushed in and slammed the drawer shut. She paid no attention to Damon's condition, but merely hurried to grab her briefcase and snake hook. From then on it was a case of getting everything in place to capture the snake, a task that was her specialty, and she did so again with exacting precision even though, in this case, the strain was insufferable.

When she left the room Damon was unconscious and would most likely die from the snake bit within minutes, she reasoned. In her mind, she figured that the police would determine the man had suffered a seizure and cut his hand and arm on the ragged edge of the desk's glass top. With no medication, such a seizure can be deadly. No one would ever suspect that he was attacked and bitten by a snake in his office . . . a perfect ruse.

Being sure no one noticed her, Lynn followed the same route she'd taken before and reached the Herpetology Lab at a few minutes before noon. She reversed her routine and placed the Black Mamba back into his tank, put away the snake hook and the sack, closed the briefcase and casually walked out of the Lab, locking the door behind her. She strolled down the corridor as if nothing had happened. Just prior to reaching the lobby she stopped and leaned against the wall, breathing an exhaustive sigh of relief. He heart had been racing so that she felt as if she was about to have a heart attack, but the heavy beating subsided and after a few calming breaths she settled down. Even though Lynn's thoughts were laced with bitterness, she concluded that her actions were justified primarily because this was the only way she could rid herself of Damon, go back to Johannesburg and recapture her youth as a herpetology expert, a period in her life that she wholeheartedly enjoyed. To this end, it all had to be done!

Chapter 40

Early Friday Afternoon

Stephen awoke from the horrendous beating he took. His head throbbed and his gut felt as if someone had run over him with a truck. He pulled himself up and held onto the car door handle to steady himself for a moment before he could even comprehend what had happened. He pressed the heel of his hand against his forehead to try and stop the pain that cut across his brow, but there seemed to be no relief. He looked around but saw no one in sight. *Where in the hell are my keys?* He stumbled out of the driver's seat and checked the ground . . . first near the driver's seat then at the rear of the car. There he spotted his keys under the exhaust pipe. At least I've got keys, he thought.

Slowly and painfully he slipped back onto the seat and shoved the ignition key into place. It was not until then that he realized the significance of the attack. *The drugs . . . are they still in the trunk?* He pulled the key back out of the slot and stuffed it into his shirt pocket. Then he reached up with his right hand and clamped it onto the roof of the car and pulled himself out of the seat. Every bone in his body ached and the walk to the back of the car seemed like a hike to Johannesburg.

He had planned this final meeting with his contact for weeks. No way was he going to give up. So, clinging to his own stubbornness like a life preserver, he pulled his car keys out of his pocket and opened the trunk lid. Without thinking he cried out, "Oh no!" The eight bags of Dagga he had spent packing up were gone. He'd saved the receipts from all the other contact sales and this was to be the last batch he'd have to sell in order to have enough cash to buy The Ingwe. All told it had taken him three years to get to this point and he wasn't about to forfeit that dream now.

Luckily no one heard him cry out, for there was no one anywhere near the car. For a moment he couldn't think. He couldn't seem to concentrate. Then a rush of thoughts raced through his mind and he knew what had to be done. Now, out of sheer frenzy, he stumbled back to the driver's side door and again managed to fall into the seat, put the key into the ignition and start the engine. He'd have to get back to the lodge in a hurry.

With unflagging fortitude and ferocious determination he entered the reserve from the rear near the warehouse, since there were no guards in place. From there he made his way to the back of the lodge and proceeded down the corridor that led to Gideon's office. *What I've got to do now is to convince Gideon to give me time to make up more bags of Dagga and have it ready to exchange for the money I need to purchase The Ingwe. Besides, wait 'til Gideon finds out who stole the drugs. He'll never believe it. This time I'll be more cautious about telling anyone about the exchange of drugs for money.*

Gideon and the two wildlife game officers arrived back at the lodge at noon. Fortunately, other than the question about the number of cages in the warehouse, there were no distinct violations they could detect in their wildlife assessment, a conclusion that greatly eased Gideon's mind. He stood in the lobby for a few minutes going over the papers that had to be signed. Then he directed them to Damon's office for they wanted to have another discussion with him about the cages found in the warehouse.

As Gideon left the men and proceeded on to his own office, he hoped that Lynn had been able to take care of Damon. Maybe she got him out of the building, he reasoned. That would delay any conversation with him and allow time to have the buyers sign the contract to purchase The Ingwe, since they were coming in late that afternoon and would be there for the *Boma*. Then he and Lynn could move on with their lives and get back to Johannesburg.

Gideon had no sooner gotten into his office and was taking off his jacket when Stephen appeared in the doorway. A shocked Gideon stared at Stephen who was covered in blood. His face was battered and one sleeve of his shirt was ripped all the way to the cuff. Bewildered, he called out, "What happened to *you*?"

Stephen limped into Gideon's office declaring, "We've gotta talk!"

Chapter 41

Friday Afternoon

While Stephen confronted Gideon in Gideon's office, the two wildlife officers headed off to see Damon Greene, hoping to find out if his story about the eight cages matched the comment made by Gideon Courtney regarding the reason for having eight cages in the warehouse. Strangely enough, the report that the Magistrate had received was that eight cages, with leopards in them, had been stolen from a resident in or near Tzaneen, South Africa.

According to the report, it seems the man claimed to be a scientist who had been working on a mutation process of developing a new breed of leopards he referred to as *Mauve Leopards* for their lavender/gray color. The man, who had named Gideon Courtney as the culprit who took the leopards, was now in critical condition in the Tzaneen Medical Center suffering from pneumonia as well as what was described by the doctors as GBS or Guillain-Barré Syndrome and was paralyzed from the waist down. The officers, of course, couldn't arrest anyone on such hearsay evidence and that's why they decided to talk first to Damon Greene and other staff members before submitting their wildlife report exonerating The Ingwe from any wrong doing. So, as far as they were concerned they'd found no exacting proof that there is such a breed of leopard. However, Du Preez felt that talking to the staff and the owners at the reserve might shed some light on the matter. Obviously Gideon wasn't about to tell them about his elicit plot, and he hoped that no one would mention his having seen a *Mauve Leopard*. His greatest concern was that Damon would crack under the pressure.

When Officer Du Preez first knocked on Damon's door, he got no answer. He knocked again, this time more forcefully. "Did you hear that?" he asked, glancing at Rouz.

"Yeah, it sounded like a moan to me."

"Let's go in," Du Preez said, pushing open the door. Neither man was prepared for what they would encounter. Damon was lying on the floor about two feet from his desk. The blood from his hand injury trailed behind him.

"My God man! What happened to you?" Rouz questioned.

"Help me!" was all Gideon could to manage to say. Du Preez grabbed him by the arms and pulled him up then sat him down on the office lounge.

"What's going on here?" Rouz again asked.

Damon brushed his hand across his face which was distinctly ashen. He leaned back, taking in a lung full of air. "My wife tried to kill me with one of her damn snakes," Damon said, his voice strained and weak. He immediately coughed then bent over and vomited.

"What do 'ya mean kill you?" Du Preez probed.

Damon sat upright and wiped his sleeve across his mouth. As sick as he was he was able to tell the two men that his wife had put a snake in the top left-hand drawer of his desk. "When I opened the drawer," he said, "at her request by the way, it slashed out at me. He missed my hand, though. I must have blacked out for a few minutes for when I woke up she was gone and the desk drawer was closed." He stopped to take a breath.

Then looking as pale as a coffin lining, Damon held his hand on the side of his face as if to hold himself upright. He bit his lip and leaned back again. "I think I'll be all right," Damon said, gasping for breath. "I had a seizure—"

"You have seizures?" Rouz pressed.

"Yeah, and I blacked out before I could make it to the door, but I took one of the pills from my desk before then."

"Rouz, give the man some water from your thermos," Du Preez ordered and call the medics. This man needs medical attention."

While Rouz was calling for the medics, Du Preez continued to question Damon. "So you say there was a snake in the top left-hand desk drawer?" he asked.

"Yes," Damon said, his face still blanched.

"Rest for a few minutes while we get the medics in here. I'm going to check out that drawer." Du Preez stepped to one side, missing the vomit that had splashed onto the floor in front of Damon then headed for the desk. There, with his head leaning to one side and his hand under the desk drawer handle, he slid the drawer open a fraction of an inch and waited to see what happened. Nothing stirred inside, so he continued opening it a little at a time until the contents were fully in view. There was no snake inside, though some papers had definitely been disturbed. Du Preez looked closer and spied sawdust on a few crinkled sheets. He turned to Rouz. "We'll have this drawer gone over for evidence. Something in there looks a lot like what I've seen in snake cages."

Damon twisted his head to look back at Du Preez. "I told you there was a snake in there. The blood on my hand is from scraping it on that rough edge on the glass top. My wife likely thought the snake got me." He leaned back and took a deep breath. "I think she'd have chosen the Adder or the Mamba if she wanted me out of the way, and believe me she did."

Chapter 42

Friday Afternoon

After lunch Brad left Kyle and Gina at poolside and went to his car to get a change of clothes that he had brought with him to wear to the *Boma* that evening. He and the women planned to meet in the lobby and go up to their suite until the seven o'clock drum beat sounded, announcing the beginning of the *Boma* festivities. Kyle and Gina had remained in the restaurant a few minutes after Brad left them to finish their drinks, then they proceeded down the corridor that led to the lobby.

"I can hardly wait to see what a *Boma's* really like. It sounds like great fun. This is almost over. Will you be sorry to leave?" Gina asked apparently wondering what Kyle would say.

"I'm looking forward to tonight, and I don't even want to think about leaving. I'd love to stay here longer," she admitted as she glanced to her right and saw the sign on Gideon Courtney's office. They both stopped when they heard shouting coming from inside the half open doorway. Stephen was yelling at Gideon, something about money and drugs.

Kyle and Gina froze in place. Kyle couldn't make out all of words that the two men were hollering back and forth at each other, but some of the words were easily recognizable, and she distinctly heard Stephen call out, "I was supposed to get first bid on buying The Ingwe."

Then Kyle heard Gideon fire back, his voice even louder than Stephen's. "Listen, if those buyers coming in tonight want to take over the place they've got it. We can't wait."

"But you promised me first bid. It's not my fault that Carole's brother and another thug robbed me and took not only the money I was supposed to get from the drugs, but they took the drugs as well, and I think they killed my contact."

Kyle figured Stephen must have paused to catch his breath or something, for there was no sound coming from the room for a second or two. However, as Kyle and Gina continued to listen they heard Stephen shout, "Don't you turn your back to me. You know how long I've worked for this. Three years. That's right . . . three years!"

Right after that last statement, Kyle heard what sounded as if a physical confrontation was taking place and a lamp or a table were being kicked about. Then, she heard a thundering crash like glass breaking. Gina must have heard it, too, for she squeezed Kyle's hand as they stood in the hallway, their mouths wide open.

"Oh jeez," Gina cried, "Let's get out of here!"

They both glared at each other with fright in their eyes. Kyle immediately looked about for a place to hide. She rushed to a door marked "Storeroom" that was opposite Gideon's office. Fortunately it was open so they hurried inside. They hadn't even gotten the door completely closed when Kyle spied Stephen running out of Gideon's office. "I'm going to check and see where he went," Kyle confided.

"Don't do that Kyle!" Gina pleaded from behind a cabinet.

But there was no stopping Kyle. She already had the door open and was standing in the hallway. "He's gone, Gina. It *was* Stephen. I saw him running out. His face and clothes were covered in blood and he was heading for the back of the building. Come on let's check Mr. Courtney's office."

"You've got to be kiddin'! I'm leaving." With that Gina raced out of the storeroom and ran toward the lobby.

Kyle pulled open Gideon's office door and let out a shrill scream that echoed down the hallway. The tranquility was shaken by Kyle's outburst as the scene evolved from a peaceful environment to one of frenzied activity. Gideon was lying on the floor with one or more large bloody shards of broken glass protruding from his chest. Kyle whipped about. This time it was Kyle following Gina's lead. When she caught up with her friend, Gina was about out of breath. Then all hell broke loose.

Chapter 43

Friday Afternoon

The two Wildlife Officers must have heard the sharp ends of Kyle's shrill cries, for they rushed into the lobby, which luckily was empty but for the Holly, the clerk at the Front Desk who appeared to be paralyzed with shock. There, Kyle and Gina, both obviously shaken and out of breath, ran headlong into the two wildlife officers. "What happened?" Du Preez asked the women.

Just then Brad entered the lobby and hurried over to where Kyle and Gina were standing next to the officers. "What happened in here, I heard screaming?" Brad asked with obvious concern.

Rouz spoke up, "And who are you?"

Brad, who had his arms around Gina in an effort to comfort her, turned to the officer and responded in his usual British accent. "I'm here with Kyle and Gina. I was outside at my car and I heard a scream."

Du Preez looked at Kyle who appeared to be the spokesperson for the women. "Then what is it ladies? What happened?"

At that point Gina was bent over trying to get her breath, so Kyle stepped forward and, breathless herself, briefly explained what they'd heard coming from Gideon Courtney's office. "We heard fighting going on so we hid in the storeroom across from his office. Then," she went on, "I saw Stephen run out."

"Who's Stephen?" Du Preez asked.

"He's the game ranger here at the lodge," Kyle said, while pulling in a full breath. Her heart was beating so hard she could hear the ringing in her ears.

Rouz asked, "Where'd he go?"

Kyle pointed. "Down the hallway toward the back door. After the hollering stopped I heard a crash of glass and I looked into the room—"

Kyle was going to expand on what she'd seen in Gideon's office, but Officer Du Preez interrupted with a command to his partner to check on the backup. "I'm going down there. See to it that the medics know where to find Mr. Greene and see that these people are escorted to a safe place," Du Preez instructed. He motioned toward the Front Desk. "See that's she's out of here, too."

When Du Preez reached Gideon Courtney's office he was stunned to find the man lying in a pool of blood. Large pieces of glass had evidently ripped through his body. Most likely that had killed him in minutes, Du Preez thought. He dialed his superior and reported the death and explained the scene. "I had Rouz call SAP on this one." He continued on, "We'll need the police, for not only do we have a dead body, but we've got a possible case of attempted murder."

Officer Rouz ushered Kyle, Gina, Holly and Brad into the back office. Then he contacted his dispatcher and reviewed his request for backup from SAP and asked if the medical team was en route.

Confusion reigned for more than two hours while Kyle and the group tried to fathom what had, indeed, transpired. It seemed to Kyle that the wait was egregious and far worse than the time they spent in the Senegal Airport, for at least there they had food and drink available. But now, all they could do was wait.

During that boring time, Kyle asked Holly where Carole was, since she hadn't seen her at The Ingwe for a few days.

"I've no idea where Carole is," Holly replied. "She called in sick today and we were short handed, too."

Strange, Kyle thought.

With a delightfully humorous smile on her face Gina concluded, "Well, Kyle, I guess that *Boma* celebration won't take place. Will it?"

Kyle looked at Gina with a grin, "Leave it to you to brighten the scene. What else could possibly happen on this trip? I think we've seen it all. I can't believe Stephen was dealing drugs and was capable of doing anything like what I saw in Mr. Courtney's office. It was horrible."

"Well you two certainly can't stay here," Brad said, "and didn't you say your flight leaves late tomorrow, Gina?"

Both Kyle and Gina nodded. "It does," Kyle said. "I've no idea what's going to hap—"

Brad interrupted her as Officer Du Preez walked into the room. "What's going on?" he asked.

"So far all I can tell is that you're going to have to stay in the area for a few days until we can clear you. We've called in SAP our South African Police to handle this from now on. However, you can't stay here. This lodge is now a crime scene. Do you have somewhere else you can stay? If not we can suggest some references."

Brad immediately interceded. "No no, I'm sure the Kruger Park Lodge, where I'm staying, can accommodate Kyle and Gina for a few days." He looked at both women. "Don't worry. I'll take care of it."

"Good," Officer Du Preez stated. "We have some papers you need to sign then you can leave. You," he said looking at Holly, "will have to sign, too. Then you can go home, but none of you can leave the area until we give you permission. Is that clear?"

Everyone nodded while Holly turned to Kyle and the group. "I can't believe this happened at The Ingwe. I don't know what to say. But it's been wonderful meeting you and I hope you have a safe trip home."

It was hugging time and the women all took part, while Brad looked on smiling.

"Thanks Holly," Kyle said. "You've been so good to us. Actually I can't believe it's been only one week out of our lives. Actually, it seems like a lifetime."

Her voice trembling, Holly burst out with, "I just wish your stay had not been—"

"I know what you mean," Kyle interrupted. "But none of this is your fault. And, it still wouldn't keep me from coming back to Africa."

After all the release papers were signed giving them permission to leave The Ingwe, Kyle and Gina repacked their suitcases and, along with Brad, left for the Kruger Park Lodge. Kyle sat in the back seat of Brad's rental car, and as they drove away, she looked back over her shoulder for one final view of the lodge and its unique and colorful setting. It seemed like such an inviting spot Kyle thought, with a mesmerizing landscape that felt exotic while also managing to feel like a home you left and long to revisit. Yet it was a hotbed of mystery and intrigue. The whole place carried a veneer of respectability, where sin ran rampant leaving a long shadow.

"Remember, Gina," Kyle said, "I told you I thought something suspicious was going on. Well, it sure was! Hopefully they'll get it all figured out and we can go home."

Gina looked up at Brad. "Wish you were coming with us."

"So do I," he admitted, offering a warm glance. "But I'll be back in Tampa at the end of the month. You're coming up aren't you?"

"Just try to keep me away," Gina declared.

Kyle took in a deep breath and sighed. *Oh, that poor guy doesn't have a chance. He's hooked.*

The entrance to the Kruger Park Lodge was auspicious with the drive into the lodge itself a treat, for it paralleled a narrow river that Brad said had hippos in it.

"See," he said, "there's a viewing deck where you can watch them in the river. It's called Hippo Hide, but they warn you not to walk around here at night or you could run into one. You see there are no fences to keep them out here."

Reacting with a huff, Gina replied. "Well, you'll never see me out here at night. That's for sure."

"I'll pass on a night walk, too, Brad. We've had enough surprises haven't we, Gina?"

"That's an understatement if I ever heard one. To me The Ingwe seemed more primitive. This place has more of a commercial feel."

"It does cater to the African enthusiast who wants some adventure, but still all the comforts of home which includes golfing." Brad pointed to the golf course on their right.

The lodge was elegant and Brad was able to get the women a room in the lodge itself. There were private thatched-roof chalets there as well but since they presumed they would be staying for only a few days, they declined and decided a room would be sufficient. Besides it was close to Brad's suite and that pleased Gina.

"They've got a nice restaurant in the lodge called the Wiesenhof. It's not going to be anything like the *Boma* you were expecting to enjoy tonight, but it's fine. Then tomorrow I'll take you to The Hut in

Hazyview. They have a good variety of African and specialty cuisine. We'll play it by ear after that, okay?"

"Of course, Brad. It's great of you to step in and help us out." Kyle turned to Gina, "I'll call and tell them to cancel those tickets for tomorrow. I sure hope we find out what's going on so we can plan for another flight," Kyle said. "This is really a mess."

Though the trip had come to a drastic end, Kyle, Gina and Brad had a fabulous two days, swimming in the lodge's pool, watching the hippos in the river, the tourists playing volleyball and, on occasion, taking strolls on the Matuma Trail all around the resort during the day hours, for Gina was quick to remind them that she wasn't going walking at night when a hippo might decide to take a stroll as well.

On the second day of their stay, an officer from the South African Police unit in Mpumalanga, called Kyle to inform her that all had been completed for their clearance to return to the States. When Kyle asked what had actually happened at The Ingwe, the officer declined to give her any data. "Sorry," he said in a matter a fact tone of voice. "It's an ongoing investigation and no details have been released as yet."

At least satisfied that they could go home, Kyle called and changed the departure date to the following day.

"I'll be sorry to see you two go. I'll miss you both," Brad said while they were dining that evening. "But, as far as finding out what happened, Kyle, I'll let you know if I hear any news before I leave in three weeks."

That evening before going to bed, Kyle entered her final journal entry. Things had been moving so fast she hadn't had a chance to do so in the last few days.

Journal Entry—7 *Tuesday morning I planted a time capsule on the grounds of The Ingwe. Hopefully someone will discover it years from now and see my parents' names and know that they were in South Africa if only in spirit. The afternoon game drive with Stephen was delightful. We saw two female lions with a cub walking along a lonely road. Then by chance we finally observed a breed of leopard that is new to South Africa called a Mauve Leopard. It was hidden in the branches of a tree, but I got a shot of it. Later on while we were parked near a large pond, I photographed a giraffe bending down to drink, and then a huge hippo charged us. He just about flew out of the water. Stephen had turned off the Rover's engine, but he managed to* *get it started and we made our escape. Another close call. The tent experience in the bush was intriguing. First, we saw a glimpse of one of the Mauve Leopards, then we spied two elephants sparring in a pond, and I shot a photo of our tracker who was standing beside the skull of a cape buffalo. The tracker's name is Million. Believe it or not. I almost succumbed to my feeling of loneliness. Fortunately though, I realized my mistake in time. I won't discuss the details, for I'd rather forget the incident. During the night in my tent, which was a few feet from the electrified fence surrounding the bush camp, I heard growling noises. When I peered out I saw a white lion. Luckily my camera came through and I got off one shot of the big cat before he vanished into the night. Today, Friday, the day of the Boma, was disastrous. Gina and I almost got caught up in what I presume was an altercation if not a murder. From what I heard going on inside Gideon Courtney's office, Stephen killed Gideon, one of the owners of The Ingwe. I witnessed Stephen leaving the site. Hopefully we'll know more later on. We stayed at the Kruger Park Lodge where Brad had been residing because his brother, Patrick, is the game ranger there. It's a beautiful place, but it couldn't match the unique qualities of isolation at The Ingwe, even with all the lodge's shortcomings. Tomorrow we leave for home. Gina's happy she came along for I'm certain she met husband # 3. I'm still lonely and can't understand why Ryan cancelled the wedding. I guess I'll ever know.*

Brad took the women to the airport the next evening, and Gina and Brad kissed for what seemed to be hours. Kyle stepped aside to allow them a bit of privacy, but finally had to say, "I'm sorry you two love birds, but we've gotta go or we'll miss this flight."

Gina conceded, giving Brad a quick kiss on his cheek. "I'll miss you," she told him, "and I can't believe how lucky I was to have found you."

"And I you," he responded. "I'll miss you, too, but call me when you get home. You've got my number." As the two walked to the security checkpoint Gina gave one last wave to Brad and they proceeded on to the gate.

To Kyle it seemed like an endless flight home. Neither spoke much. Gina said she felt exhausted from the happenings the last day at The Ingwe and Kyle was perhaps more than a little depressed, thinking about her return to an empty apartment. At least the flight was smooth, and they had no delays in Senegal and no traumatic crises during the flight.

It was a long trip . . . over seventeen hours including a brief delay in Senegal. When they finally landed in Miami, they had to transfer and take another flight to Fort Myers, Florida, a flight that also was delayed for several hours. "Oh no!" Gina exclaimed. "I'll have to call Barbara and tell her to meet us later. Man, I never want to take another plane flight . . . ever!"

"I can see your point," Kyle said with raised eyebrows.

By the time they landed in Fort Myers it was 7:00 P.M. They immediately headed down the escalator to the baggage claim area. On the way, Gina glanced at Kyle. "Hey," she said, "I know you're still hurting from the wedding debacle so how about staying with my sister and me for the night."

Kyle shook her head. "No, I'll be fine. But thanks for caring."

"I feel so sorry that things didn't work out," Gina said. "If there's anything I can do to make it better just let me know, and again, thanks for asking me to come along. You know you've got to be my Maid of Honor at my wedding."

"You're what?" Kyle asked when they reached the bottom of the escalator.

"Brad asked me to marry him."

"How wonderful," Kyle exclaimed giving Gina a hug. "You know I didn't really like him at first," she confessed, "but actually the guy kind of grows on 'ya."

"I'm so glad you approve. You've always been my best friend and that means a lot to me."

Gina's luggage was one of the first to come through on the carousel and her sister Barbara showed up shortly thereafter. Gina was all hugs while she bubbled over, trying to tell her sister all that had happened on the trip. Fact is, Barbara could barely understand what

Gina was saying. Over all the commotion, Kyle cupped her hands and announced, "She found husband number three!"

"You're kidding," turning to Gina, Barbara shouted, "Tell me all about it."

For several minutes they talked. Finally Barbara stated, "We've got to go. I'm in the short term lot."

"Are you sure you don't want to stay with us tonight, Kyle?" Gina asked. "We'd love to have you."

'No, you go on. I'll call you in the morning."

Another group hug and Gina locked arms with her sister and the two headed for the door towing the luggage behind them.

Kyle smiled as she shouted out, "Hey Gina! Be sure you watch the travel channel tonight when you get home, for I read there's going to be a special on African elephants that go on a rampage."

Gina glanced back at her, shook her head and offered a cockeyed grin. "Oh, yeah, that's just what I need." That said they were gone.

Kyle heaved a melancholy sigh, grabbed her bag and her carry on and started for the door. Suddenly from another doorway down the line she heard a loud call, "Kyle!"

When she turned to look back she couldn't believe her eyes. It was Ryan. With a dubious frown, Kyle wearily looked away, and when he finally caught up with her she was not smiling. In fact, she looked perturbed. Her voice was edgy to say the least and she spat out the words, "What are you doing here?"

"You didn't answer the messages I sent to you in Africa."

"Why should I? You cancelled the wedding." Kyle abruptly pivoted on her heel pulling her bags behind her.

Ryan followed alongside her pleading, "Please Kyle I've got to tell you something."

Exasperation deepened. "What is it," Kyle said stopping short. "Did she decide she wasn't going to marry you?"

"What do you mean?" Ryan questioned as Kyle picked up the pace and started for the garage. "Please stop," he implored. "You don't think I deserted you to marry someone else do you?" He tried to walk in front of her, but she plowed right ahead, ignoring his comments.

She got to the crowded elevator just in time to squeeze on. Ryan shoved his way in beside her, his breath hot against her cheek. When she exited the elevator, he persisted in tagging along, trying to get her to stop and listen to him. But Kyle was not about to be detoured. She stopped at the rear of her car and tapped her feet on the concrete flooring while demanding that he get out of her way. "I want to open my trunk." Her words snapped like a withered tree branch.

As Ryan stepped aside Kyle noticed that his eyes were huge as if he were fighting back emotion. "Okay," he said, "I guess you wouldn't have cared if I died."

Kyle placed her suitcase and carry-on bag in the trunk and slammed the lid then swung around toward him. "What are you talking about?" she exclaimed, a cloud of a sick doubt veiling her face.

"I'm so sorry I cancelled the wedding. I thought I was dying."

It was such a soul deep shock that, sans any emotion, Kyle found herself saying, "What do you mean dying?"

Ryan turned away and rubbed his hand across his forehead. He glanced back at Kyle. "I couldn't tell you," he went on, pausing to take in a deep breath as his lips began to tremble. "I guess I couldn't face you with the fact that I had cancer."

A river of surprise rushed through her. "Cancer!" she echoed her voice barely audible.

For an instant Ryan avoided looking at Kyle. Then he straightened up and faced her, his intense blue-gray eyes glistening, a dimple biting his cheek and that wavy strand of dark black hair that she thought was so attractive had fallen haphazardly across his forehead. "I couldn't tell you before, and I can barely speak about it now, but . . ." He stopped, the words sticking in his throat. "I had testicular cancer and they said it was terminal."

Kyle took a step back and gasped, "Oh my God!" She ground her teeth against the word, "testicular."

"A co-worker of mine had the same prognosis and he died. He'd been married for only a year, so he left his wife a widow at twenty."

Pain was visible in Ryan's face, and Kyle could tell his nerves were strung as tight as a bow string. "Somehow," he added pausing to catch his breath, "I found myself afraid to tell you, and I certainly didn't want you to go through watching me die and being a widow at your age."

"Well can't they do anything for you?"

"That's what I wanted to tell you when I sent those messages to Africa." She noticed a hint of pleading with each word. "They originally told me they'd discovered the cancer too late, but I found a group of specialists who did what was necessary to cure me without any drastic measures or without removing any—"

Kyle bit her lip. "Sh-h-h," she replied. "Don't even say it, but what happened? Are you all right?"

"They tell me I'm totally free of any cancer now. That's what I wanted to tell you," Ryan said, a throaty cadence in his voice. He gently reached up and brushed few wind-blown curls from her face. "I know you'll never forgive me for putting you through this, but I just couldn't confront the possibility of never being able to give you the kind of love you deserve in so many ways. I do want you to know I missed you and that I'll always love you."

Kyle backed away. "That's all well and good, Ryan" she explained, feeling shackled by the chains of conscientiousness. "But marriage is based on trust, and I don't know if I can trust you or not. After all, we could have worked this out together." She looked to one side before turning her gaze back to him. "Those words you said that day in my apartment couldn't have cut me more brutally than if you'd used a scalpel. I felt . . . and I still feel so left out. The pain is far too raw to have it diminish in a flash." She shot him a look of pure resentment.

Then, without showing any emotion, she moved to the driver's side of the car and got in. "Matter of fact," she said, looking right at him. "I can't make any commitment now. Though I want you to know I'm happy that you're okay." With that she put the key in the ignition and started the engine. Pulling out she glanced in the rear view mirror only to see Ryan standing alone in the deserted airport parking garage, a mere silhouette against a backdrop of the bright security lights.

Epilogue

Four weeks later

"Hey, I was getting worried that you weren't going to make it," Kyle called out to Gina and Brad as she watched them ascend the steps of the court house.

"I wouldn't have missed this for the world. Besides you two need us as witnesses," Gina fired back. A smirk and a decided look of absolute joy brightening her face.

Ryan leaned forward and shook hands with Brad. "It's great of you to get the judge to perform the wedding. It must be nice to have such influence."

"Gina and I knew you were the right man for Kyle the first time I met you, Ryan," Brad admitted. "And I was happy to set this up."

They stood at the top of the stairs for a moment while Gina marveled at Kyle who looked resplendent in her simplistic yet sophisticated turquoise silk sheath dress with matching heels. "You look fabulous, girl!" Gina announced. "And those auburn curls of yours only add to the striking color contrast. But then you'd look good in rags," she said in jest. "And those earrings are dazzling. They sparkle like the crown jewels."

"They're a gift from Ryan," Kyle said as she flashed a smile his way.

"And as for you Mr. Travis, I'd say with that gorgeous black hair, that sexy dimple and those startling eyes, you're a knock out dude. I could have fallen for you myself." With that she gave Brad a big hug then sported a huge grin. "But I've already got Mr. Right."

"Personally," Kyle beamed giving the two men a once over, "I think we've found two of the best looking guys in Florida!"

Brad shook his head and jokingly directed, "Okay you two. Let's get going and make an honest couple out of Kyle and Ryan."

Gina tapped him on the shoulder. "Hush," she said as she hurried ahead to keep up with Kyle while all four entered the building.

The Judge's clerk met them at the door of Judge Hargrove's office and ushered them into his chambers.

The judge immediately got up from his desk and skirted around it to greet the group. After the introductions were complete, the judge set the stage for the ceremony that was to follow. Then, with all the pomp and ceremony one gets when being married in a court house judge's chambers, the service proceeded with the judge wearing his formal robe and holding a set of folders as well as a bible.

Kyle, five foot nine and Ryan six foot two, stood tall before the judge. With Kyle's fingers threaded in his, she gazed over at Ryan at the very moment he darted a look her way along with a flirtatious wink. His roguish smile highlighted the dimple that Gina had mentioned was cratered in his cheek and the black suit with the hairpin stripes only tended to accentuate his stunning good looks.

As Kyle noted, his wide blue-gray eyes, that sparkled whenever the light hit them, were more lucid than usual that day, and she realized how very much she loved him.

It was apparent to Kyle when Judge Hargrove began the ritual that it was going to be a lengthy service. The judge seemed prepared to follow the traditional pattern including a formidable reading of the invocation from not only the bible but from a set of poetry. His voice was, to be honest, monotone in nature and after a time the narrative seemed to drone on and on. As one word blended into another Kyle's concentration drifted back to the night she left Ryan standing alone in the parking lot at the airport garage with a forlorn look on his face.

All the while she drove back to her apartment that night she searched her conscience trying to decide if she'd make the right decision by cutting Ryan out of her life. She was tortured by the fact that he had faced such terrifying odds, yet she did feel so abandoned and betrayed.

Surprisingly when she arrived home, she found his car parked in her driveway. He was leaning against it apparently waiting for her. At the time she couldn't help noticing that the soft blue shirt he was wearing tended to highlight his glorious blue-gray eyes that were in such a contrast to his black hair that it appeared striking in the glow of the streetlamp.

"I can't bear the thought that you don't trust me, Kyle," he told her. "All of this has been tearing me apart for ten days now, and I just can't leave thinking you hate me." His voice low and rich dropped to a seductive level. It seemed to have the power to reassure all at once. The tautness of his face and the blazing need in his eyes told her he was hurting. "I know I made a mistake by not telling you the reason why I cancelled the wedding" he went on, "but I was only thinking of what was good for you. Please believe me."

As they stood under the streetlamp with the beams lighting his face, Kyle could see the pain in his eyes and a facial expression that denoted he was urgent with wanting. Deep inside her she knew she was as impatient for him as he was for her. She edged her body toward him and idly ran her fingers up the ridge of his jacket before he pulled her close. She didn't resist, but merely clutched his shoulders and strained against him. Suddenly the pain she felt inside burst like a jolt of electricity shorting out everything else . . . breaking the thread of tension that had been thickening and tightening inside her.

In a state of ecstasy it wasn't long before delicious tears of joy filled her eyes like diamonds, and she quickly led him up the stairs into her apartment. Neither spoke, for sometimes the most beautiful words are those not said. That evening both found them unnecessary.

His fingertips touched her with scalding intimacy as he traced the lines of her breasts while at the same time Kyle arched her back and rotated her hips, emitting a sinful gasp. The mix of exotic musk and perfume was hypnotizing.

His head low, his breath caressed her cheeks while his lips touched hers lightly, brushing across them like silken warmth before he gently slid his tongue over her mouth then probed deep, sending a trail of fire curling deep down within her. While he tasted the wild flavor of her body's sweetness he picked her up in his arms and gently placed her on the bed and unwrapped her.

His amorous eyes stared down at her gloriously aroused body. Then he slipped in beside her and nestled his head in her auburn curls, drinking in the ambrosia. She, in turn, stroked his bronze forearms and his sculpturally lean torso. Ryan reached out and drew her head close in an intimacy trap where mind defers to bodies and the will is weak. The lower half of Kyle's body swayed with rhythmic sensuality as he pressed his hips tight against her and wrapped his hungry legs around her, his muscles so firm to his purpose.

Kyle closed her eyes while the scent of him stirred restless feelings within her, feelings that had been locked away for far too long.

She had longed for this day and now she was on the brink of embracing it at its finest. Neither sweet reason nor sweet clarity, however, were the emotions playing in Kyle's mind at the time, only those of complete and utter surrender and, as Ryan's lips closed over hers, she was on fire with delight and amazement at the feeling of bring as one.

The love making was like scenting one's mate . . . primeval, reflective, and compulsive . . . fulfilling beyond belief.

"Will you marry me, Kyle?" he pleaded, his voice vibrating with passion.

"With pleasure, Ryan. Please stay with me," she whispered.

"Always, Kyle, always."

There was a promise of tomorrow in that moment. Somehow they both knew their love would keep the weld strong.

All of a sudden Kyle felt a tug on her sleeve. She shook her head and blinked. "Kyle," she heard Gina's prompt. "It's your turn to answer."

"Oh," Kyle admitted, glancing quickly at Gina who appeared a bit dismayed. "I'm sorry Judge Hargrove, but I didn't hear those last words. Would you kindly repeat them?"

The judge did so and the ceremony continued on with the declaration of the vows, the ring exchange and finally the pronouncement. The kiss was warm, sweet and appropriate for the occasion. Gina, Brad and even the clerk clapped as the couple thanked the judge and made their way out of his chambers. All in all, it was a quiet but serene ceremony that suited both Kyle and Ryan just fine.

"Well," Gina cheered as they left the building and headed for the parking lot. "Now I can call you, Mrs. Travis." She stopped short. "Hey, that sounds super!"

"It does, doesn't it?" Kyle agreed flashing a bright smile directed at Ryan, who returned an amorous grin before turning his attention to Brad. In any event, the women lagged behind catching up on what had happened since returning from Africa.

"Remember I told you we're taking you two to dinner," Ryan spoke up. "I've made reservations on Sanibel. We'll take our car. That okay with you?"

"Perfect," Brad confirmed. "I haven't been there in awhile, and it'll be great to find out what's going on in your lives. Besides, I'm sure Gina has instructions to give you about our upcoming nuptials. That's only a month away you know."

"What a coincidence . . . you meeting Gina on the plane and here you are getting married," Ryan said as they approached his vehicle.

"I guess it was one of those things they say was meant to be. We hit it off from the beginning," Brad admitted, "and isn't it fine that Kyle and Gina have been friends for years. Kyle says she misses Gina since she sold her business and moved to Tampa, but actually that's not so far away. We can still get together often and that's good."

During the drive to Sanibel Island, Kyle and Gina kept up a steady stream of chatter, Gina telling Kyle all about her new Day Spa near the center of Tampa and giving Kyle an update on what was happening in regards to planning her wedding which was but a month away.

"You know Kyle, if you hadn't asked me to accompany you to Africa I never would have met Brad. I've got so much to thank you for I'll never be able to repay you. He's really a great guy, and I'm so happy you decided to hang on to Ryan. What a horrible crisis for him."

"I know. I just wish he had told me," Kyle stated. "I would've understood, and loved him no matter what. But thank God he never gave up on me. He sure was persistent. I guess down deep I knew he was the only man that would ever be in my life. I'm glad everything turned out so well."

"Are you disappointed about not havin' a big weddin'?"

"Not at all," Kyle said. "Just having you two there was all Ryan and I needed."

"By the way, what were you thinkin' about durin' the ceremony? It looked like you were in another world."

"Oh, Judge Hargrove's voice almost put me to sleep. Fact is, I was deep in a flashback of the night Ryan followed me home from the parking lot at the airport." Kyle's gaze locked on Gina. "That's the night I knew I'd never want any other man . . . ever!"

"Well, I'm really happy for you two."

While enjoying dinner, Brad announced that he had heard from Patrick and that The Ingwe had been closed down for a time. It's going to be renamed, too."

"I knew that," Kyle remarked.

Gina's forehead pulled into a frown. "How'd you know?"

"I was keeping this as a surprise to tell you tonight, but what the heck, this is as good a time as any."

"What surprise. Whatcha talkin' about?" Gina questioned.

"Well, guess where Ryan and I are going on our honeymoon?"

"Oh, come on!" Gina pressed. "You're drivin' me nuts. Where are you two goin'?"

Ryan must have overheard Gina, for he leaned close, a mischievous look framing his face as Kyle smiled. "We're going to the brand new Ingwe. It's now called "Paradiso" which in Swazi spells . . . paradise."

Gina's shoulders sagged and she slumped back in her chair. "You're kiddin'."

"No," Ryan said grabbing Kyle by the waist and giving her a hug. "I want to be there with Kyle this time. We're looking forward to it."

"Oh brother," Gina said with an explosive gesture. "I sure hope the people runnin' the place are not corrupt like the last group". She shook her head, adding, "But for God's sake Kyle, trust no one."

"What I hear from my travel agent is that all has changed there now. But we'll see. I'll have to check on whether or not they're still having those *Boma* dinners. If so, I'll film it for you." She turned to Ryan. "We never got a change to enjoy that part of the tri—"

"Oh, before I forget, Kyle," Brad interrupted. "I've got something for you. It's from Karen, who still works in the kitchen. She sent you a recipe you asked for. Patrick sent it on to me."

Kyle looked at Gina. "How nice of her," Kyle remarked. "I'll bet it's that *Baked Brie*. It was out of this world."

Brad pulled the recipe from his jacket pocket. "Here it is. Maybe you can whip up a batch sometime when we're down here." He handed the sheet of paper to Kyle.

"Oh my gosh! It's for the Baked Brie, Gina!" Kyle exclaimed excitedly.

Baked Brie with Toasted Pecans

INGREDIENTS:

    1 small wheel of Brie or Camembert—9 ounces Be sure it's a wheel not a wedge
    One half cup of pecan pieces
    3 tablespoons of light-brown sugar
    3 tablespoons of pure maple syrup
    Crackers or sliced baguettes for serving

INSTRUCTIONS:

    Preheat oven to 350 degrees. Cut off the outer coating on the cheese.
    Coat the cheese along the bottom and the sides of a 6 inch rimmed baking pan or use aluminum foil by curling the edges to form a six inch round diameter. You may also use a pastry puff as a container for the cheese.
    Then place on a baking sheet.
    Bake until softened—15 to 20 minutes. Don't let the cheese get too soft.
    Transfer to a serving plate.
    Cool about 20 minutes.

    While cheese cools, place the nuts on a clean baking sheet. Bake until toasted and fragrant—7 to 10 minutes. Sprinkle the roasted nuts on the cheese.

    In a small saucepan, combine sugar and maple syrup. Bring to a boil over medium heat. Simmer until foamy—1 to 2 minutes. Drizzle warm sauce over slightly cooled cheese and nuts. Serve with crackers or baguettes.

"You've got to give me Patrick's address, Brad. I'll send him and hopefully Karen a note. That was so thoughtful of them," Kyle stated. She immediately explained to Ryan that Karen had been particularly gracious to them on the trip.

"Since you plan on going on your honeymoon to that same spot, you'll probably be interested in knowing that Marian Cummings still works there. In fact, Patrick says Holly does as well. Do you remember them?" Brad asked.

"Of course I do," Kyle said turning to Ryan. "I hope you get to meet all of them on our trip back there. Bet they'll be surprised to see us." Kyle paused to collect her thoughts. "By the way Brad, did your brother have anything to say about what happened to the owners and the rest of the staff?" Kyle asked, still puzzled by the chain of events that rocked the place to its core. "That last day there scared the wits out of us, didn't it, Gina?"

"That's for sure!"

Just then the entrées arrived and there was a lull for a time while everyone was being served, but Brad quickly resumed the conversation by explaining that he did have news from Patrick about the happenings on that disastrous day at The Ingwe. "He said that Stephen is going on trial for murder, for I think you know he killed Gideon Courtney."

Gina cut in. "Oh, I know that. Kyle had the nerve to go into Mr. Courtney's office right after she saw Stephen run out, and she said the man was lying on his back with a great big shard of the glass coffee table ripped right through his chest."

"I felt there was a low level of dread and an undercurrent of distrust and suspicion going on in that lodge. Though it was a jewel of a place, it sure held a cache of secrets. Remember Gina, I said that several times."

"She's right. She did."

"Did Patrick find out anything about Mr. Greene, the other owner and his wife, the doctor?" Kyle probed while she picked up her fork to begin eating.

"Did he ever," Brad elaborated. "Some jaw-dropping facts all right. As far as the police are concerned, they think the doctor and Mr. Courtney, along with Mr. Greene were working with some scientist by the name of Jon Leatham, who was illegally creating a mutation of the African leopard. They wanted the mutation as an added attraction for their reserve thus gaining clientele. It was all a scheme of greed to gain customers."

Kyle blurted out, "That was those *Mauve Leopards*, Gina!"

"It surely was hotbed of greed and salacious consequences," Brad stated.

"Well, apparently all of those people are in trouble with the authorities and will undoubtedly do time. Their stories are the kind that hit the tabloids for sure. Patrick says the newspapers are also filled with articles about how Dr. Greene tried to kill her husband by placing a Black Mamba in one of his desk drawers. Though from what Patrick said, it didn't work. Though I've heard that Mr. Greene's still living, he's not in good health, for he's suffered a number of severe seizures since then. The snakes and that whole Herpetology Exhibit are now in Johannesburg, and it was reported that the scientist passed away. He's the one that set all these tragedies into motion by reporting the theft of the leopards. They say that after being in a state of unconsciousness for some time, he must have awakened just long enough to call for help."

"Brad, did they say why Stephen killed Gideon Courtney?" Kyle asked.

"Per the news, he confessed. He was trying to get the money to buy The Ingwe by dealing in Dagga or cannabis which is a form of marijuana. He claimed he'd been growing the weed in a remote spot in Limpopo Province, a place he knew well."

"Remember Gina," Kyle said, "Stephen mentioned that he had grown up in the Limpopo Province and he knew every inch of it."

"He must've found a secluded place for he'd been growing the crop for about three years and had just gotten his last bags ready for sale which would have given him enough cash to buy The Ingwe," Brad added.

"But what happened to the money?" Kyle questioned, thinking how happy she was that she had stayed true to her feelings and hadn't surrendered to that sense of need she felt on that starry night in Stephen's tent in the bush camp.

"He was robbed by Carole Magone's brother and some friend of his. In fact, the police found the dead body of the dealer. According to Patrick when Stephen confronted Gideon Courtney and told him about the robbery they had an altercation and he shoved Mr. Courtney killing him. It's been all over the news in Mpumalanga."

Kyle's sat wide-eyed as she realized another piece of the puzzle had fallen into place. "Ah ha! And you say Carole's brother was involved?"

"Not only her brother but Carole. She was the instigator who set up the whole robbery. Her sister states that she hadn't been taking her bipolar medication and that she was paranoid about Stephen's attraction to other women. I guess she decided to get even."

Kyle glanced at Brad. "Did they find the cash and the drugs?"

Brad took a sip of his cocktail before stating, "Not everything, but they did catch Carole, her brother and the friend trying to board a bus out of Johannesburg. Believe it or not they had all of the cash with them. So far the authorities don't know what happened to the drugs, but I'm sure they'll find out in time."

Kyle leaned back in her chair, her face riddled with astonishment at the outcome of such a tragedy. She looked at Gina. "What a layer of respectability they tried to portray. I had a suspicion about Carole's sincerity from the beginning, and I thought she was a bit overzealous. Frankly I can't believe all that happened while we were right under the same roof."

"I'm just glad we got back alive," Gina said as she gazed directly at Brad, then leaned over and gave him a kiss. "I found you there and it was all worth it."

"They say that 'Love' conquers call," Kyle said. "Let's all look forward to Gina's and Brad's wedding next month," Kyle said. "How about, cheers to best friends forever?" They all touched glasses and repeated the words.

When they left the restaurant, Brad suggested that they stop at a club and party awhile before heading home.

Kyle looked at Ryan at the same time he gazed her way and they both grinned. "I think we'll leave you two for now," he announced as he gave Kyle's hand a gentle squeeze, his dimple prominent in a sexy smile. "We've got some partying to do together," Ryan added, his voice ardently hinting of a night of passionate lovemaking to come.

Gina giggled. "You naughty boy, you!"

Kyle wrapped her arm around Ryan's waist and snuggled close. "Listen, Gina, we'll see you at the wedding next month, but I'll call you much before then. In the meantime, as you've always told me, 'Life's for living' and we're going to enjoy every moment of it,"

A Note to Adventurers

If, per chance, you plan to travel to the heart of the Dark Continent to enjoy the unique Lowvelt's golden savannahs, the rocky Kopjes and the magnificent wild beasts that roam the plains, the one's you'll encounter on safari, be sure to look high into the trees. If you see a flash of lavender-gray color moving about among the leaves on the top branches of the Knobthorn or the Marula trees, look very carefully, for you may be able to spot a *Mauve Leopard* that is still lurking in one or more of the game reserves in this strikingly rich Land of Contrasts.

PBL

Edwards Brothers Malloy
Thorofare, NJ USA
August 26, 2014